THE SLYNX

ALSO BY TATYANA TOLSTAYA

On the Golden Porch

Sleepwalker in a Fog

Pushkin's Children:
Writings on Russia and Russians

THE
SLYNX

TATYANA TOLSTAYA

TRANSLATED BY JAMEY GAMBRELL

HOUGHTON MIFFLIN COMPANY

BOSTON   NEW YORK

2003

For information about permission to reproduce selections
from this book, write to Permissions, Houghton Mifflin Company,
215 Park Avenue South, New York, New York 10003.

Visit our Web site: www.houghtonmifflinbooks.com.

Library of Congress Cataloging-in-Publication Data
Tolstaia, Tat'iana, 1951–
[Kys'. English]
The slynx / Tatyana Tolstaya ;
translated by Jamey Gambrell.
p.   cm.
ISBN 0-618-12497-7
I. Gambrell, Jamey. II. Title.
PG3476.T58 K9713   2003
891.73'44—dc21   2002027627

Book design by Melissa Lotfy
Typefaces: Times Ten and Akzidenz Grotesk

Printed in the United States of America

QUM 10 9 8 7 6 5 4 3 2 1

GLOSSARY

Blin (*bliny,* pl): large, thin pancake, rather like a crepe.

Golubchik (m), *Golubushka* (f): my dear, my good fellow, often used ironically. In the novel it is used as a form of address, like "comrade."

Izba: small cottage or peasant hut, something like a log cabin.

Kvas: fermented drink, slightly sweet.

Lapty: shoe or slipper made of bast, usually worn by peasants.

Murza: Tatar feudal lord.

Terem: mansion or large house, often several stories high.

THE SLYNX

A · AZ

BENEDIKT pulled on his felt boots, stomped his feet to get the fit right, checked the damper on the stove, brushed the bread crumbs onto the floor—for the mice—wedged a rag in the window to keep out the cold, stepped out the door, and breathed the pure, frosty air in through his nostrils. Ah, what a day! The night's storm had passed, the snow gleamed all white and fancy, the sky was turning blue, and the high elfir trees stood still. Black rabbits flitted from treetop to treetop. Benedikt stood squinting, his reddish beard tilted upward, watching the rabbits. If only he could down a couple—for a new cap. But he didn't have a stone.

It would be nice to have the meat, too. Mice, mice, and more mice—he was fed up with them.

Give black rabbit meat a good soaking, bring it to boil seven times, set it in the sun for a week or two, then steam it in the oven—and it won't kill you.

That is, if you catch a female. Because the male, boiled or not, it doesn't matter. People didn't used to know this, they were hungry and ate the males too. But now they know: if you eat the males you'll be stuck with a wheezing and a gurgling in your chest the rest of your life. Your legs will wither. Thick black hairs will grow like crazy out of your ears and you'll stink to high heaven.

Benedikt sighed: time for work. He wrapped his coat around him, set a wood beam across the door of the izba, and even shoved a stick behind it. There wasn't anything to steal, but he was used to doing things that way. Mother, may she rest in peace, always did it that way. In the Oldener Days, before the Blast, she told him, everyone locked their doors. The neighbors learned this from Mother and it caught on. Now the whole settlement locked their doors with sticks. It might be Freethinking.

His hometown, Fyodor-Kuzmichsk, spread out over seven hills. Benedikt walked along listening to the squeak of fresh snow, enjoying the February sun, admiring the familiar streets. Here and there black izbas stood in rows behind high pike fences and wood gates; stone pots or wood jugs were set to dry on the pikes. The taller terems had bigger jugs, and some people would even stick a whole barrel up there on the spike, right in your face as if to say: Look how rich I am, Golubchiks! People like that don't trudge to work on their own two feet, they ride on sleighs, flashing their whips, and they've got a Degenerator hitched up. The poor thing runs, all pale, in a lather, its tongue hanging out, its felt boots thudding. It races to the Work Izba and stops stock-still on all four legs, but its fuzzy sides keep going *huffa, puffa, huffa, puffa.*

And it rolls its eyes, rolls 'em up and down and sideways. And bares its teeth. And looks around . . .

To hell with them, those Degenerators, better to keep your distance. They're strange ones, and you can't figure out if they're people or not. Their faces look human, but their bodies are all furry and they run on all fours. With a felt boot on each leg. It's said they lived before the Blast, Degenerators. Could be.

It's nippy out now, steam comes out of his mouth, and his beard's frozen up. Still—what bliss! The izbas are sturdy and black, there are high white snowdrifts leaning against the fences, and a little path has been beaten to each gate. The hills run smooth all the way up and back down, white, wavy; sleighs slide along the snowy slopes, and beyond the sleighs are blue shadows, and the snow crunches in colors, and beyond the hills the sun rises, splashing rainbows on the dark blue sky. When you squint, the rays of the sun turn into circles; when you stomp your boots in the fluffy snow it sparks, like when ripe firelings flicker.

Benedikt thought a moment about firelings, remembered his

mother, and sighed: she passed away on account of those fire-lings, poor thing. They turned out to be fake.

The town of Fyodor-Kuzmichsk spreads out over seven hills. Around the town are boundless fields, unknown lands. To the north are deep forests, full of storm-felled trees, the limbs so twisted you can't get through, prickly bushes catch at your britches, branches pull your cap off your head. Old people say the Slynx lives in those forests. The Slynx sits on dark branches and howls a wild, sad howl—*eeeeennxx, eeeeennxx, eeenx-a-leeeeeennnxx!*—but no one ever sees it. If you wander into the forest it jumps on your neck from behind: *hop!* It grabs your spine in its teeth—*crunch*—and picks out the big vein with its claw and breaks it. All the reason runs right out of you. If you come back, you're never the same again, your eyes are different, and you don't ever know where you're headed, like when people walk in their sleep under the moon, their arms outstretched, their fingers fluttering: they're asleep, but they're standing on their own two feet. People will find you and take you inside, and sometimes, for fun, they'll set an empty plate in front of you, stick a spoon in your hand, and say "Eat." And you sit there like you're eating from an empty plate, you scrape and scrape and put the spoon in your mouth and chew, and then you make to wipe your dish with a piece of bread, but there's no bread in your hand. Your kinfolk are rolling on the floor with laughter. You can't do for yourself, not even take a leak, someone has to show you each time. If your missus or mother feels sorry for you, she takes you to the outhouse, but if there's no one to watch after you, you're a goner, your bladder will burst, and you'll just die.

That's what the Slynx does.

You can't go west either. There's a sort of road that way—invisible, like a little path. You walk and walk, then the town is hidden from your eyes, a sweet breeze blows from the fields, everything's fine and good, and then all of a sudden, they say, you just stop. And you stand there. And you think: Where was I going anyway? What do I need there? What's there to see? It's not like it's better out there. And you feel so sorry for yourself.

You think: Maybe the missus is crying back at the izba, searching the horizon, holding her hand over her eyes; the chickens are running around the yard, they miss you too; the izba stove is hot, the mice are having a field day, the bed is soft . . . And it's like a worrum got at your heart, and he's gnawing a hole in it . . . You turn back. Sometimes you run. And as soon as you can see your own pots on your fence, tears burst from your eyes. It's really true, they splash a whole mile. No lie!

You can't go south. The Chechens live there. First it's all steppe, steppe, and more steppe—your eyes could fall out from staring. Then beyond the steppe—the Chechens. In the middle of the town there's a watchtower with four windows, and guards keep watch out of all of them. They're on the lookout for Chechens. They don't really look all the time, of course, as much as they smoke swamp rusht and play straws. One person grabs four straws in his fist—three long ones, one short. Whoever picks the short one gets a whack on the forehead. But sometimes they look out the window. If they spot a Chechen, they're supposed to cry "Chechens, Chechens!" and then people from all the settlements run out and start beating pots with sticks, to scare the Chechens. And the Chechens skedaddle. Once, two people approached the town from the south, an old man and an old woman. We banged on our pots, stomped and hollered up a storm, but the Chechens didn't care, they just kept on coming and looking around. We—well, the boldest of us—went out to meet them with tongs, spindles, whatever there was. To see who they were and why they came.

"We're from the south, Golubchiks," they said. "We've been walking for two weeks, we've walked our feet off. We came to trade rawhide strips. Maybe you have some goods?"

What goods could we have? We eat mice. "Mice Are Our Mainstay," that's what Fyodor Kuzmich, Glorybe, teaches. But our people are softhearted, they gathered what there was in the izbas and traded for the rawhide and let them go their way. Later there was a lot of talk about them. Everyone jabbered about what they were like, the stories they told, how come they showed up.

Well, they looked just like us: the old man was gray-headed and wore reed shoes, the old woman wore a scarf, her eyes were blue, and she had horns. Their stories were long and sad. Benedikt was little and didn't have any sense at all then, but he was all ears.

They said that in the south there's an azure sea, and in that sea there's an island, and on that island there's a tower, and in that tower there's a golden stove bed. On that bed there's a girl with long hair—one hair is gold, the next is silver, one is gold, and the next is silver. She lies there braiding her tresses, just braiding her long tresses, and as soon as she finishes the world will come to an end.

Our people listened and listened and said: "What's gold and silver?"

And the Chechens said: "Gold is like fire, and silver is like moonlight, or when firelings light up."

Our people said: "Ah, so that's it. Go on and tell us some more."

And the Chechens said: "There's a great river, three years' walk from here. In that river there's a fish—Blue Fin. It talks with a human voice, cries and laughs, and swims back and forth across that river. When it swims to one side and laughs, the dawn starts playing, the sun rises up in the sky, and the day comes. When it goes back, it cries, drags the darkness with it, and hauls the moon by its tail. All the stars in the sky are Blue Fin's scales."

We asked: "Have you heard why winter comes and why summer goes?"

The old lady said: "No, good people, we haven't heard, I won't lie, we haven't heard. It's true, though, folks wonder: Why do we need winter, when summer is so much sweeter? It must be for our sins."

But the old man shook his head. "No," he said, "everything in nature must have its reason. A feller passing through once told me how it is. In the north there's a tree that grows right up to the clouds. Its trunk is black and gnarled, but its flowers are white, teeny tiny like a speck of dust. Father Frost lives in that tree, he's old and his beard is so long he tucks it into his belt.

5

Now, when it comes time for winter, as soon as the chickens flock together and fly south, then that Old Man Frost gets busy: he starts jumping from branch to branch, clapping his hands and muttering doodle-dee-doo, doodle-dee-doo! And then he whistles: *wheeeeooossshhhh!* Then the wind comes up, and those white flowers come raining down on us—and that's when you get snow. And you ask: Why does winter come?"

Our Golubchiks said: "Yes, that's right. That must be the way it is. And you, Grandpa, aren't you afraid to walk the roads? What's it like at night? Have you come across any goblins?"

"Oh, I met one once!" said the Chechen. "Seen him up close, I did, close as you are to me. Now hear what I say. My old woman had a hankering for some firelings. Bring me some firelings, she kept saying. And that year the firelings ripened sweet, nice and chewy. So off I go. Alone."

"What do you mean, alone!" we gasped.

"That's right, alone," boasted the stranger. "Well, listen up. I was walking along, just walking, and it started getting dark. Not very dark, but, well, all gray-like. I was tiptoeing so as not to scare the firelings when suddenly: *shush-shush-shush!* 'What's that?' I thought. I looked—no one there. I went on. Again: *shush-shush-shush.* Like someone was shushing the leaves. I looked around. No one. I took another step. And there he was right in front of me. There was nothing there 'tall, and then all of a sudden I seen him. At arm's length. Just a little feller. Maybe up to my waist or chest. Looked like he were made of old hay, his eyes shone red and he had palms on his feet. And he was stomping those palms on the ground and chanting: *pitter-patter, pitter-patter, pitter-patter.* Did I run, let me tell you! Don't know how I ended up at home. My old lady didn't get her firelings that time."

The children asked him: "Grandfather, tell us what other monsters there are in the forest."

They poured the old man some egg kvas and he started. "I was young back then, hotheaded. Not afraid of a thing. Once I tied three logs together with reeds, set them on the water—our river is fast and wide—sat myself down on them, and off I floated. The honest truth! The women ran down to the bank, there was a hollering and a wailing, like you might expect. Where do you see people floating on the river? Nowadays, I'm told, they hollow out trunks and put them on the water. If they're not lying, of course."

"No, they're not, they're not! It's our Fyodor Kuzmich, Glorybe. He invented it!" we cried out, Benedikt loudest of all.

"Don't know any Fyodor Kuzmich myself. We aren't book-learned. That's not my story. Like I said, I wasn't afraid of nothing. Not mermaids or water bubbles or wrigglers that live under stones. I even caught a whirlytooth fish in a bucket."

"Come on, Grandpa," our folks said. "Now you're making things up."

"That's the honest truth! My missus here will tell you."

"It's true," the old lady said. "It happened. How I yelled at him. He clean ruined my bucket, I had to burn it. Had to carve out a new one, and a new one, by the time you hollow it, tar it, let it dry three times, cure it with rusht, rub it with blue sand—it near to broke my hands, I worked so hard. And for him, it's all glory. The whole village came out to look at him. Some were afraid."

"Of course they were," we said.

The old man was pleased. "But then, you see, maybe I'm the only one," he boasted. "The only one seen a whirlytooth up close—close as you folks there, he was—and come out of it alive. Ha! I was a real he-man. Mighty! Sometimes I'd yell so loud the window bladders would burst. And how much rusht I could drink at a sitting! I could suck a whole barrel dry."

Benedikt's mother was sitting there, her lips pressed. "What concrete benefit did you derive from your strength? Did you accomplish anything socially beneficial to the community?" she asked.

The old man was offended. "When I was a youngster, Golubushka, I could jump from here to that hill way over there on one leg! Beneficial! I tell you, sometimes I'd give a shout—and the straw would fall off the roof. All our folks is like that. A real strong man, I was. My missus here will tell you, if I get a blister or a boil—it's as big as your fist. No joke. I had pimples that big,

7

I tell you. That big. And you talk. I'll have you know when my old man scratched his head, he'd shake off a half-bucket of dandruff."

"Come on, now," we piped up. "Grandpa, you promised to tell us about monsters."

But the old man wasn't joking, he was really mad. "I'm not saying another word. If you come to listen . . . then listen. Don't go butting in. It ruins the whole story. She must be one of them Oldeners, I can tell by the way she talks."

"That's right," said our people, throwing a side glance at Mother. "One of the Oldeners. Come on now, Grandpa, go on."

The Chechen also told us about forest ways, how to tell paths apart: which ones are for real and which are a figment, just green mist, a tangle of grasses, spells, and sorcery. He laid out all the signs. He told how the mermaid sings at dawn, burbles her watery songs; at first low-like, starting off deep: *oooloo, oooloo,* then up higher: *ohouuaaa, ohouuaaa*—then hold on, watch out, or she'll pull you in the river—and when the song reaches a whistle: *iyee, iyee!* run for your life, man. He told us about enchanted bark, and how you have to watch out for it; about the Snout that grabs people by their legs; and how to find the best rusht.

Then Benedikt spoke up. "Grandfather, have you seen the Slynx?"

Everyone looked at Benedikt like he was an idiot. No one said anything, though.

They saw the fearless old man off on his way, and it was again quiet in town. They put more guards on, but no one else attacked us from the south.

No, we mostly walk out east from the town. The woods there are bright, the grass is long and shiny. In the grasses there are sweet little blue flowers: if you pick them, wash them, beat them, comb and spin them, you can plait the threads and weave burlap. Mother, may she rest in peace, was all thumbs, everything tangled up in her hands. She cried when she had to spin thread, poured buckets of tears when she wove burlap. Before the Blast, she said, everything was different. You'd go to a deportmunt

8

store, she said, take what you wanted, and if you didn't like it, you'd turn up your nose, not like now. This deportmunt store or bootick they had was something like a Warehouse, only there were more goods, and they didn't give things out only on Warehouse Days—the doors stood open all day long.

It's hard to believe. How's that? Come and grab what you want? You couldn't find enough guards to guard it. Just let us in and we'll strip everything bare. And how many people would get trampled? When you go to the Warehouse your eyes nearly pop out of your head from looking at who got what, how much, and why not me?

Looking won't help any: you won't get more than they give you. And don't stare at another guy's takings: the Warehouse Workers will whack you. You got what's yours, now get out! Or else we'll take that away too.

When you leave the Warehouse with your basket you hurry home to your izba, and you keep feeling around in the basket: Is everything there? Maybe they forgot something? Or maybe someone snuck up from behind in an alley, dipped in, took off with something?

It happens. Once, Mother was coming home from the Warehouse, they'd given her crow feathers. For a pillow. They're light, you carry them and it's like there was nothing there. She got home, pulled off the cloth—and what do you know? No feathers at all, and in their place, little turds. Well, Mother cried her eyes out, but Father got the giggles. What a funny thief— he not only took off with the goods but thought up a joke, with a twist: here's what your feathers are worth. How d'ya like that!

The feathers turned up at the neighbor's. Father started bugging him: Where'd they come from? The market. Whaddya trade them for? Felt boots. Who from? All of a sudden the neighbor didn't know this, didn't know that, I didn't mean, I didn't, I drank too much rusht—you couldn't get a thing out of him. That's how they left it.

Well, and what do they give out at the Warehouse? Mousemeat sausage, mouse lard, wheatweed flour, those feathers, then

9

there's felt boots, of course, and tongs, burlap, stone pots: different things. One time they put some slimy firelings in the basket
—they'd gone bad somewhere, so they handed them out. If you
want good firelings you have to get them yourself.

Right at the edge of the town to the east are elfir woods. Elfir
is the best tree. Its trunk is light, it drips resin, the leaves are delicate, patterned, paw-shaped, they have a healthy smell. In a
word—elfir! Its cones are as big as a human head, and you can
eat your fill of its nuts. If you soak them, of course. Otherwise
they're disgusting. Firelings grow on the oldest elfirs, in the deep
forest. Such a treat: sweet, round, chewy. A ripe fireling is the
size of a person's eye. At night they shine silver, like the crescent
moon was sending a beam through the leaves, but during the
day you don't notice them. People go out into the woods when
it's still light, and as soon as it's dark everyone holds hands and
walks in a chain so as not to get lost. And so the firelings don't
know there's people around. You have to pick them off quick,
else the fireling will wake up and shout. He'll warn the others,
and they'll go out in a flash. You can pick them by feel if you
want. But no one does. You end up with fakes. When the fake
ones light up, it's like a red fire is blowing through them. Mother
picked some fakes and poisoned herself. Or else she'd be alive
right now.

Two hundred and thirty-three years Mother lived on this
earth. And she didn't grow old. They laid her in the grave just as
black-haired and pink-cheeked as ever. That's the way it is: whoever didn't croak when the Blast happened, doesn't grow old
after that. That's the Consequence they have. Like something in
them got stuck. But you can count them on the fingers of one
hand. They're all in the wet ground: some ruined by the Slynx,
some poisoned by rabbits, Mother here, by firelings . . .

Whoever was born after the Blast, they have other Consequences—all kinds. Some have got hands that look like they
broke out in green flour, like they'd been rolling in greencorn,
some have gills, another might have a cockscomb or something
else. And sometimes there aren't any Consequences, except
when they get old a pimple will sprout from the eye, or their pri-

vate parts will grow a beard down to the shins. Or nostrils will open up on their knees.

Benedikt sometimes asked Mother: How come the Blast happened? She didn't really know. It seems like people were playing around and played too hard with someone's *arms*. "We didn't have time to catch our breath," she would say. And she'd cry. "We lived better back then." And the old man—he was born after the Blast—would blow up at her: "Cut out all that Oldener Times stuff! The way we live is the way we live! It's none of our beeswax."

Mother would say: "Neanderthal! Stone Age brute!"

Then he'd grab her by the hair. She'd scream, call on the neighbors, but you wouldn't hear a peep out of them: it's just a husband teaching his wife a lesson. None of our business. A broken dish has two lives. And why did he get mad at her? Well, she was still young and looking younger all the time, and he was fading; he started limping, and he said his eyes saw everything like it was in dark water.

Mother would say to him: "Don't you dare lay a finger on me! I have a university education!"

And he'd answer: "I'll give you an ejucayshin! I'll beat you to a pulp. Gave our son a dog's name, you did, so the whole settlement would talk about him!"

And such a cussing would go on, such a squabbling—he wouldn't shut up till his whole beard was in a slobber. He was a hard one, the old man. He'd bark, and then he'd get tuckered; he'd pour himself a bucket of hooch and drink himself senseless. And Mother would smooth her hair, straighten her hem, take Benedikt by the hand, and lead him to the high hill over the river; he already knew that was where she used to live, before the Blast. Mother's five-story izba stood there, and Mother would tell about how there were higher mansions, there weren't enough fingers to count them. So what did you do—take off your boots and count your toes too? Benedikt was only learning his numbers then. It was still early for him to be counting on stones. And now, to hear tell, Fyodor Kuzmich, Glorybe, had invented counting sticks. They say that it's like you run a hole through a chip of wood, put it on the sticks, and toss them back and forth from right to left. And they say the numbers go so fast your head spins! Only don't you dare make one yourself. If you need one — come on market day to the market, pay what they tell you, they'll take burlap or mice, and then you can count to your heart's content. That's what they say. Who knows if it's true or not.

... So Mother would come to the hill, sit down on a stone, sob and cry her eyes out, soak herself with bitter tears, and remember her girlfriends, fair maidens, or dream about those deportmunt stores. And all the streets, she said, were covered with assfelt. That's like a sort of foam, but hard, black, you fall down on it and you don't fall through. If it was summer weather, Mother would sit and cry, and Benedikt would play in the dirt, making mud pies in the clay, or picking off yellers and sticking them in the ground like he was building a fence. Wide-open spaces all around: hills and streams, a warm breeze, he'd wander about — the grass would wave, and the sun rolled across the sky like a great pancake, over the fields, over the forests, to the Blue Mountains.

Our town, our home sweet homeland, is called Fyodor-Kuzmichsk, and before that, Mother says, it was called Ivan-Porfirichsk, and before that Sergei-Sergeichsk, and still before that Southern Warehouses, and way back when — Moscow.

Б · BUKI

WHEN HE was small, Benedikt's father taught him all kinds of handiwork. Making a stone ax was a chore. But he could do it. He could build an izba — dovetailed, beveled, any old way you like. He knew how to build a bathhouse and heat the stones. True, his father didn't like to wash. Bears, he'd say, live just fine without any baths. But Benedikt liked it. He'd crawl into the bathhouse, into the warm insides, splash egg kvas on the rocks for the smell, steam up some elfir branches, and give his backside a good thrashing. Benedikt knew how to dress skins, cut a rabbit into rawhide strips, stitch a cap—he was good with his hands. But just try catching one of those rabbits. By the time you're ready to throw a stone at her—*poof!* She's flown away. So most clothes are made from mouse skins, and that's not as good. Everyone knows that you can cut something from a big piece, but you can't keep your teeth warm with a mouse skin.

In short, he could do anything around the house. And that's how it should be. Fyodor Kuzmich, Glorybe, had declared: "Household Work Is Everybody's Business—Figure It Out Yourself." Benedikt's father chopped timber right up to his death throes and was thinking about setting Benedikt up in the trade. But Benedikt wanted to try for the Stokers. It was tempting. A Stoker is honored and respected, everybody takes off his hat to a Stoker—but he doesn't bow to anyone himself, he just walks on by, all proud and conceited.

And how can you argue? Where would we be without fire? Fire feeds us, fire warms, fire sings us songs. If fire dies out, we might as well lie down on our beds and put the stones on our eyes. They say there was a time when people didn't have fire. How did they live? They just did, crawling around in the darkness like blind worrums. It was Fyodor Kuzmich, Glorybe, who brought fire to people. Oh, Glorybe! We would be lost without Fyodor Kuzmich, whew, we'd be goners! He fixed up or invented just about everything we have. That smart head of his is always worrying about us, thinking thoughts for us! Fyodor Kuzmich's terem rises high, covers the sun with its dome. Fyodor Kuzmich, Glorybe, never sleeps, he just paces back and forth stroking his fluffy beard, fretting about us Golubchiks: do we have enough to eat, are we drunk, are we upset or hurt? We have Lesser Murzas, but Fyodor Kuzmich, Glorybe, is the Greatest Murza, Long May He Live. Who thought up sleighs? Fyodor Kuzmich. Who got the idea to carve wheels out of wood? Fyodor Kuzmich. He taught us to make stone pots, catch mice and make soup. He gave us counting and writing, letters big and small, taught us to tear off bark, sew booklets together, boil ink from swamp rusht, split sticks for writing and dip them in the ink. He taught us how to make boats—scrape out logs and put them on the water—he taught us to hunt the bear with a spike, to take out the bladder, stretch it on spikes, and then cover the windows with it so there's light in the window even in winter.

Only don't try to take any bear skins or bear meat for yourself: the Lesser Murzas keep watch. A simple Golubchik has no business wearing bear skin. You have to understand: How can a Murza ride in a sleigh without a fur coat? He'd freeze solid. But we run around on foot, we're warm, if you don't watch out you'll go and unbutton your coat, you're so steamed up. But silly thoughts sometimes get stuck in your head and dig in. I'd like to have a sleigh too, and a fur coat, and . . . And that's all Free-thinking.

Yes, Benedikt really wanted to try for the Stokers. But Mother was against it. It was the Scribes and nothing else for her. Father was pushing him toward timber, Mother pushed the Scribes, and he himself dreamed of swaggering down the middle of the street, his nose in the air, pulling a fire pot behind him on a string with sparks spilling from the holes. It wasn't heavy work: you get the coals from the Head Stoker, Nikita Ivanich, drag them home, light the stove, and then sit and stare out the window. In no time a neighboring Golubchik comes knocking, or someone from the Outskirts far off comes wandering by: "Father Stoker, Benedikt Karpich, let us have a bit of fire! That idiot over there wasn't watching, and my stove went out. And we were just about to fry up a batch of pancakes, what can you do . . ."

So you frown, grunt a bit like you just woke up, take your time tearing your rear end away from the bed or the stool, stretch out sweet-like—*stre-e-e-etch!*—scratch your head, spit, and pretend to be mad: "That's the way everything goes with you! Assholes. Can't tend a fire . . . Can't keep enough coals around for all of you Golubchiks, you know that? Know where you have to go for coals? . . . Aha . . . there you have it . . . These are my own two legs here. You people, you people. Someone else would just give up, wouldn't give you the time of day. You keep coming and coming. Don't have a clue yourselves, why it is you keep coming back . . . Well then, what is it you need? Coals?" You ask that way, as if you couldn't see for yourself what he needs, and you look stern, and you make a face, as if his breath stinks and you're about to puke. That is your job. That's what the job is.

The Golubchik starts whining again: "Benedikt Karpich, Faaaather, help us out, will you? I'll never forget it . . . Here, I . . . some hot pancakes . . . I brought them . . . they've only cooled off a little . . . Forgive me, don't . . ."

At this point you need to growl under your breath, "Pancakes . . ." but you don't take them yourself, God forbid—the Golubchik knows, he'll put everything quietly in a corner, and you keep on saying "Pancakes . . . hmmph"—mean-like, but don't overdo it. So that the voice goes down, into a grumble. And then slowly, taking your sweet time, you scrape up some coals with a shovel and over your shoulder to the Golubchik you say, "Did you bring your pot?"

"Of course, of course, Father, you've really saved my skin," —and then you give him a little bit.

When you've got the governmental approach to things you get respect from people—what a strict Stoker, they say, that's our batiushka, our father, for you—and then there's always little surprises after people leave. As soon as the door closes, you check in the window: Is he gone? And go straight to the package. I wonder what he brought. It might really be pancakes. Maybe lard. A baked egg. Another guy, if he's poor, might have just picked some rusht. It comes in handy too.

Ay, gone off dreaming again! It all ended the way Mother wanted. She got stubborn: there were three generations of intellyjeanseeya in the family, she said, I won't allow trodishin to be stepped on. Ay, Mother! She would run to Nikita Ivanich to whisper, and she'd drag him by the arm to the izba so they could both work on Father together, and she'd wave her hands about and set to screeching. Father gave up: *ayyy* . . . go to hell all of you, go on and do what you want . . . Only don't come complaining to me later.

So Benedikt now goes to work in the Work Izba. It's not bad work either. You come there and it's already warm, mouse-lard candles are already burning, the trash is swept away—heaven. They give him a bark notebook, a scroll to copy from, and they mark it: from here to here. You just sit tight in the warmth and make a clean copy. Only leave room for pictures. And that sweetie Olenka will draw the pictures in later with her white hand: a chicken or a bush. They don't much look like chickens or bushes, but still, they're nice to look at.

And Benedikt copies what Fyodor Kuzmich, Glorybe, writes: fairy tales, or teachings, sometimes poems. Fyodor Kuzmich's poems turn out so good that sometimes your hand starts shaking, your eyes go all dark, and it's like you've just gone and floated off somewhere, or else like there's a knot in your throat and you can't swallow. Some poems make sense, every word of them, and some—you could get dizzy trying to figure them out. The other day, for instance, Benedikt copied this one:

> The mountain crest
> Slumbers in the night;
> Quiet valleys
> Are filled with fresh dark mist;
> The road is free of dust,
> And the leaves are still . . .
> Just wait a bit,
> And you too will rest.

Any idiot could understand that one. But:

> Insomnia. Homer. Taut sails.
> I've read the list of ships halfway:
> That long brood, that train of cranes,
> That once arose over Hellas . . .

You could only squawk and scratch your beard. And then this one:

Spikenard, cinnamon, and aloe
Are rich in alluring fragrance:
As soon as Aquilon does blow,
They'll drip aromas of incense.

Yikes! Just go and figure out what'll drip where. Yes, Fyodor Kuzmich, Glorybe, knows all kinds of words. He's a poet, after all. Not easy work. "You may extract a single word from a thousand tons of linguistic ore," says Fyodor Kuzmich. He works himself to the bone for us. And he has oodles of other things to see to as well.

They say he thought up cutting a crooked stick from a piece of wood and bending it into a bow. We're supposed to call it a yoke. It's all the same to us, the boss is the boss, he can call it a yoke, the why and wherefore — it's none of our business. And you carry water jugs on this bow so your arms won't stretch out. Maybe they'll hand out some of these yokes at the Warehouse in the spring. First to the Saniturions, may their names not be spoken at night, then to the Murzas, and then, as soon as you know it, they'll come our way. And spring's already in the air. The streams will start running, the flowers will come out, the pretty girls will put on their dresses . . . What a dream! Fyodor Kuzmich himself, Glorybe, wrote:

O spring without end or borders!
Dream without borders to yield!
I recognize you, life, I embrace you,
And greet you with the ring of the shield!

Only why is it "the ring" of the shield? After all, the shield — the one for announcing decrees — is made of wood. If you happen to get a roadwork notice, if someone takes it into his head to make his own sleigh or doesn't turn over enough mouse meat, for instance, or if they postpone Warehouse Day too many times, the shield doesn't ring, it makes a dull thud. But then, the law isn't written for Fyodor Kuzmich, Glorybe. He has something to say about this, too. "Be proud," he says, "such art thou, poet, there is no law for thee." So it's not for us to tell him.

17

Other Scribes sit next to Benedikt in the Work Izba. That sweetheart Olenka draws drawings. A pretty girl: dark eyes, a gold braid, cheeks like the sky at sunset when the next day'll bring wind—all shiny. Bow-shaped eyebrows, or, like we're supposed to say now, yoke-shaped; a rabbit coat, felt boots with soles—must be from an important family. Olenka comes to work on a sleigh, the sleigh's waiting for her after work too, and it's not a plain one either: it's a troika. Under the harness the Degenerators stomp their feet, the shaft Degenerator is skittish, watch out or he'll bite you, and the trace Degenerators are even worse. How can you approach Olenka? Benedikt only sighs and steals glances at her, and she already knows, the sweetheart: she'll blink her eyes at him or turn her head just so. A modest girl.

So Benedikt goes to work, looking all around him, bowing to the Stokers, watching out for the sleighs, breathing in the frosty air, enjoying the blue sky. He was staring at a beautiful girl mincing by, and boom—he ran straight into a post. Ooooh, may you all go to here and there and back again. Damn things are all over the place!

Ouch. Nikita Ivanich, the Head Stoker, put up these posts. An old friend of Mother's, may she rest in peace. Also one of the Oldeners. He's about three hundred years old, maybe older, who knows. Who counts time? Do we know? Winter, summer, winter, summer, but how many times? You'd lose count just thinking about it. There are ten fingers, and on the feet ten toes —though some people have as many as fifteen, it's true, and some have two, and Semyon, the one from Foul Ponds, has a lot of tiny fingers on one hand, just like little roots, and nothing at all on the other. That's the kind of Consequence he got.

Nikita Ivanich would spend time with Mother. He'd come to the izba, wipe his feet off, "May I?" he'd say, and plop down on the stool and start talking about Oldener Times. "Polina Mikhailovna, do you recall Kuzminsky? Ha, ha, ha. And how Vaisman used to drop by, do you remember? Oh ho ho. And Sidorchuk, the son of a gun, remember, he was the one who concocted all those denunciations, and where are they now? Dust, it's all dust! And how Lyalya made coffee! I wouldn't object to a cup of coffee right this minute . . ." Mother would laugh or start sobbing, and the thought of deportmunt stores and booticks would drive her out of her mind. Or she'd suddenly ask, Where did all the lilac go? Lilac — that was flowers, they grew on trees, it's said, and had a wonderful smell. The old man couldn't stand these conversations, he'd run out into the yard and start chopping wood: *Whack! Hack! Smack! Crack!* . . . You could get mad all right, but how could you say a word to Nikita Ivanich? He's Head Stoker.

Benedikt is good with his hands, he can make anything, so can the other Golubchiks, but they can't make fire. It was Fyodor Kuzmich, Glorybe, brought fire to people. Only how it all happened, where he got the fire, we don't know. You could think on it for three days and you wouldn't figure it out, you'd just get a headache, like you'd drunk too much egg kvas. Some say it was from the sky, some say that Fyodor Kuzmich, Glorybe, stamped his foot and the earth flared up in a clear fire right then and there. Anything could be true.

And Nikita Ivanich tends the fire. All the Lesser Stokers go to him, they take their coals in stone pots to their izbas. What a good job! Oh, what a job! Sit at home, look out the window, and wait for Golubchiks to come by with surprises. During the daytime the Golubchiks are at work: some are wearing out holes in their chairs in the Work Izbas, some collect rusht in the swamp, some plant turnips in the fields, different things. A stove likes tender loving care; if you're late getting home — oops, it's out. Weren't paying attention — and the coals go cold. Just now, just now a little blue flame was running about and every bit of wood shone as if it were alive inside, red, clear, as if someone were breathing or wanted to say something — and that's that . . . Then it's quiet, gray, dull, like something died.

And it did die. The fire, that is. Ahh, hard to figure it all out. A mystery.

And where there's mystery — there's government service.

B · VEDI

NIKITA IVANICH was short, with a puny body, scruffy beard, and beady eyes like a chicken. But what a head of hair—yikes. In the Oldener Times, before the Blast, he was an old, old man who coughed and was about to die. He loved to tell Mother the story; if he told her once he told her a hundred times, like it made him proud. And then, he'd say, the whole shebang goes kaboom and blows to kingdom come—and here I am. I'm alive and well, he'd say, and haven't the slightest intention of dying, Golubchiks. And you needn't try to persuade me otherwise.

Mother didn't have an intention either, but those damned firelings tricked her. After Mother died, it wasn't like Nikita Ivanich changed, but he didn't talk so much, and he started to avoid people. It was easy to see why: you could count the Oldeners in a flash, there were hardly any left except for Degenerators, who aren't really people, and with today's Golubchiks, that is, with us, you can't talk the same way. When it comes down to it, the Oldeners don't understand our words, and we don't understand theirs.

Sometimes they babble and chatter such drivel, like little kids, I swear. When Mother and the old man were still alive, the housekeeping ran better. They kept fowl, put up powdered worrums, and there was Kitty to catch mice. Mother was lazy and slow. Summer was the time to put away eggs for kvas in winter. Everyone knows when fall comes the fowl head off south, but who knows if they'll come back? So you have to be on your toes.

But one time Mother said: Let's just lock them up so they'll stay at home and lay eggs for us year-round. Sure! Just try and hold them back! Grab them by the legs! They'll peck your eyes out in a thrice. Another time she said: What a pity they aren't edible—I would love to have a nice chicken dish. Father nearly keeled over laughing. What a dimwit, he said, what a dolt—

nothing but air between your ears. Klim Danilych ate chicken once—and where is he now? He not only kicked the bucket, first he turned all black, swelled up like a hollow log and burst; and that wasn't the end of it. Then the ground around his grave sank and caved in and wicked fires flicker there, cold they are, and it stinks so bad they sent people over twice to dump sand on the grave, and even that didn't help.

Nikita Ivanich goes on the same way: he doesn't get it, but sure knows how to talk. Once he said: There isn't any Slynx, it's nothing but human ignorance. How d'ya like that? And who rips people's veins out? Who sucks the lifeblood out of the neck? Tell me! And if you don't know, then shut your trap.

Nikita Ivanich started putting signposts all over town. Next to his own house he carved one that said "Nikita's Gates." As if we didn't know. No gates there, but still. They rotted. Well, all right. In another place he carved "Balchug St." Then: "Polyanka Rd." "Strastnoi Blvd." "Kuznetsky Bridge." "Volkhonka St." You ask him: Nikita Ivanich, what's going on? And he says: I want to keep memory alive. As long as I'm breathing, he says, and I'm planning on living forever, as you can see, I want to make my contribution to the restoration and rebirth of culture. Just wait, he says, in a millennium or so, you people will finally set foot upon the path of civilized development, curse your bloody souls. The light of knowledge will finally dispel the impenetrable darkness of your ignorance, O obstinate people, and the balm of enlightenment will flow down over your coarse manners, mores, and customs. Above and beyond everything, he says, I hope for a spiritual runnysauce. For without one, all the fruits of technological civilization will turn to murderous boomerangs in your callused hands, which, for that matter, has already happened. So, he says, don't stare at me from under your eyebrows like a loutish goat; when you listen to someone, keep your mouth closed. And don't shuffle.

Well, the Golubchiks got good and mad at first. You get up in the morning, rub your eyes, and right in front of your window there's a pole sticking up: "Arbat St." There's not much light in the window in winter anyway, even less what with the bladder pane, and now there's this arbat sticking up like a stud headed for a wedding. They all want to pull it out and send it to hell in a wheelbarrow. They want to use it for kindling or flooring. It doesn't take long for a person to get worked up: a wink and a blink and he's hopping mad. You can't lay a hand on Nikita Ivanich, he's a bossman, but your neighbor Golubchik—anything goes. Neighbors aren't easy to deal with, they're not just any old fuddy-duddy, you can't get rid of them. Neighbors are there to make your heart heavy, muddle your head, fire up your temper. Neighbors make you jumpy or can give you a feeling of dread. Sometimes you think: Why is my neighbor like that and not like this? What does he want? You look at him: he comes out on the porch. Yawns. Looks at the sky. Spits. Looks up at the sky again.

And you think: What's he looking at? Like he hasn't seen it before? There he goes again, standing around, and he doesn't know what he's standing around for. You shout, "Hey!"

"Whadisit?"

"Nuthin. That's whadidis. Whadisidding are you? Whaddya whadisidding at?"

"Whasit to ya?"

"Nuthin."

"Then shudjer trap!"

"You shudjer trap or else I'll ledja have it!"

So sometimes you have a good fight, even to the death, or you just break a few arms and legs, punch out an eye or something. Because it's your neighbor. There were a lot of killings on account of these poles at first, but then, as always, people got used to it, they'd just scrape off "Arbat" and carve something new: "Pakhom lives here," or cuss words. Cuss words are fun to carve. Never boring. There aren't too many of them, but they're all so cheery. Lively. If a fellow is in a serious mood, if he feels like crying or a weariness comes over him, a weakness—he'll never say or write any cuss words. But if he gets good and mad, or falls down laughing, or if he's taken by surprise all of a sudden —then they kind of come rolling out all on their own.

Г · GLAGOL

SO NIKITA IVANICH went and put his poles all over the place, and Benedikt kept banging his head on them. Lumps would pop up. That was too bad. The girls would probably giggle and whisper. They might stick their tongues out at him. Or shout from behind the gates and tease him: "Lumpy Bumpy!" One of them might run ahead on the path, stop right in front of him, raise her skirts and show him her bare ass. It was so insulting you could cry. Others, hiding in the izbas, laughed and squealed like harpies: there would be a shrieking and screeching all around, and you couldn't see who was doing it even if you turned your head, ears, or what-have-you to all sides. From those izbas where all the racket was, the shriek would up and jump to other izbas in the back row, and from there it would go to the third row, and from there out around the whole settlement. That's the way it always goes, spreading like a plague, like a fire when the wind blows the flames from yard to yard, God forbid. You could go stick your head into any house, push the door open with your boot, and shout in a furious voice: "Whaddya squawking about like a bunch of sick goats? Whasso funny?" — and they couldn't tell you. They don't know.

So just go to hell, you insulting bareass you. Sometimes, of course, it was fun to look at bare bottoms: they gave you all sorts of ideas, your heart pounded, and you didn't notice the time flying by. Yes, other times it was fun, but times like this it wasn't. Why was that?

Well, it's because the bareass was set against you, to put you in your place—you're lower than low, and don't go getting any ideas. If someone laughs at you, it's like he's showing his power over you, and you, boy, are down in the ditch.

That's something to think on. But if it's so simple, why is it that the Lesser Murzas, who are there to watch us, never laugh? Why do they stare at you like you've been dished out of the outhouse with a ladle? They talk through their teeth like they've got something valuable in their mouths, like it might fall out, and you're gonna grab it and take off. And the look in their eyes: they make them go all muddy like they're not moving. But they still cut straight through you. And then . . . but no, no, that must be Freethinking. No, no, I mustn't think. No.

. . . So then the pesky old man puts up all these posts, God forgive him, and Benedikt gets stuck with a nickname for his whole life: Lumpy. Other Golubchiks get nicknames: Rotmouth, or Gooseshake, or something else, depending on what he has coming, what stubborn habit or especially nasty Consequence he has. Benedikt didn't have any Consequences, his face was clear, he had ruddy cheeks, a strong torso, you could marry him off any time you liked. His fingers—he counted and he had just the right number, no more no less, no webbing or scales on them or on his toes. His nails were pink. He had one nose. Two eyes. An awful lot of teeth, almost three dozen. White. A golden beard, darker hair on his head, and curly. On his stomach too. On his nipples too. His belly button was where it should be, right smack in the middle. His private business also in the middle, lower down. Nice-looking. Just like a forest marshroom. Only without spots. You could take it out and show it off anytime.

And just where did Nikita Ivanich put that post? Right by the Work Izba. Wasn't that Freethinking? The sleighs wouldn't be able to turn around! Benedikt grabbed a handful of snow, held it to his lump, and stood there, reading the inscription: "Pioneer of Printing: Ivan Fyodorov." Hunh. Fancy shmancy. Come on now, let's pull it out. Benedikt grasped the stupid thing, strained, yanked, and pulled it out. He threw it down. Kicked it. Looked around. No one. Too bad Olenka or the other girls didn't see how strong he was.

There were sooooo many people in the izba. Tons and tons. Sweetie-pie Olenka was there. Sitting, blushing, her eyes lowered. But she did glance at Benedikt. Good. And Varvara Lukinishna was there, talking to Olenka, talking their girl talk. And Ksenia the Orphan. And Vasiuk the Earful.

Soon they'll announce it: time to start working. Good that he wasn't late. Being late doesn't matter, but people start to look and whisper: has he fallen ill, God forbid, God forbid. Knock on wood. True, as far back as Benedikt can remember, no one in their izba has ever fallen ill, knock on wood. Someone might get a scratchy throat or a headache—but that's not Illness, God forbid, God forbid. A finger might break, or you might get a black eye—that's not Illness either, God forbid, God forbid. Sometimes the hiccups get ahold of you—but that's not Illness, God forbid, God forbid. If the hiccups get you, you say three times:

> Hiccup, Hiccup,
> Go see Jacob,
> From Jacob to John,
> From John on and on.

They'll go away. If you get a sty on your eye, then you need a stronger spell so it'll last. You blow three times, spit three times, stand still on one leg, grab your other leg with your hand, hold it, and God forbid don't fall. And say:

> Sty, sty,
> Fly out of my eye.
> Strap, strap,
> Don't fall in the trap.
> Fig, fig,
> You'll ne'er buy a pig.
> Buy an ax and laugh
> Chop the strap in half.

That sty will go right away. That isn't Illness.

And what it is, Illness, and when it comes, and what happens then—no one knows. They don't talk about it. And if they do, they whisper. And if they whisper, then only when Vasiuk the Earful isn't around.

Everyone knows that he eavesdrops. That's the way it is. He's got so many ears you can't count them: on his head, and under his head, and on his knees, and behind his knees, and even in his boots. All kinds: big, little, round, long, and just plain holes, and pink pipes, and something like smooth slits, with hair—all kinds. You ask him, "Vasiuk, what do you need so many ears for?"

"They aren't ears."

"Then what are they?"

Just for a laugh someone will stick a piece of bone or a rusht butt or some other kind of rubbish in one of his ears. But the main ears, the ones he eavesdrops with, grow under his arms. When he's at work, he spreads his elbows wide so it's easier to listen. Then he almost moans in frustration: what kind of secrets can he hear, when anyone can see that his elbows are spread, so he must be listening.

Varvara Lukinishna also has an affliction: she's a terrible sight, even with your eyes closed. Only one eye, not a hair on her head, and cockscombs growing all over it, waving back and forth. There's one growing from her eye too. It's called cock's fringe. But it isn't Illness either, God forbid, God forbid. It's a Consequence. She's a nice woman all the same, and she writes beautiful and clean. And if you run out of ink, she'll always give you some of hers.

And fringe isn't Illness, God forbid, God forbid. And the Saniturions don't need to come, no, no, no.

They hit the clapper: work time. Benedikt sat down at his table, arranged the candle, spat on his writing stick, raised his eyebrows, stretched out his neck, and looked at the scroll: what did he have to copy today? He got *Fyodor Kuzmich's Tales.*

"Once upon a time," Benedikt wrote, "there was a goose who laid a golden egg." There you go, another Consequence. Everyone has Consequences! Take Anfisa Terentevna, she had a lot of grief from her chickens last year. And what chickens they were: big, beautiful, choice. They laid black and marble eggs—you couldn't find better! Kvas made of those eggs went straight to your head. You drain a pitcher of that kvas, and right away— *bam!* You feel like showing your stuff. You look around—everyone's double. A girl passes by—and it seems like there's two of her. You shout, "Girls! Come on over and fool around with me" —and she runs off. You roll over with laughter! You look at Anfisa Terentevna—and there's two of her too. But don't try to fool around with her, or Polikarp Matveich will come out, and there'll be two of him, and that's no joke, one of him is scary enough.

How those chickens would sing in the summer when the twilight fell and the moon rose in the sky, the sunset smoldered, the dew began to gather, and the flowers smelled sweet! Fine young fellows and fair maids would sit out in the yard, munching pickled nuts, chewing firelings, sighing, or chatting and pinching each other. As soon as the first star rolled out in the sky, the chickens would begin to sing. At first they'd crackle like kindling, then you'd hear a *trrrrr, trrrr,* then *croo-croo-croo,* and then when they got going, they'd roll out such thundering roulades, it'd warm your heart, as if you were flying off somewhere, or running down a mountain, or remembering some strange poems by Fyodor Kuzmich, Glorybe:

On the black sky—words are inscribed—
And magnificent eyes are blinded . . .
And we fear not the mortal bed,
And for us the lounge of passion isn't sweet.
Writing—in sweat, working—in sweat!
We know a different fervor:
Light fire dancing over curls—
A little breath—and inspiration!

And when autumn came with its rains and winds, all the fowl in the whole settlement headed south. Their owners would come out to see them off, sad and glum. The head hen would move in front, stick one leg out, flap her wings—and they'd all belt out a last, farewell song. They'd soar to the skies, take a turn around their homes, stretch out into a line, and fly off in pairs. You'd wave a kerchief, and sometimes the women would start wailing.

But then those chickens just went plain mad. They stopped flying, stopped singing, autumn passed, winter was just around the corner, all the other birds had headed south, and these crazies stayed put. Anfisa Terentevna shooed them with a switch broom, but they balked, ruffled their feathers, and even seemed to start talking like people. "Walk, talk, balk, whoo, whoo, whoo?" they asked, laughing at her. And they took to laying big, scary-looking white eggs. The poor woman near to lost her mind with fright. Benedikt rushed to help her and together they smothered those evil birds. They left one egg as a curiosity. Benedikt showed it to Nikita Ivanich. The old man—he's never afraid of anything—cracked the egg open on the edge of a bowl, and inside—Lord save us!—there was a yellow ball that looked like it was floating in thick water, and there wasn't any kvas malt at all . . . Lord Almighty! The old Stoker jumped up and shouted "Where are the others?" in a terrible sort of voice. We reassured him, sat him down: Don't worry, Nikita Ivanich, we know, we're not children. We got rid of the whole foul flock, cleared the coop with birch smoke so nothing evil would sprout up, and brought Goga the Fool to cast a spell: North, south, east, west, under the green sea, under the flaming oak, under the hot stone, under the stinking goat—hey, hey, fly away fly; blow left, spit right, eins, zwei, drei. It's a strong spell, tried and true, it should last.

Nikita Ivanich sat slumped over the table. He squeezed his eyes shut, clutched his jaw, and just sat there. Then he asked what the chickens had eaten before they went mad. How do we know? He went to see Anfisa Terentevna to ask, and thought about it for a long time. And that yellow ball, the one in the egg —he fried it and ate it. Honest to God, he ate it!!! And nothing happened to him.

Come to think of it, he never eats like people do. He won't touch worrums. They made Mother sick too, for that matter. But Benedikt learned how to find them as a child. He'd be playing in the streams and puddles with the other kids—there are a lot of clay-filled streams in the town—and he'd always feel around in the water and find worrums. Worrums are blind, stupid. You can catch a couple of dozen, put 'em on a stick, dry 'em out, and then pound 'em into a powder. They're so salty! The best flavoring for mouse soup. Father praised Benedikt, and he caught worrums himself, but Mother always made a face and pushed them away. Once Benedikt gave Nikita Ivanich a whole stringful. They just hung there on that string, the old man never touched them. A neighbor dropped by to ask for some fire and couldn't believe it: valuable goods were going to waste. Nikita Ivanich just gave them to her, each and every one of them. And it's so much work to catch them, you have to sift through a lot of mud till you feel the worrum, and then it wiggles around, nips at your fingers. Just try digging for them yourself! You won't go giving them away to neighbors.

One time Benedikt dropped in to see the old man, and he was sitting and sucking on a spoonful of yellow glue, the kind you see dripping down the trunks of elfirs. "What're you up to, Nikita Ivanich?"

"Eating honeycomb."

"Hummycum?"

"What bees make."

"Are you crazy?"

"Just try it. You people eat mice and worms, and then you're surprised to see so many mutants."

Benedikt got scared, he froze and finally left feeling a bit queasy, in a fog. It was frightening: the old man had gone by his own self and messed with the bees in the tree hollow . . . Then, of course, Benedikt told the others. They only shook their heads. "Sure. The bee shits, and we're gonna eat it?"

And One-and-a-Half—he has one and a half faces and a third leg—said, "What's Nikita Ivanich up to, egging us on to do things like that? And him a Stoker . . . Remember how he used to take the fellows to Murka's Hill, he wanted them to dig up the ground . . . He said there were mustardpieces buried there. And stone men, humongous white Rowmans and Creeks. We got plenty of our own rowmen, and only one river anyway."

That's right, he did take them. He said that in Oldener Times there used to be a Moozeeum on Murka's Hill, and there were shameful white stones buried in the earth. They were carved like men and women, with nipples and everything. It would be interesting to take a look, of course, but what about Freethinking? And you'd never finish digging there. And what do you need stone women for when there's plenty of live ones? The old man was playing tricks. For a long time kids ran after him and teased him: "Old Man Ivanich, wonders why his pants itch; takes them off at night, puts them on first light."

Nothing came of it.

Benedikt sighed, flicked a fleck of dust off his writing stick, and quickly finished copying the tale of the Golden Goose. He left space for Olenka to draw a goose. Then the booklet would be taken to market and traded for mice. You could trade a string of mice for a booklet. There's only government trade, though, don't dare copy anything yourself—if they find out, you'll get a thrashing.

They also say . . . but wait till Vasiuk the Earful moves away. They also say that somewhere there are Oldenprint books. Who knows if it's true, but there's a rumor. Those books, they say, were around before the Blast.

And they tell other lies: that in the woods there's a glade, and in the glade there's a white-hot stone, and beneath that stone there's a treasure. And on a dark night, when there's no moon or stars in sight, if you come to the glade barefoot, walking backward, and say, "I won't take what isn't found, but only what is underground," and when you get to the place, you turn three times, blow your nose three times, spit three times, and say, "Earth, don't conceal yourself; treasure, now reveal yourself," then a dark fog will come down and you'll hear a squeaking and a creaking from the woods, and that white-hot stone will roll back and the treasure will appear.

And that's where the books are buried. They glow like the full moon. But don't grab more than one, and when you've got one, run for your life, and if you do it wrong, then, they say, a veil falls over your eyes, and when you wake up you'll be sitting on the roof of your izba with empty hands.

And they also say these books have been seen at people's houses.

Д ▪ DOBRO

THE BELL RANG: lunch. It was too far to go home, so Benedikt went to the Food Izba. For two chits you could have a lunch of two dishes. Not as rich as at home, though at home the soup wasn't that thick anyway. But it wasn't far. Olenka ate at home, they sent a sleigh for her. The sweetheart.

Varvara Lukinishna latched on to Benedikt. She'd been keeping an eye on him for a long time. Are you going to the Food Izba? I'll go with you. And the fringe on her head quivers. If we're going, then let's go. Doesn't take long to lick your finger and put out the candle, does it?

There was such a crowd at the Food Izba! Benedikt nudged Varvara Lukinishna up to the counter with the bowls so she'd get in line, or else another bunch would come in. He rushed to a table and grabbed two places. He put spoons down: these places are taken. And he blocked them with his leg, so no one could push in. And he spread his elbows out wide and made threatening faces: it helps.

If a stranger ran up to steal a place, he'd take one look at Benedikt, and if he was a weakling, he'd turn away: Who needs to cross someone with a face like that, he'd think, God forbid; I'll sit in the corner, farther away . . . You have to know how to go about everything in its own way.

Smoke floated in the air. The bowls steamed, the spoons thudded, the candles crackled. It was hot. The cooks screamed with bloodcurdling voices, "Whoever's smoking rusht in the hut —get out! We can't breathe!"

No one moved, of course.

Varvara Lukinishna made her way over with the bowls. She didn't spill too much, even though there was a lot of pushing.

So. Mouse soup again. Governmental food, of course, is no match for homemade. The mice are the same, but the taste isn't. It's watery. There were so many worrums plunked down in the soup it could curdle your cheekbones. They don't begrudge the worrums. The soup's too salty. You stir it with your spoon—and all you get is a mouse tail. Well, maybe some eyes. Couple of ribs.

You can understand the cook. He probably hides the carcasses, takes the best pieces home to his kids.

Anyone would do the same. It's one thing to cook for strangers: Who knows what kind of people they are? But it's another to cook for your kids. Some people say you should cook the same for everybody. But who ever does that?

A stranger is a stranger. What's so good about a stranger? If the stranger's not a woman, of course. What's so good? Maybe

31

he doesn't even get that hungry. Maybe he'll manage without. Change his mind about eating.

But one of your own—he's cozy. His eyes are different. You just look at him and you can see he wants to eat. You can feel his stomach grumbling. One of your own is almost like you.

Varvara Lukinishna sighs. "I see they're not gutting the mice."

"They say there's not enough people to do the job."

"I understand, but still. Come and visit me, Benedikt, I'll treat you to some good soup."

"Thank you, Varvara Lukinishna. I'll definitely do that sometime."

Poor thing, that cockscomb just sticks straight out of her eye. Hard to look at it.

"I've been meaning to ask you, Benedikt. I'm copying poems by Fyodor Kuzmich, Glorybe. And I keep coming across the word 'steed,' 'steed.' What is a steed, do you know?"

Benedikt thought for a moment. Then another. His face even reddened from the effort. How many times he'd written that word himself, and had never thought about it. "It must be a mouse."

"What makes you think that?"

"Because 'Don't I take care of you, don't I fill your trough with oats?' That's it, a mouse."

"Well, then, what about 'The steed races, the earth trembles'?"

"It must be a big mouse. Once they start running around, you can't get to sleep. You remember, Fyodor Kuzmich, Glorybe, also wrote, 'Life, you're but a mouse's scurry, why do you trouble me?' It's a mouse, that's for sure."

"Still, it's strange. No, you haven't convinced me."

Varvara Lukinishna knows a lot of poems by heart. And she's always wanting to understand something. Who can count all the hard words! Someone else would shrug it off, but she needs to understand. Go figure. And she talks like a book. That's the way Mother talked. Or Nikita Ivanich.

Varvara Lukinishna lives alone. She catches mice, takes them to market, and trades them for booklets. Reads all the time.

"You know, Benedikt, poetry is everything to me. Our job is pure joy. And I've noticed something. Fyodor Kuzmich, Glorybe, he's different at different times. Do you understand what I mean? It's as though he speaks with different voices."

"That's what makes him the Biggest Murza, Long May He Live," said Benedikt cautiously.

"No, that's not what I mean . . . I don't know how to explain it, but I can sense it. For example: 'The reed pipe sings upon the bridge, and apple trees do bloom. The angel lifts a single star on high, of greenish hue. And on that bridge it is divine to gaze into those depths, those heights . . .' That's one voice. But, say—"

"On the bridge?" Benedikt interrupted. "That must be Foul Bridge. I know it. I caught worrums there. It really is deep as can be there. Watch out! If you bump your head and topple over, all they'll remember is your name. There'll only be bubbles left. The boards are rotten there too. When they herd the goats over it, one always falls through. I know that place." And he sucked on a bone.

"No, no, that's not what I mean. Listen: 'In the district where no feet have passed, save assassins' / Your herald the aspen is lipless and hushed, a specter far paler than canvas . . .' That's an entirely different voice, you must admit. Entirely different."

"I know that neighborhood too," cried Benedikt. "That's where Pakhom cracked his skull open."

Varvara Lukinishna shook her head, looked at the candle, and the blue flame wavered in her only eye.

"No, no . . . I keep reading and reading, and thinking, thinking . . . And I've divided the poems into different categories. And re-sewed the notebooks. And you know what's interesting?"

"Vasiuk the Earful over there is interested too," said Benedikt. "Huh, look how he's spread out. And you're wasting your time sewing poems back and forth. That's Freethinking."

"Oh, my God . . . Let's go back to work. They'll be ringing the clapper any moment now." Varvara Lukinishna looked around the hut. Rusht smoke was so thick you could cut it with a knife. It hung down blue to the floor. In the corner, Golubchiks who had had their fill were playing thwackers. Two of them had already drunk a lot of kvas and lay on the floor. Vasiuk wrote down their names.

"This restaurant is rather noisy," said Varvara Lukinishna, sighing. " 'I sat by the window in a crowded ballroom, while the bows in the background sang about love . . .' What do you think bows are?"

"Some kind of fast women?"

"No . . . You know, I so long to talk about art . . . Come visit me. Really, do come!"

"All right, I'll drop by sometime," said Benedikt unwillingly. If she weren't so ugly, he'd be happy to, of course. Take a steam bath and then go visiting. But in this case—there's plenty of time.

Maybe if he squinted it wouldn't be so bad. She was a nice woman. And she'd feed him soup. Then again, all of these conversations unsettled Benedikt.

Everyone had gathered in the Work Izba, but Olenka wasn't there. Benedikt waited, chewed on his writing stick. She wasn't coming. That happened sometimes: she was there before lunch, but didn't come in the afternoon. That must be the way it had to be. None of his business. But it made things boring.

He sat down to work on a new fairy tale, "The Gingerbread Man." What a funny story. This Gingerbread Man ran from a husband, he ran from a wife, and from a bear and a cow. He ran all on his lonesome through the forest, singing little ditties: "Run, run, as fast as you can, you can't catch me, I'm the Gingerbread Man." Benedikt was happy for the Gingerbread Man. He laughed. His mouth hung open as he wrote.

But when he got to the last line, his heart skipped a beat. The Gingerbread Man died. The fox gobbled him up! Benedikt even set his writing stick down and looked at the scroll. The Gingerbread Man died. Such a jolly little fellow. Singing songs. Enjoying life. And then—he was gone. Why?

Benedikt swallowed and looked around the izba. Everyone was writing, leaning over. The candles flickered. The bear bladders on the windows let in a bluish light. It was evening already. A storm was probably coming. It would sweep the snow into high drifts, whistle through the streets, bury the izbas up to the windows. The high trees would moan in the northern forests, the Slynx would come out of the woods, head for the town, hiss sadly, wail mournfully: *Slyyyyynx! Slyyyynx!* And the snowy wind would rage over the village, whirl over the terems, carrying the wild plaint into the distance.

Benedikt imagined himself sitting on the stove as a child, his boots hanging down and a blizzard carousing outside the window. The bluish mouse-oil candle crackled, shadows danced on the ceiling, Mother was sitting by the windowsill, embroidering a bed curtain or a towel with colored threads. Kitty crawled out from underneath the stove, soft, fuzzy, and jumped on Benedikt's lap. Mother doesn't like Kitty: if he claws her skirt she always brushes him off. Says she can't stand to look at his bare pink tail, the trunk on his face. And she doesn't like his pink, childlike fingers either. It seems these animals were completely different when she was young. So what, a lot of things have changed! If not for Kitty, who would catch so many mice for them, and where would they get lard for candles? And Benedikt loves him. If you reach out your finger, he'll grab it with his little hands and purr.

Mother supposedly had an Oldenprint book. But she kept it hidden. Because, they say, they're contagious. So Benedikt hadn't ever touched it or even seen it, and Mother strictly forbade him to talk about it, as if it didn't exist.

Father wanted to burn it. He was afraid. Some kind of Illness came from them, God forbid, God forbid.

And if it came, then the Red Sleigh would come.

And in the sleigh would be the Saniturions, may they remain nameless at night. They fly about in Red Sleighs, knock on wood, in red robes and hoods, slits where their eyes should be, and you can't see their faces, knock on wood.

And there's Benedikt sitting on the stove, and Mother embroidering, and the blizzard wailing outside the window, and the candle flares a bit, like the flickering lights above swamp rusht, and it's dark in the corners, and Father has already gotten ready for bed and undressed.

And suddenly Father screamed: *A-a-a-a!* And his eyes bugged out and he stared at his stomach, and kept on screaming and screaming. And there was a sort of rash on his stomach, like someone had patted him all over with dirty hands. And he screamed, "Illness! Illness!"

Mother pulled on her felt boots, threw a scarf on her head, and ran out for Nikita Ivanich.

Father: "He'll tell! He'll tell!" And he grabbed her skirts.

He meant that Nikita Ivanich would tell the Saniturions. All in vain. She pulled away from him and ran out into the blizzard.

She came running back with Nikita Ivanich. He said, "What is it now? Show me. What do we have here? Neurodermatitis. Don't eat so many mice. It'll go away on its own. Don't scratch it."

And it really did go away. And Father did find the Oldenprint book and burn it after all. He wasn't as afraid of the contagion as he was of the Saniturions, may they remain nameless at night.

Because they take you away and treat you, and after treatment people don't come back. No one ever comes back.

It's scary to think about. You walk down the street and suddenly there's a whistle and a whoaing. The Red Sleigh rushes by, with six Degenerators hitched to it. And whatever you're wearing, a caftan or a padded jacket, or a shirt in summer—you fling yourself to the side, into the snowdrifts or mud, cover your head with your hands, and shrink back: Lord, let them pass! Save me! You'd like to hide in the ground, disappear into the clay, become a blind worrum—just don't take me! Not me, not me, not me, not me! . . .

And they come closer and the clatter grows louder—here they are! There's heat and whistles, and the six Degenerators wheeze, and clods of mud fly up from the runners . . . and then they're gone. Silence. In the distance the dull thud of felt boots dies down.

I'm not ill, I'm not ill, no, no, no. No, no, don't let the Saniturions come, no, no, no. God forbid, God forbid, no, no, no.

E · YEST

WHEN KITTY DIED, there was no one to catch mice. You won't catch too many with bare hands. Of course science doesn't stand still, it just keeps inventing things. Benedikt would sometimes make loops, noose traps. He'd twist threads into a stiff string, rub it good and well with mouse lard, wind a special loop on one end so that it would slide, try it out on his finger—and he was off to the hunt. Our floors are all cracked and gaping, not so much on account of being poor, but so it's easier for the mice to come out. Come on out now, little critters!

> I have seen you, little mouse,
> Running all about the house,
> Through the hole your little eye
> In the wainscot peeping sly,
> Hoping soon some crumbs to steal,
> To make quite a hearty meal.

They say that the rich Golubchiks who have tall, painted terems two stories high—Murzas, for instance, or someone who has grown fat from a dishonest life—those ones have all the cracks stuffed up so there's no draft even in the deepest winter. And how do they get their food? They've got special serfs sitting in the cellars, and those serfs are trained to attack mice. That's all they know how to do. People say they sit there in the cellars day in and day out in the pitch dark, but they can see like it's high noon. They can't even come out into the light, they'd go blind right off, and their mice-catching days would be over. Who knows? Could be.

But we're simple folk, we lie down on the floor on our bellies, stick the noose in a crack and give it a tug. Mice are stupid critters. They're curious: what is that noose doing over there? And they'll stick their heads right in the loop and then: *whoop!* You give it a jerk.

Fyodor Kuzmich, Glorybe, made a scientific invention for us. The mouse trap. Well, people do have those too, but they just stand there idle. You have to put a piece of food in the mouse trap for it to work, otherwise the mice aren't interested and won't go near it. Thieves, on the other hand, are very interested. As soon as you've left home, a thief will find out that you have food lying about, and he'll come take a look. He'll clean you out of house and home and won't even say thank you.

That's just what thieves do: they take everything. Meat, noodles, nuts, goosebread, marshrooms, if you've got them saved up — everything. But they don't take rusht. There's plenty of it everywhere. You have to be a real lazybones not to have enough rusht! True, if it's really good rusht, dry and fluffy — then they might go after it. They might take the rusht too.

You can understand a thief. Here he is, walking through the village and he sees the izba door is closed with a stick. The owners aren't home. They're out, but there might be some rabbit meat in the izba. Mightn't there? It is possible, isn't it? Yes indeed, there might! Maybe the owner managed to hit a rabbit with a rock, or maybe he traded eggs or horsetail with his neighbors. Maybe he's got a knack for catching rabbits! The idea gets into your head and stays there. If you walk on by you'll never know. You can't help taking a peek. So the thief goes in, looks around. If he guessed right and there's meat — he'll take it. If not, he gets mad that there isn't any and he'll take whatever he can find, even worrums. And once he's pinched one thing, what's to hold him back? The izba's already been burgled, he figures, and so he'll go and clean the place out.

But Benedikt doesn't have anything to steal. He doesn't keep provisions, he eats what he catches. All that's there is a full trunk of rusht.

What's so good about rusht? Well, it's good for all sorts of things. You can smoke it, and drink it, and make ink out of it, and dye threads with it if someone wants to embroider a cloth. It makes good mead, especially when winter's coming. You can use it to keep the house warm by sticking it between the logs to fill the cracks. Some people have tried to cover the roof with it, but that doesn't work. The bunches are round and stiff—it just falls apart. Straw is good for a roof. If you're rich, you can use wood planks.

You can find rusht in the bog. On weekends everyone grabs a basket as soon as it's light and sets off in different directions. Benedikt found a good place. Nikita Ivanich put up a post there that says "Garden Ring." There's no ring of course, just izbas in rows. The town ends there. And right beyond the izbas there's a bog full of rusht. More than you can pick. Even the locals won't shoo you away; other Golubchiks would beat you up for going near their place, but these people don't care. So you hurry along just after dawn, in winter it's murky, red, and blows cold.

> From the dawn a luxurious cold
> Pierces the garden.

Just like Fyodor Kuzmich wrote.

We don't have gardens, of course, only maybe a Murza might, but the part about the cold—that's true enough. It goes straight through you. Benedikt's felt boots have thinned out, his feet can feel the snow. You run quick quick over Foul Bridge to the top of the hill, then down again past the Cockynork neighborhood. If a Cockynork sticks his head out you throw a rock at him to warm yourself up, and keep running. You throw the rock because the Cockynorks, they don't talk like us: all they say is blah-blah-blah and blah-blah-blah—you can't understand a thing. Why do they talk like that, why don't they want to talk like we do? Who knows. Maybe on purpose. Or maybe it's just a bad habit, that kind of thing can happen.

They're just cutting off their noses to spite their faces. What can they say in Cockynork? Our language is handier any way you look at it: you can sit down, talk things over, discuss them: such and such and thus and so. And everything's clear as day.

The Cockynorks are just plain stubborn and that's all there is to it. Some say that their noses get in their way; that they'd be happy to sit down and chat in our language, except for their noses. Their noses practically touch the ground—it's really funny. That's the Consequence they have.

When our people don't have anything to do, they sometimes get together in the evening at the Cockynork settlement, climb up on the fence, look all around, and laugh. Hey, Cockynorks, how come your noses are hanging down? Trying to smell your shoes? We'll wipe your noses for you! They run out and they're all mad. It's so funny—they close their shutters tight, hustle the children into the house, chattering blah-blah-blah all the while. And if you throw a rock and hit one of them on the forehead, he yells *ouuuuch!* But he doesn't grab the lump with his hand, he uses his nose instead, and that's really hysterical. Our lads nearly fall off the fence laughing.

Ivan Beefich, who has a little hut on Rubbish Pond, loves these kinds of pranks so much that he collects rocks—he digs them up in his garden and saves them in a barrel. If the lads are heading off to the settlement, they can't sneak by him, he knows, he keeps watch out the window. Wait, guys, take me with you, I won't make it on my own!

Ivan Beefich has really bad Consequences. His head, arms, and shoulders are all strong, straight, and powerful, it would take three days to unscramble them, as they say. But right after his underarms come the soles of his feet, and in the middle there's an udder. That's what Nikita Ivanich called it: an "udder," but we don't have a word like that, why would we, what do we need it for, it's not in any books. We just call it titties.

Sometimes there's a mix-up of course. Once the guys went to tease the Cockynorks and one of them carried Ivan Beefich piggyback. He had two whole capfuls of rocks, and was singing. He's master singer of old songs. He starts off with: "Hey, Dunya, Dunya, Dunya, die, she clobbered Vanya in the eye!" And he wiggles his shoulders and rolls his eyes, his teeth sparkle all white—a real dashing daredevil, that fellow. Of course, since he was singing, the Cockynorks heard him coming, they shut their windows and doors and hid out, only they forgot one old man in the yard. Well, he got it from everyone. And that nasty old man got so mad, he picked up a rock with his nose, just like it was his hand, and *pow!* He bonked Ivan Beefich right on the udder. Ivan Beefich went plop—and lay there. Our lads got furious: how dare they hit one of our guys—and they tore up half the Cocky-nork settlement.

That kind of thing happens mostly on holidays when people are in a good mood; on weekdays everyone's plenty busy, our people work in government service, then they make soup or smoke rusht. The Cockynorks weave bags and baskets from mouse tails, very fancy, intricate—and then they trade them at the market. Cockynorks aren't good for anything else.

Sometimes when you're running by their settlement, you'll throw something and then head for the bog. It only takes a week for fresh rusht to sprout, reddish or with a hint of green. It's good for smoking. And the older stuff is browner, it's better for paint or mead. You stuff fine rusht into a dry leaf, roll a smoke, and knock on an izba door to ask for a light. If they don't sock you in the forehead right away, they might grumble a bit, take pity, and give you a light. You walk along puffing, and you feel warmer, like you're not alone, and it seems like the faces of the Golubchiks you run into along the way aren't so beastly after all.

Ж · ZHIVETE

BENEDIKT IS MOODY, he knows that himself. No two days are ever the same. Some mornings he's full of boundless energy, every muscle is ready to spring into action. Feels like turning half the world upside down. That's when he wants to work with his hands. In that kind of mood you look for something to do: chop or plane logs, or fix something at home, make an ax or a jug, maybe hollow out a bucket. Once, in a mood like that he smoothed out a dozen planks for the roof. Honest! A whole dozen! Well, maybe not a dozen, but three for sure. That's a lot too. At times like that you feel like singing. Loud.

Sometimes the doldrums get him. Usually in the evening. Especially in autumn, and almost every day in winter. But it happens in summer too.

In the evening, when the sun starts to set beyond the wavy fields, beyond the blue mountains, beyond the far woods where no one walks — as soon as the long shadows fall and the silence comes down, that's when it happens. You're sitting on the porch, smoking, arguing with your neighbors. Gnats are swarming in the air. All the birds, all the forest scaries have settled down. Like someone walked by and wagged a finger at them. Then they start up again suddenly, but with different voices, night voices. From the groves you hear a rustling, a coo-booing, a squelching, and sometimes something whirtles or meows in a nasty way.

The neighbors say: "It's a mermaid, damn it."

And others: "Yeah, sure. It's a woodsucker, she has a nest over there."

Then some stupid woman will croak: "Maybe it's a blindlie bird."

Everyone yells at her: "What an idiot! A blindlie. A blindlie doesn't have a voice, that's why he's a blindlie!"

The silly woman opens her mouth again: "Maybe he's blind, but he has a voice like a horn, I can hear it, I'm not deaf."

Everyone: "He can see blind better than you can! He sees what he needs to see! His claws are where he's strong, not his voice!"

The man of the house — the woman's husband — says to her: "All right, woman, you've had your gabble — go on, now. Go cook something. You've started thinking too much."

Everything's like always: people are chattering, speaking their minds, discussifying about nature. And Benedikt suddenly feels queasy. Like somewhere here, in the middle, heartburn is fixing to bubble up hot. Around it, like a ring, there's a kind of cold. And there's an unease in his back. And a pulling on his ears. And his spit's bitter.

If you complain, they say: "That's the Slynx staring at your back."

No. Not likely. Couldn't be. It's something slinking around on the inside, or maybe, like Nikita Ivanich says, it's feelosophy.

You look at people—men, women—like you're seeing them for the first time, like you're a different creature, or you just came out of the forest, or the other way around, you just walked into the forest. And everything seems strange, sad and strange. Take that woman. You think: What's she for? She's got cheeks, a stomach, she bats her eyes, she's talking about something. Turning her head, smacking her lips, and what's inside her? A meaty darkness, squeaking bones, strings of guts, and nothing else. She laughs, she's scared, she frowns—but does she really have any feelings? Thoughts? What if she's just pretending to be a woman and she's really a swamp monster? Like the ones that hoot in the bushes, crackle the old leaves, creak the branches, but never show themselves. What if you went over to check? You could set your fingers like horns and poke her in the eyes. What would happen? Plunk. She'd fall, right?

You wouldn't get away without a fuss, the men would give you a thrashing, they wouldn't care that you're a government Scribe, an official Golubchik—they'd beat you black and blue, and if some Lesser Murza started asking questions, they'd swear up and down that that's how you were, that your blue face was just a plain old Consequence, that your parents had the same ugly mugs, and your grandmother too.

Today, for instance, toward evening, right at work, who knows why, feelosophy suddenly churned up inside Benedikt. Dimly, like a shadow under the water, something in his heart started to turn, to torment and call him. But where? Hard to say. There was a tingling in his back, and he felt tears rise. It was either like you were fixing to get good and mad, or wanted to fly. Or get married.

He couldn't get the Gingerbread Man out of his head. What a scary story. He sang and sang . . . He ran and he ran and he ran . . . You can't catch him, he's the Gingerbread Man . . . And then he got caught. Snap.

It was Varvara Lukinishna with all her vague talk too. She's gotta know what "steed" means. Discontent, that one. Who knows what Fyodor Kuzmich, Glorybe, might do in poems. That's what poems are for, so you don't understand a thing. And if Fyodor Kuzmich, Glorybe, is speaking in different voices, well, that's just . . . Everybody does that. Take Benedikt: this morning he left home, walking in the sunshine, the snow squeaking underfoot, lots of pleasant thoughts swirling in his head, not a care in the world. But now, with night coming, it was like he was someone else: weak, scared, and it was so dark out that going out on the street was like wearing a boot over your head—but he had to. And Olenka wasn't there, and it was even more miserable in the izba without her.

The clapper clunked: work's over.

The Golubchiks jumped up, tossed their writing sticks down, pinched the candle flames, hurried to pull on their coats and crowded around the door. Jackal Demianich, a Lesser Murza, made the rounds of the tables, put the finished scrolls in a box, stuffed the empty ink pots in a basket, and wiped the writing sticks with a rag. He grumbled that we're using up a lot of rusht, that you can't keep enough sticks on hand, and that's what a Murza does, he grumbles and gripes at people, and Jackal Demianich is given that power over us because he's a Veteran of the Ice Battle. What sort of Battle it was, and when, and just who Jackal Demianich fought, and whether he struck down a lot of Golubchiks with a cudgel or a bludgeon, we don't know, and don't want to know—and even if someone told us we'd forget.

So the day's over, it's gone, burned itself out. And night has fallen on the town, and Olenka sweetie disappeared somewhere in the winding streets, in the snowy expanses, like a vision, and his fleeting friend the Gingerbread Man was gobbled up, and now Benedikt hurried home, making his way over the hills and drifts, tripping and falling, shoveling the snow with his sleeve, and feeling a path through the winter, parting the winter with his hands.

What is winter, after all? What is it? It's when you come into the izba from the cold, stomping your felt boots to knock off the snow, shaking it off your coat and slapping your frozen hat against the door jamb; you turn your head, and your whole cheek listens to the warmth of the stove, to the weak current from the room. Has the stove gone out? God forbid. Undressing, you go all wobbly in the warmth, like you're thanking someone; you hurry to blow on the fire, to feed it with old, dry rusht, with wood chips and sticks, you pull the still warm pot of mouse soup out of the swaddle of rags. Fumbling in the hiding space behind the stove, you grab the bundle with the spoon and fork and feel grateful: everything's in order, they didn't steal it, there weren't any thieves, and if there were, they didn't find anything. You gulp down the usual thin soup, spitting the claws out into your palm, and start thinking, looking at the feeble, bluish flame of the candle, listening to the scuttering and scurrying under the floor, the crackle in the stove, the wail just outside the window, begging to be let in; something white, heavy, cold, unseen. You suddenly imagine your izba far off and tiny, like you're looking down at it from a treetop, and you imagine the whole town from afar, like it was dropped in a snowdrift, and the empty fields around, where the blizzard rages in white columns like someone being dragged under the arms with his head arched back. You imagine the northern forests, deserted, dark, impassable; the branches rock in the northern trees, and on the branches, swaying up and down, is the invisible Slynx—it kneads its paws, stretches its neck, presses its invisible ears back against its flat, invisible head, and it cries a hungry cry, and reaches, reaches for the hearth, for the warm blood pounding in people's necks: *SSSLYYYNNXXX!*

Fear touches your heart like a cold draft or a small paw, and you shudder, shake yourself and look around, as if you don't know who or where you are. Who am I?

Who am I?

Ay. Ugh. This is me. I just let things get out of hand for a moment, I almost dropped myself, just barely caught hold . . . Ugh . . . That's what it does, that Slynx, that's what it does with you even from afar, it sniffs you out, senses you, fumbles for you through the distance, through the snowstorm, through the fat log walls. And what if it happened to be nearby?

No, no, I shouldn't think about it, to hell with it, scare it off, I should start laughing or dance a squatting dance like on the May holidays. Sing a loud, happy song.

Ay, tra-la-la, tra-la-la. Ay, tra-la-la-la la! Tra la-la la la! Faldi-rol-fiddle dee faddle. Hey diddle diddle dum dee!

There you go. That's better . . . Fyodor Kuzmich, Glorybe,

teaches us that art elevates us. But art for art's sake—that's no good, he says. Art should be connected to life. "My life, or are you just a dream? . . ." Maybe . . . I don't know.

What do we really know about life? Even if you think hard about it. Who told it to be? Life, that is. Why does the sun roll across the sky, why does the mouse scuttle and scurry, the tree stretch upward, the mermaid splash in the river, the wind smell of flowers? Why do people hit each other over the head with sticks? Why is it that sometimes you don't feel like hitting, but want to go off somewhere in the summer, without roads, without paths, toward the sunrise, where the greengrass grows all around, shoulder high, where the blue rivers play, and above the rivers the golden flies swarm, the branches of unknown trees hang down to the water, and on those branches, white as white can be, sits the Princess Bird. And her eyes take up half her face, and her mouth is human, red. And she's so beautiful, that fancy Princess Bird, that she can't get over herself. Her body's covered with lavish, delicate white feathers, and she's got a tail seven yards wide that hangs like a braided net, like lacy goosefoot. The Princess Bird turns her head this way and that, admiring herself, kissing her lovely self all over. And no one in his life has ever been harmed by that white bird. And no one ever will be. Amen.

3 . ZELO

RICH PEOPLE are called rich because they live rich.

Take Varsonofy Silich, a Greater Murza. He's in charge of all the Warehouses. He decides when to have a Warehouse Day, whose turn it is, and what to hand out.

Varsonofy Silich has a governmental turn of mind, and he looks that way too: he's a blubbery sight, even for a Murza. If you took six Golubchiks and tied them together, it wouldn't even make for half of Varsonofy Silich, no, it wouldn't!

His voice is deep, rough, and kind of slow. For instance, you might need to tell the workers that on the Sunday before the May Holiday they have to open the Central Warehouse and hand out half a pood of goosefoot bread to the Golubchiks, and two skeins of uncolored thread. Some other simpler fellow would just open his mouth, say what he had to say, and close it again till next time.

But that wouldn't be the governmental approach to things, and no one would listen to him. Someone who talked that way wouldn't be a Murza.

But Varsonofy Silich does it like he's supposed to: in the morning he calls in the Lesser Murzas and the Warehouse Workers, and starts: "D-i-s-t-r-i-b-u-t-e . . ." But what exactly they're supposed to distribute he doesn't get to until evening because he doesn't like to give away official goods.

And how could you? You give one Golubchik a half pood, and then you have to go and give one to his wife, and one to the kids, and to the old, blind, limping grandma and grandpa, and to all the relatives or workers in every household. Don't you have to feed the Degenerators?—yes, you have to. In the Central Settlement alone there's at least a thousand izbas, you can count 'em, and if you take all of Fyodor-Kuzmichsk, the whole town will want to be fed, and well, you couldn't ever save up enough for everyone!

And don't you want to eat too? And your family? And the Warehouse Workers? And their serfs? Well, there you have it! You can't do it without the right approach.

You need to be smart, to think things through. Lids, for instance. Now, a simple Golubchik, one of the soft-hearted ones, what would he think? Just take the lids and hand them out. In a flash, the rumor would spread, a crowd would gather—you wouldn't be able to breathe, there'd be a crush, a stampede, cries, shouts, cripples riding piggyback on people with two legs —cripples who were trampled the last time—and they'd scream: "I'm an Invalid! Give a Lid to an Invalid!!!" Little kids would weave through the crowd pickpocketing; some would drag cats in on a string, or a goat, so as to get an extra lid; this is my brother-in-law, they'd say, he wants one too. So what if he's

47

got fur or horns or an udder—well, Golubchiks, that's Consequences for you, or are you all squeaky clean yourselves?

They'd murder each other, take off with as many lids as they could carry—some would have heart attacks from lugging the load, and afterward they'd sit in their izbas looking at what they'd got, and wouldn't know what to do with them. What do you cover with them? This one's too big, and that one's too little, they don't fit anything. They'd turn them over and over, smash them in disappointment, and throw them out in the backyard under the fence.

No, you can't do things that way with us.

So Varsonofy Silich, figuring all this out, taking stock, thinking deep, decided not to give out any lids. Better for the people and for the lids.

And he thought: If you boil soup without a lid it will come out thicker, it kind of settles down. It's tastier.

He also thought: Since there aren't any lids, everyone will have a secret longing: If only I had a lid for my pot! Life is better when you've got a dream, and sleep is sweeter.

Now that's governmental thinking.

That's why Varsonofy Silich lives rich, he's got a two-story terem with onion domes, he built a porch around the top floor, it's called a gallery, and serfs walk around and around the gallery —to scare everyone—keeping watch to make sure there isn't any evil intent toward the owner, to make sure no one's wanting to go and throw a rock at his house or something worse . . .

In the courtyard there are different services and trades; barns, warehouses, a sty for Degenerators, barracks where the serfs live. There are tons and tons of serfs: mouse-catching serfs, flour-grinding serfs, kvas-brewing serfs, marshroom gatherers, horsetailers, as many as you like. There are floor-washing serf-girls, spinners and weavers, and there's one special woman who just makes snowballs, rolls them in crushed fireling flour, and serves them at meals, and Varsonofy Silich partakes of them.

One time Benedikt got to see Varsonofy Silich in all his glory. Benedikt was walking along and some Lesser Murzas were blocking off the road—"Halt, don't pass"—barking at the Golubchiks and warming some backsides with spikes—"Don't get pushy." Then the plank gates opened, bells clanked, Degenerators stomped their felt boots, a sleigh creaked—*maaaaama!*—and there was Varsonofy Silich himself sitting in the sleigh like a great mountain. The people were happy, they tossed their hats in the air, and bowed low: "Good day, and Long May You Live, Varsonofy Silich, our dear provider, and the same to your wife, and your children as well! What would we have to eat and drink without you, our dearest one, sweet golden light of our lives!"

Everyone shouted this at him—Benedikt too—so that he would soften a bit, the Herod, and add more food next time—some lard, perhaps, or turnips and horsetail for holidays—and not eat everything up himself.

But Benedikt had never seen Fyodor Kuzmich in the flesh. And he didn't dare hope to.

And then today, the most ordinary February day you could pick, a gray, dull, powdery blizzard day with a boding north wind—blowing and sweeping the snow powder from the roofs down your collar, freezing the Golubchiks' necks and painting their ears the color of poppies—in a word, it was an ordinary, everyday sort of day, today! Today! A sleigh drove up to the Work Izba, and in it were Heralds all decked out in belts and hats and sleeves and leggings, they were wearing everything you could possibly imagine—and they made an announcement: Fyodor Kuzmich himself, Glorybe, desires to honor your izba with a luminous visitation.

And in the Work Izba, wouldn't you know it, all the stoves had gone out that morning. The night Stokers, instead of tending to the kindling and blowing on the fire, got drunk on rusht, or maybe kvas, or maybe they snorted a bunch of bog bilberry—though that's Freethinking—and slept through everything. When they rubbed their eyes open they raced to the stoves—but there was only cold ashes, and even those had gone and blown out through the chimney pipes.

What a ruckus! There was such a hullabaloo of choice cuss words—you normally wouldn't hear so many in a whole year.

But what to do? Nothing. They ran to the neighboring Work Izba for fire, but they wouldn't give it to them. You didn't give us any last time, so we won't give you any now. "Housekeeping Is Everyone's Business, Figure It Out Yourself." What do we care that you're official; we're even more official than you. Get out, get out of here, you goats' asses! Or else we'll beat the fish out of you.

So our people ran off empty-handed, and now here come the Heralds. Our people got scared, mad, they almost started bawling; some were wringing their hands, some pissed on themselves out of fear. Konstantin Leontich, who sits in the corner near the window, lost his senses for a time; he started screaming, "I see, I see a column, incorporeal, luminous, horrendous, humongous, with eyes fourscore in number, and in that pillar there's a spinning, and a flowing, and wings, and a beast heading in all four directions."

And what do you know, the bosses went berserk and ran in all four directions shouting and hollering: Where's Nikita Ivanich, the Head Stoker? Bring Nikita Ivanich here immediately!

And Benedikt got worked up with all the others, he ran around till his temples pounded and he saw dark spots before his eyes: Nikita Ivanich! Where is Nikita Ivanich! Right here, right now, what an event, good Lord, it's maybe once a century Fyodor Kuzmich decides to show himself to the people, Glorybe! Once in a blue moon he comes out of his terem, his bright terem adorned with sharp spires, eaves trimmed with carved curlicues, crimson onion domes painted with young rusht, decorated with whorls, embellished with frillery and frippery! Lord-a-miiiighty! . . . What joy, fear, joy! I . . . where should I . . . Lordy! Where is Nikita Ivanich, the old . . . damn him . . . Doesn't he understand?

The Heralds jumped off their sleigh and went about setting up their stuff. They unfurled rug runners, ornamented and woven, throughout the whole izba: a rug on the porch, and leading from the porch; in the wink of an eye they trampled down the snow around the izba and laid out a sort of half circle of bear skin. Such a grand sight, you could die now with no regrets. Vasiuk the Earful fell to the ground with all his ears and listened: Are they coming? Then he cried out: "I hear them! They're coming!" Right away you could see a sort of white cloud trembling in the distance: snowdust flew up. The cloud grew, headed our way, and people almost fainted, but to no account; it was only the Lesser Murzas, riding by to make an impression, as if to say, you can start trembling now.

They rode on by, scaring the people for no good reason. Then some time passed. Suddenly—hark!—it sounded like stone bells were ringing. The birds startled and everything died down, and then it was like a great snowstorm was moving toward us, full of twisting windwhirls. Everyone stood on the porch—the lazy Stokers and all the Scribes. Benedikt caught a glimpse of Olenka, the cooks from the Food Izba, passersby, everyone ran out to see. They all crowded around, fell down on their faces, and Benedikt with them, so that when the retinue arrived and got out of the sleigh, exactly what happened and what kind of ceremony or fuss there was—Benedikt couldn't tell. He could only hear his heart thumping in his ears: *thub-dub, thub-dub.* He came to when they kicked him to get up out of the snowdrift and herded him into the izba to pay obeisance. Inside it even seemed warmer: how beautiful, everything covered with rugs, even the stools. Rugs on the benches, the windows festooned with transparent lace, all the garbage swept into a corner and covered with bark so you couldn't see it, though it did stink a little. But horrors, there were candles everywhere, only none were lit. No fire. No Nikita Ivanich. Someone nudged Benedikt in the back: Sit down, Golubchik, Fyodor Kuzmich doesn't like it when people stand. Benedikt sat down, rooted to the spot, and watched.

Everyone froze. It was quiet as the grave. Outside the door they heard little footsteps: *trip-trap, trip-trap.* Fyodor Kuzmich, Glorybe, stepped onto the crimson rug, into the twilight of the izba.

"It's me, Golubchiks," he said.

From the fear and joy in his head Benedikt felt a rush of heat, and in his chest it was like a space had opened up, but a clenched fist was stuck smack in the middle of that space, and he couldn't breathe. Benedikt felt like he was looking through a fog and was amazed: Fyodor Kuzmich was not much taller than Kitty, he barely reached Benedikt's knee. But Kitty had teeny hands and pink fingers, and Fyodor Kuzmich's hands were the size of stove dampers, and they never kept still.

"Weren't expecting me, were you?" said Fyodor Kuzmich, laughing. "I want to paint a painting like that: *They Didn't Expect Him,* that's right. I think you'll like it. It's got one fellow coming into the room, and the others, you see, have jumped up out of their seats in surprise. Well, then, let's have a little chat. How is life, how's work going, what are you doing?"

"We're copying, Fyodor Kuzmich," the Golubchiks clamored, and Fyodor Kuzmich laughed. A lot of people laughed with him, like they were relieved: Fyodor Kuzmich, Glorybe, turned out to be a simple fellow. Maybe there's nothing to be afraid of, except for those hands that keep clenching and unclenching.

"Why don't I sit down too," said Fyodor Kuzmich, laughing again. "I want to get closer to the people, you know."

He looked all around and then jumped up on Olenka's lap. She caught him around the stomach, like Kitty, and held him. She wasn't afraid.

"Hold me tighter, or else I'll tumble off. That's it," said Fyodor Kuzmich. "Hold me with two hands, under my arms. But no tickling."

"We're happy to meet you, Fyodor Kuzmich! Long May You Live!" said the Golubchiks. "You deserve it! Thanks be to you!"

"Thank you, Fyodor Kuzmich, for your art!" cried Vasiuk the Earful.

"Thank you for being! Thank you," added the women.

"I'm always glad to meet with the intelligentsia, don't you know," Fyodor Kuzmich said, turning his head and looking up at Olenka's face from below. "Especially when you've got such sweetie pies to hold me under the arms. Only no tickling, now."

"That's right, Fyodor Kuzmich," replied the Golubchiks.

"I'm thinking of painting a lot of paintings," said Fyodor Kuzmich. "If, of course, there's enough rusht."

Everyone had a good laugh; whatever you said, there was always enough rusht to go around.

"I'll build an enormous-humongous izba, make a lot of paintings, and hang them on the walls with nails," Fyodor Kuzmich told them. "And I'll name it after myself: Kablukov Gallery. In case you don't know, Kablukov is my last name."

Everyone chuckled: Who doesn't know that?

"Do you have any questions? Maybe I said something you didn't understand, you just ask me. No harm in asking, isn't that right?"

"That's right! Oh, that's so right, Fyodor Kuzmich, Long May You Live!" cried the Golubchiks. "Right as rain! You hit the nail on the head! You're right on target, you hit the bull's eye! That's it, that's how things are!"

"What are paintings?" Olenka spoke up.

Fyodor Kuzmich, Glorybe, turned again, and looked at her.

"You just wait and see. I have a surprise for you. It's sort of like a drawing, but painted. I thought up one funny picture, hilariously funny. One Golubchik is eating a mouse, and another, you see, is walking into the izba. And the one who's eating, he hides the mouse so that the other guy doesn't steal it, yes siree. I'll call it *The Aristocrat's Breakfast,* that's it. I thought up another one too. I painted one painting, I called it *The Demon,* but it didn't turn out too well, so I brushed over it with a lot of blue paint, yes siree, I did . . . So I'm thinking of giving it to you here in the Work Izba. You can hang it up somewhere, why should it take up space at my house." And he waved his hand at the servants: "Bring it here."

One of them fumbled under his coat and brought out a birch-bark box. He took a cloth out of the box and unfolded it—it was kind of like a scroll—maybe birch bark, maybe not, a bit whiter. Very, very thin. Folded in fours. He unfolded it, and there, bright as could be, was the picture; they looked at it and you couldn't tell what it was painted with, and sure enough it was all blue. They handed it to Fyodor Kuzmich; he smoothed it out with his enormous hands and gave it back: "Who's in charge here? Hang it on the wall."

Konstantin Leontich had just taken the gag out of his mouth

—he'd almost come to his senses. He shouted "Thank you" louder than anyone, in a high voice like a goat, very loud and right in Benedikt's ear, downright deafening, dammit. Benedikt didn't know what to think: the first fresh fear had receded, and in its place he felt glum. He should feel more awe, he thought, but somehow he didn't. Everything felt all wrong. Now, if he prostrated himself on the ground, stood on all fours, his knees bent and his hands stretched out in front and to the sides, and beat his forehead on the floor—that would be better. That's why they thought it up. When you do that, the awe just spurts out of you like a burp; like what happens sometimes if you eat too much marinated horsetail—your stomach burns and grabs you, and from inside your throat bubbles keep bubbling up. But what thrill could there be sitting on a stool? You're on the same level with the Greatest Murza. He seems just like you, a simple Golubchik: you sit there, and he sits there; he says something, you say something. That's no way to go about things. A kind of insolence and envy get born inside you: Hey, Murza, what are you doing sitting on Olenka's lap? Go on, get off. Or else I'll let you have it. You start thinking thoughts like that and it's downright scary! What on earth was he thinking just now about Fyodor Kuzmich? What's happening?

Then Varvara Lukinishna spoke up timidly. "Fyodor Kuzmich, I wanted to ask . . . In your poetry, the image of the steed frequently appears. Can you please explain what a steed is?"

"Hunh?" asked Fyodor Kuzmich.

"A steed . . ."

Fyodor Kuzmich smiled and shook his head. "So you can't do it yourself . . . Can't figure it out. Hmmm . . . Come on, now, who wants to take a guess?"

"A mouse," Benedikt said hoarsely, although he had sworn he'd be quiet: he felt all mixed up inside.

"There you go, Golubushka. You see? The Golubchik here managed to do it."

"And a winged steed?" Varvara Lukinishna asked in a worried voice.

Fyodor Kuzmich frowned and shook his arms. "A bat."

54

"And how to understand: 'He brushed the steed with a curry'?"

"Well, now, Golubushka, you wouldn't eat a mouse raw, would you? You'd skin him, isn't that right? If you wanted to whip up a soufflé or a blancmange, you'd clean him, right? If, for example, you got it into your head to make the mouse into petit-fri à la mode with nut mousse, or to bake it in a béchamel sauce with croutons. Or you might catch a lot of mouselings and make yourself a schnitzel wrapped in pancakes or flaky pastry. Wouldn't you clean them first?" Fyodor Kuzmich chortled and turned his head. "How now? What can I teach you? Do you think it's easy for me to compose? 'A thousand tons of linguistic ore I mine for the sake of a single word,' you know. Have you forgotten? I composed something about that. 'Artist, do not ever slumber. Do not give yourself to dreams.' And besides art there's plenty to do: day in and day out you invent things, figuring, figuring, thinking so hard your brain swells up. The whole state is on my shoulders. No time to sit down. I just composed a Decree, you'll get it soon. A good one, yes siree, real interesting. You'll thank me for it."

"Glory to Fyodor Kuzmich! Long May He Live! We're grateful in advance!" cried the Golubchiks.

Then the doors opened and Nikita Ivanich walked in. Everyone turned to look at him. Fyodor Kuzmich too. He walked in like he was at home, all grumpy, unkempt, rusht stuck in his beard, his hat still on. He didn't fall down on his knees, didn't roll his eyes back up under his forehead. Didn't even blink.

"Good morning, citizens." He was irritated. "I've implored you on more than one occasion: Take precautions with the stoves. You have to keep them under constant observation. You're always working this old man to the bone."

"Stoker Nikita, know your place, light the stove!" shouted Jackal Demianich in a terrible, sonorous voice.

"Now you listen to me, Jackal, don't be so familiar," said Nikita Ivanich in a huff. "And don't tell me what to do! I'm three hundred years old, and I saw enough bureaucratic nastiness in the Oldener Times to suffice! You have a job, an elementary responsibility to maintain a minimum level of order! You allow your colleagues to become inebriated, and you have the gall to badger me with trifles. The mass alcoholism we are experiencing, Jackal, is partly your fault. That's right! This isn't the first time I've brought this issue to your attention! You are not inclined to respect the individual human being. Like many people, for that matter. And your veteran status"—Nikita Ivanich raised his voice and tapped on the table with a crooked finger— "please don't interrupt me! Your veteran status does not give you the right to harass me!! I am a *Homo sapiens,* a citizen and mutant, like you! Like all these citizens!" he said, gesturing broadly with his hand.

Everyone knows that there's no point in listening to Nikita Ivanich: he just rambles on, probably doesn't understand half the words he says himself.

"Nikita Ivanich! You are in the presence of Fyodor Kuzmich himself, Glorybe!" cried Jackal Demianich, shaking.

"You are in my presence," said Fyodor Kuzmich with a cough. "Fire up the stove, Golubchik, for heaven's sake, my legs are frozen. Fire it up, what's there to get mad about?"

Nikita Ivanich just waved his hand. He was annoyed. He went over to the stove. He didn't seem to care that the head of state was there and not just anyone, that he'd deigned to honor them with a luminous visitation, that he was chatting with the people, sharing his governmental thoughts with them, that he made them a gift of a painting, that guards with staffs and halberds stood at attention, that Konstantin Leontich once again sat with a gag in his mouth, all tied up with ropes so he couldn't scream, that all Varvara Lukinishna's cock's combs were fluttering from the tension, that the floor was adorned with crimson rugs. No, he didn't care. He walked straight over those governmental rugs in his lapty. Everyone froze.

"Well, all right, where is the kindling?" he grumbled, disgruntled.

Lesser Murzas ran up with kindling and tossed it in the stove. Everyone watched: Fyodor Kuzmich watched, and Benedikt watched; he'd never seen the Head Stoker light the fire. There wasn't anything in his hands. And nothing sticking out of his pockets.

Nikita Ivanich squatted. He sat there for a while. Thought a bit. He turned his head and looked around at everyone. Thought some more. And then he opened his mouth wide, and out came a blast: *Whoooooossssshhhhhh!* A column of fire blew out of him like the wind, in great puffs, and went in the stove. With a burst everything caught fire in the wide stove, and the yellow tongues of flame crackled like a jeopard tree in spring blossom.

What with all the fear and people shouting, everything went all fuzzy in Benedikt's head. He only managed to notice that Fyodor Kuzmich pushed off Olenka's lap with his huge hands, jumped on the floor, and disappeared. When Benedikt regained his senses, he rushed out on the street, but all you could see was a cloud of snowspouts reaching from the earth to the sky. And the Lesser Murzas galloping off in the other direction.

Back in the izba the rugs and the skins were gone, the walls were bare and dusty with smoke, the floor was covered with trash, the stove hummed and radiated waves of warmth. The warmth made the blue Demon on the wall stir, as though he wanted to get down.

И · IZHE

OH, HOW Benedikt envied Nikita Ivanich! That evening, arriving home after work, all worried, he checked the stove as he always did. As if to spite him, as often happened, the stove had gone out. If he'd gotten home an hour earlier, it might have been all right, a little bit of life might still have warmed the embers, he could have probably gotten down on his knees and, turning his head like he was praying, blown and blown till a live flame came out of the gray, ashen sticks. Yes, just an hour earlier it could have still been done. The workday is long, and by the time you get to work and then run home afterward—it's like on purpose, like someone figured it out so that you couldn't make it in time! The soup, of course, wouldn't be cold yet if it was wrapped in rags the way it ought to be; you can fill your belly, but the taste is sad, twilightish. You're in the dark—there's nothing to light a candle with. You feel sorry for yourself, so sorry! The izba isn't cold yet either, you can hit the hay in your padded coat and hat. But it will start freezing up at nighttime: winter will creep up to the thin cracks and the notches, it'll blow under the door, breathe cold up from the ground. By morning there will be death in the izba, and nothing else.

No, you can't go that long. You have to go ask the Stokers for fire—and you'd better get some little surprises ready for them, Golubchik. Or you can knock on your neighbor family's door and beg, if they aren't too mean. Family people have it easier: while the husband works, the wife sits at home, keeps house, watches the stove. Makes soup. Bakes. Sweeps. Maybe even spins wool. You can't go on begging like that day after day, the neighbor ladies will lose all patience: they'll smack you on the head with a shaft. Or maybe they've gone to bed, maybe they're barking at each other like family folk do, or fighting, pulling each other's hair out, and here you show up: Could you spare some coals, kind Golubchiks?

But Nikita Ivanich now, he doesn't need a family, or a woman, or neighbors; his stove could go out a hundred times—what does he care? He puffs up—and lights it again. That means he can smoke when he wants, in the forest or the fields or wherever— he's got fire with him. If he wants, he can start a campfire and sit down by the flames, tossing on dry storm kindling, branches, forest garbage, fallen thicket rubbish; he can stare into the live, reddish-yellow, flickering, warm, dancing flame. He doesn't have to ask, or bow, or scrape, or be afraid—nothing. Freedom! Benedikt would like that! Yes, he would! . . .

Once again, in the pitch dark, he felt for the pot with the warm soup and fumbled around: Where is the spoon? Who the devil knows, he stuck it somewhere and forgot. Slurp it over the rim again? How much could he take, he wasn't a goat after all.

He went out on the porch. Lordy! How dark it was. To the north, to the south, toward the sunset, the sunrise—darkness, darkness without end, without borders, and in that darkness, pieces of gloom—other izbas like logs, like rocks, like black holes in the black blackness, like gaps into nowhere, into the freezing hush, into the night, into oblivion, into death, like a long fall into a well, like what happens to you in dreams—you fall and fall and there's no bottom and your heart gets smaller and smaller, more pitiful and tighter. Lordy!

And over your head is the sky, also blacker than black, and across the sky in a pattern are the bluish spots of the stars, thicker sometimes, or weaker, it looks like they're breathing, flickering, like they're suffocating too, they're withering, they want to break away, but they can't, they're pinned fast to the black heavenly roof, nailed tight, can't be moved. Right over Benedikt's head, always overhead wherever you go—the Trough, and the Bowl, and the bunch of Northern Horsetail, and the bright white Belly Button, and the strewn Nail Clippings, and dimly, crowded, thickened, in a stripe through the whole night vault, the Spindle. They've always been there, as long as you can remember. You're born, you die, you get up, you lie down, you dance at your neighbor's wedding, or in the morning, in the stern raspberry dawn you wake in fright as though someone hit you with a stick, like you alone remain alive on earth—and the stars are still there, always there, pale, blinking, indistinct, eternal, silent.

Behind your back the izba grows cold. Soup. Bed. On the bed—a cloth: a boiled felt blanket left by Benedikt's mother, a summer coat to cover his legs; a feather pillow, kind of filthy. There should be a table at the window, a stool at the table, on the table a candlestick with an oil candle, and extra candles in the closet, and a half pood of rusht, and in the safe place, hidden from thieves, extra felt boots, knitted socks, lapty for spring, a stone knife, a string of dried marshrooms, and a pot with a handle. They were there this morning, anyway. Everything you could want. Everything. And still, something's missing. Something gnaws, gnaws at you.

...Is it riches I covet?...Or freedom? Or I'm scared of death? Where is it I want to go? Or have I gotten too big for my britches, reached the heights of Freethinking, fancy myself a Murza, or some ruler—who knows what—or a giant, magical, all powerful, the most important of all, who tramples Golubchiks, dwells in a terem squeezing his hands, shaking his head? Think how Fyodor Kuzmich, Glorybe, walked into the mud room and everyone fell on their knees...Think how Nikita Ivanich roared fire...

That old man isn't afraid of anything. He doesn't need anyone—no Murzas, no neighbors. Because he has such power, such an envious Consequence: fire comes from his innards. If he wanted, he could burn down the whole settlement, or the whole town, all the woods around it, even the whole flat pancake of the earth! That must be why the bosses avoid him, they don't mess with him like they do with us, simple Golubchiks; he has strength and glory and power on earth! Aye, aye, aye, but we poor small folk have to stand on our porches at night, inhaling the freezing darkness, exhaling a slightly warmer darkness. We stomp our feet, turn our faces to the distant heavenly Spindle, listen to tears tinkling like frozen peas, rolling into the thickets of our beards, we listen to the silence of the black izbas on black foothills, the creak of the high trees, to the whine of the blizzard, which brings in gusts—barely audible, but still clear—of a distant, pitiful, hungry northern wail.

Й ▪ I KRATKOE

FYODOR KUZMICH, GLORYBE, didn't let them down—exactly a week after his luminous visitation, he issued a Decree and it was handed out to all the Work Izbas to be copied over and over. Benedikt had to make a copy too.

Jackal Demianich called everyone together and announced —as if we didn't know ourselves—that the governmental resolution must be made available to all Golubchiks immediately, and so he therefore hereby commanded that the Decree be copied swiftly and with beautiful calligraphy and flourishes and that a copy be nailed on every corner that has a Decree board.

DECREE

Since I am Fyodor Kuzmich Kablukov, Glory to Me, the Greatest Murza, Long May I Live, a Seckletary and Academishun and Hero and Captain of the High Seas and Carpenter, and seeing as I am constantly concerned with the people's welfare, I hereby command:

That the Holiday of New Year be celebrated.

That this here holiday be celebrated the First of March kinda like the May Holidays.

It's a day off too.

That means nobody goes to work. Drink and make merry, do what you want, but within reason, and not like sometimes happens when you go to town and burn everything down and then have to mend all the fences.

The New Year Holiday should be celebrated like this: chop down a tree in the forest, not too big but full, so that it will fit in your izbas but if you want you can put it in the yard. Stick this tree in the floor or wherever you can, so it stands up, and hang all sorts of stuff on its branches depending on what you've got. It could be colored threads braided together, or nuts, firelings, or whatever you can spare around the house, all kinds of junk always piles up in the corner and it might come in handy. Tie this stuff on tight so it doesn't fall off on top of you.

Light candles so that everything's bright and cheery.

Cook up lots of yummy dishes, don't be stingy after all spring is coming soon and all kinds of things will grow in the forest.

Invite guests, your neighbors, kinfolk, feed everyone, don't be stingy, they won't eat you out of house and home. You'll get to eat too you know.

Play on pipes whoever has the knack, or on drums, you can dance if your legs are fit.

61

*Put on good clothes, dress to the teeth, also put things in
your hair.*

*Some of you might want to bathe, so I order the Baths to
open in daytime, be my guest, drop in and bathe only bring
your own firewood with you cause there won't be enough to go
around otherwise.*

It will be interesting, you'll see.

Kablukov

Benedikt copied the Decree four times, gave Olenka the
bark so she could decorate the letters to make them pretty—
with plaited ribbons, birds and flowers, since this was serious
business, or as Jackal put it, fateful affairs. He perked up and
felt cheerful. The rest of the Golubchiks working in the izba also
seemed to brighten and straighten up. Why not be happy: spring
was on the way! Spring! Who doesn't love spring! Even the
most miserable lousy Golubchik looks better, grows kinder, and
hopes for something in spring.

You spend the whole winter lying on the stove bed in soot
and peelings, not even taking your lapty off; you don't bathe or
brush your hair; you can't tell your feet from your felt boots with
all the dirt, they're grimy enough to boast about or show off to
your neighbors. Your beard is full of knots and rats' nests—
mice would be happy to take up house; your eyes are overgrown
with scales so you have to push them open with your fingers and
hold them or they'll snap shut. But when spring comes, you
crawl out in the morning, into the courtyard, to do your business
or whatever—and suddenly a strong sweet wind will blow in, as
if there were flowers somewhere around the corner, or a girl
sighed, or someone invisible were standing at your gate with
presents—the stinky fellow stands there, stock-still, and thinks
he hears something but can't believe his ears: could it really be?
Really? He stands there, his eyes glassed over, his beard rattling
in the breeze like rusht or like tiny bells; his mouth wide open
'cause he forgot to close it; he grabs his britches and freezes, and
his feet have already melted two black circles, and the shitbird
has already messed on his hair and he keeps standing there, innocent, bathed in the first wind, the golden light, and the shad-

ows are blue, and the icicles are burning with the heat and working overtime: drop-drip, drip-drop, ding dong! He stands there until a neighbor or a co-worker walking by shouts: "Whatcha hanging out for, Beauregard, whatcha lookin at? Chokin' or somefin?" and laughs in a friendly way, kindly, springlike.

The First of March is soon. Right around the corner. True, it freezes up good and hard at night still, there'll be more snowstorms, the snow will have to be dug out more than once, a path beaten down to the izba, and the main road shoveled out if it's your turn to do roadwork—but things are already easier, you can see the end of it, and the days already seem longer.

> Winter shows its anger still—
> Its time has almost passed.
> Spring knocks on the windowsill
> And shoos it from the path.

That's right. That's the way it is. Now it's time to choose a tree in the forest, like Fyodor Kuzmich, Glorybe, decreed, and dress it in whatever's to hand. During lunch break the Golubchiks discuss the Decree. What to use for decoration? They're worried.

Ksenia the Orphan says: "I have two nuts and about five yards of thread in my cupboard."

Konstantin Leontich dreams: "I'll make doilies and confetti from bark, and symmetrical garlands."

Varvara Lukinishna: "I see it this way: a fireling on the very top, and spirals of beads descending the tree."

"Beads of what?"

"Well . . . You could roll balls of clay and string them on a thread."

"Clay? In winter?"

Everyone laughed.

"You could thread peas if you have some."

"Peas would be perfect. Enjoy looking at it a bit, and then eat some. Enjoy a little more—and eat some more."

"Maybe they'll give out something from the Warehouse for the holiday."

"Yeah, sure. Hold your pockets open. They need it for themselves."

"Golubchiks! Maybe we could trade with the Cockynorks for plaited baskets?"

"Trade what? By spring everything's eaten up."

"Speak for yourself."

"And you, Olenka, what will you decorate with?"

Olenka, as always, blushed and looked down at the ground.

"Us? We, well, we . . . something, some kind of . . ."

Benedikt was charmed. He started imagining how Olenka, in a new dress with full sleeves would sit at some bountiful table, lowering her eyes to the tabletop or glancing at him, at Benedikt, or gazing at the candles—and those candles would make her eyes shine and glisten and a blush cover her cheeks. And the part in her fair hair was clean, even, milky, like the heavenly Spindle. Colorful braided bands adorned her brow, beads and decorations dangled from them, temple rings hung on either side, and in the middle was a blue stone, deep and murky like a tear. She wore stones around her neck too, threaded on a string, tightly tied right under her chin. Her little chin was so white, with such a sweet little dimple right in the middle. There she'd be, sitting straight up like a New Year's tree, all decked out, still as can be, glancing here and there . . .

The other Olenka, the one here, in the Work Izba, was drawing pictures and her tongue stuck out. She was really sort of ordinary—her face, and clothes, and manner. Both of them were one and the same Olenka, and how she splits in Benedikt's head, how he conjures one of them up like a vision—it's not easy to understand.

It's as though a sort of sleepy image splits off from the simple Olenka, and hangs in front of his eyes like a mirage, a fog, an enchantment. Hard to figure . . . You can poke the simple Olenka in the ribs, like regular people do, and tell her a joke, or play a trick on her: while she's drawing you can sneak up and tie her braid to the stool, for instance. Her braid goes down to the floor, so it's easy as pie. When she gets up—to go to the privy or to lunch—the stool will fall over with a clatter! It's a funny joke, he's done it lots of times.

You can't joke that way with the other Olenka, the magical vision, you can't elbow her in the ribs, in fact he's not sure what to do with her, but he can't get her out of his head. The vision turns up everywhere — on the street, especially in the evening, when he makes his way home in the dusk, and in the izba . . . That's how he imagines it: he opens the stiff, frozen door, steps inside. There in the dim, smoky air, in the warm pancake steam, in the midst of all the izba smells — sour, wet wool, stuffy ashes, something else familiar, homey — in the midst of all of this, there's a gleam like a feeble torch glow, and there's Olenka floating right in the air all fancy like an idol. Motionless, wrapped stiff in beads, the milky part on her head combed straight, her eyes sparkle, her eyelashes tremble, and in her gaze there's a secret and the light of a bluish candle flame.

Ugh. He can't shake it.

Well, the Golubchiks will probably celebrate the New Year Holiday dancing and feasting, and Benedikt has nothing saved up in his izba but old socks. And it's a lot of work to invite guests and feed them. What to offer them? Spring is the hungriest time. Benedikt always thins out in the spring, his ribs even stick out. All day long at work, and you had to work in the summer too — early morning in the fields to gather provisions. You get such blisters you can't hold the writing stick tight. Your hands shake and your handwriting's bad. That's why Scribes get a vacation in the summer: they're no good for work anyhow. In the summer the Scribe is like an ordinary Golubchik — a sickle on his shoulder and into the fields and glades to cut goosefoot, horsetail. Bring in the sheaves. You tie them up — lug them to the shed, and go back again, another time, once more, all over, run, run, run. While he's gone the neighbors or a stranger will filch a couple of sheaves for sure, sometimes from the field, sometimes straight from the shed. But that's all right: they steal from me, and I'll get good and mad and steal from them, those guys will steal from these guys — and so it goes in a circle. It comes out fair. Everyone steals, but everyone ends up with their own. More or less. As Nikita Ivanich says, it's a basic redistribution of personal property holdings. Maybe that's what it is.

Used to be, when Mother was still alive, the old man would

drop in and chat. He took to teaching Benedikt all sorts of ideas. Think, think for yourself, young man, use your head: wouldn't it be more efficient without all this thievery? How much time and effort would be economized! How many fewer injuries there would be in the settlement! And he'd argue, and explain, and Mother would nod her head in agreement: I always tell my son the same thing, I try to explain the elamentree preeceps of more-ality. But, alas, to little effect.

More-alls are a good thing, who can argue. But good's only good if something good comes of it. Besides more-allity, there's a lot of other things in life. Depends how you look at it.

If Golubchiks didn't steal my goods—of course that's more-allity for me. Everything would be calmer.

On the other hand. Suppose a Golubchik has cut a bunch of horsetail, right? Now he has to carry it back to the izba, right? As soon as he's started, here I come by, winking at him. He's worried, of course, he covers his sheaves, hides them from me, frets, makes a mean face, furrows his eyebrows and peers out from under them. I see all this, and stand nearby, my legs spread out. I open my mouth and start teasing him: So, what's the matter Demian? Scared to lose your provisions? Is that it? Worried? That's right, you ought to be! That's the way things go, Demian, just turn your back! Right? What do you say? Worried about your stuff? Hunh!

So the Golubchik grumbles, and paces back and forth, or maybe roars at you: What're you after, you dog! Off with you or I'll tear you to pieces! And I just laugh, of course. I move over to the side, lean against the fence or whatever's there, cross my legs, have a smoke, and keep an eye on him, wink at him, drop hints here and there, just keep worrying at the Golubchik. If he doesn't have the time, he'll drop it, gather however many sheaves he can, dragging them along on his back, if his health allows, and keeping an eye out: What am I doing, have I ruined something? Have I run off with anything? Is it his? Have I relieved myself on his provisions? Wiped my nose on his valuables? I might!

You could die laughing, it's so funny! You just have to swipe at least one sheaf from a worrywart like that.

And if I give him a more-ality? Then there's no fun in it. What do you have then? Just walk by frowning, like you didn't have breakfast? Not even look at someone else's stuff? Not even dream about it? That's awful! Really terrible. After all, that's how the eyes work: they just wander around and run into other people's stuff, sometimes even pop out. Legs can trip up and still walk on by, but the eye just sticks like glue, and the whole head turns with it, and thoughts get jammed like they ran straight into a column or a wall: damn, if only that were mine! Wouldn't that be . . . I would . . . ! For sure I would . . . ! You start to drool, and sometimes it runs down onto your beard. Your fingers start moving on their own, as if they were grabbing something. There's a buzzing in your chest. It's like someone's whispering in your ear: Take it! So what? No one will see!

Well then, after all that sweat and hard work, when you've played your pranks, you store up edibles for the winter. And by the springtime you've eaten it all up. So you either take yourself to the Food Izba and eat their garbage, Golubchik, or you make do with food for the soul.

That's what they always say about booklets: food for the soul. And it's true: you start reading and your belly doesn't growl as much. Especially if you smoke while you read. Of course books are different. Fyodor Kuzmich, Glorybe, works day and night. Sometimes he writes fairy tales, or poems, or a novel, or a mystery, or a short story, or a novella, or some kind of essay. Last year Fyodor Kuzmich, Glorybe, decided to write a shopping-hower, which is kind of like a story, only you can't make heads nor tails of it. A long sucker, they read it for three months, copied it a dozen times, wore themselves to the bone. Konstantin Leontich bragged that he understood everything—but he always brags: everyone just laughed. So you think you understood it, Golubchik—then tell us the story: who goes where, who do they see, how're they gonna do that shopping, what hanky panky do they get up to, who do they murder? Huh? You can't? Well, there you go. It was called *The World as Will and Idea*. A good name, inviting. After all, you've always got a lot of ideas in your head, especially at bedtime. You wrap your coat around you so there's no draft, cover your head with a cloth, draw up one leg, stretch out the other, put your fist or your elbow under your head; then turn over, flip your pillow onto the cold side, wrap your coat up again if it slipped, toss and turn—and start to drift off.

And the ideas come.

You might have an idea about Olenka, all decked out, white, immobile, enough to give you butterflies in your stomach; or about how you're flirting with a woman, or with a beautiful girl, you grab her, and she squeals, and you both have fun; or you're walking along the street and you find something valuable: a purse with chits or a basket of food. Or your dream might really take off and you go somewhere you've never been: along a path through the forest, toward the sunrise, and farther, into the glade, and even farther, to an unknown forest where bright streams burble, where the golden branches of the birch tree plash in a stream like long threads, like a girl's hair gleaming in the sun—they splash and play, curling in the warm wind; and under the birch tree there's greengrass, fancy ferns, beetles with shiny blue backs, and poppies—you pick them, breathe deep, and you feel sleepy, a far-off chime rings in your ears, and clouds are floating in your chest, and it's like you're on a mountain, and from the mountain you can see a white road, twisting and turning, and the sun shines, plays tricks on you, blinds you, gets in the way of seeing, and in the distance something sparkles. Is it the Ocean-Sea they sing about in songs? Or islands in magic waters, islands with white cities, gardens, and towers? Or a strange, lost kingdom? Or another life . . . ?

There you go, your head fills with all sorts of ideas—and you fall asleep.

Fyodor Kuzmich, Glorybe, doesn't write about anything like that in his shoppinghower, and, to tell the truth, it's a yawn, Lord knows. But people bought all the copies anyway, that is, they traded for it, and so now somewhere someone must be reading the thing, spitting as he goes. People love to read; on weekends at the market they always go to trade mice for booklets. The Lesser Murzas come out, set up the governmental stalls along the fence, set out birch-bark booklets, a tag stuck in each of them that says how much they'll take for it. The prices are different: five mice, ten, twenty, or if it's really interesting or has pictures, it can go as high as fifty. The Golubchiks crowd around, checking prices, discussing whether to buy or not to buy, what the book is about, what's the story, are there a lot of pictures? But you can't look inside: pay up first, then look as much as you like. The Lesser Murzas stomp their boots in the cold, slap their sleeves, hawk their goods.

"A new one, who wants a new one? *The Eternal Call!* A humongous novel!"

"Who'll take *The Fundamentals of Differential Calculus,* a popular brochure, incredibly interesting!"

Another one will put his hands to his mouth like a cup so the sound's louder and cry out: "*The Three Billy Goats Gruff!* Last Copy! A thrilling Epic! This is the last copy, come and get it!"

He does that on purpose, but he's really lying, he has another dozen under his counter. That's just how he gets the Golubchiks interested, so a crowd gathers: if it's the last one they don't want to miss it. If someone has a passion for trading books, he'll pay.

"What? They're all sold?" And the Murza, pretending to hesitate: "Well, there is one . . . I put it aside for myself . . . I don't know . . ."

The Golubchik says: "Maybe you'll let me have it? I'll throw in a couple of extra mice . . . What do you say?"

And the Murza says: "I don't know . . . I wanted to read it myself . . . But I guess if you throw in another five . . ."

"Five? Come on, now! My mice are fat, each is worth a mouse and a half!"

"Well, let me take a look." They bargain, and it's all gravy for the Murza. That's why their faces are fatter and their izbas are taller.

But Benedikt's face is ordinary, not too big, and his izba is tiny.

I · I DESIATERICHNOE

BENEDIKT SPENT the whole night catching mice. Easy to say: catching mice. Not so simple. Like everything, you have to know how. You think: Here I am and here's the mouse, I'll just grab him. Noooo.

He caught them with a noose, of course. But if the space under the floor was empty, the mouse would run over to someone richer, and then you could wiggle the noose till you were blue in the face and you wouldn't catch anything. You have to feed a mouse. That means you have to think things out ahead of time.

He got paid on the twentieth. Fifty chits. All right. The tax on them was 13 percent. That means six and a half chits of tax. Early in the morning the Golubchiks stood in line at the Payday Izba. It wasn't dawn yet. It's dark in winter—like someone poked your eyes out.

That really happens sometimes. A Golubchik might be feeling his way along in the dark to get his pay—and suddenly he falls in a ditch, or a branch pokes him in the eye, or he'll slip and break a leg, get lost, wander into a strange settlement where vicious dogs will tear him to shreds, or he'll trip and freeze to death in a snowdrift. Anything can happen.

But let's say he makes it where he's going, thank God. Good. He lines up. The first guy to get there is in the hall, or mud room. Whoever's at the end stands on the street, stomping his feet in the cold. Everyone is cursing or chatting, trying to guess whether the Paymaster Murza will come or whether he drank too much mead or kvas or hemp mash again the night before. Or they play pranks: if one of the Golubchiks in the hallway dozes off from the warmth and takes a nap, they'll pick the sleepyhead up carefully under the arms and carry him out to the end of the line. When the Golubchik wakes up, he can't figure out what happened, where he is or why he's there. He rushes back to where he was and everyone says: Don't butt into the line! Go to the end! And he says: But I was first in line! And we say: Don't know what you're talking about! Then there's a lot of shouting and fisticuffs and injuries of all kinds.

It passes the time. The dawn comes up pink and hazy, the darkness moves over. Chigir, the morning star, shines with untold beauty, like a fireling up high. The cold seems stronger. The snow sparkles.

So we wait for the Murza. Will he come? If anyone sees snowdust in the distance or catches a glimpse of a sleigh, the shout goes up: "He's coming! He's not coming! It's him, you can see his hat," and things like that. There's a real ruckus.

If he doesn't come by evening time, we go our own ways, but if he managed to unstick his eyelids the Golubchiks will get their pay.

So you stand and stand—and suddenly you make it to the window. You're the one who's lucky, it's your pay, so you're the one who has to bend over. And why do you have to bend over? Because the tiny, narrow little window is right smack at the level of your belly button. And that's because the Murza on the other side is sitting on a stool, to make it comfortable for him. He does it that way so we bow down to him, show our respect, so the body is humbled. After all, if you stand up straight when you're counting your chits, who knows what ideas you might get. Like, why so few? or why are they torn? or did he give me all of them? or did he keep a handful, the damned creep? and all kinds of Freethinking. But when you lean over at the waist, your head turned to the side so you can see what's going on, and your arm is stuck waaaayyy into the window slot—it's deep—and your fingers are spread out to grab the chits, and your shoulder aches—well, then you get a feeling for what government service means, its power and glory, and authority on earth, for all time, amen.

So if you're in luck again, you grab the chits. If you've got short arms, of course, or an ailment in your joints, then you'll never grab hold of 'em all. There's a wise proverb about that:

His arms are short. The other Golubchiks are pushing from behind, rushing you, shoving, they're plastered to your back,
breathing down your neck. It's hard. Benedikt, now, he's young,
he can fend for himself, hold his chits tight, and pull his arm
back out of the window fast enough, only scraping his knuckles a
bit, but that's nothing, it happens all the time. If you put a warm
compress on at night and wrap the hand up, the blood will
thicken. And by next payday, just wait and see, new skin will
grow over it.

When you've grabbed your chits from the government, then
you have to stand in another line to pay taxes. That's what they
say, go stand in line, but who would do it of their own free will?
So of course there's a guard with a poleax who herds the Golubchiks along into another hall, hup two, line up, one-two, left
right, and stone chains block the way on every side: that's the
way it's supposed to be.

The rest is all the same, only the Murza in the window isn't a
paymaster, he's a tax collector, and the window is wide and spa-
cious—a sleigh could get through.

Things go quicker here—you can finish in four hours. Count
out six and a half chits to the Murza and hand them over. But
you can't tear a chit in half, can you? Who needs it torn? So that
means you hand over seven. By the end of the day these Murzas
have thousands of extra chits. So they all take some for themselves, to buy some food, or to add a floor to the terem, or a bal-
cony, or to get a fur coat, or a new sleigh.

That's why he's a Murza, the tax collector.

People who don't have any government know-how, just silly
thoughts, like Nikita Ivanich, for instance, they say: Why can't
one and the same Murza give you your salary and keep back the
taxes? So things go faster.

Jeez, what idiots! You just have to laugh at them! Why? Because the Paymaster Murza is a Paymaster Murza, and the taxes
are collected by the Tax Collector Murza! How could one Murza
both give and take? Huh? Why would he even bother coming to
work with that kind of money around? He could just lock himself in the house, eat and drink, or hop in his sleigh and head off
hunting, and that'd be the last you'd see of him, right?

72

Anyone would do the same.

If the Tax Murza weren't sitting in his izba collecting money, would the Paymaster ever stick his nose out the door? Of course not, the drunken bastard, he'd never remember that the twentieth is payday or that the fifth is advance day! The Tax Murza's probably been bugging him since last night: Where are the chits? Did he spend them all? Have my interests been harmed? Are the baskets tied tight, did the mice get in them? That happens too, then they don't pay us. They just say: they're all gone, we don't know where they got to, wait till next time. And we wait.

But let's say everything goes all right, you get your pay, you've got your chits in hand. With these chits, which some people call "rubles," or "greenbarks," or "cash," you can't buy a darned thing, of course. If there were a lot of them, then maybe. Then you could buy something. But you can't. Only lunch if you're lucky.

Mice are a whole different story. There are lots of them, they're fresh every day, you can catch them if you've got the time, and trade them as much as you like, help yourself. No one will say a word. Of course, there's a tax on mice too, or duty— and there's a house tax, pillow tax, stove tax, so many you can't count them all, but that's another story.

Benedikt had his chits in hand, so he was halfway there. Now he had an idea: buy lunch in the Food Izba with those chits, but don't eat the bread, save it, take it home and feed the mice. Crumble up a little piece for them every day—scads of the lovely little critters will come running.

And this time everything worked out! The plan worked! All night Benedikt caught mice and by morning two hundred seventy-two of them dangled from his string—careful don't break it—gray, chubby cheeks, silky fur! Well, maybe not two hundred seventy-two, but one hundred fifty-six! A lot! He lost track counting. And why such success?—because everything was thought through ahead of time, everything was planned carefully, with real smarts.

Goodness gracious! How marvelous is the mind of man! Who could sing a song to it, a loud, happy song with hoots and hollers, the kind of song where you go out on a hummock or a hill, plant your feet firm, spread your arms wide, and stomp!—taking care not to fall, of course—stomp, I say! With a hey and a ho! And a fee-fi-fiddle-dee-dee! There was a tailor had a mouse, hi diddle um cum fee-doe. They lived together in one house, hi diddle um cum tarum tantrum, hi diddle um cum over the lee. And the greengrass grows all around all around, and the greengrass grows all around!

Not quite like that, but something rakish, joyous, so that the song jumps from your breast, so that your head fills with happiness, so that the happiness bubbles between your ears like soup in a pot and tickles the nape of your neck. And a knickknack paddiwack, give the mouse a crumb! This Golubchik will have some fun. So that the whole settlement, the whole world can hear: Praise be to the reason, the season, the reckoning and the beckoning of man. Hooray for the head! Hooray!!

Fyodor Kuzmich himself, Glorybe, probably never saw such a bunch of mice in his life, and isn't he the greatest hunting master of all? Isn't he a poet, a real buff, a gourmand?

Three blind mice, three blind mice.
See how they run, see how they run.
They all run after Fyodor Kuzmich
Who cut off their tails without a hitch.

Benedikt didn't sleep all night. He was so happy he couldn't sleep. His knees felt a little weak and his back ached a bit. But otherwise—he wasn't the least bit sleepy. Now it was time to take his riches to market.

The market is wonderful in the morning. A fairer sight you never did see! The snow is cleared with shovels, flattened down like a floor. If it's very, very cold, then the snow is all blue, it sparkles. Of course, once the Golubchiks run in they'll mess it up, ruin it, toss their butts on it, but it's still beautiful. If the weather's getting warmer, if there's a bit of a thaw—then it's like an ice clearing underfoot and the snowdrifts next to the fence are sunken and black, spongy, with toothy crusts. It smells of spring.

What a crowd—ooooo—eeee! It's packed to the gills. Everyone wants to trade something. Everyone's lugging goods.

There are rows of salted and pickled food: all the stands are packed with barrels, clay pots, buckets, and tubs, taste if you like, but don't grab too much, or you'll get your ears boxed. If the past summer's harvest was good, the stands sometimes reach to the horizon, and the last far-off Golubchik looks like a bug in the forest: distant, teeny tiny, waving his arms, shouting, hawking his marshrooms. He thinks he's a big shot too, but from this end it looks like you could smush him with your foot.

Another guy over there is bragging about his pickled reeds, shouting, screeching—and there are marinated ferns, cookies, and other things.

There are pickled nuts, cloth with plain threads, colored threads, bunches of lapty tied in pairs; rabbit hides or goat wool: buy it and boil yourself some boots, or knit a pair of socks if you know how; there are bone needles, stone knives, stone buckets and wooden ones, tongs, poleaxes, brooms—whatever you fancy.

And there's a whole row of fireling peddlers: these traders are important, silent, they stand with their arms folded on their stomachs, looking out from under their eyebrows, their faces all red. They're mysterious. They don't talk. And why are they so quiet? It's their habit. You have to be quiet to pick firelings, so they're used to it. You stand, look the goods over. You feel small and timid, but oh how you want to eat those firelings! You ask the trader: "How much?"

He doesn't answer, just chews on his lip. Then he says: "These, five each. These—seven."

Jeez, expensive! . . .

"They're not fakes?"

Again, he doesn't answer right away. "People've bought them, they're still alive."

Should you believe him or not? You just don't know. You shuffle around . . . You count out five mice. You take one fireling. Put it in your cheek. So sweet! Maybe you won't croak from just one. Maybe you'll just vomit. Or your hair will fall out. Or your neck will swell up. Or maybe you'll live. What did

Mother die from? She ate a whole bowl at one sitting. Nikita Ivanich always told her: "Polina Mikhailovna, why such lack of restraint?! Don't eat those figs! They're radioactive!" But would she listen? No, she stuffed herself.

Right now Benedikt didn't want to start thinking about anything sad. Spring was running in from the south like the Gingerbread Man. The New Year was bringing it! A Holiday was around the corner. Jokes and laughter. The blind men were there too. They crowded around the fence—some played on spoons, others tooted on whistles—and they sang:

> For we are jolly good fellows,
> For we are jolly good fellows . . .

They feel spring coming too. Their guide is also full of vinegar, he keeps an eagle eye out, watches the Golubchiks sternly: Come on now, who's listening to the song? Pay up, don't pass by! There's plenty of you who listen and don't pay. Blind people are blind because they can't see a darn thing. They sing and sing, sing their hearts out, and sometimes a Golubchik will listen, grab his pleasure and run off without paying. How can the blind catch him? They can't! They're in the dark. Even a midsummer's day is dark for them. If not for the guide, they'd die of hunger.

Benedikt adored folk songs. Especially in a chorus. Or when they were real lively. Now the blind people belted out:

> The heart of a beauty!
> Is wont to betray!
> It's ever as fickle,
> As the warm winds of May!

Your feet just can't keep still, they start dancing on their own. There are other good ones. Black Eyes. The Outlaw Stenka Razin. I Wanna Hold Your Hand. Down by the Riverside. And many more.

But this morning Benedikt felt a new feeling. He felt smart and rich. Rich because he was smart. Look how he planned everything—and it all worked. He tied the mice up in bunches—five in each; braided their tails, strung them on a rope and belted it around his waist. He was walking tall. Things were great. And kind of different for a change.

Usually you shuffle along, looking around: are there any bosses in sight? If they're riding in sleighs, you jump to the side of the road, take your hat off and bow. You slap a sweet smile on your face. Then you crinkle up your eyes like you're bursting with joy. You look like you're all surprised—how is it that you, a simple Golubchik, are lucky enough to get to see a Murza? Even if you bump into the same creep forty or fifty times a day, just look surprised, like he wasn't a Murza, but Grandma come visiting with a basket of goodies.

You bow, of course, depending on the rank. If it's a Lesser Murza, you put your hand on your stomach and lower your head.

If it's a Greater Murza, you bow at the waist; your hair should touch the snow or the dust, and your arm should arch back.

If it's a red sleigh ... God forbid ... No. No. No. Knock on wood, knock knock, knock. No. No.

The Murza will drive past, cover you with dust and dirt—then you can put your hat back on, wipe your face with your sleeve—and you're free at last. You can wear your plain, mean, everyday face, you can spit, cuss a bit, throw some insult after him—it's up to you. Or you might just grumble: "Sitting pretty are you ... ?" But what for? He can't exactly stand up in a sleigh, can he? Or you might say something a bit longer: "Riding, they're always riding and riding, who the hell knows where they're going." That's just to let off steam: the Murza probably knows where he's going.

You just say things like that to make yourself feel better. When you growl through your teeth, grumble and grouse—the anger feels good, it kind of rolls around all prickly warm inside you. You wanna show off your strength. Kick a fence. Or a dog if you meet one. Or smack one of the guys around. Whatever. There are all kinds of things you can do.

But sometimes you don't feel like getting mad. It's like there's a sadness inside. Like you feel sorry for someone. Must be feelosophy.

But this morning Benedikt had a new feeling. He felt smart

and rich, and he wanted everyone to see: there he goes, Benedikt, smart and rich. And generous. He stopped, listened to the blind people. They were singing a rousing old song: "Two one two, eighty-five oh three!" He listened and threw them a bunch of mice. That's right, a whole bunch. We're out on the town!

Then he threw the beggars a bunch—here you go! They almost started fighting, tore the offering to bits in a thrice. What a hoot! Then he walked along the rows, tasting the goodies. Oh, he could feel the respect, they noticed him . . .

The merchants bowed: "Over here, please! . . . What's your pleasure? Pickles, sir, try them, our pickles are the best! . . ."

He tried the pickles. Bought some. He bought everything that struck his fancy—plain and pickled and stuffed. Bought a quarter pood of goosefoot crackers, some goat curd, half a dozen firelings to bake sweet rolls. Marinated noodles. Turnips. Red and blue peas. A pitcher of kvas. He bought a bunch of baskets and put all his provisions in them. Then he rented a serf to carry all this stuff home, though, truth be told, it wasn't all that heavy. But he wanted to show off how important he was. Like, I'm a head above this humble servant, higher than the Alexander column, I won't dirty my hands carrying baskets. I have a servant. You're no match for me.

But it went all wrong. People who didn't know Benedikt thought that such a rich man would surely ride in a sleigh, but did Benedikt have a sleigh? So some of the creeps giggled at him. And people who knew him decided that this wasn't a serf, but a chum of Benedikt's, and they were surprised that this chum was lugging all the boxes, was all bent over, while Benedikt was walking along with his hands in his pockets, whistling, and not helping a whit. He wanted to enjoy a bit of boasting, but it didn't work out.

And Benedikt was afraid to get too far ahead of the serf. The second you turn around, one step to the side, he'd be off into a lane with all that stuff. Benedikt wasn't taking any chances!! You'd never find the serf again. So he walked right behind the serf, step for step. Every once in a while he shouted: "Not that way, that way! Turn! Turn, I tell you, you s.o.b.! Left. I see everything, everything! I'm right behind you! I'm watching." Things like that.

It was nerve-racking. But they got there all right. Maybe the serf, even though he was a serf, realized that you couldn't run far with all that stuff. Benedikt would catch up and give him a thrashing. When Benedikt hired him at the market, in the serf's shed, he made sure to show him his fists, and he made a mean face full of enough fury, suspicion, and dissatisfaction for all the Golubchiks and serfs in town. Gave him a good scare.

While he was walking he didn't forget to think: Just look how well you can do when you put your mind to something. In one night he made enough for a whole table of food. How about that! Now there were sweet rolls to bake, guests to invite. It would be nice to invite Olenka, but if she won't come, then Varvara Lukinishna, and maybe someone else from work. Bartholomich would be good, he's a fine storyteller. Ksenia the Orphan, though she's kind of boring and nothing much to look at. What about the neighbors? That's right, invite a dozen or so Golubchiks, sweep the izba, set out candles . . . No, hire a woman to sweep the floor . . . Why should he do the bending over? And let the woman bake the sweet rolls too. Pay her with mice. And hire the blind men! That's it! Hire the whole group. A surprise for the guests! They'll drink, eat, dance, and then, maybe, play leapfrog or choker. Not to the death, just halfway. Right. And sweep the crumbs under the floor and a zillion mice will come running again—he'll catch them again—and buy more food—and the food will drop back under the floor again! And more mice— more trading! More and more and more!

Gracious! What would happen? Thataways Benedikt would get so rich that just watch, he wouldn't have to work! That's right! He'd have mice coming out of his ears. He'd start loaning them out for a cut. He'd hire servants to stand guard, and he'd have a bright, tall, two-story house with gewgaws on the roof! He'd have another servant to watch the guards, to make sure they didn't steal anything! And more to watch those! And others to . . . But he could figure it out later . . . He'd hire women to cook . . . And blind singers to play all the time and make music, to entertain Benedikt . . . He'd build them a little platform in the corner so they could sit there and sing day in and day out . . . And build a good bathhouse . . . And have music in the bathhouse too . . . more blind people. You could listen while you took your bath . . . And he'd hire a back-scratcher girl to scratch his back . . . And another to brush his hair and hum songs to him . . . Well, and what else? That's right! A sleigh! And a wide entrance to the house, and gates that lock . . . Hey there, serfs, open the gate, the master's home! And they all throw themselves down on the ground. Benedikt's sleigh drives into the yard and right up to the terem . . . And Olenka, the snow-white swan, comes out of the terem to greet him: Hello, light of my life, Benya, come sit at the table, I've been waiting for you, keeping my eyes peeled.

They made it back to the izba. Ugh . . . What a vision he'd had . . . and his little izba wasn't exactly a terem, to put it mildly. The serf put the baskets down in the snow. He laughed. Benedikt unfastened his pay: a string of mice. Disrespect showed on the serf's face, he was sure of it. And right away the conversation went sour.

The serf said: "Who do you serve?"

Benedikt gnashed his teeth. "Serve, what do you mean, serve? I'll give you serve! I'm a state worker. And I don't serve."

The serf replied: "Who's the food for?"

Benedikt: "Who for? Me! I've got my own place! I'm going to eat now!"

The serf: "Yeah, sure. It's all yours."

He took the pay, blew his nose on the snow, right next to Benedikt's boot, and walked off.

What can you expect from a serf? A serf is a serf!!! He should catch him, take back the mice, sock him in the nose, kick him for good measure, for the Freethinking! . . . The swine!!! Benedikt was about to take off, but he was afraid to leave the baskets alone: Golubchiks had begun coming over to look at the food. Ugh. He spat, and lugged the baskets into the izba.

That rat, that cockroach turd, he hinted that Benedikt wasn't Benedikt, but someone's serf like him, that he didn't buy all that food for himself, but for his master, and his izba wasn't an izba, but a little shack, a cage. Some kind of storage hut . . . That his dreams were empty. So you want a sleigh for yourself, do you? No, he couldn't leave it be! Catch the bastard quick, give him a kick in the ass. Benedikt ran out on the street and looked around. The serf was gone, like he'd never been there . . . Maybe he'd just imagined him?

He went back into the cooled, chill twilight of the izba. How time had flown. What with one thing and another, the sun was already setting. He felt the stove: it was cold. But it shouldn't be, right? He opened the damper—so that was it . . . Thieves had been there. They'd gone and filched his coals. Nothing but cold ash. What can you do . . .

Suddenly everything was dull and boring. He didn't want any of it anymore. He sat down on the stool. He got up. He opened the door, stood there, leaning against the door jamb. Something sour rose in his chest and he felt weak. It was already dark. The middle of the day and it was evening; that's winter for you. The pale sunsetting sky, tree branches etched against it like you drew them with coals. The nests looked like tangles of hair. A rabbit flitted by. Below, the sad blue of the snow ridges, hillocks, drifts. The dilapidated black pickets of the fence sticking up like an old comb. It was still visible, but when the sunset went out you wouldn't be able to see anything at all in the pitch dark. The stars would come out, their milky, feeble light would pour across the vault of the sky as though someone were mocking him, or didn't care, or these heavenly lights weren't meant for us: What can you see in their dim, dead twinkling! That's it, they're probably not meant for us! . . .

That's the way it always is! Like someone went and cut a tiny little sliver of boundless nature out for us, for people: here you go, Golubchiks, a little bit of sun, a bit of summer, some tulip flowers, a tiny bit of greengrass, a few small birds thrown in for spare change. And that's enough. But I'll hide all the other creatures, I'll wrap them in the night, cover them in darkness, stick them in the forest and under the ground like a sleeve, I'll bury them, starlight's enough for them, they're just fine. Let them rustle, scamper, squeak, multiply, live their own lives. And you, well, go and catch 'em if you can. You caught some? Eat your fill. And if you didn't, do the best you can.

Benedikt sighed deeply. He even heard his own sigh. There it goes again. A kind of splitting in his head again. Everything was just fine: simple, clear, happy, he was full of all kinds of nice dreams, and then suddenly it was like someone came up behind him and scooped all the happiness out of his head . . . Like they plucked it out with a claw . . .

It must be the Slynx, that's what! The Slynx is staring at his back!

Benedikt felt sick with fear from the evil, from the feeling of something rising in his throat. He slammed the door shut without waiting until the sun went down, without inhaling the raw, blue, evening air; he hooked the door in a hurry, shut the bolt; slipped in the dank dark of the izba on the curds he had bought; and even forgot to cuss. He made it to the bed and lay down quickly, his legs numb.

His heart was pounding. The Slynx . . . that's what it was. That's what. Not any of this feelosophy. The old saying is right: the Slynx is staring at your back!

It's out there, in the branches, in the northern forests, in the impenetrable thickets—it wails, turns, sniffs, lifts one paw at a time, flattens its ears, picks . . . and it has chosen! . . . Softly, like a terrible, invisible Kitty, it jumps from the branches, treading delicately, crawling under the storm kindling, under the heaps of sticks and thorny branches, leaping over the gray, overgrown moss, the dry rot piled up by blizzards! Crawling and leaping, lithe and long; it turns its flat head from side to side so's not to miss or lose the trail: far away in a poor izba, on the bed, filled with blood warm as kvas, Benedikt lies and trembles, staring at the ceiling.

Closer and closer to the house . . . Out there where snow blankets the land, dusts the ravines, where the blizzard stands like a wall, where a snowy whirlwind rises from the fields, there it is: it flies in the blankets of snow, twists in the blizzard! Its paws won't leave a trace on the snow, it won't frighten a single courtyard dog, nor trouble any household creatures!

Closer and closer—its invisible face grimaces, its claws quiver. It's hungry, famished! It's tormented, tormented! *Slyyyy-nnnxxx!*

Now it creeps up to the dwelling, closes its eyes, the better to hear, now it will pounce on the rickety roof, on the chilled chimney; now it has tensed its muscles . . .

There was a sudden knocking and rapping at the door. Knock, knock, knock. Benedikt leaped up as though he'd been hit with a stick, and screamed out loud: *Nnnnooooooo!*

"Oh, are you busy, Golubchik? Then I'll come by later," said a wonderfully familiar voice from behind the door: Nikita Ivanich. The Lord sent him . . . the Lord sent him!

K · KAKO

BENEDIKT LAY IN BED with a fever for a week—shamed and chagrined. Just like a little kid. The old man tended the fire for him, baked the sweet rolls, and gave him hot water to drink. Together they ate up all the food. So much for the New Year Holiday. It came and went as though it never happened. What a pity, they missed everything! The Golubchiks had a grand old time, they danced and sang songs, lit candles like the Decree said, and drank rusht. After the holiday, as usual, there were more injuries and cripples in the town. You'd walk along the street and you could tell right away: there had been a holiday and a lot of merrymaking. Here a guy knocked about on crutches, there another had a black eye or a huge bruise on the side of his head.

Recuperated now, Benedikt pined: life had passed him by. That's the way it always was! What a shame, it was so disappointing. Hadn't he prepared, hadn't he used his brain to approach the whole affair? Hadn't he caught mice and traded them for provisions? He'd lived in anticipation of the bright, joyous event for two whole weeks: guests, candles, music!

What is life made up of, anyway? Work and cold, the wind

whistling in the trees! Right? How often does a holiday come along?

But he had to go and catch a cold. Maybe he overdid things. Or maybe it was hunger, or something he ate in the Food Izba— who knows?—and he fell into a fever, and where have those golden days gone now?

But Nikita Ivanich said that Benedikt had a newrottick. Well, whatever. Maybe he's got one and maybe he doesn't, maybe it's rotten and maybe it isn't, but what can you do—some people just never have any luck. Only it's so frustrating it makes you want to cry.

Nikita Ivanich also says, just thank your lucky stars, you'll be in better shape this way. Your legs are in one piece, they'll come in handy yet, you reckless, empty-headed, young dreamer gone astray, like all your kind, your whole generation—and for that matter, the whole human race! Nikita Ivanich doesn't like our holidays, not one bit.

So what if you get hurt once in a while. You could slip on the ice for that matter. Or fall in a ditch and land on a sharp branch, or eat something bad. Don't people die of old age too? Even Oldener Golubchiks—they live for three hundred years and then go and die anyway. New Golubchiks are born.

You feel sorry for yourself, of course, that goes without saying. You feel sorry for relatives and friends too, though not as much. But strangers—who really cares? They're strangers, after all. How can you compare? When Mother died, Benedikt was distraught, he cried so hard, and was so upset that he swelled up. But if someone else died—even Anfisa Terentevna, for instance —would he cry that way? Not on your life! He'd be surprised, he'd ask about it, he'd cock his ear and strain to hear, what did she die of? She ate something bad or what? And where are they burying her? And will Polikarp Matveich marry someone else now, and did Anfisa Terentevna leave a lot of things behind, and just what sort of things? He'd ask lots of questions, it's always interesting to know.

And then he'd be invited to the wake—that's fun. They'd eat. He'd be asked inside the izba—you go in, look around to see what kind of izba they had, what corner the stove was in, where the window was, are there any decorations—there might be a carved bench, someone with a lot of big ideas might have embroidered the bed curtains with colored threads, or there might be a shelf on the wall to hold booklets. You'd eat and drink your fill, walk around the izba, let your eyes wander over to the booklets on the shelf. Sometimes there might be an interesting one—you could lean against the wall, cross your legs, scratch your head, and stand there reading. You never knew what you might find!

But he didn't feel like dying himself, of course not. God forbid! The only thing scarier was the Slynx. It seemed to have moved on now, lost Benedikt from sight—maybe Nikita Ivanich got in its way and it retreated.

And why is the Slynx scarier than dying? Because if you die, well, that's it—you're dead. You're gone. But if the Slynx spoils you—you have to go on living with it. But how? What do they think about, the Spoiled Ones? What do they feel inside? Hunh? . . .

They must feel a fierce, frightful, unknown anguish. A gloom that's blacker than black, with poisoned tears pouring down! Sometimes that happens in dreams: it's like you're wandering around, shuffling your feet, going left and right—you don't want to go but you do, like you're looking for something, and the farther you go, the more lost you get! And there's no way back. It's like you're walking through empty valleys, terrible ones where dry grass rustles under the snow. It just keeps on rustling. And the tears keep running and running from your face down to your knees, from your knees to the ground, and you can't lift your head! Even if you could, there'd be no point: there's nothing to see! There's nothing there . . .

If a horrible thing like that happens to a person—if the Slynx sucks the lifeblood out of him, tears at his vein with its claw—he's better off dying quickly, better his bladder should burst, and that would be it. But who really knows, maybe those two or three days before death would be a whole lifetime for him? Inside, in his own head, maybe he's walking through the fields, getting married, having a bunch of children, waiting for grandchildren, and doing his government service, repairing the roads or paying the tithe. Right inside him? Only everything is with tears, with a soulful cry, with an unbearable, inhuman, unending wail: *SLYYYYNNXXXX!*

That's right. And don't say, "Why all the injuries?" Injuries are no big deal. You get your eye poked out—well, you can still enjoy the sunshine with one eye; you get your teeth knocked out —even a toothless man can smile at his own fortune and be happy.

Benedikt's eyes, teeth, arms, and legs are just fine. So what. That's good.

On the other hand, living alone is kind of boring, you need company. A family. A woman.

A Golubchik definitely needs a woman—how can you get along without a woman? Benedikt went to see the widow woman Marfushka about the woman business: maybe once or twice a week, but he'd always go to see Marfushka. You couldn't exactly say that she was pretty. In fact, her whole face was sort of crooked, like someone hit her with a battle ax. And one eye wandered. Her figure wasn't all that great either. She was shaped like a turnip. But she didn't have any Consequences. She was rounded out where she ought to be, and caved in where she ought to be. After all, he didn't visit her to look at her, but to take care of the woman business. If looking's what you want—well, you can go out on the street and look until your eyes pop out. This was different. Like Fyodor Kuzmich, Glorybe, wrote:

Not because she shines so bright,
But because with her you need no light.

You don't need any light with Marfushka, you're better off without it. As soon as Benedikt got to her place, he'd blow out the candle, and they'd start rolling around, twisting and turning and loving it up every which way. Squatting, and straddling, this way and that, and hopping around the izba—goodness gracious, what kinds of things got into your head sometimes! When you're sitting alone, thinking your own thoughts, stirring your cabbage soup, you'd never hop around the izba or stand on your head. It would be silly. But when you visit a woman—you can't help yourself. Your pants come off right away and there's jokes and giggles. Woman's nature, or rather, her body, is just made for jokes.

After you've had your fun, you're tuckered out. Then you're starving, like you hadn't eaten for three years. Well, come on now, what did you cook up, woman? And she says: Oh, Benedikt, where oh where are you off to now, leaving me alone? I'm ready for some more frolicking. Can't tire that woman out. She's a firestorm.

No, woman, we've had all our frolicking, give me some food, something pickled, noodles, kvas, rusht, everything. I'll eat and then I'll run, or else my stove will go out.

Don't worry about your stove, I'll give you coals! And it's true, she'll feed you, and wrap up a pie for you to take home, and put some coals in a fire pot for you.

Sometimes Benedikt would read her poems, if Fyodor Kuzmich, Glorybe, had made up something about the woman business. He's a real ladies' man himself, that Fyodor Kuzmich —no doubt about it.

> The flame's ablaze, it doesn't smoke,
> But will it last for long?
> She never ever spares me,
> She spends me, spends me gone.

That's right! And there's another one:

> I want to be bold, I want to be a scoffer,
> I want to tear the clothes right off her.

Go ahead and tear them off if you feel like it—who's to stop you? That used to surprise Benedikt: who would ever say a word to Fyodor Kuzmich, Glorybe, the Greatest Murza, Long May He Live? Go on and rip to your heart's content. The master is the boss. But now that he'd seen him in the flesh, well, he might have to think it over: after all, at Fyodor Kuzmich's height you couldn't even jump high enough to reach a woman. So he must be complaining. As if to say, I can't manage on my own, help me out!

But one time these poems screwed everything up. Benedikt copied out a poem, a particularly, how to put it, bawdy, lustful, one.

No, I do not hold that stormy pleasure dear!

That's the way Fyodor Kuzmich, Glorybe, put it. Benedikt was surprised: Why doesn't he hold it dear? Is he under the weather? Is he feeling poorly? But then at the end Fyodor Kuzmich, Glorybe, explained that he'd decided to try the woman business a wild, brand-new sort of way:

> You lie in silence, heeding ne'er a sound,
> You burn so bright, and brighter, brighter still,
> Until, at last, you share my flame against your will.

Benedikt wanted so bad to find out what it was that the Greatest Murza, Long May He Live, had cooked up, that he committed Freethinking. He copied out an extra scroll for himself, hid it in his sleeve, and later ran off to Marfushka and read her the poem. He made her a proposition: well, let's try it together. You plop down and lie there like a log, not heeding anything, but you have to really do it, just like we agreed . . . And I'll get all het up over you. And we'll see what these high-falutin ideas are all about. All right? Right.

That's what they decided. But it didn't work. Marfushka did everything just as agreed, just as she was told, not a peep, her arms along her sides, her heels together, her tiptoes apart. She didn't grab Benedikt or tickle him, and she didn't wiggle or wriggle around. But no burning brighter still ever happened the way it said, and there wasn't any flame sharing either—hunh—she just lay there like a sack of potatoes. All evening. And there wasn't really any flame, for that matter. Benedikt fussed and fiddled, but for some reason he wilted, soured, gave up, shrugged his shoulders, found his hat, slammed the door, and went home, and that was the whole story. But Marfushka got mad, she chased him, cussing and shouting. He shouted back. She shouted back again. They fought, tore each other's hair out. A couple of weeks later they made up again, but it wasn't quite the same. That old spark, so to speak, was gone.

So, he went to Kapitolinka for the same business, and to Crooked Vera. Glashka-Kudlashka invited him, and a lot of others. And now here you had Varvara Lukinishna asking around. He could go to see her, but she's awfully scary looking. What if she's got that fringe all over her body?

But all this woman's business—he'd visit and forget about it. It just didn't stay in his head. It's another story when a vision sticks to you, a marvelous image, a luminous mirage—that's how Olenka began to seem to Benedikt . . . You're lying down on the bed, smoking rusht, and she—there she is, close by, giggling . . . You reach out—and she's not there! Just air! She's not there—and there she is again. Gracious!

. . . Maybe he should go and court her. What about that? Court her? Go right up and say: So you see, Olenka sweetie pie, it's this way, my gorgeous beauty. I want you to be my blushing bride, my lawful wedded wife, to say I do right at the altar. Be my missus! To have and to hold. We'll live happily ever after! . . . What else do people say in this situation? . . . Something old, something new, something borrowed, something blue. We'll be happy as the day is long!

Why not! Even though her family are noble bigwigs—they ride in a sleigh. Even though she has a rabbit coat, there don't seem to be any suitors around her. She must be picky. Modest. But she does look at Benedikt. She looks—and blushes.

When Benedikt recovered from his fever and returned to work, Olenka lit up. She shone all over, like a candle; you could just take her, stick her in a holder, and she'd light up any darkness all the way around.

He had to think this thing through.

Л · LIUDI

THE FEBRUARY BLIZZARDS had passed. The March storms blew in. Heavenly streams poured down, piercing the snow. It looked like someone had punctured it and blackened it with stone nails. The earth showed through in some places. Last year's rubbish surfaced on all the streets, in all the yards. Swift rivers flowed, foamy and murky, carrying the rubbish from the hills to the flats, bringing out the stench from the settlement. Then, suddenly, up high, blue showed through. Clean, cold clouds ran rapidly across it, the wind blew, bare branches swayed, hurrying spring along. It was raw and bright; if you didn't tuck your hands into your sleeves they'd turn all red from the cold. But Benedikt felt fine and happy.

The earth underfoot squelched. The clay was impassable. You can't travel in a sleigh or a cart, but the Murzas still want to ride, don't they? They'd not be caught walking on foot—it doesn't suit their rank. You see the Degenerators kneading the clay mud with their felt boots, hauling the sleighs; they pull with all their might, cussing up a storm, but the sleighs won't budge. The Murza lashes them: Pull! They curse him. Such a hullabaloo. In short: spring!

Then it would freeze up again, there'd be a piercing cold day; a fine snow would fall, and the bladders in the windows would be covered with hoarfrost.

And while Benedikt lay in bed with a fever, Fyodor Kuzmich, Glorybe, wrote a new decree:

DECREE
Now hear this. Since I am Fyodor Kuzmich Kablukov,
Glory to me, the Greatest Murza, Long May I Live, Seckletary
and Academishun and Hero and Ship Captain, and Carpenter,
and seeing as how I am constantly worrying about the people, I
command:

Oh, and there's something else I remembered, I'd completely forgotten it since I was so busy with state affairs:

The Eighth of March is also a Holiday, International Women's Day.

This Holiday isn't a day off.

That means you have to go to work, but you can take it easy.

Women's Day means like a Woman's Holiday.

On this day you have to honor and respect all women since they are Wife and Mother and Grandmother and Niece and any other Little Girls and respect all of them.

On this Holiday don't give them a thrashing or a licking, they don't have to do all the usual things, but Wife and Mother and Grandmother and Niece and any other Little Girls should get up earlier in the morning and bake pies, pancakes and all sorts of things, wash everything clean, sweep the floors and polish the benches, carry the water from the well, wash out the underwear and outerwear, and whoever has rugs or mats they should beat them all well or else I know you, there'll be so much dust in the izba you'll have to hold your nose. She should chop wood for the bathhouse, light the fire and scrub herself all over. Set the table with bliny and a mountain of all kinds of snacks. Maybe there's some leftovers from New Year's you can put out on the table.

When you get to work congratulate every Wife and Mother and Grandmother and Niece and any other Little Girls with International Women's Day.

Say: "Wife and Mother and Grandmother and Niece and any other Little Girls I wish you happiness in life, success in work, and a peaceful sky over your head."

And every woman you meet, even your Neighborlady, say the same polite words.

Later on, drink and make merry, eat what you want, have a good time, but within reason.

Kablukov

Just as Benedikt thought, Fyodor Kuzmich, Glorybe, was a real ladies' man. The women at work were happy: no one could say a harsh word to them, or kick them, or pull their ears, or whack them upside the head, everyone congratulated them. Varvara Lukinishna wore beads around her neck. Olenka was all in ribbons. Even Ksenia the Orphan braided some kind of rose from rough threads and fastened it at her temple. They were all so beautified—you could just drop your britches and start the joking right now.

They thought up something else too: they picked willow branches and stuck them in a pot with water. It was warm in the izba and the leaves opened up. Maybe this was Freethinking, but it was their day, and that was it. They wanted to put a pot of branches on Jackal Demianich's table too, but he threw it on the floor: the Decree didn't say anything about willows.

Jackal Demianich knows all the decrees by heart and loves them. Even old ones, from ages ago: for instance, that Sunday is a day off. Everyone knows anyway that Sunday is Sunday and no Golubchik is going to work for love or money no matter what you do to him. You'd think: Why do you need a decree, why waste the bark? Noooo, that's not the governmental approach.

The governmental approach is to decree very strictly, so that God forbid the day off didn't fall on Saturday, nor, God forbid on Friday or Thursday, or Wednesday, or Tuesday, or Monday. They decree it and that's the way it will be, because that's what the state is for, that's its power and glory and authority on earth, for all time, amen.

No one likes Jackal Demianich much. Who could like a Murza? Maybe his woman and, well, maybe his little kids, but no one else. That's not what a Murza is there for, to like or not. He's there to keep things in order. To keep an eye on the lists of workers. To hand out ink. Yell. Dock you for absences, for drunkenness, or to give you a whipping—that's what he's for. You can't get by without a Murza, without him we'd get everything mixed up.

For example. If we're talking simple. The May Holiday—it happens in May, and so you'd think the October Holiday is in October. Right? Well, you're wrong! The October Holiday is in November! If we didn't have Murzas, you see, all the Golubchiks, all of Fyodor-Kuzmichsk, would be drunk and rolling around the whole month of October!

A lot of people can't understand: How come it's called the October Holiday if it's in November? They just don't understand the governmental approach! It's in November because in October the weather is usually good, there's no snow either. The air is strong, it smells of fallen leaves, the sun shines late, the sky is so blue. The Golubchiks, whichever ones can walk on two feet, go outside on their own without any Decrees. Some go off to gather rusht, some bring in brushwood from the forest, some dig up the last turnips. It's just beautiful. Nature is clear.

But in November the rains start falling and just keep on and on and on—*eeeeee!* Everything is murky between heaven and earth, and your soul is clouded over too! The roof leaks if it's thin; cold and damp blow in through the cracks. You cover the window with rags, you slump closer to the stove, or doze on the stove bed, and something inside cries, and just keeps on crying!

The beauty of summer has passed, you can't bring it back— it's like life itself is gone, and joy has blown away with the dust rising from the road! You take the rag off the window to look— and there's nothing, nothing at all, only rain running down and beating on the puddles. Torn bits of clouds. Even the dumbest Golubchiks won't stick their nose out the door of their own free will in that kind of weather. On that kind of day, when everyone's here, at home, no one's going anywhere, there's no one left in the forest, or in the fields—on a day like that they have the October Holiday. All the Golubchiks, healthy and crippled, are ordered to leave the house and go to the main square where the watchtower is, and march by it, six in a row, singing. The Murzas watch the Golubchiks from the watchtower and take a head count. Because we have to know how many people we have, and how many chits to cut out for payday and how much to give out on Warehouse Day, and how many people can be called for roadwork, if they aren't crippled. Stuff like that. As the saying goes: Count your chicks in autumn. And when you've counted them all, then of course you can go back home, drink and make merry, have a good time, do what you want, but within reason. That's the governmental approach for you.

But the bosses have to figure out exactly when the October Holiday should be—that's what bosses are for. They sit in the terems looking at the sky, observing the weather and discussing it. Yesterday, they say, was a bit early, but tomorrow—who knows, it might be late, whereas today, they say, is the very day. Get everybody out there for the count.

Jackal knows all this business, that's his job.

He told Benedikt about the Decree: "Congratulations."

Benedikt memorized the congratulations: he read them, and then reread them; he repeated them gazing at the ceiling; then he checked against the bark, then he squeezed his eyes shut and whispered them again, so he'd know them for sure. He congratulated Varvara Lukinishna politely: "I wish you Wife and Mother and Grandmother and Niece and any other Little Girls happiness in life, success in work, and a peaceful sky over your head."

Vasiuk the Earful spread his elbows and listened alertly from his corner to make sure Benedikt was saying everything right, like it was in the Decree.

Varvara Lukinishna blushed red all over: she liked hearing those words. "Oh, thank you, my dear. Come by and visit me this evening: I've made soup."

"Today? I don't know . . ."

"There are still some nuts . . . I'll bake a mouse."

"Well, I'm not sure . . ."

"The mouse is fresh as can be."

Benedikt hesitated.

"Do come . . . I'll show you something . . . in secret."

What an insistent woman. She's looks enough of a fright in a dress, but if she took off her clothes and showed her secret, it'd probably be really scary: grab your hat and run for the door. But it's tempting, of course. Who knows . . .

"Please, do come by . . . We'll talk about art . . . I know that you are capable of delicate feelings . . . I think your potential is enormous."

She batted her lone eye. My oh my, what a . . . Benedikt even started sweating. What suggestive conversations . . . and right at work . . .

"Well, it's not too small . . . No complaints in that department

94

... And I do feel everything ... How do you know? What kind of pudential did you say I have?"

"Now then, you can't hide that sort of thing ..."

"Someone blabbed?"

"Well, we often talk about your ... in our circle, you know ... we have our opinions ... Everyone agrees: you are developing in a marvelous direction ..."

"Oh!"

"That's right. We expect a lot from you."

"Hmm ... What kind of circle is this of yours?"

"Our own close group of ... like minds. You and a number of acquaintances."

That's just what he thought. Women! ... They sit down in a circle and gab about the woman's business. Who, with whom, and when. And they talked about Benedikt! They praised him!

"... We tell each other our little secrets," Varvara Lukinishna whispered. "We share."

?!?! Whoa! So that's what they're up to! Sure ... What can you do, they're lonely ...

"Are there a lot of you? In the circle, that is?"

"Oh, a small group, maybe six people ... We don't manage to get together very often, but the conversation is very intense, we're so close ..."

"With six of you it would be close ... Are you all on the floor or what?"

"Why, everyone's where they like."

"Then how do you ..."

"How do we fit? Well, my izba is miniscule, to be sure. I can't deny it, it's true. When everyone gets together, as you might expect, we're sometimes literally sitting on top of one another!"

"Uh huh ... I'll come," Benedikt said quickly. "I'll come, wait for me."

So! ... He had to get home right away and heat up the bath, wash, and then grab a jug of rusht—he couldn't go visiting with empty hands. Then ... then he'd see. Oy, what were they going to do! Now he had to congratulate everyone and head home; Jackal wouldn't say anything—it was decreed: work, but take it easy. Benedikt bowed to Ksenia the Orphan:

"I wish you Wife and Mother and Grandmother and Niece and any other Little Girls happiness in life, success in work, a peaceful sky over your head."

She was thrilled.

"I've heard it so many times today already, but it's so nice! Every day should be like this!"

Jackal raised an eyebrow at her from his corner: that was Freethinking, that was. But he couldn't object: today they were only supposed to congratulate, not insult or anything. He'd probably let her have it tomorrow.

"Come for some of my pancakes this evening."

"I'm busy."

"Oh, what a pity. My pancakes are so fluffy!"

"I'm sure they are."

And that was a hint too. Her pancakes, she says, are so fluffy! . . . What if he went to both places? . . . Burn the candle at both ends? Olenka was looking at him from her stool . . . He should congratulate Olenka. With the others it was easy, but he was sort of scared with Olenka: he felt all shy and weak in the knees. He sat down next to Olenka and muttered: "I wish you Wife and Mother and Grandmother and Niece and any other Little Girls happiness in life, success in work, a peaceful sky over your head."

But Olenka laughed softly. "I'm not your wife, am I? . . ."

"But in the decree . . ."

"And without the decree? . . . "

Benedikt started sweating again: here it was, Women's Day, Woman's Holiday, that's what it was all about . . . Oh, that Fyodor Kuzmich, Glorybe . . . Just wait, next thing she'd be inviting him for bliny . . .

". . . And without the Decree you mean there's no happiness in life?"

"Olenka . . . Olenka, I want happiness in life without the decree . . ."

"Well then?"

"I offer you my hand, heart, and pudential," whispered Benedikt. He didn't expect such fine, frightening words from himself: they just leapt out of him.

"I accept," whispered Olenka.

"You accept?!"

"I accept . . . I accept it all . . ."

They sat in silence for a moment . . . What else was there to say . . . His heart was jumping . . . Oy, he did it! . . . He did it! What a day!

Glorybe to Fyodor Kuzmich!

So it's farewell to the bachelor life! You didn't sow your wild oats for very long, Benedikt Karpich! But that's just fine! Time to settle down. Benedikt ran home: it was still early, the coals in the stove hadn't gone out, he had to collect them and fire up the bath . . . Whew! He hadn't bathed since last year! In the new style, that is. January first used to be the New Year, but now they'd moved it, it turns out . . . He ran, nodded to women he met along the way—not his habit, but today you had to. He shouted out congratulations. He wished them all happiness in life. Nikita Ivanich trundled by, lugging a log—and Benedikt shouted to him, jokingly: "A peaceful sky above your head, Nikita Ivanich! No rain, nothing!" The old man jerked, turned around, and spat on the ground. Aha, he's thinking Benedikt took him for a woman! . . . But it was just a joke!

Olenka lives in a different settlement . . . not in ours . . . We're way over here, and she's right there. They agreed that he'd visit her on the May Holiday to meet her parents. Let's hope the weather will be good, bright . . . A peaceful sky overhead! . . . Not like today: lots of mud and a freezing rain . . .

He ran past a sleigh stuck in the mud: hopeless to travel in this weather. Three furry Degenerators stood on the roadside: a troika. They were resting with their boots off, smoking rusht, grinning at the Golubchiks. When they saw Benedikt they burst into laughter. "Running away from a heart attack, are you? . . ."

"If he don't catch up, at least he'll warm up!"

"Faster, faster, they'll close the garage!"

Shameless beasts. They harass people. But it's not worth paying them back in kind: they swear a sight better than we do. No one gets involved with them, not with Degenerators.

From hill to hill, along the lanes, sometimes through gardens, scrambling under a fence for a shortcut, Benedikt ran all the way home, threw open the bolts, rushed into the izba, flung open the stove damper: the coals are smoldering! Smoldering, Golubchik! He made it in time! Put in a little rusht, some firewood, bark chips; blow on the fire, let it play for a while; and as soon as it catches, take it to the bathhouse. Haul the water, find the branches from last year that were in the shed somewhere. There ought to be a brand-new washcloth . . . it was here . . . Now if he were married, he'd run home from work—and everything would be ready, the spiders swept away, the branches steamed up. Yes, but married men can't really go visiting women . . . "Where are you going, Benedikt? It's nighttime." "Well, you see . . . I have to . . . to talk about art . . ." "We know your art! . . . Huh! A real artful one you are." And she'd take the branches and thrash him six ways from Sunday . . . Would he and Olenka really fight like that? Nooo. Everything would be fine between them—otherwise, what was the point?

You'd get home—everything's ready, only you wouldn't have the same freedom. Well, so what. But his wife was a real beauty! And freedom—well, what's freedom . . . Right now he was free, but he couldn't find the washcloth—could they really have pinched it? No, he was in luck again: he found the cloth in the bathhouse under a stone; a little moldy, but he found it. What a day today: everything is working out.

He sat and enjoyed the steam, rubbed himself all over with the washcloth, beat himself red with the branches, and inspected his body from every angle his eyes could reach: gorgeous! If a neighbor glanced in the window right now, he'd be envious. Benedikt even envied himself. No wonder the women praised him: "Marvelously developed, we expect a lot from you!" Just wait, I'll dry off and—I'm all yours. Would all six be there, or what? Never mind, God willing, I'll manage! They sit on top of each other . . . whew!

He scraped the coals in a pile: maybe they'd last longer that way. Probably not till morning, though. He could get some coals from Varvara. But why? In the morning he had to go to work, anyway. Oh, what a lot of fuss and bother! Benedikt scattered the coals again: God forbid there should be a fire. It was a tricky thing, fire: if it went out, you might as well lie down and die; if it flared up too much, it would burn everything right down to the ground like nothing was ever there! That's fire for you. It's skittish. It needs food, it's always hungry, just like a man. Gimme, gimme, gimme! But if you overfeed it, it'll gobble you up.

If there's a fire somewhere, the Golubchiks come running from all around, from all the settlements, sometimes from the farthest reaches. A huge crowd gathers like on the October Holiday. They surround the burning house and stand there, arms folded on their chests, watching . . . No one talks out loud, they just whisper: "Yikes, look at that pillar of flame . . ." "Look, look, over there the corner's caught!" . . . And the flames rush and tear about, not exactly like pillars, but like a tree, like the jeopard tree in spring—it dances and hums, twists and turns, but stays put. You turn to look at the Golubchiks: they stand there staring and the fire dances in their eyes too, it's reflected like in water, it splashes. The crowd has a thousand eyes, and water and fire lap in each and every one, like dawn rising on the river. It makes you feel strange and wild inside, no mistake, water and fire don't mix, but here they are together!

And if there's Oldeners nearby, they run back and forth tearing at their hair and shouting: "Put it out! Put out the fire!" But how? How can you put it out? You can put out a little flame with a bucket of water, but if the fire has showed its strength, that's it. All you can do is wait till it's over.

If the other izbas don't catch that's lucky. When the fire has eaten everything and starts to die down and settle, the Golubchiks move in with buckets, pots, whatever they've got, to collect coals to take home. Maybe their stove is warm, anyway—it doesn't matter. No point in letting good coals go to waste.

Sometimes a whole settlement burns. Well, you just have to start life all over again.

Spic and span and pleased with himself, Benedikt knocked on Varvara's door. She opened it, all decked out, and sweaty.

"Oh, it's you. How nice. What is this you've brought? Rusht? You needn't have gone to all that trouble . . ."

He looked around: there weren't any other frolickers there yet. He could wait. The table was set. There were two bowls and two spoons. A pot of soup.

"Have a seat. I'll be right there." She took a griddle of mice out of the oven. "I think they're done."

"Stick them with a splinter."

"That's it. They're done. Fresh, I caught them today."

"Great."

They poured some rusht. Took a bite.

"To your health."

They poured some more. It went down smooth.

"What lovely rusht. It has such a distinctive bouquet."

"I know where to pick it."

"And where is that, if it's not a secret?"

"In the bog. Behind the Cockynork settlement."

"Near the Garden Ring?"

"That's right."

"Gracious, how far afield you range!"

"Yeah, well, but it's good rusht."

"I should do a bit of reconnoitering myself."

The women still hadn't come. Benedikt coughed politely into his hand.

"Will the guests be coming or not, then?"

"Well, I wasn't sure . . ."

"But they promised?"

"I thought . . . you see, . . . I thought that I'd better reveal my secret alone first . . . I don't know how you'll react . . . I'm a bit nervous . . ."

"Me too, a little."

"I don't know if you'll be able to appreciate . . ."

"I'm able," said Benedikt, though he wasn't sure that he was.

"Well, all right, then. But it's a secret. You won't tell, of course . . ."

"No, no, no."

"Well then, close your eyes."

Benedikt closed his eyes. Something rustled. There was a bump. More rustling. Benedikt peeked with one eye. But it didn't seem like anything was ready yet—he could only see shadows from the candles dancing on the beams—so he closed his eyes again.

"Ready or not—here I come," sang Benedikt.

"Just a moment . . . How impatient you are . . ."

"I can't wait," Benedikt lied, letting a hint of playfulness appear in his voice. "I just can't wait."

Something fell on his lap, something not very heavy that smelled of mold.

"Here it is. Take a look . . ."

"What is it?"

A box—but not a box, just something shaped like it. Inside were whitish pages that looked like fresh bark, but lighter; they were very, very thin, and they seemed to be covered with dust or poppyseed.

"What is it?"

"Look closely!"

He brought it to his eyes. The dust was fine and even . . . like spider webs . . . He stared, amazed . . . Suddenly it was as though the web fell from his eyes and it hit him: "and the candle by which Anna read a life full of alarm and deceit . . ." He gasped. Letters! They were letters! Written teeny tiny, but so carefully, and they weren't brown, they were black . . . He licked his finger and rubbed the bark: he rubbed a hole right in it. Gosh, how thin.

"Careful, you'll ruin it!"

"What is it? . . ."

"It's a book . . . an Oldenprint book."

"Ay!!!" Benedikt jumped from the stool and dropped the poison. "What are you doing? I'll get sick!"

"No! Wait! Just wait a minute! . . ."

"The Sickness! . . ."

"No! . . ."

"Let me out of here! . . ."

"Just sit down. Sit down! I'll explain everything. I promise." Varvara Lukinishna pried Benedikt's hands away from the bolts, her cock's combs trembling. "It's completely safe . . . Nikita Ivanich confirmed it."

"What's he got to do with it?"

101

"He knows! He gave it to me!"

Benedikt quieted down and sat on the stool, his knees weak. He wiped his nose with his sleeve to stop the trembling. Nikita Ivanich. One of the bosses. And he didn't get sick. He touched a book—and he didn't get sick . . .

"It's safe . . ." whispered Varvara. "You know, he's an extraordinary old man . . . so knowledgeable. He explained it to me: it's completely safe, it's just a superstition . . . You see, when the Blast occurred, everything was considered dangerous, because of the radiation . . . You've heard about it . . . That's why it was forbidden. The books were radioactive . . ."

"To hear the Oldeners tell it, everything is radioactive," said Benedikt, shaking. "No, this is something else . . ."

"But Nikita Ivanich knows . . . he has . . . If it was truly dangerous, he would have fallen ill long ago, but you can see that he's healthier than either of us . . ."

"Then why do they . . . Why are people taken away and treated . . . knock on wood?"

"It's a tradition, knock on wood . . ."

They both knocked on wood.

. . . God have mercy and protect me . . . I'm not sick, I'm not sick, I'm not sick, no, no, no. I won't get sick, I won't get sick, no, no, no. Don't come, don't, don't, don't. The red hoods don't need to come, knock on wood. I don't want to be hooked.

"Nikita Ivanich explained it to me . . . It was thought to be extremely dangerous because paper absorbs other substances . . . You and I copy things so that they're not dangerous to the people's health . . . But now it doesn't matter anymore, two hundred years have passed . . . You and I are copying old books, Benedikt . . ."

"What do you mean, old? Fyodor Kuzmich, Glorybe, wrote all those booklets . . ."

"No, he didn't . . . Different people wrote them, but everyone thinks it was Fyodor Kuzmich. I felt there was something going on . . . You know, after I saw him, Fyodor Kuzmich, I couldn't sleep all night . . . I kept thinking, thinking . . . Then I made a decision, I worked up my nerve and went to see Nikita Ivanich. We talked for a long, long time . . ."

"He never told me anything . . ."

"Oh, Benedikt, he's an unusual man . . . We talked about you . . . He wanted to tell you, but not right away . . . He wanted to prepare you . . . I know it's a huge blow . . . but I think it's better to know the truth than to live life in darkness . . ."

Benedikt sat on the stool, hunched over. His thoughts strayed here and there, his head felt heavy. Maybe he went back to work too soon? Maybe he still had fever? He had the chills. Or was it just the bath? . . . Why did he have to bathe when there was no one to kiss?

"And what now?"

"Now? Nothing, simply now you know."

"What for?"

"Well, I mean, I thought . . ."

"Why think? I want to live."

"But what does that have . . . I want to, too . . . but I want to know the truth . . . if it's possible . . ."

"'For in much wisdom is much grief.' So you mean Fyodor Kuzmich, Glorybe, didn't write that either?"

"Probably not."

"Then who?"

"I don't know . . . You'll have to ask the Oldeners."

Varvara Lukinishna picked the Oldenprint book up off the floor, placed it on the table, and stroked it with her hand. It was strange to see such a fearsome thing up close.

"Still . . . Why are you touching it? . . . If we are copying old books, then just wait till we're told to copy it . . . Then you can hold it . . ."

"But when will that be? . . . Maybe not soon enough. Life is so short, and I just adore art . . . And it's such an interesting book! . . ."

"What? You're reading it?"

"Why, of course . . . Benedikt, there are so many interesting books. I'll give it to you to read if you like."

"No!!!" said Benedikt, flinching.

"But why are you so afraid?"

"I have to go . . . My head is sort of—"

"Wait! . . ."

Benedikt tore himself away, staggered out on the porch, into the rain, into the early, raw dark. Out of sight, out of mind . . . His head really was sort of . . .

. . . The March wind groaned in the treetops, rattled the bare twigs and the rabbit nests, and something else unknown—who knows what's up there moaning, what awakes in spring? A gust of wind blows—it whispers, it whines in the trees, it scatters raindrops on your head. There might be a savage cry up above, from the branches: startled, you race for the closest fence . . . Maybe it's a woodsucker bird.

The bladders twinkle faintly in the windows, the Golubchiks have lighted their candles, they're slurping down soup . . . They exchange glances: maybe they too have Oldenprint books hidden under their beds . . . We'll lock the doors and take them out . . . Read a bit . . . Maybe everyone has one, who knows . . . In that izba . . . and this one . . . and in that one over there, where a pale light flickers—is it a candle smoking, or people pacing the rooms, blocking the feeble fire with their mortal bodies, trying the bolts to make sure they're firmly shut? Out from under the mattress, from under a moldy pile of rags, filthy human rags, they take a booklet . . . a book . . . a book . . . and he's the only one who's acting like a frightened fool . . . The only one in the whole town . . . The letters are so black, so teensy . . . it's scary even to think about it . . .

Up above everything roared and groaned. The wind flew into his sleeve, cutting straight through him. Benedikt stood at an unfamiliar fence, thinking. The baked mouse had only teased his appetite. He wanted to eat. But at home in his izba there was no fire: he'd put it out when he left to go visiting. He didn't think he'd need it. Should he go back and get some coals? She'd give them to him, she's kind . . . No. Go back? The squeaking door . . . the warmth . . . the white, happy pancake of her face, the trembling cock's combs, the hurried whisper: this way, this way, I have some art . . . One minute, I'll just wipe the mold off . . . And the candle by which . . . full of alarm and deceit! What incredible fear! "Fear, noose and ditch," Fyodor Kuzmich wrote . . . No, they say, not Fyodor Kuzmich, Glorybe. . . . Full of alarm

104

. . . And deceit . . . Not Fyodor Kuzmich . . . Someone else, unseen, old, with a hidden face . . . Probably big, pale and white,
ancient, extinct, as tall as a tree, with a beard down to his knees
and horrible eyes . . . Terrifying, he stands amid the trunks, motionless, just turning his face, and his eyes look straight through
the March twilight, he rolls them so that he can see Benedikt in
the gloom: Where is that Benedikt? Why did he hide? Why did
he run for the fence?—and Benedikt's heart is pounding in his
neck, floating up to his tongue, roaring in his ears—where is
Benedikt? Come here now, I want to tell you something—his
hand will reach out and he'll hook a gnarled finger under Benedikt's rib, and with the frightful cry of the woodsucker, scream:
Eeeeeeeeeahhhhhhhhhhaaauuuuu!

There was a knock on the door of the strange izba. An ordinary, homey knock; plain, everyday life knocked on the door,
drunken talk and laughter could be heard in the twilight. So
someone has guests, it's a holiday and they went out on the
porch—to take a leak or just to go out and breathe the fresh air,
to live life or sing a song, or just to kick the cat!

They didn't notice Benedikt slinking along the fence, no one
could see him. The frightful, ancient inhabitant, who read, or
wrote, or maybe just hid a book full of deceit in rags, didn't notice him either; just as he'd appeared, he vanished, and he was
gone.

Home. It was dark in his izba, it smelled of ashes, and the
wedding was a long way off.

M · MYSLETE

OLDENERS look just like us. Men, women, young, old—all
kinds. Mostly old people. But they're different. They have a
Consequence—they don't get any older. That's it. They live and
live and they don't die from old age. They do die from other

things once in a while, though. There aren't many Oldeners left.

They sit in their izbas or go to work, and some have made it into the bosses—same as with us. Only their talk is different. If you run into a Golubchik stranger on the street, you could never say whether he's one of us or an Oldener. Until you ask him the usual: "Who are ya? How come I don't know you? What the heck you doin' in our neck of the woods?" An Oldener doesn't answer like other people do: "Whassit to ya, tired of lugging that mug around? Just wait, I'll rip it offa ya," or something like that. No, they don't answer so's you can make sense of it, so to speak: You got muscles and I got muscles so don't mess with me! No, sometimes you'll get an answer like: "Leave me be, you uncouth hooligan!" Then you know for sure the guy's an Oldener.

And when one of them does die, the others bury him. But not like we do. They don't put stones on the eyes. They don't take out the guts and stuff the insides with rusht. They don't tie the hands and feet or bend the knees. They don't put anything in the grave, not even a candle or a mouse, no dishes, no pots, no spoons, no bows and arrows, no little clay figures, nothing like that. They might tie a cross together from twigs and stick it in their corpse's hands, or draw an idol on bark and also put it in his hands like a portrait. But some of them don't even do that.

One of their old ladies died recently. Nikita Ivanich dropped by to see Benedikt, all gloomy: he was unhappy that an Oldener lady died.

"Benya, our Anna Petrovna has gone to meet her maker. Please, as a friend, do me a favor and help us carry the coffin. The thaw has made all the roads muddy. We won't be able to manage it."

What else could he do. He went to help. It was even interesting to see how they did things different than other people.

The crowd was small, about a dozen. Most of the people were elderly. No cussing, nothing. Just quiet talk. They all looked upset.

"Who's the master of ceremonies?"

"Viktor Ivanich."

"Viktor Ivanich again?"

"Who else? He's very experienced."

106

"But he couldn't arrange any transportation."

"They wouldn't give him any. Said the garage was closed for inclement weather."

"They always have excuses."

"As if you didn't know."

"They're just mocking us."

"Not as though you haven't had time to get accustomed to it."

Viktor Ivanich, their master of ceremonies, was fairly young. He had short, blond hair, combed to the side. He looked annoyed. Red threads were wound round his sleeve so you could see him from far away. Not a Murza, but sort of like one, so just in case, Benedikt bowed to him. His eyebrows twitched: he accepted the bow. He said to Benedikt: "Don't crowd around."

They put the coffin on the ground next to the hole. Someone put a stool nearby and placed a pillow on it. They stood by in a sparse half circle and took off their hats. Viktor Ivanich chose two of them and pointed.

"You and you. Please. Form the honor guard."

He looked over the heads of the crowd and raised his voice sternly.

"I declare the civil memorial service open. I shall begin!"

The Oldeners said to him: "Begin, begin, Viktor Ivanich. It's cold."

Viktor Ivanich raised his voice and began: "Are there any relatives, close friends? Move up front, please!"

No one stepped forward. That means she didn't have any relations, just like me, Benedikt thought. It means she caught her own mice.

"Co-workers?"

No one. One Golubushka stepped up: "I'm her neighbor. I looked after her."

Viktor Ivanich spoke to her angrily, in his everyday voice: "Don't get ahead of things! I haven't called you yet."

"But I'm freezing. Hurry up."

"If you are going to be obstreperous, I'll have to ask you to leave the premises!" said Viktor Ivanich rudely. "Order must be observed!"

"That's right!" a few shouted from the crowd. "Order has to

be observed, so let's observe it! Or it'll be a disaster. As always. We're just wasting time!"

Viktor Ivanich used his other voice: elevated and sort of ringing, as if he were calling out to someone in the forest: "Neighbors, housekeepers? . . . Take your place in the first row . . ."

The neighbor lady who'd made the fuss ran forward. Viktor Ivanich gave his expression a little more warmth: he pinched his mouth up like a chicken's rump and sort of wrinkled his eyes. He squeezed the woman's elbow and said: "Chin up."

The woman burst into tears. Viktor Ivanich again intoned: "Are there any military awards, commendations, orders? Government tributes, testimonials? Diplomas from state institutions? Medals of honor, pins? Epaulettes? . . ."

Nothing.

"Party cards, Komsomol or trade union ID? . . . State lottery tickets? Domestic loan bonds? Employment records? Writers or Artists Union cards? No? Drivers' licenses of any sort? Trucks? Passenger vehicles? Tractor trailers? No? Leases? Subscription forms? Gas or telephone bills? Collective antenna registration documents? Receipts for overpayment?"

All these words were so funny, total gibberish. Benedikt couldn't stop himself, he giggled, and turned to look at the crowd: they were probably cracking up too. No, they were all crying, tears streaming from their eyes. They all looked like they were staring at something very far away. One woman was wringing her hands, whispering: "We never appreciated . . . never appreciated . . ." Tears were welling in Nikita Ivanich's eyes too. Benedikt whispered to him: "What's wrong, Nikita Ivanich? You feel sorry for the old lady?"

"Quiet, Benya! Quiet. Please. This was our whole life . . . Lord . . . There you have it . . . A whole way of life . . ."

He trembled, and wiped his face with his sleeve. Viktor Ivanich continued: "Instructions for using household appliances? No? A television? A gas or electric range? A microwave? Kerosene stove? No? Vacuum cleaner? Floor polisher? Washing machine? Sewing machine? Kitchen appliances?"

"Yes, yes! There are instructions!" someone cried out.

"Very good! Please come up front! What kind of instructions?"

"It's for a meat grinder. With attachments."

"Put it right here. Here. On the pillow."

An old Golubchik approached and placed a tattered, soiled, frayed scrap of who-knows-what on the red pillow and put a stone on top of it so the wind wouldn't blow it away. All the women began sobbing; they howled like Spoiled Ones. One of them suddenly felt faint, so they held her up and fanned her face with their hands.

"Courage, comrades!" Viktor Ivanich intoned. "So! To continue. Who has any memorial objects? Relics? No? That's it? I'll move on to the second part. *Comrades!*" Viktor Ivanich spoke in such a hooting voice, just like some kind of blindlie bird, that Benedikt squatted down. He looked around. Jeez, the guy shouted like he wasn't talking to a dozen Golubchiks, but a whole thousand.

"Death has wrenched an irreplaceable laborer from our ranks," Viktor Ivanich went on. "A marvelous human being. A worthy citizen." Viktor Ivanich dropped his head on his chest and was silent for a time. Benedikt crouched and looked up at his face: Was he crying? No, he wasn't crying. He looked back at Benedikt angrily. He jerked his head up and continued. "It's sad, comrades. Immensely sad. On the eve of this glorious day, the two-hundredth anniversary of the Blast—"

"Viktor Ivanich, Viktor Ivanich!" cried the Oldeners. "You're talking about the wrong thing!"

"What do you mean? Oh, excuse me. I apologize. That's for a different occasion. I got them mixed up."

"You mustn't confuse things!"

"Don't interrupt! I'm being interrupted here," he said, squinting at Benedikt. "People are crowding around!"

"That's Polina Mikhailovna's boy!"

"Don't argue, ladies and gentlemen. Let's continue! On the eve . . ."

Viktor Ivanich collected himself, frowned, and stood at attention.

"On the eve of this mournful occasion, the two-hundredth anniversary of the Blast, which dispersed and then consolidated our ranks, a great, inspiring comrade, an irreplaceable citizen, a modest, inconspicuous toiler, has left us. An individual possessed of a grand soul. She has left us, but her cause is not dead. Though Anna Petrovna's contribution to the restoration of our Lofty Past may not have been large," said Viktor Ivanich, pointing to the pillow, "it is nonetheless weighty, tangible . . . Rest in peace, Anna Petrovna! . . . Who wants to speak on behalf of the settlement? You, Nikolai Maximich? Be my guest."

Another old Golubchik appeared, his hair blowing in the wind. His face was tear-stained and he blew his nose. "Anna Petrovna! You toiled in anonymity," he said, addressing the coffin directly. "How did it come to this, Anna Petrovna? Tell me! And what about us? We didn't appreciate you! We weren't interested! We thought—there's Anna Petrovna and there's Anna Petrovna again! Just another old lady. We thought you would always be with us. Why beat around the bush, we didn't give a fig about you! Who needs her, we thought, that little old mean-spirited, communal-apartment crone, she just gets underfoot like a poisonous mushroom, God forgive us!"

"Hey, watch it," the Golubchiks warned. "Go easy."

"De mortuis aut bene aut nihil!" someone cackled into Benedikt's ear.

"What did I do?" said Benedikt, startled. "What do I have to do with it?"

"It's not about you, Benya, nothing to do with you. Calm down," Nikita Ivanich said, tugging on Benedikt. "Stand still, don't fidget."

"Who, I repeat, needed you, Anna Petrovna? You were an invisible mosquito interested only in your kitchen, you never left the stove! Here's what remains of you: how to eat, and that's the sum total! But we are sorry for you, Anna Petrovna! Without you the people is not whole!"

Viktor Ivanich shook the Golubchik's hand and thanked him: "Well spoken, comrade. We thank you. On behalf of the Monument Preservation Society, Nikita Ivanich, please say a few words!"

Nikita Ivanich went up and also blew his nose. "Friends!" he began. "What does this memorial object tell us?" he asked, pointing to the pillow. "This priceless relic of a bygone era! What stories would it tell us if it could speak? Some might say: It's nothing but museum dust, the ashes of the centuries! Instructions for a meat grinder! Ha! However, my friends! However! As a former museum employee who has never relinquished his responsibilities, let me tell you something. In these difficult years—the Stone Age, the sunset of Europe, the death of the gods and everything else that you and I, friends, have lived through—at this time the instructions for a meat grinder are no less valuable than a papyrus from the library of Alexandria! A fragment of Noah's Ark! The tablets of Hammurabi. Moreover, friends, material culture is being restored hour by hour. The wheel has been reinvented, the yoke is returning to use, and the solar clock as well! We will soon learn to fire pottery! Isn't that correct, friends? The time of the meat grinder will come. Though at present it may seem as mysterious as the secrets of the pyramids—we don't even know whether they still stand, by the way—as incomprehensible to the mind as the canals of the planet Mars—the hour will come, friends, when it will start working! And Viktor Ivanich is right—it will rise before us, tangible and weighty, just as the aqueduct once devised by the slaves of Rome arrived in our former era. Unfortunately the aqueduct hasn't come back to our time yet, but even that is not far off! It will come, everything will come! The most important thing is to preserve our spiritual heritage! The object itself may not exist, but there are instructions for its use, we have its spiritual—no, I do not fear that word—will and testament, a missive from the past! And Anna Petrovna, a modest, entirely unremarkable grandmother, preserved this missive unto her deathbed! A keeper of the hearth, the cornerstone, the pillar of the whole world. It's a lesson to us all, friends. As our great poet wrote: 'O monument untouched by human hands! Harder than copper, older than the pyramids!' I salute you, Anna Petrovna, you are a saintly soul!"

He burst into tears and moved aside.

"Very well put, Nikita Ivanich. We thank you. Lev Lvovich,

please step forward on behalf of the Dissidents," announced Viktor Ivanich.

A thin, curly-headed Golubchik stood up. He grimaced. Clasped his hands over his belly. Rocked gently from heel to toe. "Ladies and gentlemen, this is symbolic: the world may perish, but the meat grinder is indestructible. The meat grinder of history. And here I beg to differ with the representative from the Monument Preservation Society," he said, grimacing again. "A meat grinder, ladies and gentlemen. With attachments. The grinder hasn't changed. Only the attachments have changed. There was no freedom back then, nor is there now. And note the saddest thing, ladies and gentlemen. How deep rooted this is. In the people's mind. Instructions for tightening the screws. The eternal rotation of levers and blades. Let us remember Dostoevsky: 'The whole world may perish, but I want to drink tea.' Or grind meat. Cannon fodder, ladies and gentlemen. In this hour I have a bitter taste in my mouth. We have already been ground to bits. And they want to do it some more. I won't even mention the present economic situation: we're all freezing. I simply wish to draw your attention to this: yes, a meat grinder. Devised long ago by the slaves of the Third Rome. By slaves! And there are no Xeroxes!"

"Very well said, Lev Lvovich. We thank you. On behalf of the female community? . . . Lily Pavlovna?"

Benedikt didn't bother to listen to the woman; he squatted on a mound and waited for them to finish. It started to freeze. The surface of the clay, stirred up by many feet, began to ice over, and a fine snow was blowing. Spring just wouldn't stick, just wouldn't hang on. It'd be nice to go into the warmth and stretch out on the bed. And for Olenka to bring him pancakes and hot kvas. Olenka! Indescribable beauty! A little scary to marry such beauty! Her braid is long. Her eyes are bright . . . Her little face is egg-shaped, like a triangle. Plump, but maybe that's all the warm clothes wrapped around her. Her fingers are thin. If only the May Holiday would come . . . She could sit at the window and embroider, and Benedikt would admire her all the livelong day.

■　■　■

Meanwhile, the Oldeners talked, cried, sang something melancholy, buried their old woman, and had begun to go their separate ways. Nikita Ivanich, sniffing, sat down next to Benedikt, opened his pouch, stuffed some rusht into a leaf and rolled it up, one for him, one for Benedikt. He puffed out a little flame and they lit up.

"What did she die of, Nikita Ivanich?"

"I don't know, Benya. Who can tell?"

"She ate something, or what?"

"Ah, Benya! . . ."

"Nikita Ivanich, I'm thinking of getting married."

"That's good. But aren't you young to be getting married?"

"Nikita Ivanich! I'm in my third decade!"

"That's true . . . But I wanted to get you involved in something . . . As old friends . . ."

"What is it? Putting up pillars and posts?"

"Even better . . . I want to erect another monument to Pushkin. On Strastnoi Boulevard. We buried Anna Petrovna, and I thought . . . by association, you know . . . He had his Anna Petrovna, we had our Anna Petrovna . . . A fleeting vision . . . Whatever passes shall be sweet . . . You have to help me."

"What kind of monument?"

"How can I explain it? We'll carve a figure out of wood, life size. A handsome fellow. Thoughtful. His head bowed, his hand on his heart."

"The way you bow to Murzas?"

"No . . . The way you listen: What is in the offing? What has passed us by? Hand on heart. Like this. Is it beating? Yes? Then there's life still there."

"Who is Pushkin? From around here?"

"A genius. He died. Long ago."

"He ate something bad?"

"Good Lord Almighty! . . . Lord forgive me, but what a dim-witted oaf you are, and Polina Mikhailovna's son to boot! However, I must take some of the blame, I should have taken you under my wing long ago. Well, now I'll have something to do in my old age. We'll fix everything. You have a good profession, no? You're well read, is that right?"

"I read well, Nikita Ivanich! I love to read. I love art. I adore music."

"Music. Hmm, yes. I loved Brahms."

"I love a good brahms too. That's for sure."

"How could you know?" asked the old man, surprised.

"What do you mean! Ha! Semyon, you see—you know Semyon, right? He has an izba on Rubbish Pond? Next to Ivan Beefich? Like this—Ivan Beefich's izba, and there's Semyon's, you know? On the right, where the big ditch is?"

"All right, all right, what about this Semyon?"

"Well, when he has his fill of kvas, he plays loud music. He turns buckets and pots upside down, and hits them with sticks—broompah, broompah, broompah-pah, and then he hits the bottom of a barrel—whack—and it makes a big *brrrahms!*"

"Right . . ." sighed Nikita Ivanich.

They sat in silence and smoked. It was nice to think about music. And singing . . . He should ask Semyon to the wedding. The wind gusted and blew down some more fine snow.

"Well, should we go, Nikita Ivanich? . . . Or else my tail is gonna freeze stiff."

"What tail?"

"What do you mean, what tail? A plain old tail, the kind that grows on your backside."

H · NASH

HOW DO YOU like that! Man proposes, God disposes. Halfway through my earthly life, I awoke in a twilit forest! Having strayed from the path in the darkness of the valley! There I was, living my life, enjoying the sun, gazing in sorrow at the stars, smelling the flowers, dreaming lovely dreams, and suddenly—what a blow! What a drama! A crying shame and a drama—

nothing this really terrible has probably ever happened to anybody, not even the Gingerbread Man!

Benedikt had lived his whole life proudly: fine and fit as a fiddle he was. He knew it himself, and people said so. You can't see your own face, of course, unless you pour water in a bowl, light a candle, and look in. Then you can sort of see something. But his body was right there in plain sight. Arms, legs, belly button, nipples, private parts, here are all the fingers on his hands and there are the toes on his feet—and all without any defect. And what's in back? His backside, of course, and on his backside—a little tail. And now Nikita Ivanich says people don't and shouldn't have tails! What? What is it then, a Consequence?

Of course, there was a time when Benedikt didn't have a tail. In childhood his backside was smooth. But when he started growing and his male strength began to show, his tail began to grow too. Benedikt thought that was the way it should be. That's the difference between a man and a woman, that on him everything grows on the outside, and in her everything grows inside. His beard and the hair on his body didn't grow at first either, but then they came in real handsome.

He was proud of his tail! A well-formed little tail, white and strong, about as long as your palm or a little longer. If Benedikt was pleased, or feeling happy, it would wag back and forth. What else was it supposed to do? And if he felt a sudden fear or sadness come over him, then his tail would kind of lay low, flat down. You could always tell from your tail what mood you were in. And so how is it that now it turns out it's not normal? All wrong? Holy moly! Maybe his privates—his pudential, in book talk—are also wrong? Take a look, Nikita Ivanich!

Nikita Ivanich examined Benedikt and he looked kind of dejected. No, he said, your privates are just fine, handsome and healthy, there's only one set, and anybody would be happy to have one like that. But your tail is completely superfluous. I'm rather surprised that someone like you, a dreamer and a neurotic, didn't catch on earlier. I always told you not to eat so many mice! Let me amputate it for you right now. That means that I'll get an ax and chop it off. Whack!

No! It's too scary! What do you mean, chop it off? It's like a hand or a foot! No! Not for anything! Nikita Ivanich kept it up: Come on, come on, maybe all your nonsense and neuroses are caused by the tail! . . . No, no! I won't give in!

But how could he get married now? How could he look Olenka, that radiant beauty, straight in the eye? After all, getting married isn't only pancakes and embroidery, or walking hand in hand in the orchard garden, it means pulling your britches down. And Olenka will look at it and take fright: What is that?! Won't she? But all the other women: Marfushka, Kapitolinka, Crooked Vera, Glashka-Kudlashka, and lots of others —they never said anything, they never fussed or griped. No siree. They always complimented him! Uneducated idiots! Don't know anything except the woman's business.

All right, but what should he do now? He was halfway there, he'd already proposed and been invited to his in-laws. He'd already agreed with Olenka and set a day to visit their izba, to pay his respects and get acquainted! Hello, dear people, I want to marry your daughter! And who exactly are you and what do you have to show for yourself? I'm Benedikt Karpich, the late Karp Pudich's son, who was the son of Pud Christoforovich, who was the son of Christopher Matveich, and whose son that Matvei was and from where—we can't remember, it's been lost in the gloom of time. What I have to show for myself is that I'm young, healthy, good-looking, and I have a good clean job, you know that . . . "Aren't you lying to us, Benedikt Karpich?" "I'm not lying." "Then why do you have a dog's name, Benedikt? Maybe it's not a name but a nickname? . . . Why would they give you a dog's name? What kind of Consequence do you have?"

That's the drama of it.

What do I care that other Golubchiks have Consequences: extra hair, rashes, blister bumps! Blisters are just water bubbles, they burst—and they're gone. Horns, ears, and cock's combs aren't comely, but what do I care? Your own bump's a proper lump, the other guy's—just a little itch! There's no secret to horns or ears, everything's in plain view, people are used to it. No one's gonna laugh and say: Hey, you over there, whatcha got horns for! They were always there, the horns, you don't even see

116

them anymore. But a tail—it's kind of a secret—all hidden, private. If everyone had one that would be all right. But if you're the only one—it's shameful.

It's not like he ended up with an amazing Consequence like Nikita Ivanich got: breathing fire! Nice and clean: people are scared, they respect you. You are our Head Stoker, they say. But about Benedikt they'd say: Mongrel! You're a stray mutt, a streetwalker! That's what they always say to dogs. For that matter, any Golubchik who sees a dog wants to crush it or kick it, throw a stick at it or poke it with something, or just swear at it, not mean-like, no, meanness is for people—but with a kind of disgust.

Nikita Ivanich said: Well, on the other hand, the tail is an original characteristic of primates. Long, long ago, when humans had not yet fully evolved, tails were normal phenomena and surprised no one; they clearly began to disappear when man began using sticks and tools. Nowadays a tail is an atavism. But what concerns me is the sudden reappearance of this specific appendage. What could the reason be? After all, we're in the Neolithic period, and not some savage animal kingdom. What could it mean?

With a tear in his eye, Benedikt said: All fine and well for you to talk and use all kinds of big words, Nikita Ivanich. You're always wanting to restore the past, to put up posts and pillars, carve pushkins out of wood, but you don't care about the past hanging off my backside and I have to get married! All you Oldeners are the same: "We'll re-create the lofty past in full measure." Well, here's your full measure! Take it! And since you love the past so much, why don't you go running around with a tail? I don't need one! I want to live!

And Nikita Ivanich said: You're right, young fellow, those are the words of a real man, not a boy. But what I mean is that I hope for the resurrection of the spiritual! It's time! I hope for brotherhood, love, beauty. Justice. Mutual respect. Lofty aspirations. I want thoughtful, honest labor, hand in hand, to replace brawls and altercations. I want the fire of love for one's fellow man to burn in the soul.

Benedikt said: Sure, right away. Easy for you to talk, you've

117

got your own fire. Everyone bows to you, kisses your feet, they probably bring you surprises in baskets: bliny or noodles! And if things don't go your way—you can just huff and puff and burn your mortal enemy down, turn him to ash! But what can the simple folk do?

Nikita Ivanich said: No, now just a minute, young man, hold your horses, you misunderstood me again. I have no intention of burning anyone up, I merely help as best I can. Of course, I have an unusual Consequence, a rather convenient one—I can have a smoke any time I like. But I too may not be immortal—look at Anna Petrovna, she left us for a better world, where there is no sorrow or lamentation. It's time for you, my good people, to cease relying on this old man and display a little—just a little—initiative. It's time to make fire yourselves!

And Benedikt said: Good Lord Almighty, Nikita Ivanich, are you crazy? Where would we get fire from? It's a mystery! It can't be known! Where does it come from? If an izba burns down, everybody will come running and grab some coals for their pot. Then, of course. But if all the stoves in the town went out? Hunh? What're we supposed to do, wait for lightning storms? We'd all croak in the meantime!

Nikita Ivanich said: Think friction, young man, friction. Try it. I'd be happy to, but I'm too old. I can't.

Benedikt said: Oh, come on now, Nikita Ivanich. You talk about how old you are, but there you go being bawdy again.

"Unfortunately," said Nikita Ivanich, "I don't have his portrait, a fact which is a constant source of grief and regret to me. I didn't manage to save it. What does one take out of a burning house? What would we want with us on an uninhabited island? The eternal question! At one time my friends and I squabbled for hours on end on summer verandahs, in winter kitchens, or with fellow travelers we chanced to meet on the train. Which three books are the most valuable in the world? Which are dearest to our hearts? Tell me, young man, what would you carry out of a burning house?"

Benedikt thought long and hard. He imagined his izba.

When you go in, on the right-hand side, there's a table with a stool. The table is pushed up to the window so there's more light. There's a candle on the table and next to the table there's a stool. One of its legs rotted, and he had never got around to fixing it. Farther along the wall there's another chair. Mother used to sit in it, but now no one sits in it, though Benedikt sometimes hangs his jacket there or throws his clothes over it. There's nothing else. The other wall goes out from that corner, and that's where the bed is. There's rags on the bed, of course. Over the bed, on the wall, there's a shelf, and there are some booklets on the shelf if the thieves haven't stolen them. Under the bed, like everyone else, he has a box for all kinds of junk, the junk you hate to throw out—tools, wooden nails and stuff. At the head of the bed there's another corner. On the third wall, the one facing you when you enter, is the stove. What about the stove? A stove's a stove. No secret there. On top of it there's also a bed if you like the warmth, and in the bottom part you cook food. Plugs, latches, chokers, dampers, handle turns, hiding pockets— everything's part of the stove. It's wrapped all around in ropes and string so you can hang things to dry, or just for decoration. And it's so wide, so fat-assed, that there's no room for anything else on the fourth wall: just a couple of hooks to hang a hat or a towel on, and that's it. Then there's the door to the pantry, where rusht and dried marshrooms are stored.

What would he carry out if, God forbid, there was a fire? Rusht? What for? You can always get some more. His new bowl? He could make another one. He'd miss the chair a bit, the chair was very old.

"I'd take the chair," said Benedikt.

"Really?" said Nikita Ivanich, surprised. "Why?"

"It was Mother's."

"Yes, of course. Sentimental value. But what about books? Aren't books important to you?"

"I love reading, Nikita Ivanich, but so what? If I have to, I can always make some new booklets. Or trade mice for them. And if there's a fire, God forbid, Nikita Ivanich, they'll be the first thing to burn. Puff! They're gone. Bark just doesn't hold up."

"But the words inscribed in them are harder than copper and more enduring than the pyramids. Isn't that right? Do you deny it?" Nikita Ivanich chuckled and patted Benedikt on the back like he was coughing. "You too, young man, are a participant! A participant!—you've no business being such a scatterbrain, such an ignoramus, a spiritual Neanderthal, a depressed Cro-Magnon! I detect a spark of humanity even in you! I do. I harbor some hope for you! Your little brain is smoldering," said Nikita Ivanich, continuing to insult him. "Your soul is not devoid of impulses . . . 'You're destined to know a noble impulse / but won't accomplish anything at all,'" sang Nikita Ivanich in a ghastly voice, like a goat bleating. "But you and I will create something fine, something edifying. You do have a certain creative streak, I think . . ."

"Nikita Ivanich," Benedikt sniveled, offended. "Why all these words! . . . You might as well just kick me, I swear, why are you calling me names?"

"Right, then. So, as I said," the old man went on, "I don't have his portrait, but I'll assist you. He wasn't very tall."

"But you said he was a giant," muttered Benedikt, wiping his nose with his sleeve.

"A giant of the spirit. 'His proud head rose higher than . . .'"

"'. . . the Alexander column.' I know, I copied it. But we don't know how many yards tall that column was, Nikita Ivanich."

"It doesn't matter, not one little bit! Now, we'll extract him from this log—sorry, but we haven't got any others. The most important thing to me is the bowed head and the arm. Like this." The Stoker showed him. "Look at me. Carve a curly head, a straight nose, and a thoughtful face."

"Was his beard long?"

"No beard."

"None at all?"

"Just on the side, like that. Sideburns."

"Like Pakhom has?"

"Good heavens, no. Fifty times smaller. So: the head, the neck, the shoulders, arms, hands, the arms are the most important. Understood? Bend the elbow."

Benedikt tapped the log with his boot. It rang; the wood was good, light. Dense and dry. Good material.

"Beriawood?"

"What? Who?!?!"

The old man cursed, spat, and sparks flew from his eyes; he didn't explain what enraged him. He turned red and puffed up like a beetroot:

"It's Pushkin! Pushkin! The future Pushkin!"

So who's the real Cro-Magnon? Who's got a newrottick now? You can't do anything with them, these Oldeners. They start shouting at the wrong time, swear in strange words, and push you around for who knows what reason. They're always un- happy: they don't understand a good joke, they don't like our dances or games, they never have a good time like people are supposed to, they're no fun, and all you hear from them is "Oh, horrors!" when there's nothing horrible happening at all.

What's really horrible? Horrible is when the Red Sleigh rides, knock, knock, knock on wood, no, no, no. Not me, don't take me. Or when you think about the Slynx, now that's horror. Because then you're alone. Completely alone, there's no one. And it's heading toward you ... No!!!—I don't even want to think about it ... But what's so horrible about dancing and singing together, or playing leapfrog?

It's a fun game. You invite guests, then you clean up the izba. You scrape the crumbs off the table with your elbow: Hey, mice, come on over here! You push the trash that's piled up in the house under the bed with your boot, and cover it so it doesn't stick out. You smooth the bedclothes, straighten the sheet or blanket or whatever. If the sheet is really dirty, then you wash it. If not—well, it'll do. If there's an embroidered dust ruffle lying around, or a bed curtain, you shake them and lay them out pretty on the stove like they were always there. You light can- dles all over the place, and don't be stingy, so everything's bright and festive. You rustle up a mountain of hot snacks, and put eve- rything out on the table in rows. You set out a jug of mead on the table and put some more at the ready out in the cold pantry. The guests will bring something too, no one goes visiting empty-handed, unless he's a miserable midget or some kind of freakin' nincompoop. You have to bring a gift to the house. So everyone is all clean, combed, and dressed in fresh clothes, whoever has them. Jokes, laughter. First you sit at the table. The table's a sight to behold! Baked mice, poached mice, mice in sauce. Marinated mouse tails, mouse-eye caviar. Pickled mouse tripe also goes well with kvas. Goosefoot rolls. Marshrooms, if they're in season. If a Golubchik is richer, then there's bliny. Really rich tables have sweet rolls. Everyone sits down, says thanks, the mead is poured, the first round is gulped down right away. Now to the second. It goes to your head, starts getting to you. That's right! If it's good rusht, choice rusht, you'll never notice that there's not a lot of food. You've eaten, already put away the third and the fourth—you've forgotten when that was, we're already on the tenth. We smoke, laugh. Gossip some gossip, who was with whom, tell a few shaggy dog stories. If there are women we flirt with them: pinch them, or grab them, have a little feel. We stomp our feet and sing in unison:

> Pease porridge hot!
> Pease porridge cold!
> Pease porridge in the pot!
> Nine days old!
> Some like it hot!
> Some like it cold!
> Some like it in the pot!
> Nine days old!

And then we start to play. Leapfrog is a good game, lots of fun. It goes like this. We put out the candles so it's dark. You sit or stand wherever you want, and one guy gets up on the stove. He sits there, sits, and then—bam, he jumps down with an ear-splitting yell! If he lands on one of the guests, he'll always knock him over, give him a bruising or pull an arm out of joint or something. If he misses—then he'll hurt himself: his head, or his knee, or elbow, or maybe he'll break a rib: the stove is high. You can hit the stool in the dark—ouch! Or hit your head on the table. If he doesn't crash, he gets back up on the stove. If he's out of the game, the others are impatient: my turn, my turn, I get to jump this time! The squeals, shouts, laughing—you could piss in your pants it's so much fun. Then you light the candles and take a look at the damage. There's even more laughter then: just a few minutes ago Zinovy had an eye—now he doesn't! Gurian over there broke his arm, it's hanging down like a loose strap, what kind of work can he do now?

Of course, if someone hurts me or my body, it's not funny. I get mad, no kidding. But that's if it's me. If it's someone else, it's funny. Why? Because me—that's me; and him—that's not me, it's him. But the Oldeners say: Oh, horrors! How could you! And they don't understand that if everything went their way, no one would ever laugh or have any fun, we'd all just sit at home all gloom and doom and there wouldn't be any adventures, or dancing, or squealing women.

We also play smothers, and that's fun too: you stuff a pillow in someone's face and smother him, and he flails and splutters and when he gets away, he's all red and sweaty, and his hair's sticking out like a harpy's. People rarely die, our guys are strong, they fight, there's a lot of strength in their muscles. Why? Because they work a lot, they plant turnips in the fields, crack stones, gather sheaves, chop trees into logs. There's no need to go insulting us, to say that there's still some brains smoldering in us: our brains are smart enough. We aren't quick, but we figure things out. We've figured out that the beriawood tree is a good tree for pinocchios and buckets, and it makes fine barrels. The elfir is also a wonderful tree, just right for bathhouse switches, and its nuts are tasty, and a lot of other things, but you can't carve a symbol from it because it's got too much resin, it bleeds all sticky. Birch, now, it's nice to look at, but the trunk is thin and crooked, it's hard to carve. The jeopard tree is even thinner, all knots and bumps, in a word: the jeopard tree. The willow won't do, the beantree is stringy, and the grab tree is wet year-round. There are a lot of other kinds when you count them, and we know them all. So now we'll strip the bark, mark the holes with a stone chisel . . . and whip up an idol before the wedding.

Benedikt sighed, whispered, and spat just like they tell you to —God bless!—and went at the beriawood tree with an ax.

O · ON

YOU COULDN'T SEE the terem of Olenka's family from the street. The fence was high and deep, with sharp spikes on top. There was a gate in the middle. In the gate was a stone ring. To one side of the gate was a booth. In the booth was a serf.

When Benedikt proposed to Olenka, he told her he wanted to send matchmakers ahead of him. It was easier that way—the matchmakers would say everything that needed to be said about you, make a deal, settle everything. They'd praise you to the skies behind your back: he's so this and so that, they'd say, and you should see him do this, he's not a man, he's a rose in bloom, a fleet falcon. But Olenka objected: No, no. No matchmakers, we're a modern family . . . don't send them. Just come yourself. We'll sit and chat of this and that. We'll eat . . .

He took some presents: a string of mice, a jug of kvas—so as not to go empty-handed—and a bouquet of bluebells.

Everything was going right. But he was nervous. What would happen?

He went up to the gate and stood there. The serf came out of the booth, irritated.

"Who do you want?"

"I'm Olga Kudeyarovna's co-worker."

"By appointment?"

"By appointment."

"Wait here."

The serf returned to the booth and rustled some bark for a long time.

"What's your name?"

Benedikt told him. The serf rustled something again.

"Go in."

He opened a small gate in the fence and Benedikt entered. There was another fence about five yards from the first. And another booth with a serf, even more irritated than the first.

"Who do you want?"

"I'm Olga Kudeyarovna's co-worker."

"What've you got there?"

"Presents."

"Hand over the presents."

"Why . . . how . . . I was invited, how can I go without presents?"

"Hand over the presents and sign here." The serf didn't even seem to hear Benedikt. He unrolled the bark and wrote: "Mice —one dozen ordinary household. Kvas, small wooden jug— one. Blue wildflowers—one bunch."

Benedikt suddenly balked. He got mad. "I won't hand over the flowers!!! You have no right!!! I was personally invited by Olga Kudeyarovna!!!"

Before signing, he crossed out "flowers."

The serf thought for a moment. "Go to the dogs. Go on, get outta here."

How mean he put it—"to the dogs." But he let him in. They let him through the second fence—and then there was a third. Two serfs rose from the bench at the third gate and without saying a word, bad or good, they patted Benedikt all over. They wanted to see if he had hidden something in his pants or under his shirt. But the only extra thing he had was a tail.

"Go on."

Benedikt thought there would be another fence, but no, there wasn't, instead an enormous garden opened up with trees and flowers and all kinds of huts and sheds and little paths of yellowish sand. At the back of the garden stood the terem. Benedikt hadn't been really scared before, but now he was petrified: he'd never seen such wealth and magnificence. His heart thudded and his tail wagged back and forth, back and forth. His eyes clouded over. He didn't remember how they led him into the house.

The serfs brought him and left him alone in a room. Some time passed and he heard a scraping sound behind the doors. There was more scraping, the doors opened—and He Himself came out. Olenka's Papa. The owner of all this. His future father-in-law.

125

He smiled. "Welcome. We're expecting you. Benedikt Karpich? My name is Kudeyar Kudeyarich."

And he looked at him. Benedikt looked back. But he couldn't move—his legs seemed rooted to the floor.

Kudeyar Kudeyarich was big—that is, long and tall. His neck was long, and his head was small. The top of his head was sort of bald, and around his bald spot there was a pale crown of fair hair. He had no beard, and a long, sticklike mouth, whose corners seemed to turn down. He kept opening and closing his mouth as though he wasn't used to breathing and had decided he'd try it out every which way. His eyes were round and yellow, like firelings, and at the bottom of his eyes there seemed to be a light burning.

He was wearing a big white shirt, unbelted. His britches were wide, even wider at the bottom. He wore plain old house lapty on his feet.

"Why are you standing there, Benedikt Karpich? Come and sit down at the table."

He took Benedikt by the elbow and moved him into another chamber. The table was set. Wooow! There was so much food! From one end to the other—bowls and more bowls, all kinds of dishes, pots and plates! Countless pies, bliny, pancakes, twist rolls, pretzels, colored noodles! And peas! And sheaves of pickled horsetail set in the corners! And the marshrooms . . . bucketfuls, brimming over, any minute they would jump off the edge. And whole birds, tiny ones wrapped in dough: the legs stuck out at one end and the head at the other! And in the middle of the table—a roast. Whoa, a goat! They've got a whole goat on the table, and they had to raise that goat too! So the serfs had been right to take away his gifts: what was he doing with a bunch of mice when there was a whole goat!

Olenka sat at the table all decked out, her cheeks rouged, her eyes lowered. That's the way Benedikt saw her in his visions, sitting like that: wearing a white blouse, her neck wound with beads, her hair combed smoothly, a ribbon on her brow! And as soon as Benedikt entered the dining room, Olenka blushed even redder. She didn't lift her eyes, but smiled to herself.

Yikes!

And on the other side of the dining room another door opened and his mother-in-law came in. Rather, floated in: the woman was wide as a house, half of her was in the dining room saying hello while the other half hadn't even made it through the door, you had to wait.

"And this," his father-in-law said, "is our wife, Fevronia. One of the oldest families, descended from the French."

"That's the family legend," said his mother-in-law.

Benedikt bowed with one hand, presented the bouquet of bluebells with the other, and fell at his mother-in-law's feet.

"The vittles are getting cold," said his mother-in-law. "Eat up, don't be shy."

They sat down on the benches. Benedikt opposite Olenka, Father- and Mother-in-law side by side.

"Help yourself," said his mother-in-law.

Benedikt felt shy again: how could he restrain himself? If he took a lot they'd think: "Oh, what a glutton! Probably can't ever feed him enough!" And if he took too little, they'd think: "Oh, what a weak son-in-law! Probably can't even drive a nail in." Should he take a little meat pie? He stretched out a hand for the pie, and everyone looked at his hand. He jerked it back.

"We like to eat a lot," said his mother-in-law. And she served herself. So did Kudeyar Kudeyarich. And Olenka. Benedikt stretched out his hand again — to the pancakes. Everyone stared again. He jerked it back once more.

They chewed.

"So," said his father-in-law, "it seems you want to get married."

"I do."

They chewed in silence some more. For the third time Benedikt thought of helping himself to something, but as soon as he'd raised his hand they all stared at it! A fire seemed to flare in the father's eyes. What was going on?

"Getting married is serious business . . . When I married my wife, Fevronia, that's what I told her: This is serious business."

"That's right, we ate a lot at the wedding," said the mother.

"We ate very well at the wedding," said the father.

Was this a hint? Benedikt's tail began to tap lightly against the bench from anxiety.

"Why aren't you eating?" said the mother again.

Oh, well, what would be would be. He reached out, grabbed a goat leg and plopped it down on his plate, and added noodles on top. And horsetail. As soon as he'd done it, a light flared in all their eyes again, like a lantern.

"So that means you want to join our family," said the father.

"I do."

"Not afraid of family problems, then, are you? Running a house is harder than catching a mouse, as the saying goes."

"I'm not afraid. I'm handy at a lot of things."

"A lot of things?"

"Uh huh."

Something scrabbled under the table. Must be a mouse.

"And what if it's serious business?"

"I'm ready. Sure."

"Oh ho!"

Once again it grew lighter around the table. Benedikt made himself lift his head and look—there was definitely something shining in the father's eyes. As though a fireling was glowing. And in the dining room—the evening had already turned to twilight—rays of light shone from his eyes. Like from a torch, if you look at it through a fist: you roll your hand up in a fist and look through it. Like a moonlit path. The father was looking at his plate, and even though it was twilight, you could see everything on it. When he looked at the table—it was like it was lit up by fire. When he looked at Benedikt he gave off even more light, so bright that Benedikt blinked and jerked his head away.

Olenka said, "Papa, control yourself."

Benedikt stole a sideways glance at the mother: she gave off the same rays. And Olenka, too. Only weaker.

There was a scrabbling sound under the table again. And Benedikt's tail tapped harder than ever.

"Help yourself to more," said the mother. "Our family likes to eat a lot."

"One of the oldest families, descended from the French," affirmed the father.

"Have some more noodles."

"Thank you kindly."

"Now, you aren't having any bad thoughts, are you?" asked the father.

"What kind of thoughts?"

"All kinds of bad thoughts—Freethinking or malice aforethought of any kind . . ."

"I don't have any thoughts like that," said Benedikt in a fright.

"How about murder most foul?"

"What kind of murder?"

"Who knows . . . Maybe you're thinking: I'll marry, get my father- and mother-in-law out of the way, and take all their property for myself?"

"Goodness, how could you—"

"No? You aren't thinking: If I could just do away with them and take their place, I could feast my fill day in and day out?"

"What are you talking about? . . . Why? . . . Kudeyar Kudeyarich! Why, I—"

"Papa," said Olenka again, "control yourself."

Once again there was a scratching sound under the table—this time right nearby. Benedikt couldn't help himself, he knocked a piece of bread off the table on purpose with his elbow and bent down as though to pick it up. Under the table he saw the father's feet in their lapty. And through the lapty he saw claws. Long ones, gray and sharp. Olenka's father was scraping the floor with those claws and had already scraped up a huge pile of shavings—they lay there like hair or light-colored, curly straw. Benedikt looked and saw that the mother had claws. Olenka too. But hers were smaller. There was a small pile of scrapings under her.

Benedikt didn't say anything—what could you say? He tore off another piece of goat for himself. And gulped down a lot more horsetail. A lot more.

"But tell me," the father continued, "don't you sometimes

think: We aren't doing things right, our life is all wrong?"

"No, I don't."

"Don't you sometimes think thoughts like: We should figure out who's to blame, and crush him or stick his head in a barrel?"

"No, I don't."

"Or break his back, or throw him off a tower?"

"No, no!"

"What's that tapping?" the mother suddenly spoke. "Sounds like someone's knocking."

Benedikt quickly stuck his hand under him to hold his tail still.

"And don't you have thoughts like: The Murzas are to blame for everything, they should be overthrown?"

"No!!!"

"You never thought of overthrowing the Greatest Murza?"

"Goodness, no!! No!!! I don't understand what you're talking about!!!"

"What do you mean you don't understand? The Greatest Murza, I mean Fyodor Kuzmich, Glorybe. You never dreamed of overthrowing him?"

"Kudeyar Kudeyarich, how could you?"

"Control yourself, Papa . . ."

"Oh, all right . . . Let me show you something . . ."

The father got up from the table, went into another room, and returned with a book. An Oldenprint book. Benedikt sat on both hands and held his tail tight.

"I'll show you . . . Ever seen one of these?"

"Never!"

"You know what it is?"

"No!"

"Think about it a minute."

"I don't know anything, I've never seen anything. Never heard anything. I don't understand anything, don't want anything, haven't dreamt anything."

The father laid the book on his lap, shone his light on it, and turned the pages.

"Do you want one of these? Should I give it to you? It's a good one! . . ."

"I don't want anything!!!"

"Don't even want to get married, then?"

Get married! Benedikt had almost forgotten—from fear and longing, from the incredible, unending shame of what was held tight in his hands under his body—that he was supposed to get married. Married! How could he ever have gotten that idea in his head? Got too big for his britches, the knucklehead, the mongrel stray! Wasn't enough for him to have Marfushka, Kapitolinka, Crooked Vera, Glashka-Kudlashka, and all the others! Had to try for a girl like this: meek eyes, a white face, a braid five yards long, a chin with a dimple, and claws on her feet! Run! That's right, run—toss a knapsack over your shoulder and run as far as you can, toward the sunrise, or the south, no looking back, to the Ocean-Sea itself, to the blue expanses, to the white sands!

But Olenka raised her eyes, turned on the light in them, a reddish light, faint like a fake fireling on a dark trunk. She raised her eyebrows right up to her ribbon, laughed with her red mouth, straightened the white blouse on her breasts, and wiggled her shoulders. "Papa, you're such an incorrigible rascal. We've already settled everything. Embrace your son-in-law."

"So . . . It's all settled, is it? Made up your minds behind Papa's back. Papa works day in and day out, without a moment's rest . . . Wants what's best . . . I see right through all of you . . . !" the father suddenly shouted.

"Papa, you're not the only one who—"

"He's not one of us!" shouted the father.

"Papa, you're not at work!"

"What kind of work does he do?" whispered Benedikt.

"What do you mean, what kind of work?" asked the mother in surprise. "Don't you know? Kudeyar Kudeyarich is the Head Saniturion."

Π · POKOI

BENEDIKT STOPPED going to work. Why bother? He was a goner however you looked at it. Luckily for him, summer had arrived and the Scribes were on vacation. Otherwise he would have been pressed into roadwork as an idler. It was time to plant turnips, but he was overcome with such heartache that he didn't have the usual stomach for turnips. He went to the far settlement and bought some bog bilberry from the Golubchiks there. He snorted it. It didn't help much. He lay on his bed. Cried.

He went to see Nikita Ivanich, and worked on carving the pushkin from the log, bit by bit. The idol's head was already big and round, like a cauldron. Dejected looking. His nose hung on the chest. The elbow stuck out, as requested.

"Nikita Ivanich. What did you call my tail?"

"An atavism."

"What other kinds of atavisms are there?"

"Hmmm. Hairy women."

"How about claws?"

"I haven't heard of that. No, probably not."

He thought of going to see Marfushka. Decided not to. He didn't feel like joking, and he wasn't so interested in her squeals or pancakes anymore.

He went to the house where Varvara Lukinishna lived. Looked through the fence. There was underwear hanging on ropes. Yellers were blooming in the yard. He didn't go in.

He drank about three barrels of rusht. He wanted to forget everything. The rusht didn't go to his head, it just made his stomach bloat. He felt slightly deaf and his vision was dimmer too. But there was an unbearable clarity in his head, or rather, an expanse, and the expanse was empty. The steppes.

He wanted to take his sack and head south. To carve a big stick—for fighting off Chechens—and head for the sea. And which sea it is—who knows? You can imagine whatever you like. Three years to get there on foot, they say. Benedikt imagined it this way: he climbed a tall mountain, and from the top you could see forever. He looked down and there was the sea: a big body of water, warm and blue, and it plashed, the water played and plashed! A small wave ran along it, a curly wave, coiled white. There were islands everywhere in the sea—poking up like pointed hats. All of them were green, seething with green. Amid that green, unimaginable colored gardens grew. The lilac tree that Mother told him about grew there too. The flowers of the lilac were a blue froth of bell-like flowers hanging to the ground and fluttering in the wind. On the very tippy top of those islands were towns. White stone walls encircled them. The walls had gates, and behind the gates were cobbled roads. If you walked along the road up the mountain there would be a terem, and in the terem a golden bed. On that bed there was a girl braiding her hair, one gold hair, the next silver, one gold, one silver . . . Her feet had claws . . . She hooked you with her claw . . . with her claws . . .

Sometimes he wanted to head for the sunrise. To walk and walk . . . the grasses would grow higher and brighter, the sun would come up, and its light would shine through them . . . He imagined himself walking along, jumping over little streams, wading through rivers. And the forest would become denser and denser, like a fabric, and the bugs whirred and whirled about, buzzing. And in the forest there'd be a glade, and in the glade there'd be tulip flowers, a red rug of tulips covering the whole glade so you couldn't see the ground. And on the branches there'd be a lacy white tail that folded and spread out like a net. Above that tail its mistress, the Princess Bird, would gaze longingly, admiring herself. Her mouth is red as a tulip. And she'd say to him, "Hello, Benedikt, my fleet falcon, did you come to take a look at me? . . . I never harm anyone, but you already know that . . . Come closer, Benedikt, let's kiss . . ."

He didn't head south or toward the sunrise. His head felt clear and dull at the same time. He packed his sack and then unpacked it. He looked at his things: What did I put in there? The stone knife I used for carving the pushkin. Another knife. A chisel. He'd taken some wooden nails, who knows why. Why did he need nails in the south? He took them out. An extra pair of pants. Still good, almost no patches . . . A bowl, a spoon. He took them out. What was he going to eat with them? How was he going to make food? Without fire?

You couldn't go anywhere without fire.

Now, if he could take Nikita Ivanich along . . . They'd walk together, and talk. At night, they'd light a fire. Catch some fish, boil up some soup if they weren't poisonous.

Only you couldn't go far. They'd miss him and come looking. As soon as someone's stove went out, they'd come looking to find him right away. They'd run, shouting: Nikita Ivanich! Bring Nikita Ivanich here now! And they'd find Benedikt too. They'd catch up, give him the what for, twist his white arms behind his back: You're supposed to get married! Married, married! . . .

Maybe that's what he should do: get married. So what if she has claws? Claws can be clipped. You can clip them . . . That's not the point . . . Man isn't without defects. One has a tail, one has horns, someone else has a cock's comb, or scales, or gills . . . A sheep's hole and a human soul. But that wasn't the way he wanted it to be . . . He imagined strolling in the orchard garden, smelling the bluebells together. Talking about serious things, about life, or nature, about what you can find in it . . . Reciting some poetry . . .

> But the hand behind your back is stronger
> The coachman's whistle more alarming,
> And the moon in its insanity,
> Is reflected in your eyes, I see.

She would be amazed and listen. Her eyes would be glued to him. And in the evening he'd catch a mouse and hide it in his hand. Playfully, he'd say: Come on now, what have I got here? . . . Pussy cat, pussy cat, where have you been? Go on, guess. Who's been nibbling at my housekin? . . . And she would blush: "Control yourself, fleet falcon . . ."

Or he could go back to work. Copying books. You stretch

your neck out and copy . . . It's interesting . . . What are the people in those books doing? . . . They travel somewhere . . . Murder someone . . . love someone . . . Whew, there are so many people in books! You just keep on copying and copying. Then he'd spit on his finger, put out the candle—and go home . . . Autumn would come, the leaves would fall from the trees . . . The earth would be covered in snow . . . the izba would be buried up to the windows . . . Benedikt would light a mouse-oil candle, sit down at the table, prop his head in his hand, hunch over, and gaze at the thin flame. Dark beams would run above his head, the wail of the snowy emptiness would be heard beyond the walls, the wail of the Slynx on the dark branches in the northern thickets: *Slyyyynxxx! Slyyyyynxxxx!* It would wail as though it hadn't gotten something, as though its life were ended if it didn't get a drink of a live soul, as if it couldn't find peace, and hunger had twisted its innards. It would turn its invisible head, and splay its invisible paws, and scratch the dark air with its invisible claws, and smack its cold lips, looking for a warm human neck to suck on, to drink its fill, to swallow something living . . . It shakes its head and sniffs. It catches the scent and jumps from the branches, and it's off, crying and whining: *Ssslllyyynxxx! Slyy-ynxxx!* And the snowspouts rise from the dark fields where there's nary a light above your head nor a path in the impassable expanses, no north no south, only white darkness and blizzardy blindness, and the snowspouts will rush forth and grab the Slynx and a deathly plaint will fly over the town, and my faint, unseeing heart that only wanted to live will be buried under a heavy snowdrift! . . .

Olenka's family is getting ready for the wedding. It's set for fall. You'll come live with us, they say. You'll eat well, build up your strength, and later we'll set you up in a good business. What kind of business could they have, the Saniturions? . . . He didn't want to think about it . . .

Should he go and finish the pushkin? Old Nikita Ivanich now has two ridiculous dreams: to chop off Benedikt's tail, and to put the pushkin up on the crossroads, on White Hill. What did he need this pushkin for? He trembled over it, and he ordered Benedikt to tremble as well, like he worshipped it. He wrote a lot of poems, said Nikita Ivanich, he thought the people's path to him would never be overgrown—but if you don't weed, then it's sure to grow over. Fyodor Kuzmich, Glorybe, said Nikita Ivanich, sits there on top of those books and copies them. He's littering the people's path. Wants all the glory for himself, and what about more-ality. That's not right. You see, Benedikt, don't you, that that's not right? You and I, young man, will erect an idol on the crossroads, and that will be our challenge and our protest. Work with inspiration and devotion, and if I shout every now and then, don't pay attention to my outbursts.

When the hand and fingers showed up out of the log, Nikita Ivanich applauded. You have real talent, Benedikt, real talent! Just shave off a tad here. Let him stand, his head lowered, listening to the mice scurrying, the breeze blowing, to life hurrying somewhere, it just goes on and on, on and on, day in and day out! Day in and day out!

Summer adorned itself in luxuriant colors. The days grew longer. Pushkin's caftan was already visible. During the day Benedikt chipped away at the pushkin, in the evening he gathered the chips for kindling, heated up soup, gulped it down, and sat out on the porch to smoke. You smoke, sigh, gaze off into the distance, and your head is empty. But once again visions fill it.

Again, toward evening, when the sunset grew yellow and went out, when the fog gathered in the lowlands and the first star came out in the sky, the woodsucker began yowling in the grove. Benedikt began imagining Olenka again. Here he was, sitting on the porch, smoking, watching the sky go out; the air was about to turn blue and cold. Silence. Near the ground everything was blue as blue could be, and up above, the sky shone even and yellow, smoldering its last; every now and then a swipe of pink would tint the yellow, or a gray cloud would stretch like a spindle, hang there a bit until its top would stain raspberry, flare, and be gone. Like someone was rubbing the sunset, smearing it with his fingers.

Once again, Olenka would emerge from the twilight, as though she were painted on the air. She glistened like a fireling, but you could see through her, faintly, dimly. Her hair was combed smooth, her part shone. Olenka's face was white as the moon, and it didn't budge; her neck was veiled in a dozen rows of beads, up to the very dimple in her chin. On her forehead and her ears there were beads and more beads, and little tassels. Her eyes took up half her face, from under the eyebrows to the temples on the sides, dark eyes, but they sparkled like water in a barrel at midnight. And she looks straight through you with those eyes, looks like she wants to say something but never will, not for anything. She never takes her eyes off you, seems like she's going to laugh, or is waiting for a question, or like she'll start singing with her mouth closed. Olenka's mouth is red and she's white, and this vision is fearsome, like it wasn't Olenka, but the Princess Bird herself, only not kind and good, but like she killed someone and was happy about it . . .

And Benedikt fell into such a daze, he felt like he'd snorted a lot of bog bilberry. His legs and seat had goosebumps and there seemed to be a ringing in his fingers. In his chest, or rather, his stomach, there was a ringing too, a dull one, like someone had stuck an empty stone bucket inside him. This daze, which looked like Olenka, would blink its eyelashes and stare at him again. Its eyes got even bigger and its black eyebrows ran straight across, and between the eyebrows was a little stone, like a moon teardrop.

What the hell does she want from him?

Old pushkin-mushkin probably didn't want to get married either, was probably dead set against it, cried, resisted, but then married—and it was all right. Right? His proud head rose higher than the Alexander column. He rode in sleighs. Was bothered by mice. Ran around with girls, got his rocks off. He was famous: now we're carving a pinocchio of him.

We're just as good as him. Isn't that right? Or is it?

"I'll have you know that Immanuel Kant," the Head Stoker instructed him, "and by the way, since you're so inclined to philosophizing, you'd do well to remember that name. Now, as I was saying. Two things surprised Kant: the moral law inside man and the starry heaven above our heads. How do we interpret this? Well, it means that man is the crossroads of two abysses, equally bottomless and equally inaccessible: the outer and inner worlds. And just as the stars, planets, comets, nebula, and other heavenly bodies move according to laws that we understand but poorly, though they are strictly preordained—are you listening to me, Benedikt?—so it is that moral law, all our imperfections notwithstanding, is preordained, etched with a diamond blade on the tablets of the conscience! Inscribed in fiery letters in the Book of Being. And even if this book is hidden from our myopic eyes, even if it is hidden in the valley of mists, behind seven gates, even if its pages are mixed up, its alphabet barbaric and indecipherable, it still exists, young man! It shines even at night! Our life, young man, consists of the search for this book. It is a sleepless path through the dense forest, groping our way, an unexpected acquisition! Our poet—the one to whom you and I are erecting a modest altar—our poet knew this, young man! He knew everything! Pushkin is our be all and end all—the starry sky above and the law in our heart!"

"All right, all right," said Benedikt. He tossed his butt and stamped it out with his shoe. "To hell with it, Nikita Ivanich. Go on and cut off my tail."

And he lay down across the bench.

P . RTSY

FATHER-IN-LAW has a huge menagerie, almost a whole street, cages and pens running down both sides. First there's a big shed, and in that shed a stable, and in the stable Degenerators. Hairy, black—yikes. All the fur on their sides is matted. Nasty faces. Some scratch their sides on the fence branches, some guzzle swill from jugs, others chew hay, some sleep, and three in the corner play birch cards and quarrel.

"Are you bonkers, lead with a diamond?"

"You shut up!"

"Oh, so that's it. Here's a stud fer ya."

Father-in-law didn't like it, he scratched the floor.

"Card games again, is it? And the stalls haven't been cleaned!"

The Degenerators don't give a hoot.

"Don't freak, boss. Everything's hunky-dory. Your play, Valera."

"Ha. Trump you."

Father-in-law swore and led Benedikt further on.

"Swine . . . Lazy so and sos . . . I'll give you Terenty, son, he'll be quieter. Only watch out, don't overfeed him. I wanted to give you Potap, but he's skittish. Chews on the bit, insults you . . . So . . . Here are the goats. I keep these for meat. Those are for wool. They make a fine jersey, very warm. Women like them."

"What's a jersey?"

"A knitted thing. Here are our chickens. I built an outdoor cage here, I keep rabbits."

"How about that!"

Benedikt craned his neck. There it was: a cage of woven sticks, tall as could be. A whole tree grew in the cage and on the very top was a nest, and in the nest, there they were, rabbits. One stuck his tail out and wagged it like he was teasing. Benedikt didn't have anything to wag anymore. And his sitting bone ached . . . On and on, cages and more cages . . . His father-in-law walked along, pointing left and right.

"Here we got some curiosities. All kinds of animals. We don't go hungry here. I got bird catchers sitting in the forest all day long, they bring back full snares. Sparrows and nightingales are good in pies. My wife, Fevronia, she fancies them. You can't eat every single kind of bird, of course. First we try 'em out on the serfs. One time they caught a tiny little bird, red, beady eyes; it smelled good and had a pretty voice. We wanted to marinate it, but then had second thoughts: Let's feed it to a serf, we decided. He took one bite, fell down on the floor, and kicked the bucket. We laughed so hard! What if it'd been us? Well, there you go! You have to keep an eye on nature."

There's another cage and there's a moss-covered tree in it too, with a hollow.

"What's here? I can't see anything."

"Ah . . . Here I got a woodsucker."

"You caught a woodsucker?"

"Uh huh. It's in the tree hollow."

"Wow . . ."

Father-in-law raised the whip he used to keep the Degenerators in line, stuck it through the branches, and knocked on the trunk.

"Woodsucker! Come out! Come out, listen up!"

Silence. It didn't want to come out.

"Come out, you bitch!!" Father-in-law poked the tree hollow with the whip.

And sure enough—it darted out like a shadow, and then hid its head.

"You see it?" said Father-in-law, happy.

"Amazing . . ." Benedikt said in wonder.

"That's right. We want to use this one for soup. Let's see . . . What else do we have here?"

In the cages and wicker sheds everything whistled, cackled, and ruffled like some kind of jungle. Over there on a branch a dozen nightingales were lined up like mice. A blue feather flashed by over there, and in the far cages there was another tree, bare, gnawed, with no bark. Something white and rumpled, like a worn sheet with holes in it, hung on a limb of that tree.

"I got some of everything stored up . . . There you have it, son! Summer, winter—the cup is full. Come on, I'll show you the barns."

He showed Benedikt the barns where the thistledown grain and goosefoot bread were stored, he showed him the fish farms, the gardens. It was a rich, sizable household—no doubt about it. Benedikt had never known such wealth existed. So how's that now—he's sort of like the owner of this property? Great!

It really did turn out well, it'd be a sin to complain. And he had been scared of something . . . What had he been scared of? It wasn't scary. A friendly family, everyone has meals together. The table is always set wall to wall with dishes, and they eat every last crumb. Benedikt can't keep up with them.

Mother-in-law serves herself more than anyone, of course,

140

or, as Kudeyar Kudeyarich put it, she takes the lead. After her comes Father-in-law, and then Olenka, and Benedikt hangs somewhere at the end of the line. They laugh at him all the time! But in a good-natured way.

And we don't just put everything on our plate at the same time, but in a certain order. First come the pasties. We toss about forty in our mouths, one after the other, one after the other—like peas. Then it's time for pancakes. Can't keep count of the pancakes. Then we snack on ferns. After we've warmed up, we move on to soup. After about five bowls, we say: Aha, now that we've finally worked up an appetite—it's time for the meat. After the meat come the bliny: with sour cream, a dollop of marshrooms, then you roll it up and—Lord bless us! We finish off a whole tray of bliny. Then come all kinds of sweet rolls with powdered firelings, doughnuts, crullers. Then cheese and fruit.

Benedikt didn't want to go near the cheese and fruit. He resisted.

"After sweets? Cheese? What do you mean?"

They laughed at him.

"I told you: my wife, Fevronia, is of French extraction! Didn't we explain that?"

These French sure are out to get you: you eat cheese and your stomach turns and you can say goodbye to your dinner. Even if you eat it first. And gooseberries are a sour fruit, horrible, fuzzy, even worse. You chew and groan: you feel like a goat.

That's dinner. But besides dinner we have other meals: breakfast, midmorning breakfast, snacks, supper—each and every day. And at nighttime you get a bowl of food: you might wake up at night to take a leak or something—and what if your innards are growling from hunger? God forbid.

After eating, you rest. Lie on the bed. Doze. Next to the stove.

Or we might take a ride in the sleigh: in autumn when there's a bit of frost, it's great. In the morning, after you wake up, you open the bladder on the window and look out: what's nature doing? Is winter coming? The air is so fresh, so cold, and the sky's murky white. The first snowflakes, big, white, and jagged, fall on the ground. Slowly at first, just a little bit, or one by one: you can even count them. Then more and more—and then you see they've thickened in the air: first you can't see the fence, then the nearby huts disappear, and when it gets going—you can't see anything at all, only a white net dancing in front of your eyes. And in the dining room it's all clean and warm; the stove crackles and hums, the bed is wide and soft, Olenka has flopped on the bed, the lazybones, she doesn't want to come out from under the covers.

"Come here, Benedikt, let's love it up . . ."

You hang the window back in place, and jump under the covers with Olenka. After making love, you crawl to the table, have breakfast—and it's into the sleigh with you. The sleigh is wide and soft too: it's lined with fur and piled with feather pillows. And the serfs bring more skins to put on top like blankets. They tuck you into the fur on all sides and you lie there like you're in bed. Mother-in-law runs up with a bowl full of pasty pies: "You might get hungry on the road."

The Degenerator stomps and grumbles.

"What weather! . . . A good master wouldn't let his dog out in this kind of weather . . ."

What's the bastard hinting at?

"Come on, Terenty, don't think. Just go. I want to take a ride."

"Been a long time since you walked, eh, chief?"

"How dare you! Come on, get a move on!"

Here's a nasty breed for you: all they want to do is argue, object, and whistle. Benedikt ended up with a lazy cur, a real slacker. He wouldn't race flat out like a whirlwind, the way Benedikt liked. No, he had to prance around putting one foot after the other, whistling and grinning. If a girl passed by he'd even allow himself to make comments: "Whoa, what a voluptuous broad!"

Or: "Now there's a cadre for you!"

Or he'd say to Benedikt: "Maybe we should give them a hayride? Hey, baby! Hey, you ginches! Over here!"

He scares people, the swine. And attracts disrespect. Sometimes he just plunks down in the middle of the road and sits there.

"What's going on, Teterya?"

"Some can call me Teterya, and some Terenty Petrovich."

"I'll give you a Petrovich! Get a move on! . . . Stop. Where the hell're you going?"

"Back to the garage. I'm off duty!"

And he bursts out laughing, the rat.

But all in all, life is good. Everything's all right. Well, almost everything. At night Benedikt would sometimes wake up suddenly, and at first he couldn't understand: Where am I? The room was big, the windows were bright with moonlight, and the moonlight lay in stripes on the floor. Someone snored lightly nearby. Oh, that's right, I'm married. You get up, walk around barefoot, quietly. The floor in the room is warm—that's because we sleep on the second story, and under the floor are stovepipes that warm it. What will they think up next? The floors are smooth, only here and there are little piles Olenka has clawed up. You stand, listening to the silence. It's quiet . . . Well, Olenka is snuffling, a snore can be heard somewhere far off in the house, someone suddenly cries out in his sleep, but still, it's quiet. And that's because the mice aren't scampering around. There aren't any mice.

At first it was kind of strange. A mouse scurries, life hurries, goes the saying, and poems say the same kind of thing: "Life, you're but a mouse's scurry, why do you trouble me?" "Hickory dickory dock . . ." "There was a crooked man who walked a crooked mile . . ." But here—nothing. Benedikt wanted to ask, but it was kind of awkward to ask all kinds of silly questions. There aren't any, so they must have caught them all.

Yes, things are good: it's warm, his stomach's full, his wife is nice and fat. And he's used to his in-laws now, they're not so bad. They have faults, but who's perfect? Everybody's different, isn't that so? Mother-in-law, for instance, she's . . . well, kind of boring. There's nothing to talk about. All she says is "eat," and "eat." I got it, I got it, I'm eating. I open my mouth, put food in, close it, chew. Now I want to talk about life or art or something.

I chew, and was just about to ask something, when she says: "Why aren't you eating?" I open my mouth again, more food—it's hard to talk with your mouth full—and swallow, in a hurry to say something, and she says, "Why aren't you eating anything? Maybe it isn't tasty? Just tell me."

"No, everything's delicious, I just wanted to—"

"If it's delicious, then eat."

"But I—"

"You don't like our food?"

"No, I didn't—"

"Maybe you're used to delicacies, and you're turning up your nose at our food?"

"I—"

"We don't have any dainties, of course, we get by with what we have, but if you don't care for our . . ."

"But—"

"Olenka! Why is he so picky . . . If he won't taste my cooking, then I just don't know what to feed him!"

"Benya, don't upset Mama, eat . . ."

"I'm eating, I'm eating!!!"

"You're not eating well enough, then." As soon as the bickering starts, all thought of art, or poems, or anything else, disappears.

Father-in-law is a little different. He really likes to talk. You could even say he wants to talk all the time, so you start thinking: It would be nice if he'd be quiet for a change. He likes to teach and ask questions, like he's testing you. He opens his mouth, takes a few breaths, and starts asking. There's a bad smell from his mouth, it kind of stinks. And he sort of stretches his neck out. Benedikt thought that his collar was tight, but no: his collar is always unbuttoned. It's just a habit. When Benedikt has eaten his full, he sits down by the window to look out—and there's Father-in-law sitting down next to him, ready for a chat.

"So, how about it, son, no thoughts popping up?"

"What thoughts?"

"All kinds of bad thoughts?"

"No, nothing popping up."

144

"Think about it carefully."

"I can't think. I'm stuffed."

"Maybe you feel like committing some villainy?"

"No, I don't."

"But if you think about it?"

"I still don't."

"Maybe you've planned some homicide?"

"No."

"But if you think about it?"

"No."

"If you're honest about it?"

"For heaven's sake, I told you. No!"

"No dreams of overthrowing the bosses?"

"Listen, I'm going to sleep! I can't take this!"

"And what if you have some murderous dreams?"

Benedikt gets up, goes to his room, slams the door and flops on the bed. Then the door opens noiselessly: Father-in-law pokes his head in.

He whispers, "Haven't thought up any malicious acts against the Big Murza, have you?"

Benedikt doesn't answer.

"Against the Murza, I said?"

Benedikt doesn't answer.

"Hey? No ideas? I'm asking. Son? Hello . . . son? Against the Murza, I'm asking you, have you dreamt up—"

"No! No! Close the door! I'm sleeping! Don't bother me, what is this? I want to sleep!"

"So, no ideas've popped up, is that it?"

That's how time passes. Eat, sleep, bicker with your relatives. And ride in the sleigh. Look out the window. Everything's just fine, all right—it doesn't get any better. But something is missing. Like you need something else. Only he forgot what.

After the marriage Benedikt didn't need anything at first. For about two weeks, maybe three. Well . . . four. Maybe five. While he got used to things, had a look around at this and that. But then—it felt like there was something—and it was gone.

C · SLOVO

AT FIRST Benedikt thought that he missed the sound of scurrying mice. After all, the mouse is our be all and end all. It's food, and clothes you can make from the pelts, and trading at the market for whatever you want. Remember how he'd caught two hundred of them at New Year's? His soul sang, people sang with him! He remembered how he walked along almost dancing, stomping on the collapsed snowdrifts, splashing his heels in puddles to make them spatter rainbows! Honest pay for an honest job. And how much he got when he traded all those mice! He and Nikita Ivanich ate that food for a whole week and they couldn't finish it. The old man baked sweet rolls . . . Somehow, they became friends over those sweet rolls. That is, if you could be friends with an Oldener. He's a bad cook compared to Mother-in-law. The sweet rolls came out lopsided—raw on one side, burned on the other, and in the middle not curds, but who knows what. Mother-in-law's sweet rolls just melt in your mouth.

Then he thought maybe he missed his izba. Sometimes he dreamt he was walking around a house that seemed to be his father-in-law's, from one gallery to the next, from one floor to the next, and it was like the same house, but not the same: it was longer, sort of sideways, everything was warped sideways. He walked and walked and kept being surprised: there was no end to this house. He had to find one special door, so he opened all the doors. But what he needed behind that door wasn't clear. He opened one door and there was his izba, but it wasn't quite the same either, it had gotten bigger: the ceiling went way up into the darkness, you couldn't see it. A bit of dry hay fell from the ceiling with a whoosh and a crackle. He stood and looked at that hay, and he was full of fear, as if someone had grabbed his heart with a paw, then let it go again. He would find out something any minute now. He was just about to find out. Then Olenka walked by and seemed to be lugging a log. She was unfriendly, sort of dry. Where are you lugging that log to, Olenka, why aren't you friendly anymore? And she laughed nastily and said, "Olenka? I'm not Olenka..." He looked again: and it really wasn't Olenka, but someone else...

...When you wake up from a dream like that, your mouth's dry and your heart goes boom-boom, boom-boom. You can't understand where you are. You touch yourself: Is this me? And the moon shines through the bladder window, bright and horrible. And the lunar path on the floor has stretched out. Some people walk in their sleep when the moon's full: they call them lunatics. The moon speaks to them, or so they say. We don't know why they stretch their arms out. It looks like they're asking for handouts or some kind of help, but if you take them by the hand, they flinch. They look surprised. And they listen: heads cocked, they listen. Their eyes are open but they don't see us. Golubchiks like that get up out of bed, go out in the yard, wander around, and then scramble up on the roof, one-two-three like it was stairs. They get right up on the roof, at the very tippy top, and walk back and forth. It's closer to the moon up there. They stare at the moon and she stares back at them: you can see a face on the moon, and that face is crying: it looks at us, at our life, and it cries.

That's what it is, Benedikt thought, he missed his izba. He even rode over to take a look: he hitched up Teterya and rode to his native settlement. But no, it wasn't that. He looked at his izba, at the straw roof: it had completely dried out. The door was open, there was burdock growing in the yard, which hadn't been weeded since springtime, and grabble grass, and biteweed, and some other strange weed with long black stems and withered leaves. The first snowflakes were whirling about, falling, indifferent to everything. He stood there awhile, took off his hat like he was standing by a grave. Everything was probably torn up inside. It was kind of a pity, but not really: his heart didn't care. It had broken away. But he shouldn't have taken the sleigh: after that trip Teterya got completely out of hand and lost all respect for Benedikt. While Benedikt stood at the fence, that furry pig stood by and smoked, he even spat on the ground, and then said, "Ha! I had a dive in Sviblovo that was better than that place."

"Teterya, watch how you talk to your betters! Your place is in the bridle!"

"And yours is—you know where . . . I had a mirrored buffet. And a color TV with an Italian tube . . . My brother-in-law managed to get a hold of a Yugoslav cabinet set, I had a separate bathroom and toilet, Golden Autumn wallpaper."

"Talking again! Go on, bridle up!"

"The kitchen was linoleum, but the rest was parquet tiles. I had a three-burner stove."

"Teterya! Who am I talking to!"

"A fridge with a freezer, beer in cans . . . lemon vodka, nice and cold . . ."

And he stands there, the rodent, on his hind legs like he was an equal, leaning on the fence, chatting, and there's a dream in his eyes, and it's clear as day he doesn't think of Benedikt as his master at all! He's lost in memories!

"Tomatoes from Kuban, Estonian cucumbers with bumps . . . We ate pressed black caviar and thought the regular stuff was shit . . . There was dark rye bread for twelve kopecks . . . Herring with onion . . . Tea with lemon . . . Pink and white meringues . . . Cherries in liqueur from Kuibyshev . . . Samarkand melon . . ."

Once he got started, he just kept on, who was there to stop him! Nikita Ivanich is right when he says there should be respect for people, and justice too! But this swine doesn't respect people, he doesn't give a fig for them! Benedikt got mad and beat him on the sides with the whip, slapped him on the ears and kicked him good and hard. And his father-in-law says Terenty's the calm one, it's Potap that's skittish! What's Potap like, then, if this one is obedient? . . . After that trip, you gotta call him Terenty Petrovich, like he was some kind of Murza. Yeah, sure.

Then he had another thought. Maybe he missed his tail? He'd had a tail a long time, he'd wagged it, enjoyed it. When you wag your tail sometimes it makes your ears tickle. It was a good tail, smooth, white, and strong. Sure, it's embarrassing to have a tail when others don't, but it wasn't a bad tail. That's a fact. And now Nikita Ivanich had gone and chopped it off, almost to the very root—jeez it was scary. Nikita Ivanich crossed himself: God bless me! And . . . whack . . . but it didn't hurt as much as he'd feared. And that's because it's all cartilage, says Nikita Ivanich. Not bone. "Congratulations," he said to Benedikt, "on the occasion of your partial humanization." That was probably a joke. "Maybe you'll get smarter," he joked again.

Now, in place of a tail he had a callus, like a bump, and it ached. Afterward Benedikt walked around for a whole week with his legs apart. He couldn't sit down. But it healed before the wedding. And now it was kind of strange: you couldn't wag it or anything. So that must be how everybody else feels, he thought. Hmmm.

But on the other hand—what does that mean, everybody else? Who is everybody else? After all, each and every one has his own special Consequence. His relatives have claws, for instance. They ruin the floor. Mother-in-law is bulky, descended from the French—she can scratch up the floor so bad it looks like a whole head of hair fell out on it. Olenka is more delicate, her piles are smaller. Father-in-law scrapes up long thin strips of kindling, you could start a fire with them. Benedikt suggested to Olenka that he clip her claws. He was afraid that she would scratch him in bed. But she started howling: What are you talking about? Look at what he's after now! My organism! No!!! Ay!! . . . And she didn't let him.

But the Degenerators don't have claws, even though they're probably not really people. They have feet at the end of their legs and hands on their arms. Very dirty ones: they wear felt boots all day long, when they're not playing cards. Sometimes they sit down, stretch their legs out, and scratch behind their ears, real quick, but if you catch a glimpse you can see that they don't have claws.

All in all, it was kind of sad at first. His rear end felt orphaned, and he stared at every tail he came across, whether a goat's, a bird's, a dog's, or a mouse's.

■ ■ ■

He went to check out the pushkin. Just a week before the wedding Benedikt had decided: That's enough, it's ready. What else is there to do?

Toward the end he wasn't really carving the figure but fixing details. He chiseled the curls, shaved down the back of the neck so it looked more like the genius was hunched over, like he was saddened by life. He touched up the fingers, the eyes. He had carved six fingers to begin with. Nikita Ivanich got mad as a hornet, shouted all kinds of things at him, but Benedikt was used to his shouts and explained calmly that that's what carpentry science requires: a bit extra never hurts. Who knows how things will turn out, what kind of mistake you might make, if you're drunk and you hit the wrong place with the ax. You can always cut off the extra. He'd finished the work now, you could say, he'd rubbed it with dry rusht—polishing, they call it—so it would be smooth and wouldn't have any splinters. Then, of course, he offered the commissioner a choice: which finger did he wish to cut off of freedom's bard? There's a lot to choose from, it made him feel good, take your pick! If you want—this one, or maybe that one; oh, you don't like that one, well, then this one, we could take off this one or that, or that one or this. Well? When everything is done scientifically, the way it's supposed to be—with extra to spare and no stinting—the soul rejoices.

But Nikita Ivanich got all tied up in knots and couldn't choose, he ran around and around and pulled out his hair—and he had a ton of hair. How could he, so to speak, dare to have the Freethinking temerity to blasphemously hack off the poet's hands at his own caprice? A tail was one thing, but this is a hand!!! He buried his face in his palms, shook his head, peeked out with one eye, then squeezed it shut, fretted and fretted, and couldn't decide. He left all six fingers. And the pushkin didn't have any legs, they decided not to bother with legs. They didn't have time. Only the trunk, just down to the sash around his shirt. After that it was like a stump, all smooth.

It took six of them to drag it—they hired serfs and paid them with mice. One of the Oldeners, Lev Lvovich of the Dissidents, a friend of Nikita Ivanich, decided to help. He approved of the idol.

"He looks like a pure retard. A six-phalanged seraphim. A slap in the face of public taste," he said. But he wasn't much help pulling, he was so skinny, he was more of a director, so to speak, the way bosses always are. "Come on, come on. Stop! Move it! There you go. Not like that! To the left!" They wanted to put the pushkin where Nikita Ivanich showed them—for some reason he liked that spot. They started digging a hole under him. But the owner there turned out to be ornery: he ran out waving his arms, spitting and frothing at the mouth—they trampled his dill, you see. That dill is useless stuff, no taste, no smell, it's more for looks' sake; but of course if you're starving you'll eat dill too.

Nikita Ivanich had to go and put his symbol right in the middle of a Golubchik's garden, of course, and he argued with him and tried to shame him and bribe him with getting fire without standing in line, and then appealed to the serfs to raise a ruckus so that the people's voice could be heard. But the serfs didn't give a hoot: they stood there frowning, crossing their legs, smoking, waiting for their pay, for the boss to shout himself out, for his heart to burst so he'd quiet down, that's what always happens. In the end, the chunk of beriawood had to be lugged across the street. There was a place between the fences that didn't belong to anyone.

So there he stands, the poor dear, listening to the noise of the street, like Nikita Ivanich wanted—you turn the corner and see him on a hill, in the wind, all black. This wood, beriawood, always blackens from the rain. The pushkin stands there like a bush at night, a rebellious and angry spirit; his head bent, two meat patties on the sides of his face—old-fashioned sideburns—his nose down, his fingers tearing at his caftan. A shitbird had settled on his head, of course, but that's just what they do, shamelessly: whatever they see they shit on, that's why they got that disgraceful nickname, for their disgracefulness.

So Benedikt went. He looked at the pushkin. Shooed away the kids so they wouldn't climb on it. He wanted to tamp down the snow around it but was too lazy to get out of the sleigh. He looked around . . . and that was it. So let it stand there, it's not bothering anyone.

∎ ∎ ∎

He thought and he thought. What was missing? Suddenly he realized. It hit him. Books! He hadn't read any books for a long time, or copied them, or held them in his hands! Since May! He stopped going to work of his own will, then he had vacation, then the wedding, then family life, and now another fall was already breaking into winter but hadn't broken through. That always happens with nature, it can't make up its mind. One day rain, the next snow. The October Holiday is already over. Only this year he didn't go for the head count. His father-in-law had to go for work—he complained, but he went, and he told us: Stay at home, I know there are three of you, anyway, I'll put you on the list.

Benedikt couldn't stand the October Holiday. Who could like it, except for maybe some Murza, and even then as part of his job? Still, it was some kind of entertainment, and you could look at the people and they might hand out something from the Warehouse. Only now he didn't need anything. So there was trouble in nature, and trouble in his head too. There's nothing to do. It's boring.

You wander around the house, skulk, and loaf around looking for things to do. You spit on your finger and run it along the wall. You keep on, tracing the whole room, or at least go as far as you can till the spit dries out. Then you spit on your finger again and start over.

What else? You squat, put your elbows against your knees grab your beard with your fists and rock: back and forth. Back and forth.

Or you stick out your lower lip and flap it with your finger. It makes a funny noise, bub bub bub.

Or you sit on a stool or a bench and rock back and forth, stick out your tongue, close one eye, and look at your tongue with the other one. You can see part of your nose, and the tip of your tongue. But only just.

Or else you pull the skin around your eyes back till they're skinny slits just to see what happens; and what happens is that you see everything, but kind of blurry.

You can hang your head between your knees to the floor, and wait until the blood rushes down. There'll be a roar in your head, things'll go all foggy; and there'll be a buzzing and thumping in your ears.

You can weave your fingers together, one after the other, and then turn them inside out and wiggle them: here's the terem, here's the steeple, open the door, and there are the people. Or you can just wiggle your fingers. That's on your hands. But if you try it with your toes you'll get a cramp in your foot. Who can figure it? Your hands work this way and your feet that way. Well, hands are hands, and feet are feet. That's probably why.

Or you can just look at your fingernails.

And you don't see any visions: somehow they're all gone, the visions. Too bad. Benedikt used to see Olenka: beads, dimples, ribbons. And now what? Now there she is, Olenka herself. Right by your side. Dimples—she's got dimples over her whole body. Dimples so big you stick your finger in and it almost disappears. Stick your fingers in as much as you like. She won't get mad. You could even say she welcomes it: "You rapscallion, you. Why such a hurry?"

Only she used to kind of sparkle. Like a secret. And now there she is, sitting on the stool, her face spread thick with sour cream—to make it whiter; only the sour cream makes her look awful. She scratches her head. "Take a look, Benedikt. What is this here? Is it a rat's nest?"

There never used to be any rats' nests: her braid went all the way down to the ground. But now she's not supposed to wear a braid. Since she's a married Golubushka, Olenka has to have a woman's hairdo. And this is a lot of trouble. She divides her hair into locks, wets them down with water or rusht, and then starts winding the hair on wood bobbins. She wraps her whole head up this way and walks around with the bobbins rattling, knocking against each other all day long. She has to have curls, you see. And her face is smeared with sour cream: she looks like a real ghoul.

"Why did you wind all those things on yourself?"

"What do you mean? To be beautiful. It's for you."

She plops down on the bed. "Come here, Benedikt, let's make love."

"That's enough, enough."

"Just come here, come over here, don't talk."

"I feel sort of weak. I ate a bit too much."

"Don't make things up, you haven't eaten since breakfast."

"You'll scratch me."

"What do you mean, scratch you? Don't invent things."

"Your face is covered with sour cream."

"You've always got excuses! I'm sooo unhaaaappy . . .!"

And she starts wailing. But then she stops.

"Benedikt! Come here. Something itches. Over there, right there, what is it? Did something pop up?"

"Nothing popped up."

"No, look again, you didn't look carefully. Carefully now! Something itches, it's tingling."

"There's nothing there."

"What's tingling then? It's not a carbuncle, is it?"

"No."

"Maybe a blister? Is it swollen?"

"No."

"Is it red?"

"No, no!"

"Then what is it? It keeps on itching and itching, and then it stings so bad! . . . And over here? Benedikt! Pay attention! Right here—no, farther! Between the shoulder blades!"

"There isn't anything."

"Maybe scales?"

"No!"

"Some dandruff, then? It's itching. Brush it off me."

"It's all clear, I said! Don't invent things!"

"Maybe I broke out in freckles all over?"

"No!!!"

"Maybe it's a pimple or a wart! You have to be careful—they can pop up and that's it, you're dead!"

"Your back is fine, I tell you! You're imagining everything!"

"Of course, since I'm the one suffering, and not you, you don't care! But I've got an ache here under my arm, Benedikt."

"It'll stop."

"Other men would be sympathetic! . . . If I raise my arm this way and turn it that way, it starts aching! And if I lean over like that, and put my foot there, I get a stitch in my side right away, come on now, take a look, what's on my side, I can't see it!"

He was sure of it. If only he could lie around now with a book! Snow was falling softly in the yard, logs were crackling in the stove—it was the perfect time to lie in bed with a book. Put a bowl of firelings or something else delicious nearby, to stick behind your cheek, and let yourself go . . . into the book . . . Right now it's winter outside, for instance, and there it's summer. Here it's daytime and there it's evening. And they'll describe that summer for you and pretty it up, and tell you what kind of evening it is, who went where, what they were wearing, who sat on which bench by the river, who they're waiting for—it's always a lover—what birds are singing in the sky, how the sun goes down, how the gnats swarm . . . And you can hear something beyond the river, a song of some sort. And everything will be in the book: how there was a noise in the bushes—the lover arrived for the tryst. What they said to each other, what they settled on . . . Or who built a big ship and sailed it on the Ocean-Sea, and how many people crowded on that boat, and where they set sail for, and how the boat works, they'll tell you about everything. And about how the voyage goes, who argued about what with whom, about the chip one guy had on his shoulder, how he grew blacker than a storm cloud and got all sorts of ideas in his head . . . and who realized it and said, Ay, why is he looking at us like a stray dog that wants to bite, let's set him down on a desert island . . .

You read, move your lips, figure out the words, and it's like you're in two places at the same time: you're sitting or lying with your legs curled up, your hand groping in the bowl, but you can see different worlds, far-off worlds that maybe never existed but still seem real. You run or sail or race in a sleigh—you're running away from someone, or you yourself have decided to attack—your heart thumps, life flies by, and it's wondrous: you can live as many different lives as there are books to read. Like a werewolf or something: you're a man, and all of a sudden—you're a woman, or an old man, or a small child, or a whole battalion on guard, or I don't know what. And if it's true that it wasn't Fyodor Kuzmich, Glorybe, who wrote all those books, well, who cares? Then it means there were other Fyodor Kuzmiches, ancient people, who sat, and wrote, and saw visions. Why not?

And just about now, the candles have probably been lighted in the Work Izba, the scrolls rolled up, Jackal Demianich is looking watchfully around. Konstantin Leontich is writing fast as can be, copying, from time to time he tosses down his writing stick, claps his hands and cries out! He always gets very worked up about what happens in books. And then he grabs his writing stick again, and goes on ... And Varvara Lukinishna bends her head, her combs tremble, she's thinking about something ... maybe that at home she has a book hidden? There was something there about a candle, about deceit ... But neither Benedikt nor Olenka are in the Work Izba anymore ... Olenka lies on the bed whining, covered in sour cream, and Benedikt is rocking on the stool. If only he could catch some mice right now, and trade them at the market for a book. Only there aren't any mice in the house.

What sort of book was it that Father-in-law shoved at Benedikt? Should he go and ask? Since Father-in-law didn't get sick, knock, knock, knock on wood, then it was true: you can touch them.

T · TVERDO

FATHER-IN-LAW sat down right next to him again, opened his mouth, and asked: "Haven't been having any bad thoughts, have you?"

Benedikt answered boldly: "Yep. I have."

Father-in-law was overjoyed. "Come on, come on, let's hear them!"

"What sort of book did you show me a long time ago? When I came courting?"

"How do you know it's a book?"

"I just know."

"Where from? Someone showed you one?"

"Maybe someone did."

"Who was it?"

"What sort of book was it?"

"No, who showed you?"

Benedikt thought about telling him, but thought better of it: who knows what . . .

"Don't ask a lot of questions, just let me read it."

"Then you tell me who showed it to you."

"We had one at our house," said Benedikt, and he wasn't even lying.

"Where is it?"

"They burned it. My old man burned it."

"Why?"

"So no one would get the Illness, knock on wood."

Father-in-law thought for a moment, his eyes blazed, and his feet scraped. "You people are so backward. A backward people . . ."

"Why are we backward? . . . We obey the Decrees. We adopt all the scientific achievements: the yoke, the sun clock. Nails."

"You're backward because you can't see past your own noses," Father-in-law explained, "and you don't understand the governmental approach to social questions."

Benedikt's spirits fell. It was true, he had a hard time with the governmental approach to things. Until the explanations came in Decrees, he didn't get the governmental, state approach, he understood things the simple way. When they'd explained it all, then, of course, he understood. But the governmental approach was never straightforward. You think this is the way things should go, but no, it's like this, not like that. No way you could guess for yourself.

"Take Illness," continued Father-in-law, "the view you hold is incorrect."

"I heard it's tradition," said Benedikt carefully.

"What tradition?"

"To treat people. That there used to be radiation from books, and they treated the ones who had books. But now two hundred years have gone by and it doesn't matter. That's the tradition. That's what I heard."

Father-in-law's eyes gave off a strong light. He scratched the floor, almost ripping out the floorboards.

"Benediiiikt! Come heeeere, let's make love!" Olenka called from the next room.

"Lie down and wait!" cried Father-in-law. "We're having a governmental conversation! About worldviews! So now, this is the way things go: Illness isn't in books, my dear boy, it's in people's heads."

"Like a cold?"

"Worse. Now, you talk about nails. All right. We didn't use to know about nails, right?"

"That's right."

"And was it better when there weren't any nails, what do you think?"

Benedikt thought a moment. "It was worse."

"That's right. So. Things used to be worse. And now they're better. You get my drift."

"I think I get your drift."

"And before that, they were even worse. And before everything—well, there was the Blast. Was that a good thing, what do you think?"

"Heavens no!"

"That's right. So, which way do we need to go? Forward, of course. When you're walking down the street, would you start stepping in place? No. You go straight on ahead. Why are our eyes on our forehead and not on our rear ends, right? Nature is giving us directions."

"That's true," Benedikt admitted.

"Only forward, no other way. So, for instance, since I'm Head Saniturion, I am going to light the way." And he gave off rays as bright as full-moon light. "Do you follow me now?"

"No," said Benedikt.

"No again. Well, what can you do . . . All right, then. There's a lot of backwardness in society," Father-in-law explained. "And all people are brothers. Now then, can a brother refuse help to his brother? What would he be if he did that? A bad guy, a sleazeball. Helping and fixing come first. But how do some people think? 'Oh, it's none of my beeswax.' Is that good?"

"It's kind of bad. That's not more-alls."

"Right. And how to help?"

"I don't know."

"Think about it."

"Well . . . I don't know . . . Feed someone?"

"Ha! You call that thinking! If you feed and feed and feed people, and keep on feeding them, they'll stop working. You'll be the only one sweating, all for them. How're you gonna come up with all that food? Where are you gonna get new food? Where's the food coming from if no one's working? No. Think again."

Benedikt thought about how to help his brother. True, he didn't have a brother, and thinking was uncomfortable. He imagined someone tall, lanky, and irksome: he sat on a stool and whined: "Brooother . . . He-e-l-l-p me . . . Pleeease help me, brooother . . ." And you don't feel like it, so you whack him on the head.

"Maybe by keeping a lookout while he's off?"

"Sure. You stand there like a pillar all day long. And he's out chasing skirts."

Benedikt got mad at this brother: What a bastard! What more did he need?

"You give up," Father-in-law said, shaking his head. "Well, all right. Let's think it through together. You ever planted turnips?"

"Yes."

"You've planted them. Good. So you know how it works: you plant the turnip and you wait. You're waiting for a turnip—but who knows what will sprout up? Maybe half turnips, half weeds. You ever weeded grass?"

"Yes."

"Good. So you know. What's left to explain? If you don't weed the turnip in time, the whole field will be covered in weeds. And the turnip won't be able to push through the weeds. Isn't that right? And there won't be anything to eat, or to guard. So there you have it!"

"True," Benedikt admitted.

"Of course it's true. Now, follow me. You read the story 'The Turnip'? Copied it?"

"The story? I read it: Grandpa planted a turnip. The turnip grew and grew and grew till it couldn't grow anymore."

"Right. Only it's not a story. It's a fable."

"What's a fable?"

"A fable is a directive rendered in a simplified form for popular consumption."

"And which direction do they cook the turnip in?" asked Benedikt in surprise.

"And you call yourself a careful reader, do you? Grandpa pulls and pulls on the turnip, but he can't pull it out. He calls Grandmother. They pull and pull and pull, but they can't pull it out. Then they call a lot of others. No go. Then they call in a mouse—and they pull the turnip out. How do we interpret this? I'll tell you how. It means we can't do without mice. Mice Are Our Mainstay."

And it was true! As soon as Father-in-law explained it that way, it was suddenly all clear, it all fit together. What a smart man.

"So, in general, and all in all," concluded Father-in-law, "this is the picture: the collective depends on the mouse, because the mouse, you see, it's the cornerstone of our happy existence. I'm explaining social science to you, don't turn your head away. This way, leaning against the cornerstone, people grab what they can and pull. If you get a turnip, fine. If there's no turnips, then horsetail, or rusht at worst."

"You're right there. It's true. Last year someone grabbed all the rusht in my pantry. I got home—the door was open, they'd pulled everything out!"

"Good. You've finally started to think. So then, how do you see your job?"

"Which one?"

"Which?! Weeding!"

Benedikt thought hard. "Weeding? Hmm . . . Do you have to weed? Aha! You mean catch thieves?"

"What thieves! . . . Figure it out! Who are the thieves?"

"Thieves? Thieves are the ones who steal."

"Well, and who steals?"

"Who steals . . . who steals . . . Well, everyone steals."

"That's the whole point," said Father-in-law with a laugh. "Everybody steals! So who are you gonna catch? Your own self? My, my, my, you're so funny."

Father-in-law opened his mouth and laughed hard. Benedikt turned his head: a really foul smell came from Father-in-law's mouth.

"So, then, what's your job? You give up? To treat them, of course. You have to treat people, my fine boy!"

Benedikt felt a chill pass through him.

"Who—me?"

"And who else? Of course you! We'll feed you up a bit—I'll give you a little hook, and when you're used to it, when you've got the hang of it—you'll get a big one."

"I can't, no, no, no I can't. What do you . . . I can't hook people, no, no, no . . . knock, knock, knock on wood, no no no—"

"There you go again! I explained it to you, and I thought you were listening up good, and then I hear this 'I can't, I can't.' You just forget that 'I can't.' Do you have a duty to society or not? Should the people move toward the bright, lofty future or not? Should we help our brothers? Yes, we should. Don't argue. Our job, dear boy, couldn't be more noble, but the people are backward, they don't get it. They've got all these silly fears, they spread gossip. Savages!"

Benedikt was dejected. He had only just understood everything and then Father-in-law sort of turned it all topsy-turvy—and once again everything was all mixed up and he was in the doldrums.

"So what does that mean: We can't read books?"

"What do you mean you can't read books?" said Father-in-law in surprise. "Why not? Read to your heart's content, I have a whole library of Oldenprint books, some of them have pictures. I'll get you a pass."

"Then why treat people?"

"Again all this why oh why! Because of Illness!"

"I don't get it . . . ."

"Not all at once. You'll get it, you will."

"Well, but you said Mice Are Our Mainstay. Then why aren't there any mice in our house?"

"We don't have any mice because we lead a spiritual life. We don't need mice."

Y . UK

FATHER-IN-LAW had a whole storeroom full of Oldenprint books. When Benedikt got his pass to the books—*ooooeeee!*—his eyes popped out, his knees went weak, his hands shook and he nearly had a fainting fit. The room was huge, on the very top floor, with windows, and shelves, shelves, and more shelves, all along the walls, and on the shelves were books, books, and more books! Big ones, little ones, all kinds. Some fit in your palm but the letters were big. Others were big but the letters were tiny. There were books with pictures, not just plain ones, but color! Honest to God. Color pictures! There was a whole book of color pictures, with lots of naked women, all pink—sitting on the grass, and on stools, and squatting, and every which way. Some were thin as brooms, others not bad, nice and plump. One of them had climbed onto a bed and thrown off the blanket—pretty good, that one.

He turned the pages—some men were walking along with rakes—they must be going to plant turnips.

Then there was the sea, and on it a boat, and over the boat a sheet on sticks. They must have decided to do the washing and hung it out to dry. That's handy: look how much water there is in the sea.

He turned the pages back to where the woman climbed on the bed. A fine woman. Kind of like Olenka, only no sour cream on her face.

Then there were a lot of Golubchiks sitting on animals—animals that looked something like goats, but with no beards. Father-in-law said they're steeds. Steeds. Aha. So that's what a steed is. Scary looking. But these guys rode them and weren't afraid.

Then there were colored flowers. A pot, and flowers sticking out of it. Boring. Then everything was all slathered on and mushed around and you couldn't figure out what it was. That was boring too. He turned some more pages and there was this picture: nothing on it, just a white page, and in the middle, a square-shaped black hole. Nothing else. Kind of like the end of everything. He looked and looked at the hole—and suddenly got scared, like in a dream. He clapped the book shut and dropped it.

There were lots of pictures in other books too. Benedikt sat on the floor for three days turning the pages. There were drawings of everything you could imagine. Good Lord! Pretty girls with babies sat laughing, and off in the distance were white roads and green hills, and on the hills were mountain towns, bright blue, or pink like the dawn. There were serious men, all important, with pancake-shaped hats on their heads, yellow chains across their chests, and puffy sleeves like women wear. Or a huge crowd of Golubchiks, and a bunch of little kids, only the kids are naked, they've only got colored rags wrapped around them. They're flying up somewhere, and they're taking lots of flowers and wreathes with them. The whole family must have gone weeding together, and some tricksters robbed them, took off with their coats while they were in the fields.

Once something familiar caught his eye. It was none other than *The Demon*. For sure. The one Fyodor Kuzmich gave them. Benedikt sat for a long time looking at it and thinking, so long that his feet went to sleep. It's one thing to listen to others, and another thing altogether to see for yourself. So it was true, they weren't lying, it wasn't Fyodor Kuzmich who wrote books, but other Golubchiks. Fyodor Kuzmich, Glorybe, must have seen this Demon, painted by a Golubchik named Vrubel, and he just up and tore the picture out of the book. So that's what he's like: dinky but daring. It was sad, somehow: he had deceived Benedikt, set him up, taken him for a fool.

After these books Benedikt started dreaming in color, and his heart pounded. It was all big green hills, covered with green-grass, and a road, and Benedikt was running along the road on light feet, amazed at how easy it was to run. And there were trees on the hills, and their shadows were lacy and fleet: the sun played through the leaves, danced on the greengrass. He ran and laughed: it's so easy to run, I want to tell someone! But there wasn't anyone, everyone was hiding. That's all right: they'll come out in time and laugh together with Benedikt! He didn't know where he was running, only that someone was waiting for him happily, someone wanted to praise him: Good boy, Benedikt, good boy!

He dreamt he knew how to fly. Not very high, and not for long, but still, he was flying. This was on a road too, but it was dark. And warm. It must be summer. Benedikt seemed to be dressed in white pants and a white shirt. And somehow he just knew that if he pushed off the ground with his feet, and then arched his back like this, and waved his arms to the side like a frog, that he could float in the air for about ten yards. Then that power seemed to dry up, and he pushed off again, and floated again. Benedikt showed someone and explained. You see how simple it is, just arch your back, point your stomach to the ground, and do this with your arms, there, like that. Then he'd wake up—and what a pity: he had known how to fly, and now he'd forgotten.

Once he dreamt that his tail had grown back ornate and patterned, all white, like the tail of the Princess Bird. He looked over his shoulder and gazed at his tail . . . It was dark and cool in the room and the window was low. The light of the morning sun hit the window and the white feathers, splintering into tiny rainbows, sparkling splotches. He would fan out his tail and gather it up again, and watch how the sparks played on the white feathers, as though they were made of fluffy, flying snow. He liked this tail so much, so much—he'd like to squat and jump through the window onto a branch right now, and walk along the branch: *ko-ko-ko*. Only the tail ached a little bit, and it was hard to walk with it. Then he was no longer by the window, but going down a staircase, the tail rustling behind him, bumping along the stairs, stiff and cold, and even fuller than before. Benedikt went into a room where the family was waiting for him. They're sitting at the table and watching... They're creeping around in lapty. And they look at him so sternly, judging, angry. Benedikt looks too and sees he's naked. He forgot to put his pants on, or he lost them or something. It's time to eat. So he sits down at the table and wants to cover his privates with his tail. He tries this way, and that, but nothing works because the tail's too short. How could that be? Just now it was so long it thumped on the stairs, and suddenly it's too short. He reached for it with his hands, turned his head, and looked at it under his arms. It wasn't the same tail anymore. It was dark and speckled, and the feathers stuck to his hands: he touched them and they fell off ...

You dream the strangest things, but who knows what to think about all these dreams? When he'd looked at all the books with pictures, he started on the others. In the beginning his eyes couldn't follow the Oldenprint letters, they jumped around. Then they got used to it, like it was the way things ought to be. As if Benedikt had been reading forbidden books his whole life! At first he grabbed anything and everything, but then he decided to put them in order. To count up everything. He piled all the books on the floor and rearranged them his own way. At first he arranged them by color: yellow books in this corner, red books in that corner. That wasn't quite right. Then he organized them by size: big ones over there, little ones over here. He didn't like that either. Why? Because every book said who wrote it on the cover. Jules Verne, for instance. He wrote a big brown book, and a little blue one. How can you stick them in different corners? They should be together. Then he tripped up: there are books called journals, and more than one Golubchik wrote in them, maybe ten of them, and each wrote something different. These journals need to be together too, by numbers: first number one, then two, then — but what's this? — it should be number three, but there isn't any three, the next one is seven. What happened? It's gone! That's upsetting. Maybe it's around here somewhere, he'll find it later. There's all kinds of journals, and they have wonderful names. Some make sense and others don't. Take *Star*, for instance, that's clear. You'd have to be a complete idiot not to understand that one. But then there's *Cadries*, and what is "Cadries"? It must be a mistake, it should probably be "Cadres." That's what Teterya calls girls he meets on the street. Benedikt brewed some ink from rusht, whittled himself a writing stick, and fixed everything. There was a lot about girls written in that journal, it was true.

Then there's *Questions of Literature*. Benedikt took a look at it: no questions at all, only answers. The issue with questions must have got lost. Too bad.

There's a journal called *Potatoes and Vegetables*, with pictures. And there's *At the Wheel. Siberian Lights*. There's one called *Syntaxis*, which seems like a bad word, but who knows what it means. It must be a cuss word. Benedikt skimmed it: there you go, there are cuss words in it. He put it to one side: interesting. He'd have to read it before going to bed.

There's *Heartfelt Words; European Herald; Scales*. These are sort of different, they smell moldy. That doesn't matter, but some letters, a couple in almost every word, are strange, different. Benedikt thought that maybe it wasn't in his language, but in Cockynork instead. Once he got used to reading it, though, it wasn't so bad. He stopped paying attention to the extra letters, like they weren't there.

Some Golubchiks tried real hard, they wrote neat little books the same size and color, called "collected works." There was Zola, for instance. Or Antonina Koptiaeva. The collecteds also had a portrait of the Golubchik who wrote them drawn right in the book. Such funny portraits, unbelievable. Take Golubchik Sergei Sartakov: such an awful-looking face, if you met him on the street, you'd jump. But he sat around writing things. He wrote a lot.

Some books are worn and dirty, pages fall out of them. Some are so neat and clean, seems like they were made yesterday. A real pleasure to look at. Take Anton Chekhov. His book was so worn! Seems he was all thumbs, a real loser. Maybe a little blind. Look at his face, he's got a Consequence on his eyes: two shiny circles and a string hanging down. Now Koptiaeva, you see, is a clean woman, she takes care of herself. Her book looks untouched. He set Koptiaeva aside to read before bed too.

Father-in-law came by, watched Benedikt rearranging everything and said approvingly, "I see you love culture."

"I adore culture."

"It's good stuff. We like to read too. Sometimes we sit in a circle and read."

"Hmmm."

"But there are some people who don't respect culture, who ruin it."

"Hmm."

"They tear pages out, turn the pages with dirty hands."

"Oh no . . . Who?"

"They're all around."

Father-in-law stood there for a while, breathing heavily—the whole room smelled terrible—and then he left.

First thing in the morning, without eating or drinking, Benedikt splashed water on his face and began reading. He'd be called to lunch—too bad, they interrupted the most interesting part! At first he'd run in quickly, grab a bite, and go back to the books. Then he realized that he could read at the table. The food tasted better and you didn't lose time that way. The family was insulted, of course. Mother-in-law was hurt that Benedikt didn't praise her cooking that much, Olenka thought he was reading about women, and she's sitting right there like some kind of fool. Father-in-law stood up for him: Leave him alone, this is art.

Olenka wailed: "He just reads books and doesn't pay any attention to me!"

Father-in-law defended him: "It's none of your business. Shut up! If he's reading, that means he needs to read . . ."

"What is he reading all the time? He's reading about women! And he won't look at his own wife! I'm going to tear up all those books of yours!"

"There's nothing here about women! Here, look, it says: 'Roger pulled out a pistol and listened. A door creaked.' No women."

"You see, no girls there!"

"Yeah, sure! No women! Why'd he pull his pissdoll out then, the filthy old man?"

"Because now Mister Blake will go inside, and he'll hit him on the head with a pistol—Roger will. He's hiding behind the portier. Leave me alone," said Benedikt.

"What Mister Blake?"

"The family notary. Don't bother me."

"Why is he pulling out his pissdoll in front of a family man? Get your own family and show it to them!"

"Well, that just shows to go what an idiot you are," Father-in-law said to her. "Family is family, but you've got to realize there's such a thing as research. Your husband isn't here just for fun and games, he's a citizen of society, a breadwinner and protector. All you wanna do is giggle, but he needs to study. Son!"

"Hmm?"

"Have you read *Hamlet* yet?"

"Not yet."

"Read it. Mustn't allow gaps in your education . . . you have to read *Hamlet*."

"All right, I'll read it."

"*Macbeth* too. Oh, now that's a good book, very useful . . ."

"All right."

"*Mumu* is a must. Very exciting story. By a fellow called Turgenev. They put a stone around the dog's neck and throw her in the water . . . *The Gingerbread Man* is good too."

"I read *The Gingerbread Man*."

"You've read it? Great, isn't it?"

"Uh huh."

"That fox really gives it to him . . . Snap! Yes, brother, that fox, you know . . . That's a real fox for you . . . Snap!"

"It's kinda sad . . ."

"What do you mean, sad! . . . It's art! It's not sad, it's a hint . . . You have to know how to read between the lines . . . You read Krylov's *Fables?*"

"I started them."

"There are some good ones . . . 'The Wolf and the Lamb.' That's good. 'It's your fault that I'm hungry!' Pure poetry."

"I like adventure stories better."

"Ah, I see, you mean so they draw it out, don't do it all at once . . . That yellow one, *The Head Hunters,* you have to read that one too."

"Listen, leave me alone! I'll read it! You're bothering me! Let me read in peace."

"That's it, that's it! Not another word!" Father-in-law put his finger to his lips. "Go on, do your work, study in peace. Not another word, not another word."

Φ . FERT

SPRING HAD COME with its huge flowers. Beyond the window everything was bright blue—but Benedikt noticed only because light poured in and it was easier to read. He pulled aside the bladder covering the window—there it was! All the meadows and glades had long been covered with greengrass, the little azure flowers were wilting, the yellow ones were coming in. Honey waves of wind blew, calling stout hearts to set off for faraway lands, to explore wondrous kingdoms, launch dugouts on clean rivers and hold course for the Ocean-Sea. But Benedikt didn't need any of this. He had everything in books, rolled up, buried in little secret boxes: sea and meadow, deep blue and sandy winds, foul winds and snow, and the wind they call Zephyr. Starless nights and nights of passion, velvety nights and sleepless nights! Southern, white, pink, sweet as could be, dreamy, draining nights! Golden and silver stars, blue and green as sea salt, shooting and falling stars, foreboding stars, glittering diamond and lone stars, stars that herald woe, and stars that shine like beacons—there you go, beacons! All the vessels on all the seas, all the kisses, islands, roads and all the cities those roads lead to, all the city gates, nooks, crannies, dungeons and tunnels, towers, flags, all the golden curls and jet black braids, the thunder and clash of arms, the clouds, the steppes, and again the wind, sea, and stars! He didn't need anything else, it was all here!

A rich man—that's who he was. Rich as rich could be! Benedikt thought about himself. I'm rich, he thought, and he laughed. He even yelped. I'm my own Murza! My own Sultan! Everyone's in the palm of my hand, in little letters: the bounty of boundless nature and the lives of countless people! Old-timers, youngsters, and indescribable beauties!

There was another good thing about books, he thought. The beauties rustling their dresses between the pages, peering from behind shutters and from under lace curtains, the beauties wringing their white hands and throwing themselves with loosened hair under the hooves of steeds, their eyes sparking fiercely —she's crying and her waist is the size of an hourglass—beauties who lounge on divans with pounding hearts, and leap up to cast a wild gaze around the room; who step fearfully, lowering their dark blue eyes; who dance fiery dances with roses in their hair—these beauties never have to answer nature's call, they never have to bend over to pick things up, they never get gas, no pimples pop up on their faces, and their backs never hurt. Their golden hair never has any dandruff and lice never nest or lay eggs in it, they leave them alone. And those golden curls—they curl for days on end, and no one ever says anything about these beauties spending half the day with bobbins in their hair. They don't chomp, sneeze, or snore. Their cheeks don't squelch; no Isabelle or Caroline ever wakes up puffy with sleep; their jaws don't clack when they yawn, they awake refreshed and toss back the curtains. And they all throw themselves joyfully into the arms of their beloved. And just who is their beloved? Why, it's Benedikt, of course, whether he's called Don Pedro or Sysoy.

It's spring! Why does he need spring? Well, there's one good thing about it: there's more light for reading. The day is longer, and the letters are clearer.

In summer Benedikt had a hammock hung for him in the gallery. Above the hammock he hung a light sheet to protect him from the shitbirds. They have no shame, not the least bit: wherever they see a cornice, that's where they sit, cooing and shitting. It's not so bad if it falls on your hair, but what if it falls on a book? He had two serfs stand on either side of him to fan him and shoo away gnats and mosquitoes. He had a rocking girl sit there to rock the hammock ever so gently, not too hard, just a little bit. Another girl brought him cool drinks: she crushed dogwood berries, stewed compote from them, and added lots of chopped ice. The ice was left over from winter: all winter long workers chopped ice and stored it in cold cellars. And this compote was good to drink through a straw: they'd cut some grass, and if it wasn't poisonous they'd dry it, and inside there was a little hole, and you could drink through it.

The flies had grown mean and big, their wings shimmered blue, their eyes were rainbows. Two workers stood next to Benedikt fanning them away, while a third ran to help. It must be fall. He raised his eyes: it really was fall, rain was dripping from the clouds. God forbid a book should get wet. He moved back inside the house.

X · KHER

IT WAS AN ordinary day, Thursday. A bit of snow was falling, and nothing foretold anything. And that's the way it is in books: if nothing foretells anything they always tell you special. And if they tell you, hold on: birds will cackle, the wind will take to howling, and the mirror will crack. A mirror is what people had in Oldener times, sort of like a board, and they looked at that board and could see themselves, like when we look in the water.

They all sat down to eat.

Benedikt opened issue number seven of the *Northern Herald*. It was a very strong book, sewn with threads and glued together; he cracked the spine so it wouldn't close, leaned on it with his elbow, and held it down with a bowl of soup.

Mother-in-law said: "Eat up, son, the meat patties are getting cold."

"Mmm . . ."

"They're tasty, juicy."

"Mmm . . ."

"Steamed with marshrooms. Try them, they should be good, I steamed them in the oven for an hour."

Olenka said: "Mashed turnips are good with patties."

Father-in-law: "Puree goes good with everything."

"No, especially with meat patties."

"Well, that's for sure—it's not every day we steam patties."

"It sure isn't."

". . . . ," Benedikt read, his eyes already accustomed to racing across the lines, ". . . ."

"Last year, remember, we gathered biteweed and cooked up some macedoine with turnips."

"Uh huh."

"If you slopped some goat cheese into the macedoine for the taste, it would be even more delicious."

"That's right."

"And noodles are good too."

"How could they be bad?"

"It's really good when you put butter in the noodles, add some forest herbs, a bit of kvas, bake it and then let it simmer, and as soon as it sizzles, you serve it."

"With ground marshrooms on top."

"That's right."

"And a flaky roulette stuffed with nuts."

"And ferns."

"Ferns, yep."

"Then spice cookies. Braided ones."

"Why braided? Broiled are better."

"Yeah, sure, broiled. Broiled they come out a touch bitter."

"So? So what? That's good."

"What's good about it? Woven ones are way better. There's an egg in them."

"What do you know. Woven! . . . Next thing you'll be talking about bliny again."

"Bliny, so what? What about bliny?"

"What about, nothing about! Bliny! What'll it be next?"

"What's it to you?"

"Nothing! That's what!"

"Well, then, don't say nothing. But I say: bliny!"

"I'll give you bliny!"

"You're a real blin yourself."

"That's right, I'm a blin. So what does that make you?"

"Nothing!"

"Then shut up!"

"Shut up yourself!"

"I'll just shut up, then!"

"So just go ahead and shut up!"

"So there, I'll shut up! Bliny!"

"Then just shut up! Give us some peace and quiet!"

They shut up. Chewed. Benedikt turned the page, resettled his bowl, and held the journal down again.

"Eat your patties, son."

"I'm eating."

"Take some more. Olenka, serve him some more. Pour some sauce on them, for heaven's sake! There you go. Pour some more."

"Give him some marshrooms."

"And some fried steak."

They were silent again.

"Too bad Eudoxia croaked. She knew how to whip up the best nut soufflé."

"You're not kidding."

"There was a kind of crust on top, but it was soft inside."

"That's right . . ."

"And her charlottes . . . Who can make a charlotte like that nowadays?"

"Which one? With turnips?"

"That's right, turnips."

"I know how to make one from turnips."

"Yeah, sure."

"What does that mean?"

"Nothing."

"You don't think I can?"

"Nope."

"Well, I can."

"You're lying."

"Oh, yes, I can. First you steam it, then you mash it. Then you add eggs, nuts, and goat milk and pop it in the oven. On a high heat. Like for bliny."

"There you go with your bliny again."

"What's wrong with bliny, you creep? Just wait, you'll be asking for them next thing you know!"

"Yes, I will! Puffy, flaky ones."

"To hell with you."

"What's that supposed to mean?"

"Just what I said."

"Just you wait, I swear I'll smack you on the forehead with a ladle — then you'll have your bliny!"

Benedikt turned another page.

"Son!"

"Mmm . . ."

"Put the book down. As soon as you're at the table you've got your nose in a book. Can't sit with you or have a proper conversation."

"Mmm . . ."

"Son!"

"Mmm?"

"What're you reading there? Read it out loud."

"What? Art, that's what!"

"So go on and read it."

Olenka pursed her lips. "He's just reading about women. Wants an adventure."

"Fat chance you'll understand. Well, why not ... Here goes: 'Liudmila wrapped her shivering body in the fluffy shawl, covering her thin, shaking shoulders. Her blushing cheeks blazed brightly with a crimson fire. Her starry eyes shot arrows of alarm at Vladimir. Under her silk blouse, her high breasts rose and fell like the ocean waves. "Vladimir," she whispered. "Vladimir ..." Vladimir gritted his teeth. Stern muscles bulged under his tanned skin. He turned away. Liudmila's delicate fingers played nervously with the fringe of her shawl. "Vladimir!" she cried, reaching out with her palms ...'"

Olenka frowned stubbornly. "And just how many hands does she have, that Liudmila?"

"Just the right number. Two!"

"Well, she's fiddling around like she's got six. Is that a Consequence or what?"

"Take a look at yourself!" said Benedikt angrily. "This is art."

Women—they're all the same. They'll go and spoil your whole dream. Just riles you. Benedikt turned some more pages. "'Liudmila rubbed her tired temples with delicate fingertips. "Never," she murmured, wringing her hands. A deathly pallor filled her face. She released herself from his embrace. "It's all over," muttered Vladimir. The stern line of his lips betrayed extreme emotion.'" Oh, jeez, it's true ... Liudmila has a Consequence ... Why didn't they say anything about this before? Benedikt turned the page. "To be continued ..." Damn! In the most interesting place. He felt the journal, turned it over, thumbed through the pages: maybe he'd find the next part at the end—it happens sometimes. But it wasn't there. He pushed back the stool to go have a look in the storeroom.

"Where are you going? What about the meat patties?"

Benedikt had arranged all the shelves in the storeroom a long time ago: you could see right away what was where. Father-in-law had Gogol right next to Chekhov—you could look for a hundred years and you'd never find it. Everything should have its own science, that is, its own system. So you don't have to fuss around here and there to no good end, instead you can just go and find what you need.

Number eight wasn't there. Well, maybe he made a mistake and put it in the wrong place . . . that happens . . . Here's *The Northern Herald,* here's *The Herald of Europe, Russian Wealth, The Urals, Lights of the Urals, Beekeeping* . . . no, not here . . . *Banner, Literary Bashkortostan, New World* . . . he'd read them, Turgenev, he'd read it, Yakub Kolas, read it, Mikhalkov, *A Partisan's Handbook,* Petrarch, *The Plague, The Plague of Domestic Animals: Fleas and Ticks,* Popescu, *Popka-the-Fool—Paint It Yourself,* Popov, another Popov, Poptsov, *The Iliad, Electric Current,* he'd read it, *Gone With the Wind, Russo-Japanese Polytechnical Dictionary,* Sartakov, Sartre, *Sholokhov: Humanistic Aspects,* Sophocles, *Sorting Consumer Refuse, Sovmorflot—60 Years,* Stockard, *Manufacture of Stockings and Socks,* he'd read that one, that one and that one . . .

Chalk Farm, Chandrabkhangneshapkhandra Lal, vol. 18, Chaucer, John Cheever; *The Black Prince,* aha, a mistake, that didn't go there, Chekhov, Chapchakhov, *Chakhokhbili in Karsian, Chukh-Chukh: For Little People.*

Chen-Chen: Tales of the Congo, Cherokee Customs, Chewing Gum Stories, Chingachguk the Giant Serpent, Chipmunks and Other Friendly Rodents, Chkalov, *Chrysanthemums of Armenia Part V, Chukotka: A Demographic Review,* Chukovsky, *Chum—Dwelling of the Peoples of the Far North, Churchill: The Early Years,* read it. Kafka, *Kama River Steamboats, Kashas Derived from Whole Grain. Dial M for Murder, Murder in Mesopotamia, Murder on the Orient Express, Kirov's Murder, Laudanum: The Poetic Experience, Lilliputians and Other Little People,* Limonov, Lipchitz, *Lipid-protein Tissue Metabolism* . . . he'd read it all.

The Red and the Black, Baa Baa Black Sheep, The Blue and the Green, The Adventure of the Blue Carbuncle, The Blue Cup, Island of the Blue Dolphins, The Chocolate Prince, The Crimson Flower . . . that's a good one . . . *The Crimson Letter, Crimson Sails, Little Red Riding Hood, The Yellow Arrow, The Five Or-*

ange Pips, The White Steamboat, White Clothes, White Bim—
Black Ear, T. H. White, *The Woman in White, The Purple Island,*
The Black Tower, Black Sea Steamboats: Registry, this is where
The Black Prince goes. Now . . .

Appleton, Bacon, Belcher, Blinman, Cooke, Culpepper,
Honeyman, Hungerford, Liverich, Pearson, Saulter . . . Baldwin,
Beardsley, Hatcliff, Morehead, Skinner, Topsfield, White-
head, Whisker . . . Bairnsfather, Childe, Fairbrother, Mother-
well, Littleboy . . . Ambler, Bulstrode, Chatterley, Doddleton,
Dolittle, Fleetwood, Gabbler, Golightly, Hopkins, Sitwell, Skip-
with, Standon, Swift, Talkien, Walker, Whistler . . . Hammer-
stein, Hornebolt, Ironquill, Newbolt, Witherspoon . . . Canby,
Mabie, Moody, Orwell, Whowood . . . Bathurst, Beerbohm,
Beveridge, Brine, Dampier-Whetham, de La Fontaine, Dewey,
Drinkwater, Dryden, Lapping, Shipwash, Washburn, Water-
house . . . Addicock, Cockburn, Crapsey, Dickens, Dickinson,
Fullalove, Gotobed, Hooker, Longfellow, Lovelace, Loveridge,
Middlesex, Sexton, Simpkiss, Sinkin, Strangewayes, Sweetecok,
Toplady . . . Fairweather, Flood, Fogg, Frost, Haleston, Rain-
borough, Snowdon, Sun Yat-sen, Weatherby, Wyndham . . .
Middleton, Overbury, Underhill . . . Coffin, Dyer, Feversham,
Lockjaw, Paine, Rawbone . . .

The Vampire's Embrace, The Dragon's Embrace, The For-
eigner's Embrace, The Fatal Embrace, Passion's Embrace, Fiery
Embraces, The All-Consuming Flame of Passion . . . The Dag-
ger's Blow, The Poisoned Dagger, The Poisoned Hat, Poisoned
Clothes, With Dagger and Poison, Poisonous Mushrooms of
Central Russia, Golden-haired Poisoners, Arsenic and Old
Lace, Death of a Salesman, Death Comes for the Archbishop,
Death Comes at Midnight, Death Comes at Dawn, The Bloody
Dawn . . .

Children of the Arbat, Vanya's Children, Children of the Un-
derground, Children of the Soviet Land, Kids in Cages, Children
on Christ, The Boxcar Children, Nikita's Childhood.

Marinina, *Marinating and Pickling, Marine Artists, Marinetti*
—the Ideologist of Fascism, Mari-El Grammar: Uses of the In-
strumental Case.

Klim Voroshilov, Klim Samgin, Ivan Klima, K. Li, *Maximal*

Load in Concrete Construction: Calculations and Tables (dissertation).

Anaïs Nin, Nina Sadur, *Nineveh: An Archeological Collection. Ninja in a Bloody Coat, Mutant Ninja Turtles Return,* Papanin, *Make Life from Whom?*

Eugenia Grandet, *Eugene Onegin,* Eugene Primakov, Eugene Gutsalo, *Eugenics: A Racist's Weapon, Eugene Sue.*

Hamlet, Prince of Denmark, Tashkent—City of Bread, Bread —A Common Noun, Urengoi—The Land of Youth, Uruguay— An Ancient Land, Kustanai—The Steppe Country, Scabies—An Illness of Dirty Hands.

Foot Hygiene on the Road, F. Leghold, *Ardent Revolutionaries, The Barefoot Doctors, Flat Feet in Young Children, Claws: New Types, Shoe Polish Manufacture, Grow Up, Friend: What a Young Man Needs to Know about Wet Dreams, Hands Comrade!, Sewing Trousers, The Time of the Quadrupeds, Step Faster!, How the Millipede Made Porridge, Marinating Vegetables at Home,* Faulkner, *Fiji: Class Struggle, Fyodor's Woe,* Shakh-Reza-Pahlevi, Shakespeare, Shukshin.

Mumu, Nana, Shu-shu: Tales of Lenin, Gagarin: We Remember Yura, Tartar Women's Costumes, Bubulina—A Popular Greek Heroine, Boborykin, Babaevsky, Chichibabin, Bibigon, Gogol, *Dadaists Exhibition Catalogue,* Kokoschka, *Mimicry in Fish, Vivisection,* Tiutiunnik, Chavchavadze, *Lake Titicaca, Popocatepetl, Raising Chihuahuas, The Adventures of Tin Tin.*

Afraid of guessing, Benedikt went through the treasures with shaking hands; he was no longer thinking about issue number eight. It's not here, I'll live. But book after book, journal after journal—he'd already seen this, read this, this, this, this, this . . . So what did this mean? Had he already read everything? Now what was he going to read? And tomorrow? A year from now?

His mouth went dry and his legs felt weak. He lifted the candle high; its bluish light parted the darkness and danced on the shelves along the books' covers . . . maybe, up on the top . . .

Plato, Plotinus, Platonov, *Plaiting and Knitting Jackets,* Herman Plisetsky, Maya Plisetskaya, *Plevna: A Guide, Playing with Death, Plaints and Songs of the Southern Slavs, Playboy. Plinths:*

A Guidebook, Planetary Thinking, Plan for Popular Development in the Fifth Five-year Plan. Plebeians of Ancient Rome. Plenary Sessions of the CPSU, The Horn of Plenty in Oil Painting, Pleurisy. Pliushka, Khriapa, and Their Merry Friends. Plying the Arctic Waters. The Pilgrims at Plymouth Rock. He'd read them all.

That was it. "It's all over," muttered Vladimir. Nothing foretold this. Benedikt stood there, dripping candle oil on the floor, trying to take in the full horror of what he'd just realized. A guy is feasting at a rich banquet, wearing a crown of roses, laughing, carefree, his whole life lies ahead: he doesn't have a worry in the world and everything's bright; he takes a bite of sweet roll in play, reaches out for another—and all of a sudden he sees that the table is empty, cleared, there are no leftovers and the room is dead: no friends, no beauties, no flowers, no candles, no cymbals, no dancers, no rusht, maybe even the table itself is gone, there's only dry straw ... slowly drifting from the ceiling ... rustling and drifting ...

Slowly, slowly he returned to the dining room and sat down; they talked and grumbled, served him food ... Patties ... On his plate—a meat pattie. It lay there. A pattie ... There's a meat pattie on Benedikt's plate. He looked and looked ... the pattie lay there. He couldn't understand ... what should he think ... about the meat pattie?

"Eat! Eat, while it's still warm! Do you want some sauce?"

They're saying words; who's talking? He looked and saw a huge woman, a female. A big head, a little nose in the center. On either side of the nose, cheeks—red, rubbed with beets. Two dark, worried eyes that looked as though they were full of autumn water; just like when you step on moss in the woods and leave a footprint—brown water fills it up right away. Black eyebrows arching over the eyes. A stone hung between the eyebrows, clear, bluish from the candlelight. On either side of the eyebrows—the temples, with woven, colorful temple rings, and above the eyebrows no forehead, only golden hair, all twirled and plaited, and above the hair a headdress. Small stones set in the headdress like stars, a blizzard of ribbons and beaded threads falling like rain—they hang, jangle, reach all the way to the chin. Under the chin, under its dimple—right away there's the torso, wide as a sleigh, and on the torso—three-story tits. Wow! Unbelievably, horribly beautiful: could this really be Olenka? The Queen of Sheba.

"Olenka!" said Benedikt in amazement. "Is that really you? How beautiful you've become! When did this happen? My forest rose! My Siren!"

"Control yourself," said Olenka, heaving and jiggling. But her eyes didn't leave him for a moment.

Benedikt didn't try to control himself, and Olenka was just saying that out of habit, just for appearances, as they say. For three days running, or maybe it was four, or five, or perhaps six . . . why beat around the bush—for an entire week Benedikt and Olenka frolicked and capered every which way as if in some sort of daze—and, well, you couldn't keep track of what they did. Seeing what was going on, Mother-in-law rolled a barrel of egg kvas out of the granary, strong stuff, take a gulp—you gasp— and tears spring to your eyes; it's good kvas. They romped and rollicked royally—got up to all sorts of antics, and played leapfrog. They ran around on all fours, Olenka in her birthday suit. Benedikt had a sudden hankering to wear Olenka's headdress and rattle her beads, and where his tail used to be he tied her bobbins on so there'd be more of a clatter—you tie on a string, thread the bobbins on it and it makes a regular racket—my oh my, like a thunderstorm at the beginning of May. Then he'd start bleating like a goat.

But after a while—how to put it? There was a pause. A kind of grimness set in.

Щ · SHCHA

"IN THE CITY of Delhi there lived a wealthy water-bearer. His name was Kandarpaketu . . ." Already read it.

What to do now? What to live for? Once again, he had a feeling of alarm, as if he'd lost himself, but where and when—he hadn't noticed. It was frightening . . . Just recently he'd thought: I'm a rich man. But then he caught himself—all his wealth was now behind him, it had leaked out like water. Ahead lay a great drought, a desert. In the city of Delhi there lived a wealthy water-bearer . . .

He looked around. Silence. No mice scurrying. Quiet. Then sounds began to come through: the regular click-clack of a knife. Someone was chopping meat for dumplings; over there he heard a smooth, womblike sound—someone was rolling dough. Outside the window nature fussed and complained. It droned and squeaked; it would suddenly send the wind wailing, blizzarding, hurling snow at the windows; then it began to drone again; it droned and droned, on and on in the tops of trees, rocking the nests, tossing the tree crests. Dense, heavy snows surrounded the terem, swept over the three fences, through the sty and the warehouses, everything was engulfed in a swift, nocturnal burst of snow. There's no heart in it, in the snow, and if there is, it's mean, blind. The snow billows like great sleeves, sweeps up to the roof, throws itself across the fences, courses through the settlement, along the lanes, through the plaited fences, the thin roofs, to the outskirts, across the fields, to the impenetrable woods. Trees fall there, dead and white, like human bones; the northern juniper bush spreads its needles to prick pedestrians and sleigh riders. The paths wind like nooses and grab you by the legs, swaddling you in snow; branches knock your hat off; prickly vines have hung themselves up to rip at your collar. The snow will pound your back, ensnare you, knock you down, string you up on a branch; you'll jerk and struggle. But the Slynx has already sensed you, the Slynx knows you're there . . .

Benedikt flinched, shook his head to get rid of the thoughts, squeezed his eyes shut, plugged his ears with his fingers and bit his tongue to chase the Slynx from his thoughts, chase it, get rid of it! Its body is long and supple, its head flat and its ears flattened back . . . Shoo! The Slynx is pale, muscular, colorless — like the twilight or like a fish, or like the skin on Kitty's stomach, between the legs . . . No, no! . . . No!!!

Its claws itch, it's itching to . . . But you can't see it, you can't see it . . . He began to beat his head against the wall so stars would glitter in his eyes, so that some sort of light would break the darkness. Eyes are tricky, though: you squeeze them shut tight, yet something creeps into the reddish gloom under your eyelids, flashes across it: from left to right little hairs flit by or there's a shimmering you can't get rid of, or some uninvited object will run out and seem to laugh at you and then, poof! — it melts. He squeezed his eyes and opened them again: red and yellow rings whirled, his head spun, and there it was, he could see it with eyes wide open. It champed and grimaced.

He began stomping his feet: boom, boom, boom! He waved his arms about, and then grabbed his hair and pulled! Again! *Heyyyy!!* he cried. *Heeeeyyyyy!* In the city of Delhi there lived a wealthy water-bearer, and his name was Kandarpaketu!!! There lived a wealthy water-bearer, lived a wealthy water-bearer! Lived — lived, lived — lived, lived a wealthy water-bearer! With a hi and ho and a derry down-o! Through the town of Ramsey . . . And a twee dum fiddle dee dee! A wealthy water-bearer, don't you know, a rich and wealthy water-bearer!

He felt like slugging someone to dispel the fear and rage; maybe he should go and wallop Olga — here's for your bobbins! Or run and kick Mother-in-law in the ass; let her wibble-wobble for a couple of hours . . .

He ran down the stairs recklessly, knocked over a flowerpot, ran into his father-in-law, and shouted:

"There's no more books! Let's go, dammit!"

"Let's go!!!" replied Father-in-law like an echo. His eyes

blazed, he stomped and thrust a double-edged hook—who knows from where—into Benedikt's hand. He threw open the door of the closet and tossed a robe to Benedikt; it blinded Benedikt for a moment, but the slits settled right over his eyes. He could see everything through this crevice, all human affairs, trivial, cowardly, fussy: all people want is a bit of soup and to bed, but the wind howls, the snowstorm shrieks, and the Slynx is in flight; it soars, triumphant, over the city. "Art is in danger!" shouted Father-in-law as the sleigh swerved and screeched at the bend in the road. Our robes gleam with red light in the blizzard wail—watch out!—the storm's red cavalry flies across the city, and two pillars of light, a bright force, shine from Father-in-law's eyes, illuminating the path: our hope, protection, force—the Slynx withdraws, we won't surrender, we are legion!—forward, Saniturions, else art will perish! The white pancakes of frightened faces appear in the open door of an izba—"Ha, ha, so scared you're pissing in your pants, are you? The book! Give us the book!" The Golubchik squeals, shields it with his elbow, braces his foot, the shadows romp. "Hold him!!! He's stuffing it in the stove!!! Aha, you want to burn art, do you? Get him with the hook, the hook. Turn it!" comes Father-in-law's savage cry, or someone else's, you can't tell under the robes. "Turn the hook, for crying out loud." He turned it, yanked, something burst and streamed out, there were shouts and cries, he grabbed the book, pressed it to his heart, trembling—I'm alive! He pushed something away with his foot and leapt out into the blizzard.

. . . Benedikt lay in bed and sobbed. The tears flowed and flowed. Mother-in-law changed the pillows, Father-in-law ordered the women to walk on tiptoe, speak in whispers, and not worry the patient with troubling questions. He himself sat on the edge of Benedikt's bed, gave him warm drinks, hung right over him, shaking his head, sympathizing, consoling him.

"Now, how did that happen, tell me? How come you were so clumsy? . . . I told you to turn the hook carefully, gently . . . From the shoulder, the shoulder . . . And you go and: whack! That's what did it."

Benedikt choked on his tears. He wailed softly, delicately, his weakened fingers trembled; he could feel the cold and the slippery turn of the hook although he no longer held any hook, only a mug with compote.

It didn't happen—and yet it had happened. His arm could still feel the crunch up to the elbow, the way you squash a beetle: instead of just grabbing the book, jerking it, tearing it away, he caught the Golubchik right on the neck, on the vein, and since he whirled the hook with unpracticed fingers, the vein snapped and something streamed out, something black. The head flopped to one side, the eyes dimmed, and vomit gushed from the mouth.

Benedikt had never killed anyone, that is, Golubchiks, and it had never even occurred to him. He might hit someone or knock him around, but that was different, just ordinary, everyday stuff. You get him, he gets you, and you're quits. A bruise here, a sprain there—the usual. And before hitting a Golubchik you have to get yourself worked up against him, store up a gloomy weight in your heart. The bruises or sprains balance out this gloominess like weights on scales: goods on one side, weights on the other. Then you belt him one—and it's justified.

But he'd never even met this Golubchik, the one he crushed. He'd never even seen him, wasn't worked up against him, didn't have a grudge against him—he was living and let him go on living, planting turnips, talking to his woman, bouncing his little kids on his knee.

Benedikt just wanted to take the book away. Because society is backward, the people live in the darkness of ignorance, they're superstitious, they keep books under the bed, or even bury them in damp holes. You can destroy a book this way. It rots, falls apart, gets covered in green mildew, gets worm holes. Books have to be protected, they belong in a dry, bright place, they have to be cherished and cradled, preserved and kissed. No one else will bother, there's no one else to take care of them, the ancient people who wrote these books have turned to dust, they've died out, not a shadow remains. They won't return, they'll never come back! They don't exist anymore!

But our ignorant Golubchiks—just look at them—they won't admit to themselves or others that they've hidden books. Books are rotting, being lost forever, and they'll never admit they've hidden one. They're backward and afraid of Illness, and Illness has nothing to do with it. Benedikt has read a thousand books and he's just fine.

But he hadn't gotten mad at that Golubchik, it was all the fault of the water-bearer from Delhi, whose name was Kandarpaketu, it was all his father-in-law's fault—he handed him the hook at the wrong time, when his heart was blinded, when the snow raged, and that distant wail deprived him of reason! . . . Look, just look what it does with people: flushes the reason clear out of them, flies through the storm, hungry, pale, and you can't hear yourself think. You see rings of stars in your eyes, and your hand turns the wrong way. Crunch!—and everything flows out.

. . . But he saved the book. The book! My precious treasure! Life, the road, the sea's expanses, fanned by the wind, the golden cloud, the blue wave! The gloom parts, you can see far away, the wide open spaces unfold, and those spaces hold bright forests with sun filtering through them and glades splattered with tulips. The spring wind Zephyr rocks the branches, waves like white lace, and the lace turns, spreads open like a fan, and in it, as in a decorated cup, is the white Princess Bird, with her red, innocent mouth. The Princess Bird doesn't eat or drink, it lives only by air and kisses, never harms anyone, and never brings sorrow. And when the Princess Bird smiles with her tulip mouth, she raises her bright eyes to the heights—she always thinks luminous thoughts about herself; she lowers her eyes and admires herself. When she sees Benedikt, she'll say: Come here, Benedikt, it's always spring here with me, I always have love . . .

"My dear sweet boy . . . you've got a heart of gold . . ." His father-in-law lamented, "I taught you, didn't I, I taught you . . . Ay, my boy . . . Turn it, I said, the hook, turn it . . . Didn't I tell you? I told you! And you? . . . What have you gone and done?"

Father-in-law shook his head. He sat, dejected, leaning on his hand. He gazed reproachfully at Benedikt.

"In a hurry, were you? Well, you went too fast . . . you didn't protect life . . . Now he'll never be treated! I mean, how could we treat him now? Huh?" Father-in-law leaned over, shined his light into Benedikt's eyes, and his foul breath enveloped Benedikt.

"It was an accident!" Benedikt whined through his tears. The words came out in a squeak. "It scared me!"

"Who scared you?"

"The Slynx! . . . It scared me! And I missed!"

"Get out of here, women," said Father-in-law. "My son-in-law is upset, don't you see? What bad luck he's had. He'll survive. Don't get underfoot. Give him some more compote. Bring some soft white patties."

"I don't want any, noooo!"

"You must. You have to eat. Some broth too. Listen to your heart . . . it's beating so hard . . ." Father-in-law touched Benedikt's heart, feeling it with hard fingers.

"Don't touch me! Leave me alone!"

"What do you mean, leave you alone? I'm a medical worker. Am I supposed to know your condition? I am. Just look: you're shaking all over. Come on, now. Come on, like that. Eat up! Take some more."

"The book . . ."

"The one we confiscated? . . . Don't worry. I've got it."

"Give it . . ."

"You can't have it! Not now! What are you thinking of? Just lie down. You're very upset. How could you read yourself? I'll read it to you aloud. It's a good book . . . A book of the highest quality, my dear . . ."

Benedikt lay there wrapped in blankets, swallowing broth and tears, while Father-in-law, lighting the pages with his eyes, running his fingers under the lines, read in a thick, important voice:

> Hickory, dickory, six and seven,
> Alabone, Crackabone, ten and eleven,
> Spin, spun, muskidun,
> Twiddle 'em, twaddle 'em, twenty-one . . .
>
> A duck and a drake,
> And a half-penny cake,

With a penny to pay the old baker.
A hop and a scotch
Is another notch,
Slitherum, slatherum, take her.

Ц . TSI

THEY TOOK ONE from Theofilactus, one from Boris, two from Eulalia. Klementy, Lavrenty, Osip, Zuzya, and Revolt were all a waste of time, they didn't find anything, just bits and pieces. Maliuta had three books buried in the barn, all covered with black spots so you couldn't make out a word. Vandalism pure and simple . . . Roach Efimich—who would have thought?— had a whole trunkful right out in the open, two dozen books, dry and clean. Only there wasn't one word in our language, all the letters were strange: hooks and bent nails. Ulyana only had ones with pictures. Methuselah and Churilo—the twins who lived behind the river and loaned mice for a living—had one tiny torn book. Akhmetka managed to burn his: they scared him . . . Zoya Gurevna burned hers. Avenir, Maccabe, Nelly the Harelip, Ulcer, Riurik, Ivan Pricklin, Sysoy had nothing. January used to have one, but he didn't know where it was, though his pantry walls were all hung with pictures, and there were indecent women on the pictures.

Gloom and doom.

"There's so much nastiness among the people," Father-in-law said, "just think. I mean, at one time they were told: Don't keep books at home! Were they told? Yes, they were. But no, they keep holding on to them. Everyone wants things their own way. The books rot, they get them dirty, they bury them in the front garden. Can you imagine?"

"Yes, yes."

"They poke holes in them, tear out pages, roll them up like cigars . . ."

"That's horrible, I can't even listen!"

"They use them as tops on soup pots . . ."

"Don't make me sick! I can't stand it!"

"Or they stick them in a dormer window and when it rains, the pages slip and you end up with mush . . . Or they use them in the stove—what do you get? Smoke, soot, and then poof—it burns up . . . There are people who don't want to waste firewood, and they just heat the stove with books . . ."

"Stop, please, I can't stand it!"

"And then—do you hear me, son?—there are people who tear out the pages and use them in the privy, hang them on a nail for nature's calls . . . And we know what that means . . ."

Benedikt couldn't take any more. He jumped up from the stool. Running his hands through his hair, he paced the room: there was a tight knot in his heart, his soul was dazed and dizzy as though he were on a steep incline, as though the floor under his feet were tilting like in a dream and any minute now everything would roll off it into a bottomless pit, into a well, who knows where. Here we are sitting around, or lying on the bed in a warm terem, everything is clean and civilized, you can smell bliny cooking in the kitchen, our women are decent, they're white, rosy, steamed in the bath; all decked out with beads, headdresses, sarafans, first, second, and third petticoats with ribbons, and they also thought up wearing shawls that swish, with clean, lacy, patterned feathers. But down there in town are Golubchiks in unswept izbas, living in constant soot and filth, with black and blue faces, dimwitted gazes, they grab books without wiping their hands; they crack the spines, tear out pages crosswise and top to bottom; they tear off the legs of steeds, the heads of beauties. They crumple the Ocean-Sea's wine-dark waves and chuck them into the greedy fire; they roll white roads into cigars and squeeze them: blue-gray smoke winds around the paths, the flowering bushes crackle and go up in flames. Cut down at the root, the lilac tree falls with a moan, the golden birch topples and the tulip is trampled, the secret glade is soiled. With a fierce cry, her mouth torn, Princess Bird tumbles from her branch, her legs upside down, her head smashed against a stone!

What's burned can't be returned, what's dead can't be fed. And what would you take out of a burning house? . . . Me? You don't know? And you call yourself a Stoker! You asked the riddle, what you call a dilemma. If you had to choose, what would you take: a pussy cat or a painting? a Golubchik or a book? Questions! And he worried about it, wallowed in doubt, shook his head, twisted his beard! . . . "I can't decide, I've been thinking about it for three hundred years . . ." Really now, a pussy! A cat, to be scientific, his job is to hunt, to fly like spit on the wind, stay out from underfoot, to know his business—catching mice! Pussy cat pussy cat what did you there? And not paintings! Golubchiks? Golubchiks are ashes, entrails, dung, stove smoke, clay, and they'll all return to clay. They're full of dirt, candle oil, droppings, dust.

You, O Book, my pure, shining precious, my golden singing promise, my dream, a distant call—

> O tender specter, happy chance,
> Again I heed the ancient lore,
> Again with beauty rare in stance,
> You beckon from the distant shore!

You, Book! You are the only one who won't deceive, won't attack, won't insult, won't abandon! You're quiet—but you laugh, shout, and sing; you're obedient—but you amaze, tease, and entice; you're small, but you contain countless peoples. Nothing but a handful of letters, that's all, but if you feel like it, you can turn heads, confuse, spin, cloud, make tears spring to the eyes, take away the breath, the entire soul will stir in the wind like a canvas, will rise in waves and flap its wings! Sometimes a kind of wordless feeling tosses and turns in the chest, pounds its fists on the door, the walls: I'm suffocating! Let me out! How can you let that feeling out, all fuzzy and naked? What words can you dress it in? We don't have any words, we don't know! Just like wild animals, or a blindlie bird, or a mermaid— no words, just a bellowing. But you open a book—and there they are, fabulous, flying words:

O city! O wind! O snowstorms and blizzards!
O azure abyss all raveled and tattered!
Here am I! I'm blameless! I'm with you forever . . .

. . . Or there's bile and sadness and bitterness. The emptiness
dries your eyes out and you search for the words, and here they
are:

But is the world not all alike?
From the Cabbala of Chaldaic signs
Throughout the ages, now and ever more,
To the sky where the even star shines.

The same old wisdom — born of ashes,
And in that wisdom, like our twin,
The face of longing, frailty, fear, and sin,
Stares straight across the ages at us.

Benedikt ran out onto the gallery, looked at the settlement
from the heights, at the city, its hills and valleys, the paths worn
between the fences, the snow-covered streets. Snow blew and
swirled all around, it slid with a swish from the roof beyond the
gates. He stood there, his neck craned, turning his head this
way and that, staring hard, blinking away the frost: Who was
hiding them? Who had them wrapped in a cloth on the stove, in
a box under the bed, in an earthen pit, in a birch chest — who? If
only he knew! There are books out there! I know there are, I
can sense them, I can smell them: they're there! Only where?
Squinting, he gazed into the blind gloom: it was twilight, lights
were coming on in the izbas; little people below were hurrying,
running, rushing to the stove warmth, to their benches, to their
soup, their thin mouse stew . . . How do they eat that slop, isn't it
disgusting? . . . A murky water . . . like when you wash your feet,
the same color . . . Bits of flesh settle on the bottom, spiced salty
worrums. The people's anchovies . . . That was what Nikita Ivanich called worrums . . . Was the old man still alive? It would be
good to see him . . . Maybe he has a book? Maybe he'd let him
read it? And he wouldn't need to be treated, he'd hand it over
himself . . . If I had my way — I'd turn the whole city upside
down. Hand over those books, right now! But Father-in-law

won't allow it, he holds back, all in good measure, son, if we take them all off for treatment—who's going to work? Who'll clear the roads, plant the turnips, weave the baskets? That's not the governmental approach: all in a rush. In one fell swoop! Right away! Really, now! You'd only scare people, they'd run off! You caught mice? You know the science? Well, there you go! . . .

It's true, he used to catch mice. He'd feed them first. That's right. He was even rich for a whole hour. And then? It all disappeared, like it was never there! All that was left of his riches was some sweet rolls—and they were burnt!

He needed to stretch his legs. He went into the stalls. No culture . . . A heavy animal smell. The goats are bleating. Teterya and his pals, as always, are playing cards: "Here's a jack for you!"

"We'll play a ten."

"Are you nuts?"

"It's trump!"

"So what if it's trump?? The ten takes it. He dropped a ten! He's cheating, guys!"

As always—they haven't mucked out the stables or anything.

"Teterya! Over here. Bridle up."

"Wait a minute, we're not finished."

"What do you mean, wait? You've had enough rest."

"So, no . . . then . . . A dame, and another dame! There you go!"

"Teterya!"

"I'm between shifts. You'll take it? Here's a jack for change."

"Teterya!!!" Benedikt shouted, stamping his foot.

"Now, now, there he goes, shouting up a storm. The sleigh runners are bent."

"Don't lie! It's always the same old thing! Get your boots on, I'm going for a ride. You've got five minutes to tack up! . . ."

Benedikt walked along the cages. Here were the sparrows. A small bird, like a mouse, but tasty. Only it has a lot of bones. There were nightingales in this cage. They ate them, need to catch some new ones. In springtime. Right now they're all hiding. Here—what's this? Here's the woodsucker.

"Woodsucker!" Benedikt called. "Come out!"

It didn't come out.

"Come out of there, you bitch!"

It didn't want to. Terenty pulled up, smirking. "Shout louder."

He shouted louder.

"Even louder."

"Woodsuuuuuuccker!!"

It won't come, what's going on!

"Shout like your guts are gonna split. She'll come out. From the gut."

Benedikt looked at him doubtfully: the pig is laughing, happy: "Ha ha! You ate it already!"

"Did we? Then what the hell are you . . ."

Idiotic jokes . . . You could ruin your voice in a frost like this. Benedikt checked out the cage. All the weaker birds were in the hollow. The blindlie had hidden his head under his wing. The shitbirds had flocked together and were warming each other. They were suffering! There you go! That'll teach you to shit on people's heads! What a trashy bird! And its meat is rubbish — stringy, tough, they only feed it to Degenerators, but people don't eat it. And it doesn't want to live in the forest, only in town.

In the farthest cage, where the bare tree and branch stood, you couldn't see anyone. Who knows who lived there. Whatever it was, it was in the hollow. Or maybe there wasn't anyone: the cage was clean, no droppings, no feathers. Maybe they ate it already.

Jeez, they ate the woodsucker. And he hadn't even noticed, he was so busy reading. He never got a good look at it. Who knows when they'd catch another one. They don't just come and fly into your hand, woodsuckers.

"Let's go," Teterya hurried him. "I'm freezing."

"Don't give me orders, you pig. If you have to—you'll freeze!"

He kicked the louse in his side, sat down in the sleigh, and covered himself with a bear skin. "Off with you! At a gallop—and I want songs!"

Ч · CHERV

... NIKITA IVANICH and another Oldener, Lev Lvovich of the Dissidents, were sitting at the table drinking rusht. They'd been drinking awhile and were feeling fine: their faces were red, and they were mumbling a lot of nonsense.

Benedikt took off his hat. "And a good day to you."

"Benya? Benya! Is it really you?" Nikita Ivanich was pleased. "It's been so long! How long has it been? A year, two? ... Extraordinary ... Do you know each other? Benedikt Karpov, our sculptor, the people's Opekushin."

Lev Lvovich looked at him skeptically, as though he didn't recognize him, as if he hadn't helped to carry the pushkin himself. He made a face. "Kudeyarov's son-in-law?"

"That's right."

"I heard about it, I heard about your mesalliance."

"Thank you," said Benedikt, feeling touched. So they had heard about his marriage.

He sat down and the Oldeners moved over. It was crowded, of course. The izba seemed smaller than the last time he'd been there. The candle smoked and dripped, shadows danced. The walls were black with soot. Poverty showed on the table too: a jug, a couple of mugs, a plate of peas. They poured some rusht for Benedikt.

"So what are you up to? How are you? Just think ... Here we were, sitting, drinking ... talking about life ... about the past ... That is, we were talking about the future too, of course ... About our Pushkin ... How we sculpted him, hey? How we erected him! What an event! A milestone! The resuscitation of the saints! An historical landmark! Now he's with us again. And Pushkin, you know, Benya, Pushkin is our be all and end all! He's everything to us. You just think about it, remember, and assimilate it ... But what a pity ... can you imagine? He already requires restoration ..."

"What does he require?" asked Benedikt, standing up.

"Fixing, Benya, he needs fixing! The rain, the snow, the birds . . . they've all taken their toll. If he were only made of stone! I won't even mention bronze, we're nowhere near having bronze. And then there's the people—people are utter savages: they tie a rope around him, and hang their laundry on freedom's bard! Underwear and pillowcases—barbarians!"

"But Nikita Ivanich, you were the one who always said the people's path to him should never be overgrown. And now you're complaining."

"Oh, Lord . . . Benya . . . That was a figure of speech."

"All right, we can put that figure wherever you want. I'll send some serfs. We could use the sleigh too."

"O Lord in Heaven, help us."

"We need a Xerox," said Lev Lvovich gloomily.

"It was only about a hundred years ago that you said we needed a fax. That the West would come to our aid," replied Nikita Ivanich.

"That's right, but the irony is that—"

"The irony is that there isn't any West."

"What do you mean there isn't any West!" snapped Lev Lvovich. "There's always a West."

"But we don't know anything about it."

"No, no, no. Excuse me! You and I know. It's just that they don't know anything about us."

"And that's news to you?"

Lev Lvovich became even more gloomy and scraped at the table. "Right now the most important thing is a Xerox."

"But why, tell me why?!"

"Because it was said: be fruitful and multiply!" Lev Lvovich raised a long finger. "Multiply!"

"Well then, just how do you envision this?" Nikita Ivanich asked. "Let's just suppose, for the sake of argument, that you have your fax and your Xerox. Under current conditions. Let's just suppose. Although it's highly unlikely. What would you do with them? How to you intend to fight for freedom with a fax? Go on, tell me."

"My pleasure. It's quite simple. I take an album of Dürer's work. That's just an example. Black and white, but that doesn't matter. I make a copy. I multiply it. I fax it to the West. They receive it and say: 'Wait a minute, what's going on here! That's our national treasure.' They fax me back: 'Return our national treasure immediately!' And I say to them: Come and get it. Take charge. Then you've got international contacts, diplomatic negotiations, everything you could hope for. Coffee. Paved roads. Nikita Ivanich, remember shirts with cuff links? Conferences . . ."

"Confrontations."

"Humanitarian rice."

"Porno films . . ."

"Jeans."

"Terrorists."

"Of course. Complaints to the UN. Political hunger strikes. The International Court in The Hague."

"The Hague doesn't exist anymore."

Lev Lvovich shook his head so hard the candle flame flickered: "Don't upset me, Nikita Ivanich. Don't say such terrible things. That's just nationalistic claptrap."

"There is no Hague, Golubchik. There never was."

Lev Lvovich started crying drunken tears and banged his fist on the table. The peas jumped on the plate. "It's not true, I don't believe it! The West will come to our aid!"

"We have to do it ourselves, all on our own."

"This is not the first time I've noticed your nationalistic tendencies! You're a Slavophile!"

"You know, I'm really—"

"A Slavophile, a Slavophile! Don't deny it."

"I hope for a spiritual renaissance."

"Samizdat is what we need."

"But Lev Lvovich! We have lots of samizdat, it's flourishing. If I'm not mistaken, you yourself used to insist it was the most important thing. And just look—no spiritual life. So apparently it's not the main thing."

Benedikt coughed politely to interrupt. "My life is spiritual."

"In what sense?"

"I don't eat mice."

"Well, and what else?"

"Not a single bite ... Only birds. Meat. Pasties once in a while. Bliny. Marshrooms, of course. Nightingales dipped in batter, horsetail à la Savoy. Bullfinch stew. Fireling parfait à la Lyonnaise. Then—cheese and fruit. That's it."

The Oldeners' eyes bugged out and they stared at him silently.

"And cigars?" Lev Lvovich finally asked, grinning.

"We go into another room to smoke. Near the stove. Fevronia, my mother-in-law, doesn't let us smoke at the table."

"I remember Pigronia," remarked Lev Lvovich. "I remember her father. An imbecile. And her grandfather. Another imbecile. Her great-grandfather too."

"That's right," affirmed Benedikt. "She's from one of the oldest families, of French origin."

"They were fruitful and multiplied," giggled tipsy Nikita Ivanich. "There you go! Hmm? Lev Lvovich!"

"And there's your spiritual renaissance for you, Nikita Ivanich!"

They poured some more rusht.

"All right, then ... Here's to returning to sources, Lev Lvovich!"

"To our freedom!"

They drank. Benedikt drank too.

"Why is it," said Nikita Ivanich, "why is it that everything keeps mutating, everything? People, well, all right, but the language, concepts, meaning! Huh? Russia! Everything gets twisted up in knots."

"Not everything," argued Benedikt. "Now, if you eat cheese, then yes, your insides will mutiny, and your stomach'll get tied up in knots. But if you eat a pasty—it's all right ... Nikita Ivanich! ... I brought a present for you."

Benedikt fumbled inside his coat and pulled out the book with "Slitherum Slatherum" wrapped in a clean cloth. He really didn't want to give it up, but it wouldn't work without a sacrifice.

"Here. It's for you. A book."

Nikita Ivanich was taken aback. Lev Lvovich ruffled: "It's a provocation! . . . Careful, Nikita Ivanich!"

"It's a poem," explained Benedikt. "Everything about our life is all written down here in poems. You're arguing, next thing you'll start fighting—but why don't you read it instead. I learned it by heart." Benedikt looked up into a dark corner of the ceiling—it was always easier to remember things that way, when nothing distracted you. "Hickory dickory six and seven. Alabone, Crackabone—"

"That's enough," said Lev Lvovich.

"You like to read to yourself? I do too, with my eyes. When there's no one to bother me . . . I just pour myself a cup of compote—and read!"

"Where did you get it?" asked Nikita Ivanich.

Benedikt's face expressed a certain vagueness: he stuck his jaw out, screwed up his mouth, as if ready to kiss someone, raised his eyebrows as high as he could, looked over his shoulder, and flapped his hands around in different directions.

"I got it . . . well, I just got it. We have a big library at home."

They poured some more rusht. The Oldeners didn't look at Benedikt, and they didn't look at each other. They stared at the table.

"Special Reserves," said Lev Lvovich.

"A spiritual treasure trove," corrected Nikita Ivanich.

"But I've already read everything," said Benedikt. "I, well, I have a favor to ask. Maybe you have something to read, no? I'll be careful . . . no spots, nothing. I respect books."

"I don't have any books," replied Nikita Ivanich. "I truly don't. Would I lie?"

"I could give you mine, for a little while . . . Kind of like an exchange. If you'll be careful . . . Wrap them in something . . . a cloth or rags . . . I have good books, they don't have any Illness or anything . . ."

"Interlibrary with Leviathan. I wouldn't get involved."

"You're in a conspiratorial phase . . . Where are your democratic values?"

"We shouldn't cooperate with a totalitarian regime . . ."

Benedikt waited for the Oldeners to stop their gibberish. "What do you think, Nikita Ivanich?"

Nikita Ivanich waved his hands around like he hadn't heard the question. He poured some more mead. It went down smoothly . . .

"I have interesting books," Benedikt tempted them. "About women, and nature, and science too . . . they tell you all sorts of things . . . You were talking about freedom—well, I've got one about freedom too, about everything. It teaches how to make freedom. Should I bring it? Only you have to be careful."

"Really?" Lev Lvovich said with interest. "Whose book?"

"Mine."

"The author, who's the author?"

Benedikt thought.

"I can't remember right off. I think It starts with Pl."

"Plekhanov?"

"No . . ."

"It couldn't be Plevier?"

"No, no . . . Don't interrupt . . . Aha! It's *Plaiting and Knitting Jackets.* 'When knitting the armhole we cast on two extra loops for freedom of movement. We slip them on the right needle, taking care not to tighten them excessively.'"

"We've always known how to tighten things excessively around here . . ." said Lev Lvovich with a grin.

"So should I bring it? It's all right?" said Benedikt, rising.

"Don't bother, young man."

Benedikt had been sly: he himself didn't like *Plaiting* very much—it was a boring sort of essay; but he thought maybe it would do for Oldeners—who knows what they like? He himself liked *Embraces* better. Since he'd already gotten up, Benedikt pushed the door open to let in some of the blizzardy air—they'd smoked up the place something fierce. He wanted to keep an eye on Teterya: Had he gone and committed Freethinking, and crawled up into the sleigh? There was a bear skin there, and sometimes the stinking scum did that: he'd get up under the skin to get warm, and after that just try airing it out! Degenerators have a strong smell: dung, straw, unwashed feet. No, he hadn't crawled in, but what was he doing? He was standing on his legs. He'd taken the felt boots off his hands and was scratching swear words onto the pillar that said "Nikitsky Gates."

"Teterya!!!" Benedikt croaked. "You hairy rat! I see everything!"

He immediately darted back on all fours, as if he hadn't been doing anything, and raised his leg on the pillar as if to say, yeah? I'm just relieving myself, the way we do. I'm pissing.

"You pig . . ."

Nikita Ivanich looked out over Benedikt's shoulder. "Benya! Why don't you invite your comrade inside? Good Lord, he's outside and in such cold weather!"

"Comrade? Nikita Ivanich! That's a Degenerator! Don't tell me you haven't seen Degenerators before!"

Lev Lvovich hadn't taken a liking to Benedikt: he looked at him with disdain and kept his mouth squinched to one side. He also got up from the table, crowded behind the Stoker's back, and looked out. "Appalling exploitation . . ." he muttered.

"Call him, call him into the house! That's inhumane!"

"But he's not a human! Humans don't have felt boots on their hands!"

"You have to look at it more broadly! Even without him the people is incomplete!" Lev Lvovich instructed.

"We won't argue about definitions . . ." The old man wrapped a scarf around his neck . . . "Who are you and I . . . ? Bipeds without feathers, with articulate speech . . . Let me out, I'll go and invite him . . . What's his name?"

"He answers to Teterya."

"But I can't speak to an adult like that . . . What's his patronymic?"

"Petrovich . . . Don't be crazy, Nikita Ivanich, watch out, for God's sake!!! Invite a Degenerator into the izba? He'll muck the whole place up. Wait!"

"Terenty Petrovich," the Stoker said, leaning over into the snowdrift, "kindly come in to the izba! Come sit at the table and warm up!"

The deranged Oldeners unhitched the Degenerator, took off his shaft, and led him into the izba. Benedikt spat.

"Please, let me have your reins, I'll help. Hang them on the nail."

"They'll filch the bear skin! No one's watching the hide," screamed Benedikt and ran to the sleigh. Just in time: two Golubchiks had already wrapped the bear skin in a rug and thrown it on their shoulder. Everyone would have done the same — why not? Who leaves goods like that in the middle of the street without an owner nearby! Seeing Benedikt, they ran into a lane with the rug. He caught up with them, gave them a thrashing, and recovered the goods, huffing and puffing. Oohh, what thievery!

"... I came home, everything was quite civilized, the floors were covered with goddamn Polish varnish!" cursed a soused Teterya. "I took off my shoes, put on my slippers, and there was figure skating on the tube. Irina Rodnina! A double lux ... Maya Kristalinskaya was singing. She gets on your nerves, doesn't she?"

"I ..." objected Lev Lvovich.

"I, I, I, it's always I. 'I' is just a letter of the alphabet! Gone to seed under Kuzmich, Glorybe! He's let everyone go to pot, frigging dwarf! Reading books, all a bunch of smart alecs all of a sudden! Under Sergeich you wouldn't have done all that reading!"

"Excuse me, but I beg to differ!" Lev Lvovich and Nikita Ivanich broke in, interrupting each other. "Under Sergei Sergeich there was utter terror! He trampled the rights of the individual! ... There were arrests in broad daylight! Have you forgotten that more than three were forbidden to gather at one time? ... No singing or smoking on the streets! ... Curfew! ... And what happened if you were late to the recount? — And the uniforms ...."

"There was law and order under Sergeich! All the terems were built! All the fences! They never held up Warehouse packages! A basket for holidays, my ration was fifth category, and I got a postcard from the local committee! ..."

"You've got it all mixed up, all confused ... postcards were before the Blast! ... But just remember — a mere forty years ago private mouse-catching was forbidden!"

"...A co-op apartment in Skabl...in Sviblovo," said Teterya, tripping over his own tongue, "five minutes from the metro. A park zone, you got me? We weren't a bunch of rabinoviches living in the center!...They were right to put you all in jail!"

"I beg your pardon...we're talking about Sergei Sergeich!"

"...They stick a pair of glasses on and then they start thinking!...I won't let you weeds hit me with a wrench. Don't you shake your beard at meeee! Abraham! You're an abraham! The government gives you a quota and you're supposed to stay within it...Jeezus F....Christ...and not go wagging your butts in front of a bunch of foreigners..."

"But—"

"Gone and multiplied like rabbits, shit! Supposed to be two percent and not a cent more so you don't crush the working class!...Who ate all the meat? Epstein! Huh? Who bought up all the sugar...and we're supposed to make hooch from tomato paste, right? Isn't that right? You're a hitler! There's no Zhirinovsky for you guys anymore!"

"But—"

"Made your son a nice liddle blue shoot, suit, a hunnert percent wool! Then you made a deal to sell the Kuriles to Reagan! ...Not an inch will we yield!..."

"Terenty Petrovich!"

"I said not one inch!...We won't give up the Kuriles... And you can stick your pillars up your rear end! You parasites, tried to turn the country into a museum. Pour gasoline over you and—just one little match!...and your pppparliament, and your books, and your academic Ssssssakharov! And..."

"Now you've done it, you s.o.b.!" A crimson Lev Lvovich suddenly hauled back and punched him. "Don't you dare touch Andrei Dmitrich!!!"

There wasn't any Andrei Dmitrich in the izba; but that happens when you drink too much: your eyes see everything double, and strange figures and faces watch you from the corners. Then you blink—and they're gone.

"You bastard!" shouted the Head Stoker as well. "Get out of here!"

"Don't touuuuch me!" Teterya yelled, flailing his furry elbows. "Help! They're beating Ruuuussssssians!"

"You prison slime . . . Terrorist! Tie him up!"

They knocked over the table and the jug rolled away. Benedikt jumped in too, and helped them tie the drunken pig with the reins; they rolled him up, threw him outside in the snow, and kicked him for good measure.

"I had a chrome faucet in Sviblovo!" they could hear from the snowstorm. "And you can't even get it up, you queers! . . ."

If this one is quiet, what is Potap like?

Ш . SHA

> Bright thoughts ascend
> In my heart's battered torch
> And bright thoughts descend
> By a dark fire scorched.

"Under Sergei Sergeich there was law and order," said Benedikt.

"You said it," replied Father-in-law.

"No more than three people gathered at a time."

"No way."

"But now everybody's too smart for their britches, they read books, they've gone to seed. Fyodor Kuzmich, Glorybe, has let everything get out of hand."

"Words of gold!" Father-in-law exclaimed joyfully.

"Sergei Sergeich built fences, but what've we got nowadays?"

"A crying shame!"

"Holes everywhere, fences falling down, the people's path is overgrown with dill!"

"That's right!"

"A useless weed, no taste, no smell!"

"Not a smidgen."

"People hang underwear and pillowcases on the pushkin, and the pushkin—is our be all and end all!"

"Right down to his itty bitty toes!"

"He's the one who wrote the poems, not Fyodor Kuzmich!"

"Never a truer word spoken."

"He's higher than the Alexander column!"

"Oh, my dear, the column can't compare!"

"But Fyodor Kuzmich, Glorybe, is only knee high to a grasshopper! And he wants to be the Greatest Murza, Long May He Live. Sits right down on Olenka's lap and makes himself at home!"

"Yes, yes . . . tell me more . . ."

"What do you mean, 'yes and tell me more'?"

"Take the next step, think it through."

"Think what where?"

"What does your heart tell you?"

Benedikt's heart wasn't telling him anything. His heart was dark, dark as an izba in winter when all the candles have gone out and you live with your hands outstretched. There was an extra candle somewhere, but just try and find it now in the pitch dark.

You stumble and your hands fumble, they're blind, frightened: who knows what you might find or touch, not seeing what it is. Your soul will freeze: What's this? There's never been anything like this in the izba. What is it?

Your insides are like to pop with fear and you throw the thing away, whatever it was . . . You stand there, petrified, scared to breathe . . . Scared to take a step . . . You think: If I move, I'll step on *it* . . .

Carefully . . . sideways . . . along the edges . . . against the wall. One step, two steps . . . and you make it to the door. You yank the door open and run as fast as your legs will carry you!

You collapse under a tree or next to the fence; everything inside is pounding. Now you have to pull yourself together, ask someone for coals or maybe a candle. If they give you a candle it's easier, not so scary; you'll go back to the izba and take a look.

What was that thing? And there doesn't seem to be anything there.

Nothing at all.

Could be your neighbors were playing a trick on you, the jokesters: while you were out, they put who knows what there, to ruin your reason with fear; and while you were running back and forth, trying to get some fire, they go and fetch whatever it was they stuck there. So there's nothing there now, and you never know what it was.

His heart wasn't telling him anything. But his head—yes, his head was telling him something. That's why reason is up there in the head. His head told him that a long time ago, before his wedding—yikes, ages ago—when he was still a wild young man, an uneducated greenhorn with a tail and no sense, he saw a book at Varvara Lukinishna's place. He couldn't remember what book it was, big or little, or what it was called: the fear and the strangeness made it so he didn't understand anything at the time, he only understood that he was scared stiff.

Now, of course, as an educated man, sophisticated, you might say, he'd know how to appreciate such a treasure. He'd fondle it, turn it over, count the number of pages and see what the letters were like: big or small. Is it a quick read or not? Having read it, he'd know which shelf to put it on, with a kiss.

Now, refined and wiser, he knew that a book is a delicate friend, a white bird, an exquisite being, afraid of water.

Darling things! Afraid of water, of fire, They shiver in the wind. Clumsy, crude human fingers leave bruises on them that'll never fade! Never!

Some people touch books without washing their hands!

Some underline things in ink!

Some even tear pages out!

And he himself used to be so barbaric and clumsy, such a Cro-Magnon, that he rubbed a hole in a page with a spit-covered finger! "And the candle by which Anna read a life full of alarm and deceit . . ." Idiot. He'd rubbed a hole in it, Lord forgive him. It was the same as if you'd found the secret glade in the forest by some miracle—all covered in crimson tulips and golden trees—

and finally embraced the sweet Princess Bird, and while embracing her you'd gone and poked your dirty finger in her bright, self-admiring eye!

Varvara Lukinishna said that Nikita Ivanich gave her the book. So, he was caught out in a lie, the old man! You do have books, you old drunk, you hide them somewhere, bury them, won't let good people read them . . . They aren't in the izba, Benedikt knew that izba like the back of his hand, he'd spent a lot of time there . . . They aren't in the shed, we carved the pushkin in the shed . . . There's only rusht in the pantry . . . In the bathhouse maybe?

Benedikt thought about the bathhouse and got mad. He could feel his face puffing up with anger: the bathhouse is damp, books would mildew there. Here he'd come, asking nicely, offering to trade. He'd brought a valuable present. He didn't begrudge anything; he sat with the Oldeners for half a day, listened to their nonsense—but no, they had to go and lie, had to pretend, and pull the wool over his eyes, look away, brush him off, deny everything. No, no, not us, we don't have any books, don't even bother to look for any! . . .

And they invited that stinking bastard, that Degenerator, to sit at the table with them. Yes, Terenty Petrovich. What do you think, Terenty Petrovich? Would you care for some rusht, Terenty Petrovich? They fed him and got him drunk, and then they got mad at him for some reason, and threw him out in the snow like a sack of turnips . . . Served him right, of course.

But they treated Benedikt the same way: they laughed and left him with nothing to show for his trouble . . .

The old man said: the heavens and the heart, it's all the same, and you remember that. What's in the sky? There's darkness and blizzards, stormy whirlwinds. In summer, stars: the Trough, the Bowl, Horsetail, Nail Clippings, the Belly Button, there are tons of them! They're all written down in a book, he said, and that book lies locked behind seven gates, and that book holds the secret of how to live, only the pages are all shuffled . . . and the letters aren't like ours. Go and look for it, he said. Pushkin looked for it, and you go and look too. I'm looking, I'm looking, just think how many people I've shaken down: Theofilactus, Eensy Weensy, Zuzya, Nenila the Hare, Methuselah and Churilo, the twins; Osip, Revolt, Eulalia, Avenir, Maccabee, Zoya Gurevna . . . January, Ulcer, Sysoy, Ivan Pricklin . . . They caught them all with the hook, dragged them across the floor, all of them grabbed the tables and stools, all of them howled bloody murder when they were taken away to be treated . . . Noooooo, that is, dooooooon't . . . !

What do you mean, don't? It says: Books shouldn't be kept at home, and whoever keeps them shouldn't hide them, and whoever hides them should be treated.

Because everything's gotten out of hand under Fyodor Kuzmich, Glorybe. And who grabbed the main book and hid it — the one where it says how to live? Roach Efimich had books with letters that weren't like ours right out in plain view, two dozen of them, all clean and dry. Is that where the precious writings are? Probably not. Nikita Ivanich said they're locked behind seven gates, in a valley of fog . . . So keep on thinking, Benedikt . . .

Go and hitch up Teterya. To make sure he wouldn't swear the whole time or give anything away, so he'd keep his mouth shut, Benedikt made him a plug, that is, a gag: you take a rag, roll it up, tie it with a string, and stuff it in between the blabbermouth's teeth; then you fasten it around the ears. And off you go, at a gallop, but without songs!

"Where ya going so late, Benny?"

"I've got, I have to . . . go talk about art . . ."

> From the threshold of the gate
> Let the wilting beauty gaze
> Whether gentle or depraved
> Whether spiteful or quite chaste.
>
> Who cares about her charming hands!
> Who needs her bed's warm heat
> Come on, brother, let's retreat,
> Let's soar above the sands!

But the weather is bad: the air is heavy and full of alarm. The blizzard is rotten, like it was mixed with water, and the snow no longer sparkles as it did, it sticks to things. On the corners, at the crossroads, on the squares, the people stand around in bunches —more than three at a time. They huddle, looking at the sky or talking, or just standing there fretting.

Why is there unrest among the people? . . . He just passed two Golubchiks with worried faces, their eyes flitting back and forth. Others run past, waving their hands. And those guys over there were chatting, then they ran back in their houses and slammed the gates. Benedikt stopped in the sleigh, watching people he knew. Poltorak whizzed by like a wheel and was gone: he has three legs, you could never catch up with him.

There's a woman being led by the elbow: she can't walk on her own, she beats her breast with her hand, and cries out: "Oh, woe is me! Woe is me! . . ." She slumps. What's going on . . . ?

"Konstantin Leontich!" Benedikt cried out. "Stop, Konstantin Leontich! . . . What's wrong, what happened?"

Konstantin Leontich, agitated, hatless, his coat buttoned wrong, answered in a strange voice: "There was just an announcement: it's a leap year!"

"What, again?"

"Yes, yes! We're all so upset . . . They let us go home early."

"Why?" worried Benedikt. "They didn't give any reason?"

"We don't know anything yet . . . I'm in a hurry, Golubchik, forgive me. My wife doesn't know yet. Our livestock is still in the yard, the attic window has to be closed shut, you know how it is . . ."

So that's it . . . leap year: await misfortune! Furry stars, a bad harvest, hungry livestock. Grain comes up withered in the fields, if there's a drought. If there's a flood and storms, on the other hand, horsetail will take over like it's swelled with water, it'll grow higher than the trees, its roots will dig down into the clay on which the city stands: it will bring on mudslides and carve out new ravines. The woods will be sprinkled with fake firelings. If you don't watch out the Chechens will attack, and what an affliction that will be! And if the summer turns out to be cold and stormy, with winds, nothing good'll come of it, and the harpies will awake! God forbid!

Why is it that some years are leap years and others are just plain years? Who knows! What can you do? Nothing at all, you just have to put up with it!

But the people get anxious. Hostility and dissatisfaction rise. Why? Because a bad year is never shorter, just the opposite: they deliberately mock us, they make it longer. They add an extra day: here you go, all yours! And an extra day means extra work, extra taxes, all kinds of human vexation—you could just cry! And they put that day in February. There's a poem that goes:

February! Grab the inks and cry!

Well, that's what the Scribes do. So do cooks and woodcutters, not to mention the people who get called up for roadwork.

Some say: Well, it's extra work, but it means you live longer, right? You get an extra day on earth, get to eat an extra pancake or pie! Is that so bad? You think you're about to die—but no, there's another dawn to greet, another sun to shine, and in the evening you can dance and drink! Though it would be better if this day wasn't added in winter, when life seems dreary, but in the summer, in the good weather.

Yeah, sure! Don't hold your breath! Good weather. If they wanted to make things easier for people, they wouldn't add this day to a leap year but to a regular year, and not just one day, but two or three, or a whole week, and make it a holiday!

Meanwhile, they'd arrived at the izba where Varvara Luki-nishna lived.

"Wait here."

Teterya grunted under the gag and rolled his eyes.

"I said: Wait and be quiet."

No, there he goes, moaning again, waving his felt boot.

"So what is it now? What is it?"

He took off his boot, freed his hand, untied the gag, and spit with a hiss.

". . . I said, I know this place."

"So what? So do I."

"You know how to get your rocks off, but I know that there used to be a gas station here."

"Who cares what was where."

"And a gas station means fuel. Underground. Throw a match in, and boom—we all go up in a puff of smoke."

Benedikt thought a moment. "What for?"

"Not what for but where to. To hell and gone."

Benedikt opened his mouth to remind him: shut your trap, your place is in the bridle. But he knew what the answer would be and decided not to go asking for the rude cracks; his foot already had a callus from kicking, and you could kick the pig as much as you liked—he didn't care. So Benedikt didn't say anything, he just opened his mouth and shut it again.

"Gasoline, I tell you. Up to your ass in gas. Gasoline, gasoline, capish? It's like water, but it burns." Tetery laughed. "Tiger, tiger, burning bright, don't forget to leave the light . . . Eeny meeny miny moe, catch a tiger by the toe . . . Gimme a cigar while you're in there doing your business."

"What'll it be next?"

"Then screw you. Fascist!"

Worse than dogs, those Degenerators. You swear at a dog and it can't talk back. Woof, woof, that's all; you can put up with it. But Degenerators never shut up, they keep bugging you . . . As soon as you sit down in the sleigh it starts: he doesn't like the route, and that's the wrong lane, and that road is blocked, and the government doesn't run things right, and he don't like the way the Murzas look, and you better believe what he'd do to them you just wait give him his way and you'll see, and who's to blame, and how in the Oldener days he drank with his cousins, and what they drank, and how they pigged out, and what he bought, and where he went on vacation, and how he caught fish at his mother's in the country, and what a good place she had: her own milk, her own eggs, what else do you need; and all the cats he ran over, the nasty pests should all be drowned so they know their place. And what women he fooled around with, and how there was one lady General couldn't live without him and he told her: Tough luck, sweetheart, love has flown the coop, don't get your hopes up, don't wait, and she said: No, my heart will break, I'll give you whatever you want. And what cost how much when, and to hear him tell it was all cheap, just take what

209

you want and be gone. He shouts at passersby, and screams obscenities at women and girls, and after all that it turns out that he can't even go straight where he's going, he always has to take a roundabout way.

Now he's saying: guzzelean. It's water but it burns. Just where has anyone ever seen water burning? That's never happened and it never will. Water and fire don't mix, they can't. Except, of course, when people stand watching a fire and the flames lap in their eyes like in water, reflected; and the people stand there like pillars, frozen, like they were under a spell—well then, yes; but that's just a mirage, just illusion and nothing else. Nothing in nature says for water to burn. Unless the Last Days are coming? . . . But that can't be. I don't even want to think about it . . . On the other hand, it's a leap year, so that means bad omens, and the blizzard is sort of sticky, and there's a buzz in the air.

He yanked the swollen door. It smacked like a kiss. Behind it was a second door: she had a mud room between the two. He stood for a while, leaning against the second door, listening. He didn't bother to put on the robe, although he was supposed to: he allowed a little Freethinking. It's government service, of course, but every job lets you bend the rules a little for your friends or relatives.

He hesitated. Should he leave the hook in the mud room or take it with him right off? If he takes the hook with him, the sick Golubchik guesses and starts shouting right away; and where there's shouting, there's a commotion. Some of them bang their heads on the table or the stool or the stove; the place is crowded, you can't move around much, so your hand doesn't have the same flair, the same freedom. It's all well and fine to go polishing your art outdoors, training, that is. How do they teach the Saniturions? They make big dolls, huge idols, from rags and cloth; and you work on technique on the greengrass: thrusting from the shoulder, catching with a turn, pulling, or whatever. Outdoors it's easy, but in the izba, in real life, so to speak, it doesn't work that way. Nope, it doesn't.

First of all, there's the doll: it doesn't run around the izba, does it? It doesn't let out bloodcurdling screams, does it? It doesn't grab the table or chair for dear life, does it? One whack and it just lies there quiet, not feeling anything, just like the instructions say. But a Golubchik—he's alive, he makes a racket.

That's one problem. And the other, of course, is that it's always crowded. That's really an oversight. Yep. Needs more work.

So you can't always follow all the government rules; that's where the bending comes in. Some might argue with that, but "theory is dry, my friend, and the tree of life grows green and full."

Benedikt thought about it and left the hook in the mud room. He opened the second door, and stuck his head in: "Peek-a-boo! Who came to see you?"

Not a sound.

"Varvara!"

"Who's there?" came a quiet whisper.

"The Big Bad Wolf," Benedikt joked.

There was no reaction, just some rustling. Benedikt moved into the room and looked around: what was she doing? She lay on the bed, wrapped in tatters and rags, but you could hardly tell it was Varvara Lukinishna: one eye was visible through the rags, and the rest was all cock's combs—and more combs, combs, combs, combs. It seemed that since Benedikt had last seen her, she'd sprouted cock's combs all over.

"Oh, is it really you? Come for a visit?" she said. "And here I am, a little sick . . . I'm not working these days . . ."

"What?" said Benedikt, worried. "What's wrong?"

"I don't know, Golubchik. Some kind of weakness . . . I can hardly see, everything's dark . . . I can barely walk . . . Please sit down! I'm so happy you're here! Only I'm afraid I've nothing to offer you."

Benedikt didn't have anything with him either. You're not supposed to go visiting without a gift, it's true, but he couldn't come up with anything to give. A book was out of the question, better to die than give away a book. Like an idiot he went and gave the Head Stoker the one with "Slitherum Slatherum," and then he was sorry, so sorry! He kept imagining what a good book it was, how beautifully it stood on the shelf—clean and warm, and how, poor thing, it was probably lying around at the Stoker's somewhere now in a messy, gloomy, smoky izba. Maybe it fell on the floor and the old man didn't notice with his bad eyesight; maybe there was nothing to cover the soup with, and he . . . Or maybe Lev Lvovich, the lecher, asked to borrow it and took it home, hid himself away from everyone, put out the candle, and xeroxed it: I want to multiply, he said! There are insatiable rakes like that, women aren't enough for them! They fool around with goats and dogs, Lord forgive me, and even with felt boots! He felt so bad he banged his head against the wall, wrung his hands, and bit his fingernails; no, he'd never give another book to anyone.

Flowers—now Golubchiks do give flowers sometimes when they go visiting women. They pick a bunch of real bright ones in the garden or, so they smell good, put a lot of them together—and you've got a bouquet. They give the woman the bouquet: you're so beautiful, so to speak, you're a regular bouquet yourself. And you don't smell too bad either. Hold it tight and we'll mess around. But what flowers could you find in winter?

Most people bring rusht when they go visiting, or even better, mead brewed from rusht. Because you're going to want to drink some too, and that way you don't have to think about it.

Mead is good for two reasons: you can drink it right away without waiting for anyone to brew, steep, filter, and clarify it, or cool it down and then filter it again! It's all ready, help yourself and drink.

Second, it's good because if you came visiting, and the guests didn't get along—say you argue with the Golubchik who invited you, or fight, or spit at someone, or they spit at you, or something else—well, you think, at least I had a drink, it wasn't a complete waste.

But Benedikt hadn't done his own housekeeping for a long time, he didn't have his own mead, and the Kudeyarovs, well, as soon as you started making some . . . no, better not to have anyone asking questions. So he came empty-handed. And left the hook in the mud room. He pulled up a stool and sat down next to the bed, put an expression of sympathy on his face: he cocked his eyebrows up, turned his mouth down. No smile.

"How are you?" said Varvara in a weak voice. "I heard that you married. Congratulations. A wonderful event."

"Yes, a real mesalliance," Benedikt bragged.

"How lovely it must be ... I always dreamed ... Tell me ... tell me something moving and exciting."

"Hmm. Oh, they announced that we're having another leap year."

Varvara Lukinishna burst into tears. Well, no doubt about it, nothing happy in that news.

Benedikt shifted his weight and cleared his throat, not knowing what else to say. The book was hidden somewhere. Under the bed? He stretched out his leg, real casual, stuck it under the bed and felt around with his foot. There seemed to be a box.

"You know, you read in books: fleur d'orange, fate ... flowers pinned at the waist, filigree lace ..."

"Yep, they all start with the letter Fert," said Benedikt. "With Fert I noticed you can hardly ever make any sense of the words." Through his felt boots it was hard to feel what kind of box it was and where the top was. There you go: without a hook you might as well be missing your hands.

Varvara Lukinishna's one eye filled with tears.

"... the altar ... the choir ... the incense ... dearly beloved ... the veil ... the garter ..."

"Just what I said, can't make sense of it!"

Benedikt stuck his second leg under the bed, pulled his boot down on his heel, and pulled his foot out. The foot wrapping got stuck—it must have been poorly wound. No, better to take off both boots. But how hard it was with no hands! What now? To take the first boot off, you have hold down the heel with the second, but to take the second one off, you have to press it down with the first one. But if you've gone and taken off the first one, then it will be off, won't it? How are you supposed to hold the other one? Now there's a scientific question they don't answer in books. And if you try to learn by watching nature, then you have to move your legs like a fly—quick quick rub them against each other. Then the legs get kind of mixed up, you can't tell which is first and which is second: but all of a sudden the boots fly off.

". . . and my youth flew by without love!" Varvara Lukinishna cried.

"Yes, yes!" agreed Benedikt. Now he had to unwind the foot wrappings: they got in the way.

"Take my hand, dear friend!"

Benedikt guessed more or less where Varvara Lukinishna's hand must be, took it, and held it. Now his hands were occupied, there was nothing to help his feet. That meant he had to keep turning his foot around and around, so the wrapping would unwind, and had to hold it to one side with his second foot. You could get downright bushed and work up a real sweat that way.

"Don't tremble so, my friend! It's too late! Fate did not deign to let our paths cross! . . ."

"Yes, yes, that's true. I noticed that myself."

A bare foot is so much more agile than a foot in a shoe! Almost like it had eyes on the soles! There's the wall of the box, fuzzy, but with no splinters: birch doesn't splinter, it's not like pulpwood. And not every bark works for a box: thin bark is used more for letters, and thick bark, that's for baskets: we know our carpentry. Here's the top. Now he had to raise the top with his toes . . .

"You're equally distraught? Dear heart! Could it be . . . is it true? . . ."

Benedikt grabbed Varvara Lukinishna's hand, or whatever it was, even harder, for support. He spread his toes, stretched out his big toe, and flipped the top. Aha! Got it!

Suddenly his eyes squeezed shut, he jerked upward and then fell, grabbing on to something. A damned cramp! He forgot that feet don't work like hands, that's for sure!!!

It passed. Whew!

. . . Varvara Lukinishna lay there without moving, her eye open, staring at the ceiling. Benedikt was taken aback and looked closely. What was going on? His elbow had kind of pressed down on her somewhere . . . he couldn't figure out where. Did he bump her or something?

He sat and waited. "Hey," he called.

She didn't answer. She wasn't dead, was she? . . . Ay, she was dead. Jeez! What from? It was kind of unpleasant . . . Dying sure wasn't fun, not like playing dead.

He sat on the stool, his head lowered. This was bad. They had worked together. He took off his hat. She wasn't an old woman, she could have gone on living and living. Copying books. Planting turnips.

She didn't really have any relatives—who was going to bury her? And how? Our way, or like the Oldeners do it?

Mother was buried the Oldeners' way. Stretched out. If it was done our way, then you had to gut the corpse, bend the knees, tie the arms and legs together, make clay figures, and put them in the grave. Benedikt had never done this himself, people who like to do that sort of thing always came out of the woodwork and he only stood to the side, watching.

"Teterya!" he yelled out the door. "Come here."

The Degenerator ran willingly into the izba: it was warm inside.

"Teterya . . . This woman died. A co-worker . . . I came to visit a co-worker and she just up and died right this minute. What needs to be done? Huh? . . ."

"OK," said Teterya in a rush. "You have to put her hands on her chest in a cross . . . like that . . . Not that way! . . . Where is her chest? . . . Christ, who the hell knows . . . it should be lower than the head . . . Anyway, the arms crossed, an icon in the hands, of course. Close the eyes . . . Where are her eyes? . . . Oh, here's one! Spartak vs. Armenia, one to zero. Tie the jaw; where's her jaw! Where's . . . oh, forget it; just let her lie there like that. You, you're supposed to call people together, rustle up a lot of grub, bliny and stuff, and make sure there's a shitload of booze."

"All right, you can go, I know what to do from here."

"Beet and potato salad, the more the better! The red stuff, you know, with onion! Ah!"

"Out!" Benedikt screamed.

. . . He crossed her arms, if they were in fact her arms, closed her eye . . . Shouldn't he put a stone on it? But where could you find a rock in winter! Now. An icon? That's what they draw on birch bark? An idol?

A bluish mouse-oil candle trembled on the table; just moments ago Varvara lit that candle. He opened the stove damper, that's where the sticks were: the fire jumped back and forth, dancing. Varvara had just put the sticks in the stove. She stoked the fire—and now it was burning in the emptiness. She wasn't there anymore. He threw in a few more pieces so that the fire hummed and there'd be more light in the izba.

On the table there was a pile of birch sheets, a writing stick, and an ink pot: she boiled her own rusht for ink, sharpened her own sticks, she liked for everything to be orderly . . . Homemade was always better than official, she used to say. Come over for some soup, she used to say. How can you compare official soup to homemade? He didn't come. He was afraid of her cock's combs . . .

> Oh, the moment, oh, the bitter fight.
> Let the beer brew with the malt.
> Life could have been pure flight,
> But rain and cold streamed from the heavens' vault.

Benedikt started to cry. The tears burned his eyes, backed up quickly and overflowed the brim, pouring down into his beard. He wiped his eyes with his sleeve. She was kind. She always gave you her own ink if yours ran out. She explained what words meant. A steed, she said, is not a mouse—truer words were never spoken. An idol in her hands . . .

Sniffling, Benedikt sat at the table, took a piece of birch bark, and turned it around. We need an idol . . . He squeezed the writing stick—he hadn't held it for so long—and dipped it in the ink. An idol. But how to draw one . . .

. . . He drew a bent head. Around the head—curls: scritch scratch, scritch scratch. Kind of like the letter S, technically, "Slovo." All right . . . A long nose. Straight. A face. Sideburns on the sides. Fill them in so they're thicker. Dot, dot—and you've got the eyes. The elbow goes here. Six fingers. Squiggle squaggle squiggle all around: that's supposed to be a caftan.

It looks like him.

He stuck the idol in her hands.

He stood there and looked at her.

Suddenly it was as if something broke through his chest, burst, exploded like a barrel of kvas: he started to sob, he shook, he gulped and gasped, he howled—was he remembering Mother? His life? Springtimes gone by? Islands in the sea? Untraveled roads? A white bird? Nighttime dreams? Go on and ask, no one will answer! . . . He blew his nose and put on his hat.

Yes! That's right. So what did I come here for? Oh, the book! . . . Where does she have the book? Benedikt got down on all fours and looked under the bed, holding the candle. There's that box. He pulled it out and rifled around in it—women's junk, nothing valuable. No book. He looked some more—nothing, just the usual garbage. He put his hand under and felt around. Nothing.

He looked on the stove. Nothing . . .

Behind the stove. Nothing.

Under the stove. Nothing.

In the closet—he held the candle up—just rusht. With a deft hand he grabbed the hook—it's so much easier with a hook—and poked everything. Nothing.

Perhaps the table, a drawer of some kind—no, nothing. A stool—does it have a false bottom? No. He stood, looking over the izba with his eyes: the shed! He ran outside into the shed with the candle: nothing. She didn't have a bathhouse, there was no one to start the fire. He went back into the izba.

The mattress! He stuck his hands under Varvara. It was awkward, she got in the way. He felt the whole mattress, but she got in the way. He dragged her off onto the floor. He felt the mattress and pillow, poked them with the hook; he checked the blanket with hurried fingers, and the quilt of crow feathers. Nothing.

The attic!!! Where was the hatch? Over there. He climbed up on the stool. Hurrying, he bumped Varvara, and the idol fell out of her hands. He bent over, stuck it back somewhere in her middle.

There was nothing in the attic. Only torn strips of moonlight coming in through the dormer window.

It should be closed: it's a leap year, you never know ...

The moon shone, the wind blew, the clouds scudded across the sky, the trees swayed. The air smelled of water. Spring again, was it? And the emptiness, the meaninglessness, and some kind of scurrying—sticks of hay fell from the ceiling, the roof was drying out. No, something else.

Ah—the mice. The mice were scurrying. She has mice in her izba. Hickory dickory dock. "Life, you're but a mouse's scurry ..."

> Who cares about her charming hands!
> Who needs her bed's warm heat
> Come on, brother, let's retreat,
> Let's soar above the sands!

... Benedikt returned to the sleigh. The Degenerator looked at him questioningly. Benedikt stuck out his leg and kicked him. He kicked Terenty Petrovich until his foot was numb.

Ъ · ER

THERE'S A GOOD RULE: Don't let a pig into the house, he'll get used to it. The dog in the yard likes the doghouse just fine. Let him stay there and guard his master.

If some Golubchik takes pity on him and lets him into the house for the winter—"Oh, the poor mutt is freezing," or something like that—the dog will never go back to the doghouse, it has already taken a fancy to life in the izba. As soon as you turn around, it will weasel its way back in.

It's a scientific rule, true for all creatures. The same for Degenerators. Where is the Degenerator's place? In the sty. Because he's a pig and swine should stay in the pigpen, the very name tells you that.

Take Teterya, for instance: he was let in people's houses a couple of times. First Nikita Ivanich got out of line, sat him down at the table, and asked his opinions about things. Then Benedikt had to call him in at Varvara's that time—out of spiritual distress, he forgot himself. So the Degenerator developed a taste for it, and now he rushed in whenever he could.

At first he looked for excuses to help carry something, open the door, pay Mother-in-law or Olenka compliments. Then he started coming to the kitchen with his advice. You know, he'd say, I have a first-class recipe for drying marshrooms. Marshrooms, no less! We've been drying marshrooms since the time of Tsar Gorokh, we're still drying them, and will be drying them until the Last Days come! You just string them up on a thread and dry them! Nothing science can add to it!

Then he pretended that he wanted to hear Father-in-law's instructions: how to put on the sleigh bells so that they ring louder, so that there was more sound from them when you ride. What songs it was best to sing along the way: merry or melancholy. Then, before you knew it, he was the senior Degenerator, and he started shouting out orders himself: Hey, clean up that dung over there. Next thing he was making himself at home in the house. All you heard was: Terenty Petrovich this, Terenty Petrovich that.

Benedikt was furious. He stomped, he pleaded, he shamed, he argued, he threatened, he dragged Teterya around by the sleeve. No, Benya, leave him be, what would we do without Terenty Petrovich? He fetches, and carries, and entertains, and whips up a great potato casserole, and compliments rosy cheeks and white face paint too.

He'd see Olenka in her curlers, slathered in sour cream, and would say, as if to himself, like he couldn't help it: "Holy Toledo! What a beautiful woman!"

He'd drive the sleigh with a whistle and a song; he braided the reins, decorated the harness strap with birch pictures; he fastened a picture of an idol right in the middle—a fellow with mustaches on both sides; to the right a naked woman with tits, to the left a sign: "Terenty Petrovich Golovatykh: AT YOUR SERVICE." He invited Olenka to admire it, and Olenka immediately said: "That's it, Benedikt. This is my sleigh! You take another one." Benedikt spat, but he gave her the sleigh and Teterya with it—he was so mad he didn't even feel like kicking him.

Benedikt was given a Degenerator named Joachim, an old man who wheezed and coughed: everything in his chest squealed and bleated, rattled and whistled; he could barely drag his legs along. He'd drive the length of two fences and stop: "Oh, Lord Almighty, heavenly queen . . . Our sins weigh heavy . . . If only the Lord would call me to him . . ."

And he'd cough . . . with a rattle, a wet cough; then he'd clear his throat and spit; not even the whip could get him going until he'd spat out everything.

"Heavenly mother . . . and the forty sainted martyrs . . . you've forgotten me . . . Oh, saint Nikolai . . . for my terrible sins . . ."

"Come on, Grandpa, get a move on! You can spit at home!"

"Oh, why won't death come? . . . the Lord is wrathful . . ."

"Let's have a song! A spirited one!"

"Chriiiiist is riiiiisen from the deeeeeeead . . ."

It was embarrassing: What if someone he knew saw him? Would he start to grin? Hey, looky there, look at Benedikt! What kind of old nag has he got? Where do they find them like that? Or even worse they'd give him a nickname!

And just as he'd feared, that's what happened. He was driving Joachim past the pushkin—he wanted to see how it was holding up—and right at that very moment Nikita Ivanich was climbing up on our be all and end all and untying another laundry line from his neck. He saw the whole shameful thing and sure enough, he shouted: "Benedikt, you should be ashamed of yourself!!! To drive an old man like that!! Just remember whose son you are!!! Polina Mikhailovna's!!! What on earth are you thinking of? You'll get there faster on foot!!!"

It was so humiliating, Benedikt turned away and pretended

that he didn't see, didn't hear, and complained to Father-in-law when he got home. Oldeners are pointing at me, I should be going along at a good clip, I'll shame my mother's memory! Give Teterya back, to hell with him! But Teterya was already busy with other work. He'd been promoted to kitchen help; he was cleaning turnips, plucking chickens, and making beet salad.

So they gave Benedikt the most plain, ordinary sort of Degenerator: no peculiarities. His name was Nikolai.

Olenka stuffed the pillows with white fluff; it was much softer to lie on. He didn't have to work at all: no chopping, no hewing. He didn't have to walk either—I'll take the sleigh. Food? Eat whenever you please. So Benedikt filled out, he bloated, his features swam. He grew heavier. Not even so much from food as from heavy thoughts. It was like his soul had been stuffed with rags, snippets of cloth and lint: it was hot, itchy, and stifling. Lie down or stand up, no peace to be found.

There must be some books somewhere. There must be.

He went out into the yard, on the greengrass—it had only just begun to push up through the snow—to give his arms a workout. That way, if they had to confiscate something, his hands and arms would be light, deft, and agile. The hook wouldn't stick, it would fly, and he wouldn't be able to tell where his arm ended and the hook began.

Father-in-law kept reproaching him, saying Benedikt was clumsy, that he'd done that Golubchik in. Father-in-law would meet him in the hallway and shake his head regretfully: ay-ay-ay-ay-ay-ay . . .

"I mean, why is it a hook? It's a hook because it isn't a spear! It has a certain line, my dear boy, see? It curves! And why? Because humane treatment is important to us in our profession. A long time ago, of course, the regime was stricter. The least little thing, a short conversation and then pop! That was the end of it. In those days, needless to say, a spear was handier. But now we take a different approach: a little crookedness, a little bending, because we don't kill them, we treat them. There's a lot of backwardness in society—I explained it all to you, remember? Art is being destroyed. If not for you and me, who would stand up for art? Who? Well, there you go."

"But Papa, art requires sacrifices," Olenka would say, standing up for Benedikt.

"The first blin is always lumpy," Mother-in-law comforted.

"There you go, talking about bliny again! How come you only talk about one thing: bliny and more bliny! . . ." Benedikt wasn't listening, he walked out, turning over the heavy thoughts in his head. Whistling to Nikolai, he plopped into the sleigh like a sack of potatoes: "To the market!" he said, leaving his robe on, just pushing the hood back. Red, bulky, gloomy, he wandered past the booths where the Lesser Murzas displayed their birch books, their clumsy, messy homemade booklets. People fell silent, terrified when Benedikt tromped through with a heavy step and heavy thoughts on his brow, dark circles under his eyes from sleepless nights, overfed jowls and a strangling collar. He knew he was scary—so be it. He took a booklet and flipped the pages disdainfully—the Murza started to say he had to pay first but Benedikt gave him such a look that he didn't open his mouth again.

He'd read it. And this one? What was this? He'd read it, the whole thing, not excerpts like here.

"Where's the whole text? The whole story should be here, thieves!" he screeched at a Murza who sat there like a shriveled old sparrow. He poked his fat finger at the bark. "Even here you stole something, what kind of people are you! Here you leave out a chapter, there you break off mid-word, and in another place you mix up the lines!"

"The government doesn't have enough bark," muttered one frightened Murza, "there's not enough people to do the work—"

"Quiiiiii-et!"

Sometimes he would find something he hadn't read: rusty looking scribbles, bent lines, mistakes on every page. Reading something like that was like eating dirt and rocks. He took it. It made him feel sick, he despised himself, but he took it.

In the evening, leaning over, running his finger over the potholes and ruts of the bark, moving his lips, he made out the words; his eyes had grown unaccustomed to script, he stumbled sometimes. His eyes wanted the straight, fleet, clear, clean black-and-white page of Oldenprint books. A careless Scribe, it seems, had copied out this one—there were blotches and smudges. If he could find out who it was he'd have their head in a barrel!

> Our eyes were glued to the tribune, (blotch)
> Our ears discerned amid the silence of the state,
> The final, equitable weighing of the summary
> Where all divisions add up to the century!
>
> Blotch . . .
> Blotch . . . and cannot lock our feelings up, remote.
> Conferred upon us by Party Card and heart, (blotch)
> Is the decisive power of the vote!

Well? The poetry was worth a mouse and a half, maximum, and they get twelve. There's thievery here too. True, Benedikt didn't pay. They just gave it to him.

He tried rereading the old books, but it wasn't the same. No emotion, no trembling or anticipation of things to come. You always knew what happened next; if a book is new, unread, you break into a sweat just wondering: Will he catch up or not? What will her answer be? Will he find the treasure or will thieves get it first? But the second time around your eyes pass lamely over the lines. You know: he'll find it; he'll catch him; they'll get married; he'll strangle her. Whatever.

At night, tossing and turning sleeplessly on the soft down, he thought about things. He imagined the town, the streets, the iz-bas, the Golubchiks. In his head he went over all the faces he knew. Ivan Beefich—does he have a book? But he doesn't even know his letters. How could that be: the Golubchik doesn't know how to read, but he has a book? Does it happen? Yes, it happens. He uses it instead of a soup top . . . Or to press marsh-rooms into a salting barrel . . . He was filled with bad blood, he thought bad things about Ivan Beefich. Should he try a confisca-tion? . . . Ivan Beefich doesn't have any legs, his feet come right out of his underarms. You need a short hook here, with a thick handle. But Ivan Beefich does have strong hands. So a short one won't do . . .

Yaroslav. Should he check out Yaroslav? They studied letters together, and counting . . . If he hid something, he wouldn't admit it. He thought about Yaroslav. He could see him going into the izba, bolting the door. Yaroslav looked around. He walked over to the window on tiptoe, pulled the bladder back: was anyone looking? Now to the stove . . . He stuck a candle in there to light it . . . Now to the bed . . . He turned around again, like he'd felt something. He stood there for a minute . . . He bent over to pull a box out from under the bed . . . He rifles around in the box for a while, fumbling . . . shifts something from one hand into the other . . . Benedikt tensed, he could see it like it was really happening. Only it was kind of see-through, transparent—the candle flickered and crackled straight through Yaroslav, as though he was hanging there in the twilight air like a sleepy shadow, rummaging and rummaging: his see-through back covered with a homespun shirt, his transparent shoulder blades moving back and forth: he was looking for something; his vertebrae moved like shadowy bumps along his spine . . .

Benedikt looked into the darkness with eyes wide open. It was just darkness, there was nothing in it, right? But no, there was Yaroslav, and he'd gotten so stuck that he wouldn't come unstuck! You toss and turn on the pillows, or get up to smoke, or to go to the privy, or somewhere else—and there he is. Yaroslav, Yaroslav . . . You tell yourself: Don't think about Yaroslav! I don't know anything about him! But no, how can you say that, I mean, there's his back, there he is, rummaging . . . You pass the night without sleep, you get up, gloomy as a storm cloud. Nothing at breakfast seems tasty, everything's wrong somehow . . . You take a bite and drop it: it's not right, not right . . . You blurt out: Maybe we should check Yaroslav? . . . Father-in-law isn't pleased, he scrapes the floor, his eyes reproach you: always obsessed with trivia, son, always avoiding the most important things . . .

By summer Benedikt's hook flew like a bird. Yaroslav was

checked—and nothing was found; Rudolf, Myrtle, Cecilia Albertovna, Trofim, Shalva—nothing; Jacob, Vampire, Mikhail, another Mikhail, Lame Lyalya, Eustachius—nothing. He bought *Brades's Tables* at the market—just numbers. He'd like to catch that Brades, and stuff his head in a barrel.

No one around. Nothing. Only a leap year blizzard in his heart: it slips and sticks, sticks and slips, and the blizzard hums, like distant, unhappy voices—they wail softly, complain, but all without words. Or like in the steppe—hear it?—hands outstretched, they shuffle along on all sides. The Broken Ones shuffle along; there they are heading in all directions, though there aren't any directions for them; they've gone astray and there's no one to tell, and if there were, if they met a real live person, he wouldn't feel sorry for them, he doesn't need them. And they wouldn't recognize him, they don't even recognize themselves.

"Nikolai! . . . We're going to the pushkin!"

A damp blizzard had thrown a heap of snow on the pushkin's hunched head and shoulders and the crook of his arm, as though he'd been crawling around other people's izbas, filching things from their closets, taking whatever he could find—and what he found was a sorry sight, all frayed, just rags—and he had crawled out of the room, clasping the rags to his chest. Moldering hay was falling from his head; it kept falling.

Well then, brother pushkin? You probably felt the same way, didn't you? You probably tossed and turned at night, walked with heavy legs over scraped floors, oppressed by your thoughts?

Did you, too, hitch the fastest steed to the sleigh and ride gloomily with no destination across the snowy fields, listening to the clatter of the lonely sleigh bells, the drawn-out song of the courier?

Did you, too, conjure the past, fear the future?

Did you rise higher than the column?—and while you rose, while you saw yourself weak and threatening, pitiful and triumphant, while you looked for what we are all looking for—the white bird, the main book, the road to the sea—did your dung heap Terenty Petrovich drop in on your wife, the bootlicker, mocker, helpful wheeler-dealer? Did his lewd, empty talk burble through the rooms? Did he tempt with wondrous marvels? "You know, Olga Kudeyarovna, there's a place I know ... Underground guzzelean water ... Just toss in a match, and fuckin' A, we'll go up in smoke. Kaboom! Would you care to?" ... Let's soar above the sands!

Tell me, pushkin! How should I live? I hacked you out of a dumb log all by myself, bent your head, bent your elbow so you would cross your chest and listen to your heart: What has passed? What is yet to come? Without me you would be an eyeless chunk, an empty log, a nameless tree in the forest; you'd rustle in the wind in spring, drop your acorns in fall, creak in winter: no one would know about you! Without me—you wouldn't be here! "Who was it, with iniquitous power, called me forth from nothingness?" It was me, I called you! I did!

It's true, you came out a little crooked, the back of your head is flat, your fingers aren't quite right, and you don't have any legs. I can see that for myself, I understand carpentry.

But you're who you are, be patient, my child—you're the same as us, no different!

You're our be all and end all and we're yours, and there's no one else! No one! Help me!

Ы · YERY

"GIVE ME the book," whined Benedikt. "Don't try to jew me out of it, give me the book!"

Nikita Ivanich looked at Lev Lvovich of the Dissidents. Lev Lvovich of the Dissidents looked out the window. It was a summer's eve, still light, the bladder off the window—you could see far, far away.

"It's too soon!" said Nikita Ivanich.

"Soon for what? The sun is already setting."

"Too early for you. You don't know the ABCs yet. You're uncivilized."

"Steppe and nothing else . . . as far as the eye can see . . . And neither fish nor fowl . . ." said Lev Lvovich through his teeth.

"What do you mean, I don't know them?" answered Benedikt in amazement. "Me? Why, I . . . I . . . Why . . . Do you know how many books I've read? How many I've copied?"

"It doesn't matter if it's a thousand."

"It's more than that!"

"Even if it's a thousand, it hardly matters. You don't really know how to read, books are of no use to you. They're just empty page-turning, a collection of letters. You haven't learned the alphabet of life. Of life, do you hear me?"

Benedikt was flabbergasted. He didn't know what to say. To be told such a bold-faced lie straight out like that. Nikita Ivanich might as well have said: You're not you, you're not Benedikt, and you aren't living on this earth, and . . . and . . . and I don't know what.

"You already said that . . . What do you mean I don't know? The alphabet . . . There's Az . . . Slovo . . . Myslete . . . Fert."

"There's Fert, but there's Theta, and Yat, and Izhitsa, there are concepts inaccessible to you: sensitivity, compassion, generosity . . ."

"The rights of individuals," piped up Lev Lvovich of the Dissidents.

"Honesty, justice, spiritual insight . . ."

"Freedom of speech, freedom of the press, freedom of association," added Lev Lvovich.

"Mutual assistance, respect for others . . . self-sacrifice . . ."

"Now that's a lot of stinking mystical blather," shouted Lev Lvovich, wagging his finger. "This isn't the first time I've noticed where you're heading with all that monument preservation! This smacks of nationalistic mysticism. It downright stinks."

It did smell bad in the izba. Lev Lvovich sure got that one right.

"There isn't any Theta," objected Benedikt. In his head he went through the entire alphabet, afraid that perhaps he'd let something slip—but no, he hadn't forgotten anything, he knew the alphabet by heart, backward and forward, and he'd never had cause to complain about his memory. "There's no Theta, and after Fert comes Kher, and that's that. There isn't anything else."

"And don't hold your breath, there isn't going to be any," said Lev Lvovich, getting worked up once again, "You, Nikita Ivanich, you've got no business sowing obscurantism and superstition. Social protest is what's needed now, not Tolstoyism. This isn't the first time I've observed this in you. You're a Tolstoyan."

"I—"

"A Tolstoyan, a Tolstoyan! Don't argue with me!"

"But—"

"On this point, old man, you and I are on different sides of the barricades. You are dragging society backward. 'To a cell in a shell.' You are a socially pernicious element. Mysticism! Right now the most important thing is protest. It's crucial to say: No! Do you remember—now when was that?—remember when I was called up for roadwork?"

"And—"

"I said: No! You must remember, you were around then."

"And you didn't go?"

"No, no, why do you say that? I went. They forced me. But I said: No!"

"Who did you say it to?"

"To you, I told you, you must remember. I believe it's very important to say no at the right moment. To say: I protest!"

"You protested, but you went anyway?"

"Have you ever met anyone who didn't go?"

"Forgive me, but what's the point . . . if no one hears—"

"And what's the point of your . . . what shall I call them . . . activities? All those posts?"

"What do you mean? Memory, of course!"

"Of what? Whose memory? It's just empty noise! Hot air! Now, here we've got a young man," said Lev Lvovich, looking at Benedikt with distaste. "Let this young man tell us, since he knows his letters so well, precisely what is inscribed on the pillar standing in the burdock and nettle patch next to your izba, and why is it there."

"It's grabweed," Benedikt corrected.

"It doesn't matter, I'm used to calling it nettle."

"Call it a pot if you like. It's grabweed."

"What does it matter?"

"Stick your hand in and you'll find out."

"Lev Lvovich," remarked Nikita Ivanich, "it's possible that the young man is right. Nowadays they differentiate nettle from grabweed. You and I don't, but they can tell the difference."

"No, no, no. Excuse me," said Lev Lvovich stubbornly, "I'm not yet blind, and let's not have any mysticism here: I see nettle and I insist that it is nettle."

"Crikey, Lev Lvovich, nettle is nettle!" Benedikt said. "And grabweed is grabweed. If it grabs you, you'll know it. You can make soup from nettle. It's not very good, but you can do it. But just try making soup from grabweed. No way you can make soup of it! No, no, no-o-o-o," Benedikt said with a laugh, "you'll never make soup of grabweed. Yeah, sure, nettle! It's not nettle. I swear. It's grabweed. That's it. Grabweed and nothing but."

"All right, all right," Lev Lvovich stopped him. "So what is written on the post?"

Benedikt stuck his head out of the window, squinted, and read everything that was on the post out loud to the Oldeners: "Nikita's Gates," seven swear words, an obscene picture, "Fedya and Klava," another five cuss words, "Vitya was here," "There is no heppinness in life," three swear words, "Zakhar is a dog," and one more obscene picture. He read everything aloud.

"There you've got it, the whole inscription, or text, exactly like it is. And there's no Theta there. Lots of the F letter, one, two . . . eight. No, nine, the ninth is in Fedya. But there's no Theta."

"Your Theta isn't there," Lev Lvovich confirmed.

"Yes, it is," cried the Stoker, beside himself. "Nikita's Gate is my Theta to you, to everyone! So that there's some memory of our glorious past! With hope for the future! We'll restore everything, everything, and we'll start with the small things! It's a whole layer of our history! Pushkin was here! He was married here!"

"The pushkin was here," Benedikt agreed. "Right here in the shed, that's where we started him. We chiseled his head out, his arm, everything was fine and dandy. You helped drag him yourself, Lev Lvovich, you forgot already? You have a bad memory! And Vitya was here."

"What Vitya?"

"I don't know, maybe it was Vitya the Fainter from Upper Maelstrom, maybe it was the Chuchin's Vitya—a big guy, a bit younger than I am. Or maybe it was Vitya Ringlegs. It's not likely, though—I don't think he could make it all the way here. No, he couldn't make it. His legs are kind of turned around, like his foot was on the inside . . ."

"What are you talking about, what Vitya, what does Vitya have to do with anything?"

"There it is, over there on the post, on the post! 'Vitya was here!' I only just read it out loud to you!"

"But that's completely unimportant, whether he was or wasn't here, who knows . . .? I'm talking about memory . . ."

"Well, he left a memory! He carved it! So that people would know, whoever walked by—so they'd remember: he was here!"

"When will you learn to differentiate!!" shouted Nikita Ivanich, who had puffed up, turned red, and begun gesticulating . . . "It's a milestone, a historical landmark! Nikita's Gates stood here, do you understand that? You Neanderthal!!! A great city stood here! Pushkin was here!"

"Vitya was here," shouted Benedikt, becoming incensed himself. "Fedya and Klava were here! Klava, I don't know, maybe Klava was at home and just Fedya was here! He carved a memory! And it's all here! Aha! I've got it! I know which Vitya! It was Viktor Ivanich, who buried your old woman. The organizer. It must have been him. That Viktor Ivanich."

"Viktor Ivanich would never go around carving nonsense on posts," protested the Oldeners, "it's difficult to even imagine . . . completely unthinkable . . ."

"Why wouldn't he? How do you know? What, is he dumber than you? You carve things, and he can't carve anything, is that it? It's all right to carve something about some gates, go ahead, but about a real person—not on your life, is that it?"

All three of them sat in silence, breathing through their noses.

"All right," said Nikita Ivanich, spreading his hands. "Let's calm down. Right now—wait—now I'll concentrate and explain. Good. In some ways you're right. Human beings are important. But! What's the point of this?" Nikita Ivanich gathered his fingers together. "The point is, that this memory—pay attention Benedikt!—this memory can exist on different levels . . ."

Benedikt spat.

"You think I'm an idiot! You're talking like I was a little baby! . . . If he's a big strapping nitwit, then of course he's at a different level! He'll do his carving right on the very top! If he's a pip-squeak—he won't be able to reach, so he'll say what he has to on the bottom! And this one's right in the middle, exactly Viktor Ivanich's height. He's the one that did it, and there's no doubt about it."

"Steppe and nothing else . . ." Lev Lvovich suddenly started singing.

"As far as the eye can seeee . . ." Benedikt chimed in joyfully. He liked this song, always ordered the Degenerators to sing it on the road. "Out on that lonesome steppe . . ."

"A coachman called to meeeee!"

All three began singing, Benedikt sang the bass, Nikita Ivanich sort of croaked along, and Lev Lvovich sang in a high, beautiful, heartfelt voice with a tear in it. Even Nikolai out in the yard was surprised. He stopped munching grass and stared at the singers.

> You, my oldest friend,
> Don't recall bad deeds,
> On this desolate steppe,
> Please do bury meeeeee!

The singing went so well, such a languid lightness set in, such a sense of accord, such wings, it felt like the smoky izba wasn't an izba, but a meadow, like nature raised her head, turned to look, opened her mouth in surprise and listened, and tears kept on falling and falling from her eyes. Like the Princess Bird forgot her beautiful self for a minute and set her brilliant gaze on the singers in amazement. Like they hadn't just been arguing, their hearts incensed, hadn't exchanged angry looks and put on grimaces of mutual disdain; like their hands hadn't been itching to punch the other guy in the kisser so he wouldn't look at me like that, so that he didn't make faces, didn't talk through his teeth, didn't hold his nose! It's hard to stay mad when you're singing: if you open your mouth the wrong way, you'll ruin the song. If you squawk, you lose track, like you've dropped something, and spilled it! If you ruin a song, you're the fool, you'll be to blame, there's no one else! The others have gone on, they're carrying the tune along nicely, calmly, and it's like you were drunk and tripped and fell face down in the mud. Shameful!

> Please go tell my wife,
> That on the steppe I frooooooooze!—

Lev Lvovich broke off, banged his head against the table, and began to cry, like he was barking. Benedikt was scared, he stopped singing and stared at the Oldener, forgetting to close his mouth, which remained open at the letter O.

"Lev Lvovich! Lyovushka!" pleaded Nikita Ivanich. The Stoker ran all around, tugged at the crying man's sleeve, grabbed a cup, put it down, grabbed a towel, dropped it. "Now what is this! Lyovushka! Come on, that's enough! We'll manage somehow! We're alive, after all, aren't we?"

Lev Lvovich shook his head, rocking it on the table, like he was saying no and he didn't want to stop.

"Benya! Get some water, quick . . . ! He's not supposed to be under stress, he has a heart condition!"

They gave the Oldener something to drink, dried him with a towel, and fanned his face with their hands.

"You sing so well!" said Nikita Ivanich comfortingly. "Did you study or is it just natural? Does it run in your family?"

"Probably . . . Papa was a dentist," sniffed Lev Lvovich one last time. "And on my mother's side I'm from the Kuban."

Ь · YER'

THEY SAY you can never have too much of a woman's body—
and they're right. Olenka expanded sideways, forward, and
backward. You couldn't have asked for anything more beautiful.
Where once she had a dimpled chin there were now eight. She
had six rows of tits. She had to sit on five stools, three weren't
enough. Not long ago they widened the doorway, but they'd
been stingy: it needed to be widened again. Any other husband
would have been proud. But Benedikt looked at all this splen-
dor without any excitement. He didn't feel like playing goats, or
tickling and pinching her.

"Benedikt, you don't understand anything about female
beauty. Terenty Petrovich, now, he appreciates . . . Go sleep in
another room."

To hell with her, then. She might squash him at night, smother
him. Benedikt made himself a pallet in the library. From there
you could hardly hear her snoring. And that way the signal
would come quicker.

He slept fully dressed, and stopped bathing: what a bore.
Dirt collected behind his ears, all kinds of garbage. Creatures of
some kind settled in: slow, with lots of legs; at night they moved
from place to place, uneasy. Maybe they were lugging their nests
somewhere, but you couldn't see who they were—they were behind the ears. His feet were sweaty and stuck together. It didn't
matter. You lie there like a warm corpse: your ears don't hear,
your eyes don't see. True, he did wash his hands; but he had to
for his work.

> . . . And where is that clearest of fires,
> and why does it not burn?

You get up, go to the kitchen, pluck a meat pattie out of a bowl
with two fingers, with a third you scoop the jelly out of the bowl.

You eat it. No emotion. You eat it—that's all. Now what? Start dancing a jig?

You open the window bladder—a fine rain drizzles, needling the puddles; the clouds are low, the whole sky is covered, it's dark during the day, as if the sun had never risen. A serf crosses the yard—he covers his head from the rain and goes around the puddles, carrying a sack of hay to the Degenerators. A long time ago, oh, how long ago it was, in a former life!—you would have tried to guess: Will he slip or not? Will he fall? And now you look on sort of dumbly: Yeah, the serf slipped. Yeah, he fell. But there's no joy in it anymore.

. . . The lamplighter should have lit them, but sleeps.

He sleeps, and I'm not to blame, my sweet . . .

From the bedroom came a clicking and clattering: Olenka and Terenty Petrovich were playing dominoes and laughing. Another time he would have burst into the room like a tornado and beat Terenty's mug black and blue, loosened a few teeth for him, and kicked him out of the family quarters! Olenka would have got what was coming to her as well: he'd have grabbed her by the hair, by those bobbins of hers, and smashed her sour-creamed face against the wall. Again! Once more! Another time for good measure! He'd have stomped on her and given her a few in the ribs, in the ribs!

But now it didn't matter; they're playing and let them play.

You lie there. Just lie and lie there. "Ne'er a drop of divinity, nor single sigh of inspiration." No tears, no life, no love. For a month, perhaps a half a year. Suddenly: hark! Something blows in on the breeze. This is a signal.

You perk up right away, on guard. Has it come, or did you just imagine it? Seems like you imagined . . . No! There it is again! Clear as clear can be! You rise up on your elbow, cock your ear to one side, listening.

There's a faint light in your head—like a candle behind a door cracked open . . . Careful not to scare it off . . .

It's gotten a bit stronger now, that light, and you can see the room. In the middle there's nothing, and on that nothing—

there's a book. The pages are turning . . . It seems to be coming closer and closer, you can almost make out what's written . . .

Then your mouth goes dry, your heart pounds, your eyes go blind: you just saw the book, and the pages were turning, they were turning! But you can't see what's going on around you, and if you do see it, it doesn't mean anything at all. The meaning is over there, in the book; the book is the only real, living thing. Your bed, stool, room, father- and mother-in-law, your wife and her lover—they aren't alive, they're like drawings! Moving shadows, like the cloud shadows running across the earth—and they're gone!

But what kind of book it is, where it is, why its pages are turning—and is someone turning them or is it moving on its own? That is a mystery.

One time he felt the pull—and rushed to check Konstantin Leontich. He was driving by, and suddenly he felt the pull: What if he's got one? There wasn't anything there, just a string of worrums. Now that was a false signal.

There are true signals and then sometimes there are false ones: if the signal is for real, then the vision you see in your head gets stronger, thicker, so to speak; the book you see in your vision gets heavier and heavier. At first it's clear and watery, and then it thickens; you see its paper, white, oh, so white, or yellowed and rough, you can see every freckle and spot and scratch on it, like you were looking at skin close up. You look and you laugh from the joy of it, just like you were about to make love.

The letters too: at first they slip and jump around. Then they settle into even rows, nice and black, all whispering. Some are open wide like they were inviting you: Come on in!

Take the letter O for instance. It's a round window, like you're looking down from the attic at a burbling, chirping spring forest: you can see streams and fields far away, and if you're lucky and you squint your eyes, you might see the White Bird— tiny, distant, like a white speck. Or the letter Π, Pokoi. Well it's just a doorframe! And what's beyond that door? Who knows, maybe a completely new life no one ever imagined! One that's never happened before!

X, Kher, or Ж, Zhivete, they block the way, they won't let you in, they crisscross and close off the passage: Stay out! Forget it!

Ц, Tsi, and Щ, Shcha, have tails, like Benedikt before his wedding.

Ч, Cherv, is like an upside-down chair.

Г, Glagol, is shaped like a hook.

Now if the signal is really true, then it all comes together: the paper, the letters, the picture you can see through them, the whispering, and the hum, the wind from the turning pages—a dusty, warm wind—it all thickens in front of your eyes, floods you, washes over you in a kind of airy wave. Then you know. Yes! That's it! I'm coming!

And in a flash it falls away and leaves you, all the heaviness stays on the bed, all the dull daze, the thick, bodily, meaty heaving from side to side. Suddenly there's no confusion, no laziness, no sticky, slurping swampy bog in you. You rise in a single surge, taut like a thread pulled tight, light and resonant; there's a goal in your head, you know what to do, you're collected and cheerful!

All that sticky weight falls away—there's only the surge! The soul!

The robe wrapped itself around his shoulders like a magic skin. The hood, his reliable protector, leapt onto his head: I may not be seen, but I see through everyone! His strong weapon seemed to grow into his hand—his trusty hook, bent like the letter Г, Glagol! "With words to burn the hearts of men!" With a birdlike, lilting cry, with one sweep of the hand, I call my comrades. Always prepared!

Wondrous comrades, a flying division! You call from the yard or from the gallery—and there they are, as if they neither sleep nor eat, each dozen in harmony like a single being! Ready. Onward! Stern, shining warriors, we rise and fly, neither snow nor rain nor sleet shall stop us—we know no obstacle, and the people part like the sea before us.

We tear them away and take them; we save them. If the signal was really true, we take them and save them, because then there really was a Book there. It called, beckoned, cried out, came in a vision.

But if the signal is false—well, then there isn't anything. That's the way it was at Konstantin Leontich's. Nothing but garbage.

But it turned out all wrong at Konstantin Leontich's. Why? Well, because Benedikt was riding along in his sleigh, darker than a thundercloud, lost in his thoughts, and his thoughts were grim and tearful like autumn clouds—clouds in the sky, clouds in the breast, it's all the same, feelosophy has got that part right. Without seeing, he knew that his eyes were red with blood, that he had dark, deep rings under his eyes, that his face and curls had darkened, stuck together—uncombed, unwashed, his head had become flat, like a spoon. His throat was sticky from smoking, as though he'd swallowed clay. He turned the corner and suddenly he felt the pull: over there. In that izba.

And then he allowed himself some Freethinking, or what you might call a violation of procedure. He went alone, right then, without his comrades. Whoa! he cried to Nikolai. He pulled on the reins and stopped him: Wait here; he threw on his hood and kicked the gate open with his foot.

They teach you: never go out on a confiscation alone—it's Freethinking, and they're absolutely right: you wouldn't go alone for firelings, now, would you? The fireling might guess that there's a human walking around, and cry out, and put out its light to warn the others, mightn't it? And what if it turns out to be a fake fireling? Well, in our business it's the same thing: science is the same everywhere.

Konstantin Leontich screamed and resisted. He hit Benedikt on the arm so hard it really really hurt. In professional terms: he complicated the confiscation.

He let out a blood-curdling yell and called his neighbors. They didn't come, they'd hidden. Then he tore the hood off and recognized Benedikt. He squealed and hit him in the face when he recognized him.

He scratched him furiously; he even knocked him over.

But he made a mistake when he grabbed the hook with his

hands; the hook is double-edged, you shouldn't grab it with your hands.

That's not what it's for.

The hook is to grab the book with, to catch it, drag it to you, to pull it toward you; it's not a spear. Why is it so sharp? So that it's dangerous for a Golubchik to hold on to the book when it's confiscated. They all clutch the book tight, so the hook is sharpened. That way, if you get out of hand, you won't be able to hold on, you'll slice your hands off in an instant, and every single last one of your fingers!

On the outside and the inside it's sharpened really sharp, that's why you need practice grabbing and turning with it; that's why every confiscated book has cuts from the hook, like little wounds. A clumsy Saniturion could carelessly slice through a book, and that must never happen, you can't ruin art. If the work is good and clean, you can pull in a book with one flick, and there'll only be a little scar.

So they work in groups or brigades: one comrade confiscates the book, the others use their hooks to catch the Golubchiks in the izba by their clothes, or by the collar, they wind him up, in rags.

And another thing the hook is useful for: if the Golubchik is rambunctious, the hook is good for knocking him off his feet, so he falls down right away, and for that there's always a set of horns handy. It's a professional instrument too, but simpler, it looks like the letter Y, or a set of tongs. When someone falls, you can hold his neck down to the floor to make sure he doesn't get back up.

Saniturions used to be given spears. One poke, and that was the end of the Golubchik. But we don't do that anymore, now we're humane.

And a Saniturion should also watch himself, his hands always have to be clean. The hook will always be dirty from the Golubchik: with blood or vomit, whatever; but the hands have to be clean. That's why Benedikt always washes his hands.

Because otherwise how are you going to hold the book after the confiscation? In the sleigh when you're on your way back?

So there you have it, that's the technique, the tricks, or the scientific organization of labor. It seems simple, but it's not so simple. It's crowded in the izba, and dark; you bump into each other—a lot of people complain.

Freethinking is out of place here, but Benedikt let it happen, as always. So he went and got wounded by Konstantin Leontich: on his hands, and on his face, and on his chest too; and he sprained his ankle. And all in vain: it was a false signal, there weren't any books.

It was the day of the October Holiday, Konstantin Leontich was getting ready for the yearly recount, he was washing rags out in the tub—pants, a shirt. Well, so there'll be one Golubchik missing, the Murzas won't count Konstantin Leontich. They'll write down in the official lists: taken for treatment.

After all, you can't count everyone, can you, Murza?

In December, at the darkest time of the year, Olenka delivered triplets. Mother-in-law came by and called Benedikt in to come look at the brood. She congratulated him. He lay there, empty and heavy-hearted, waiting for the signal; and there wasn't any. All right then, he'd go take a look.

There were three kids: one appeared to be female, she was tiny and cried. Another seemed to be a boy, but it was hard to tell right off. The third—well, you couldn't figure out what it was— to look at, it was a fuzzy, scary-looking ball. All round-like, but with eyes. They picked it up in their arms to rock it, and started singing: "Bye Baby Bunting, Daddy's gone a-hunting . . ." and with a shove it pushed away, jumped on the floor, rolled off, and disappeared into a crack in the floor. They all rushed to catch it, their hands outstretched. They moved stools and benches—but no luck.

Benedikt stood around awhile, watched, as though through a fog, congratulated Olenka on a successful delivery. Then he went back to his room. Mother-in-law ran to call Terenty Petrovich to take a look so she could brag about her grandchildren.

He lay down on the bed that had seen so many sighs and groans. He had made himself a serious rut, lying there during all those empty years, those countless, joyless nights. He frowned and thought: If the thing just stayed under the floor that wouldn't be so bad, but what if it comes out and starts chewing up books? Maybe he should spackle the cracks closed? The floor boards had gotten quite thin. The family could scrape up a big heap in a day. Sometimes you'd walk by and it looked like there was a whole head of hair fallen on the floor! You could never tell, that thing might come out from under the floor and head straight for the book room. It would gnaw on the bindings, the spines . . . There's glue in there. Leather sometimes.

As if he didn't have enough worries, and here . . . It would eat them up, it would definitely eat them! It needs to eat, right? There are threats to art all around: from people, rodents, the damp! How stupid and blind Benedikt used to be, blind as the blind men at the market: they sing, sing their hearts out, but they live in darkness, for them it's dark at midday! He didn't understand anything back then, like he was a worrum! He asked all kinds of silly questions, frowned, and opened his mouth wide so it was easier to think, but he didn't understand anything.

How come we don't have mice? How come we don't need them? Well, we don't need them because we live a spiritual life: we've got books preserved here, and art, and mice would come out and eat up our treasures! With their tiny, sharp teeth, crunch crunch, nibble nibble, they'd chew them up, ruin them!

But Golubchiks have a different life, they depend on mice. They can't do anything without mice. They need them for soup, of course, and stew, and if you want to sew yourself a coat, or trade at the market, pay taxes, that is, pay the tithe. There's the house tax, the pillow tax, the stove tax—you need mice for all of them. So that means they can't keep books at home, no, no, no! It's either one or the other.

And why is it that spiritual life is called a higher life? It's because you put books up as high as you can, on the top floor, on a shelf, so that if misfortune strikes and the vermin get into the house, the treasure will be safer. That's why!

And why do Father-in-law, Mother-in-law, and Olenka have claws on their feet?—for the same reason, of course! To protect spirituality! To be on the watch for mice! You won't slip by them. That's why there are three fences wrapped around the terem! That's why the guards are so strict! That's why they search you when you come in! Because no matter who you are, even the fanciest suitor or some other very important person, you could still bring a mouse in with you and you wouldn't even notice.

If you have a rat's nest in your hair a mouse could make its own nest there too.

It could hide in your pockets, that happens sometimes.

Or in a boot.

It couldn't have been clearer, but he hadn't understood. And he hadn't understood Illness, goodness knows what he thought. But Illness is in people's heads, Illness is human ignorance, stupidity, Freethinking, dimwittedness, it's when they think "Oh, well, who cares, it doesn't matter, mice and books can live in the same izba." Jeez! A book in the same izba with a mouse! Horrible even to think about.

And how stubborn the scum are: you'd think no one let them read, that someone took away poems and essays! And just why did the government hire Scribes, why did it build the Work Izba, teach people letters, hand out writing sticks, scrape bark clean, sew bark booklets? It's a lot of extra work for the government, extra effort, fuss and bother! It's all for the people, that's who it's for. Catch all the mice you like, go on, be my guest—then trade them for booklets and read to your heart's content!

He clenched his fists in anger, tossed and turned on the bed, and in his head everything grew clearer and clearer, like a great space was opening up! Good Lord! That's how it always was, in ancient times too! "But is the world not all alike . . . Throughout the ages, now and ever more?" It is! It is!

Beneath a canopy of fetid thatch,
In valleys far below the mountain's crest,
A web has bound both kith and kin,
Nearby, an earthly mouse now builds its nest.

Now kith and kin crowd round the valley,

They clamor, yet each one is still alone,
And each conceals in his own desert
A frozen knot, an ever precious stone.

There you go! In the Oldener days people did the same thing: they made mischief, had a spell of Freethinking, hid books in the cold somewhere, in the damp, all frozen in a knotted bundle. Now he got it!

In the stony cracks between the tiles
The faces of the mice squeezed through,
They looked like triangles of chalk,
With mournful eyes on either side—one, two.

That's right, there's no holding a mouse back! It can get through any crack or crevice!

. . . Life, you're but a mouse's scurry,
Why do you trouble me?

Ah, brother pushkin! Aha! You also tried to protect your writing from rodents! He'd write—and they'd eat, he'd write some more, and they'd eat again! No wonder he was troubled! That's why he kept riding back and forth across the snow, across the icy desert! The sleigh bells jangle ting-a-ling! He'd hitch up a Degenerator and it was off to the steppes! He was hiding his work, looking for a place to keep it safe!

Neither fire nor darkened huts,
Just woods and snow to greet me,
The whitened stripes of frosty ruts
Are all that here do meet me.

He was looking for a place to bury . . . Suddenly, everything became so clear that Benedikt sat up and put his feet on the floor. Why didn't he realize it earlier . . . ? How could he have missed the instructions? . . . A long time ago! What did they sing with Lev Lvovich?

Steppe and nothing else,
As far as the eye can see . . .

242

Out on that lonesome steppe
A coachman called to me.

Well! Why did he go racing off to the steppes, if not to hide books? — "in his own desert / a frozen knot, an ever precious stone . . ."

Please do tell my wife,
That on the steppe I froze,
And that I took with me
Her undying love!

What love is he talking about? It was a book! What else could you love but a book? Huh?

"Tell my wife . . . that I took with me." He asks his pal to tell his wife so that she doesn't keep looking, otherwise she'll be missing them . . . Now there's a poem for you! Not a poem but a regular fable! Governing instructions rendered in a simplified, popular form!

That's why Lev Lvovich was crying. He probably buried some books too, and now he can't find them. That's enough to make you cry. But he started singing and remembered!

How did they hint to Benedikt? Benedikt asked them: Are there any books around to read? And they answered: You don't know your ABCs. And he said: What do you mean I don't know them, I know them! And they said: "Steppe and nothing else, as far as the eye can see . . ." It was a hint. A fable. That's where the books are buried, they were telling him. We don't keep them at home.

All right. Where is the steppe? The steppe is in the south . . . But why did he keep saying: the west will help us? . . . And Nikita Ivanich kept telling him: No way, it won't help, we have to do it ourselves. So which is it? Where are they?

Mother-in-law knocked on the door: "Time to bathe the children! Are you going to watch?"

"Don't bother me!" screamed Benedikt, pounding his fist. "Close the door!"

"Should we bathe them?"

"Shut the door!"

She broke his train of thought, dammit! . . . Benedikt dressed hurriedly, throwing on his coat, the robe, and the hood. He dashed down the stairs and whistled to a lethargic Nikolai to hitch up.

He drove him impatiently, tapping his boot in the sleigh. He had to check the horizon. He absolutely had to. Before the faint winter light was gone, he had to survey the horizon in all four directions.

Benedikt was driving to the watchtower, that's where. He'd never been up in the watchtower before. Who would have let a Golubchik up there, anyway? It was forbidden, it belonged to the government, only guards and Murzas are allowed on the tower. And why is that? Because you can see far and wide from there, and that's governmental business, it's not meant for just anyone! An ordinary Golubchik has no call to be looking off far and wide: it's not fitting. Maybe there are warriors approaching off in the distance! Maybe a ferocious enemy wants to take a bite out of our bright homeland, so he's sharpened his sticks and marched off toward us. That's governmental business! It's forbidden! But no one would ever stop Benedikt, since he was a Saniturion.

No one stopped him. Naturally.

The watchtower was higher than the highest terem, higher than the trees, higher than the Alexander column. There was a room on the very top. In the room, set in the walls, were four small windows, four slits facing the four sides of the world. Above it sat a slanted four-sided roof, like a hat. Like the one the Murzas wear. When you look up from below — way, way up, under the clouds, the government workers and guards swarm like little ants. They crawl from one place to another, fiddling around with something. Down on the ground the guards have poleaxes. Benedikt rose heavily from the sleigh, one part of him at a time, his awful eyes looking through the crimson slits. He raised his hood — and the guards fell prostrate onto the hard, frozen snow crust. He stepped into the tower. There was a strong doggy smell from dirty coats and the acrid odor of cheap rusht: they were smoking damp, uncleaned rusht with twigs and straw. The wood steps clunked and clattered under his feet. There was a spiral staircase covered with yellow ice—this was where they relieved themselves and stamped out butts. On the walkways, sparkling with frost, someone had scratched curse words, the usual stuff. Not a whiff of spirituality . . . He climbed slowly, leaning on the hook, stopping on the landings to rest. Steam came out of his mouth and hung there, hovering in clouds in the foul, frosty air.

On the top landing the guards jumped in surprise when they saw the red robe of a government worker.

"Out!" ordered Benedikt.

The workers took off, tearing down the stairs, pushing one another, all eight legs thundering down.

From the tower you could see far away. Far away . . . There wasn't even a word in the language to say how far you could see from the tower! And if there was a word like that, you'd be scared to say it out loud. Ooooh, so far away! To the farthest of far, the edge of the edge, to the limit of limits, all the way to death! The round pancake of the earth, the whole heavenly vault, the entire cold December, the whole city with all its settlements, with its dark, lopsided izbas—empty and wide open, gone over with the fine-tooth comb of the Saniturions' hooks and still inhabited, still swarming with scared, senseless, stubborn life!

> O world, roll up into a single block,
> A cracked and broken sidewalk,
> A fouled and filthy warehouse,
> The burrow of a mouse!

A thin strip of horrible yellow sunset filled the western window, and the evening star Alatyr twinkled in the sunset. The pushkin stuck out like a small black stick in the confusion of streets, and from that height the rope looped around the poet's neck and hung with laundry looked like a fine thread.

The sunrise lay hidden in a dark-blue blanket in the other window, covering the woods, rivers, more woods, and secret fields where red tulips sleep under the snow, where Benedikt's eternal bride hibernates, dressed in frosty lace, inside an icy, decorated egg, with a smile on her luminous face, my unfound love, the Princess Bird, and she dreams of kisses, of silky grass, golden flies, and mirrored waters where her unspeakable beauty is reflected, shimmers, ruffles, multiplies. In her sleep the Princess Bird sighs a happy sigh and dreams of her beautiful self.

To the south, lit by a terrible double light—the yellow from the west and the dark blue from the sunrise side—in the south, blocking the impassable snowy steppe with its whistling whirlwinds and stormy columns, in the south, which runs, runs ever onward toward the dark blue, windy Ocean-Sea, in the south, beyond the ravine, beyond the triple moat, covering the whole width of the window, spread the red, adorned, embellished, ornamented, painted, many-towered, many-storied terem of Fyodor Kuzmich, Glorybe, the Greatest Murza, Long May He Live.

"Ha!" laughed Benedikt.

Joy spurted from him like foamy, sparkling kvas.

> Joy, thou beauteous godly lightning,
> Daughter of Elysium.

Suddenly, everything became as limpid as a spring brook. It was all right in front of him, clear as day. That's what it was! There! . . . There, right before him, unspoiled, unspent, a treasure trove full to the brim, a magical garden blooming and fruitful in its pink-white froth, a garden flowing with the sweetest juice, like a billion blind firelings! There, packed tight from its sonorous cellars to its aromatic attics, was the pleasure palace! Ali Baba's cave! The Taj Mahal, for cryin' out loud!

Of course! In the south, that's right! So the west did help! The light was from the west, the star was a beacon. It illuminated everything! He guessed, he figured it out, he understood the clues, he understood the fable—and everything fit together!

He squinted from happiness, squeezed his eyelids tight, and shook his head. He stuck his head through the window slit to feel it better; he inhaled the aroma of frost and wood, the sweet smoke curling up from the chimneys of the Red Terem. He seemed to see things better with his eyelids closed, he heard more clearly, and felt more acutely; there, there, right nearby, very close, just beyond the gully, beyond the ditch, behind the triple wall, beyond the high pike fence—but you can jump over a wall and slip under a pike fence. If only he could jump from the tower right this minute, softly softly, unheard and unseen, and be swept away in the blizzard's whirlwind, carried like weightless dust across the gully, like a snowspout right into the attic window! Crawling and leaping, limber and long, but just so he didn't miss it, didn't lose the trail; closer, still closer to the terem, without leaving traces on the snow, scaring dogs in the yard, or disturbing any creatures in the house!

And then to drink, drink his fill, drink in the letters, words, and pages with their sweet, dusty, acrid, inimitable smell! O my beauteous poppies! O my imperishable, ever-shining gold!

"Oooooooh!" Benedikt squealed blissfully.

"So, son, are you ready now?" came a quiet laugh behind him, just above his ear. Benedikt started and opened his eyes.

"Goodness gracious, Papa! You scared me!"

Father-in-law stole up quietly, the floorboards didn't even tremble. You could tell he'd pulled his claws in. He, too, wore a red robe and hood over his head, but by the voice and the smell you could tell that yes, it was Father-in-law, Kudeyar Kudeyarich.

"So what now?" whispered Father-in-law. "Shall we do a bit of tumbling?"

"I don't understand."

"Feel like doing a bit of overturning? Fyodor Kuzmich, that is, Glorybe? Ready to knock off the evil tormentor? That damned dwarf?"

"I'm ready," Benedikt whispered with conviction. "Papa! I'd do it with my own hands!"

"Oh, heart of mine! . . ." said Father-in-law joyfully. "Well? Finally! . . . Finally! Let me hug you!"

Benedikt and Kudeyar Kudeyarich embraced and stood looking down on the city from the heights. Bluish lights began to flicker in the izbas, the sunset went out, the stars emerged.

"Let's swear an oath to each other," said Kudeyar Kudeyarich.

"An oath?"

"Yep. For eternal friendship."

"Well . . . all right."

"I gave you everything. I gave you my daughter—if you want, I'll let you have my wife."

"Uh, that won't be n-n-n-necessary. We need Kant in our hearts and a peaceful sky above our heads. There's a law like that," Benedikt remembered.

"True enough. And it's us against the tyrants. Agreed?"

"Of course."

"We'll ravage the oppressor's nest, okey dokey?"

"Oh, Papa, he's got books piled high as the snow!"

"Aaah, my dear, even higher. And he tears pictures out of them."

"Quiet, I don't want to know," said Benedikt, gritting his teeth.

"I can't be quiet! Art is in peril!" Father-in-law exclaimed sternly. "There is no worse enemy than indifference! All evil in fact comes from the silent acquiescence of the indifferent. You read *Mumu,* didn't you? Did you understand the moral? How he kept silent all the time, and the dog died."

"Papa, but how—"

"Know-how, that's how. I've thought the whole thing through. We'll make a revolution. I've just been waiting for you. We'll go in at night, he doesn't sleep at night, but the guards will be tired. Okey-dokey?"

"At night, how can we do it at night? It's dark!"

"And what am I here for? Aren't I a torch-bearer?"

Father-in-law's eyes gave off a ray of light, and he laughed contentedly.

Clear and simple. The soul was icy clean. No neuroses now.

Ѣ · YAT

THE RED TEREM had a moldy smell—a familiar, exciting smell ... Unmistakable. Old paper, the leather of ancient bindings, traces of gold dust, sweet glue. Benedikt felt a bit weak in the knees, like he was on his way to a woman for the first time. Women! ... What did he need Marfushkas or Olenkas for now, when all the women of the ages, the Isoldes, the Rosamunds, the Juliets, with their combs and silks, their daggers and caprices, would be his any minute, now and forever more ... When he was just about to become the owner of the untold, the unimaginable ... the Shah of Shahs, the Emir, the Sultan, the Sun King, Head of the Housing Committee, Chairman of the Earth, Head Clerk, Archimandrite, Pope of Rome, Boyars' Council Scribe, the Collegiate Assessor, King Solomon ... He, Benedikt, he would be all of these ...

Father-in-law illuminated the path with his eyes. Two strong, moon-white rays searched the hallways. Dust swam in the beams of light, disappearing for a moment when Father-in-law blinked. Benedikt's head spun from the frequent flares, the fragrance of nearby book bindings, and the sweetish stench coming from Father-in-law's mouth—Father-in-law kept jerking his head, as though his collar was strangling him. Shadows danced along the walls like gigantic letters: Г—Glagol of the hook, Л—Liudi of Benedikt's peaked hood, Ж—Zhivete of the cautious fingers splayed to feel their way along the walls, to search for hidden doors. Father-in-law ordered him to step softly, not to shuffle his feet.

"Listen to the revolution, dammit!"

The revolutionaries crept through the corridors, turned corners, stopped, looked around, listened. Somewhere back there near the entrance lay the pitiful guards, no longer breathing: what can a poleax or a halberd do against a double-edged hook, swift as a bird?

249

They passed through two floors, climbed the stairs, ran on tiptoe across the hanging galleries where the moon shone bright and terrible through the window bladders. Their black felt boots silently crossed the moonlit floorboards; the tall, ornamented inner doors opened to show the drunken private quarter guards snoring—legs akimbo, caps on their chests. Father-in-law swore quietly: No order in the government at all. Fyodor Kuzmich, Glorybe, had ruined everything. Quickly, with a swift poke, they dispatched the guards.

After the entrance there were more corridors and the sweet smell grew nearer. Glancing upward, Benedikt clasped his hands: books! The shelves were packed with books! Lord Almighty! Saints alive! His knees gave way, he trembled and whined softly: you couldn't read them all in a whole lifetime! A forest of pages, an endless, indiscriminate blizzard, uncounted! Ah . . .! Ah!!! Aaaaa! Maybe . . . just maybe . . . somewhere here . . . maybe the secret book is here somewhere! The book that tells you how to live, where to go, where to guide the heart! Maybe Fyodor Kuzmich, Glorybe, has found it, and is already reading it: he jumps up on the bed quick as a wink, and just reads and reads! He went and found it, the monster, and he's reading it!! The tyrant! Shit!

"Pay attention!" Father-in-law breathed into his face.

The hallways branched off, turned, forked, and disappeared toward the unknown depths of the terem. Father-in-law looked every which way: all that could be seen was books.

"There has to be a simple way in," muttered Father-in-law. "Somewhere there must be an entrance. There has to be . . . We took a wrong turn somewhere."

"The Northern Herald!!! Issue number eight!!!" Benedikt cried. He rushed at it, pushing Kudeyar Kudeyarich, who tripped and fell against the wall. As he fell, he reached his hand out to break his fall: the wall yielded and turned into a shelf, the shelf collapsed and broke into pieces. Suddenly they were in an enormous hall whose walls were entirely covered with bookcases and shelves; there were countless tables heaped high with books, and at the head table, in a semicircle of a thousand candles, was a

high stool, and on that stool sat Fyodor Kuzmich himself, Glorybe, with a writing stick in his mouth: he turned his face to look at
them and his mouth opened wide: he was surprised.

"Why are you here unannounced?" he said, frowning.

"Get down, overthrow yourself, you accursed tyrant-blood-
sucker," cried Father-in-law with real flourish. "We've come to
oust you!"

"Who's come? Why did they let you in?" said Fyodor Kuzmich, Glorybe, in a worried voice.

"Who's come? Who's come? He whose time has come, that's
who."

"Tyrants of the world, tremble; but you take courage and
hark!" cried Benedikt from behind Father-in-law's shoulder.

"Why tremble?" asked Fyodor Kuzmich, as he realized what
was happening. He screwed up his face and began to cry. "What
are you going to do to me?"

"Your unjust rule has ended! You tormented the people—
and that's enough of that! Now we'll give you a taste of the
hook!"

"I don't want the hook, I don't. It huuurts!"

"Next thing you know he'll be telling us his sad story," cried
Father-in-law. "Beat him!" he cried, striking a blow in his direction. But Fyodor Kuzmich, Glorybe, rolled off the stool like a
pea and ran, so Father-in-law hit a book instead, and split it in
two.

"Why, why are you ousting meeee?"

"You're doing a bad job of running the state!" cried Father-
in-law in a terrible voice. Hook in hand, he rushed at the Greatest Murza, Long May He Live, but Fyodor Kuzmich, Glorybe,
dived under the stool again and scrambled under the table. He
ran to the other side of the room.

"I do the best I can!" sobbed Fyodor Kuzmich.

"You destroyed the whole goddamned country! You tear
pages out of books! Get him, Benedikt!"

"You stole poems from the pushkin," cried Benedikt, working himself up, "and he's our be all and end all! And you stole
from him!"

"I invented the wheel!"

"It was the pushkin who invented the wheel!"

"And the yoke!"

"Pushkin did it!"

"The torch!"

"Jeez! He's still being stubborn."

Benedikt ran after Fyodor Kuzmich from one side of the table, Father-in-law tried to head him off on the other side, but the Greatest Murza, Long May He Live, once again bolted under the books.

"Leave me alone, I'm a good boy!"

"You wily louse!" cried Father-in-law. With one hand leaning on the table, he jumped over it in a single leap. Fyodor Kuzmich, Glorybe, squealed, scampered under the bookcase, and took refuge somewhere out of sight.

"Catch him!" croaked Father-in-law, thrusting his hook under the shelves. "He'll get away! Get away! He has tunnels dug everywhere!"

Benedikt ran over to help. Together, getting in each other's way, they poked around with their hooks, huffing and puffing . . .

"I've got something here. Think I got him . . . Come on, you're younger, squat down and take a look . . . I can't quite get the hook in. It's him, right?"

Benedikt got down on his hands and knees and looked under the shelves—it was dark and there were all kinds of wisps and rags.

"I can't see anything . . . Kudeyar Kudeyarich, if you could just light it up!"

"I'm afraid to let him go . . . Come on, now, take the hook from me . . . Dammit . . . I can't figure out . . ."

Benedikt grabbed the hook; Father-in-law got on all fours, shone his light under the shelves. His joints creaked.

"There's so much dust . . . Can't see anything . . . Huge dust balls under here . . ."

Something jerked the hook, they heard the sound of clothes ripping. Benedikt jabbed and gave the hook a twist, but too late: tap tap tap—they could hear small steps running along the walls behind the shelves somewhere in the depths of the room.

"You let him get away, dammit!" cried Father-in-law in disappointment. "And I taught you, I taught you!"

"Why is it always me? . . . You were the one who hooked him by the clothes!"

"We should have squashed him. Where is he now? . . . Come on now, come out, Fyodor Kuzmich! Come out like a good boy!"

"No fair, no fair!" cried Fyodor Kuzmich, Glorybe, from below.

"There he is! Come on!"

But Fyodor Kuzmich scurried away again.

"Don't try to catch me, I'm just a little guy."

"Stick him . . . Poke over here, that way!"

"Why are you so insistent? . . . Go away!" Fyodor Kuzmich squeaked from a third place.

"You're not nice!" he cried from a fourth.

Father-in-law looked all around, Benedikt looked around, his neck craned, his head bent. Something shuffled under the far shelf; he turned his head that way; something rustled under the shelves; with a soft, long leap Benedikt jumped. If he closed his eyes, he could hear the sounds better; so he closed his eyes and turned his head from side to side; if he could only push his ears back a bit more, it would be even better. His nostrils flared—he could find him by smell too, his smell went with him when he ran . . . There he is!

"There he is!" cried Benedikt, leaping and lunging at the spot. He turned his hook. There was a piercing squeal under the hook. "I've got him!"

Something burst. It was a soft sound, but distinct. Something tensed and then went limp on the hook. Benedikt turned it and pulled the Greatest Murza, Long May He Live, out from under the shelf. So much fuss and bother for such a puny little body. Benedikt pushed back his hood and wiped his nose with his sleeve. He took a closer look. The backbone had broken; the head was twisted to one side, and the eyes had rolled back.

Father-in-law walked over and looked. He shook his head.

"The hook got dirty. It'll have to be boiled."

"Now what?"

"Clean him off it and throw him in a box or something."

"With my hands?"

"Why your hands? God forbid. Use a piece of paper. There's tons of paper around here."

"Hey, hey, don't tear up any books! I have to read them!"

"No letters here. Just a picture."

Father-in-law tore a portrait out of a book, rolled it up in a cone, stuck his hand in it, and cleaned Fyodor Kuzmich, Glory-be, off the hook. Then he wiped off the hook.

"There you go," muttered Father-in-law. "No more tyranny allowed! It was just getting too darn fashionable!"

Benedikt was suddenly exhausted. His temples pounded. He wasn't used to bending down. He sat on a stool to catch his breath. There were a bunch of books laid out on the table. Well, that was it. Now everything was his. He opened one of them cautiously.

> The trepidation of life, of all the centuries and races,
> Lives in you. Always. Right now. In all your hidden places.

Poems. He clapped the book shut and looked at another.

> He who draws the darkest lot of chance
> Is not subject to the dance;
> Like a star drowned in the skies,
> In his place, a new star will arise.

More poems! Lord and Saints Almighty. How much there is to read! He opened a third book:

> What kind of East do you favor?
> The East of Xerxes, or of Christ the Savior?

A fourth book:

> Is all quiet among our fair people?
> No. The Emperor's murdered, cast down.
> And there's someone now talking of freedom,
> On the square of the town.

It was all sort of about the same thing. The tyrant must have been putting a little collection together for himself. Benedikt opened the fifth book, the one from which Father-in-law tore a portrait that Fyodor Kuzmich, Glorybe, ruined:

> Man suits all elements, every season.
> Tyrant, traitor, or the prison.

Father-in-law tore the book away from Benedikt and tossed it aside.

"Stop that nonsense! Now it's time to think about the State!"

"About the State? What about it?"

"What? You and I have carried out a coup, that's what. And he says: What about it? We have to put things in order."

Benedikt looked around the room: true, everything was topsy-turvy, the stools were upside down, the tables were all over, books lay every which way, having fallen off shelves while he and Father-in-law chased the Greatest Murza, Long May He Live. Everything was dusty.

"So what? Send over a bunch of serfs and they'll clean up."

"Now that just shows you're a real dimwit! Spiritual, spiritual order is what we need! And you keep fretting about earthly stuff! We have to write a decree. When you carry out a coup d'état you always have to write a decree. Come on now, find me some clean bark. There ought to be some around here."

Benedikt rummaged around on the table, moving the books. He found a scroll that was nearly clean. Fyodor Kuzmich, Glorybe, had only begun to write on it.

DECREE
Since I am Fyodor Kuzmich Kablukov, Glory-to-me, the Greatest Murza, Long May I Live, and Seckletary, Academishun, and Hero and Ship Captain and Handyman, and since I am constantly thinking day and night about the people, I decree:
—Now I've got a couple of free minutes, but the whole day was nonstop.
—This is what else I thought up for the people's goo . . .

And then there were a bunch of lines and blotches: that's where he got scared.

"All right, then. Come on, let's get on with it. What have we got here? . . . Cross all that out. You write, your handwriting is better: Decree Number One."

DECREE NUMBER ONE
1. I am going to be the Boss now.
2. My title will be General Saniturion.
3. I will live in the Red Terem with twice as many guards.
4. Don't come any closer than one hundred yards, 'cause whoever does will get the hook right away no questions asked.

Kudeyarov

P.S.
Henceforth and forever more the city will be called Kudeyar-Kudeyarichsk. Learn it by heart.

Kudeyarov

Benedikt wrote it down.

"OK. Show me how it came out. 'Kudeyarov' needs to be bigger and with a curlicue. Cross it out. Rewrite it, so that the last name is in big letters, as big as a toenail. After the V twist it around in circles left and right, kind of like loops. There you go. That's it."

Father-in-law blew on the bark so it would dry; then he admired it.

"All right. What else should we do? . . . Write: Decree Number Two."

"Kudeyar Kudeyarich! You should decree more holidays."

"Ay ay ay! Your approach is so ungovernmental," said Father-in-law testily. "Has the decree been signed? It has! Did it take effect? It did! So you call me General Saniturion. Talk to me like you're supposed to. Who do you think you are?"

"And the extras? The attributes?"

"Ah, the attributes . . . attributes . . . Hmm . . . How about: 'Life, Health, Strength.' General Saniturion, Life, Health, Strength. Write it in there. All right. You need a title too . . . How about Deputy for Defense?"

"I want to be General Deputy for Defense."

"What's this now, already trying to oust me?" cried Father-in-law. "You want to oust me, is that it?"

"What does it have to do with . . . You're always going on like . . . like I don't know what! No ousting, it just sounds nice: General!"

"Of course it sounds nice! But two can't have it at the same time! There's never more than one General! If you want, you can be Deputy for Defense and Marine Affairs."

"For Marine and Oceanic."

"Whatever you like. Let's keep going. Decree Number Two."

"Holidays, more holidays."

"There you go again with an ungovernmental approach! First and foremost are civil liberties, not holidays."

"Why? What does it matter?"

"Because! That's how revolution is always done: first the tyrant is overthrown, then the new Boss of everything is named, and then come civil liberties."

They sat down to write, shuffling the bark. Light began to appear in the window. Beyond the doors you could hear a murmuring and a muttering, whispered negotiations, a commotion. There was a knock at the door.

"Who's trying to get in? What do you want?"

A serf stumbled in with a bow.

"There's a, um . . . a delegation of representatives asking: What's up?"

"What representatives?"

"What representatives?" shouted the serf, turning back toward the entrance.

"Of the People!" came the cry from the entryway. It seemed to be Lev Lvovich shouting. They'd barely had time to overthrow the tyrant and here petitioners were already besieging them. The rumor must've got around. That's the people for you! Won't give you a minute of peace!

"Some Representatives of the People."

"Tell them the revolution was successful, the tyrant has been deposed, we're working on a decree about civil liberties, don't bother us, disperse and go home."

"Don't forget about the Xeroxes!" came the cry from the entryway.

"Now he's telling me what to do! Who's the liberator here? Me! Kick him out," said Father-in-law angrily. "Close the door and don't let anyone in. We're writing fateful papers here, and he's hanging around bugging us. Come on, Deputy. Write: Decree Number Two."

"I wrote that."

"All right, then . . . Liberties . . . I've got it written down here somewhere . . . a list . . . I can't make it out. Your eyes are younger, read it to me."

"Ay . . . What bad handwriting . . . Who wrote it?"

"Who wrote it? I wrote it. I copied it from a book. I consulted the literature so everything would be scientific. Go on, read it."

"Hmm . . . freedom of the . . . left or maybe it's life and . . . I can't figure it out."

"Skip it, read on."

"Freedom . . . of ass-Ocean, is that it?"

"Let me see. That seems right . . . Yes, that's it. OK, so that when people get together, they can move around freely. Or else they'll just clump up and crowd into one place and there won't be any room to move. They'll smoke the place up, then they'll get headaches and they'll be bad workers. Write: No more than three can gather."

"And what if it's a holiday?"

"Doesn't matter."

"And what if there are six people in a family? Or seven?"

Father-in-law spat. "What's all this dialecticals you're coming up with? Then let them fill out a form, pay a fine, and get permission. Write!"

Benedikt wrote: "No more than three for heaven's sake can gather at a time."

"Now: freedom of the printing press."

"What's that for?"

"It has to be there, so that people can read Oldenprint books." Father-in-law thought a minute. "All right. To hell with them. It doesn't matter anymore. Let them read."

Benedikt wrote: "The reading of Oldenprint books is permitted." He thought a minute and added: "but within reason." That's what Fyodor Kuzmich, Glorybe, always decreed. He thought some more. No, what'll that lead to? Anybody can just take books and read them? Free to take them out of the larder and lay them out on the table? What if that table's got something spilled on it or it's dirty? When it's forbidden to read books everybody takes care of them, they wrap them in a clean cloth and are afraid to breathe on them. But when reading is permitted, then they'll probably break the spines or rip out pages! They'll get it into their heads to throw books. No! You can't trust people. But what's the big deal? Just take them away and that's it. Comb the city, settlement after settlement, house by house, shake down everyone, confiscate the books, and lock them up behind seven bolts. That's all there is to it.

Suddenly he felt: I understand the governmental approach!!! All by myself, without any decree—I understand!!! Hurray! So that's what happens when you sit in the Red Terem! Benedikt straightened his shoulders, laughed, stuck out the end of his tongue, and carefully wrote in the word "not" between "is" and "permitted."

"Now . . . Freedom of re, relig . . . religion."

Father-in-law yawned. "I'm sick of this. That's enough liberties."

"There's just a little more here."

"That's enough. Not too much of the good stuff. Let's do defense. Write: Decree Number Three."

They worked on defense until noon. Mother-in-law sent someone to ask when they would be coming home. Dinner had grown cold. They ordered bliny and pies to be brought to the Red Terem with a barrel of kvas and some candles. Benedikt, as Deputy for Defense and Marine and Oceanic Affairs, got into the spirit of things—it was interesting. They decided to build three fences around the city so it would be easier to defend themselves against the Chechens. On top of the fence at all twenty-four corners, there would be booths with guards to watch with eagle eyes day and night in both directions. They decided to make plank gates on all four sides of the wall. If someone needs to go out into the fields—to plant turnips, or gather sheaves—he can get a pass in the office. In the morning you go out with a pass, in the evening you hand it back. Serfs will make a hole in the pass, or, as Father-in-law said, they can punch it and write in the name: so-and-so was let through, he paid ten chits. And also, Benedikt thought, this fence would be a defense against the Slynx. If you built it really really high, the Slynx would never get through it. Inside the fence you can go where you like and enjoy your freedom. Peace and Freewill. The pushkin wrote that too.

Yes! And then defend the pushkin from the people, so that they don't hang underwear on him. Make stone chains and put them on pillars on all four sides around him. Up above, over his head, a little parasol so that the shitbirds don't shit on him. And put serfs at all the corners, a night watch and especially a day watch. Add weeding the people's path to the list of roadwork. That way the path would be cleared during the winter, and in the summer you could plant bluebells around it. Forbid dill throughout the land, so you couldn't smell it anywhere anymore.

Benedikt sat a bit longer, thought a bit more, and got mad: the pushkin is our be all and end all! And moreover, Benedikt is deputy for Marine and Oceanics. Here's what needs to be done: carve out a huge kind of ship, with logs and boughs. Put it by the river. And put the pushkin up top, on the very tippy top. With a book in his hand. Higher than the Alexander column, with some to spare.

Let him stand there strong and safe, his legs in chains, his head in the clouds, his face to the south, to the endless steppe, to the far-off dark blue seas.

"I really love that pushkin so much," sighed Benedikt.

"More than me?" frowned Father-in-law. "Look here! Write: Decree Number Twenty-eight: On Fire Safety Measures."

Θ · THETA

"PAPA COMPLAINS you're always moving away from him at the table. You're hurting his feelings . . ."

"He stinks, so I move over."

"Stinks? Picky, picky! And just what is it you smell?"

"He smells like a corpse."

"Well, what else? He's not going to smell like a tulip, is he?"

"It's disgusting."

"So what? That's his work!"

"Well, I don't like it. He shouldn't smell."

"Goodness gracious, aren't you the delicate one."

Benedikt answered distractedly, as usual, without looking up. He sat at a huge table in a bright room of the Red Terem. On the ceiling—he remembered without even looking—was a curly sort of mural with flowers and leaves. The ones that were outlined in rusht were brownish, the ones outlined with ground shells were green, and if they were outlined with a blue stone— then they were blue! Gorgeous! The light came right in through the window grates, it was summer outside, there were grass and flowers, but on the ceiling it was always summer. Benedikt was eating jam cakes and reading *The Journal of Horse Breeding.* He read calmly, with pleasure: there was a whole hallway of these magazines, enough to last a century. He would read a bit from the journal, and then from *The Odyssey,* then some Yamamoto, or *Correspondence from Two Corners,* or poems, or *Care of Leather Footwear,* or a bit of Sartre. He read whatever he felt like reading, everything was at hand, it was all his. For all time to come, amen.

He didn't feel like working at governmental affairs at all: it was a big bore. They gave the Golubchiks liberties, they gave them Decrees—what else do they need? They even gave them Instructions, what more is there? Who wants to work?

Strengthen defense? They strengthened it: sapling fences, picket fences, pike fences—they fixed everything as best they could, they spackled and stuffed rags in the holes, using whatever was to hand. The enemy couldn't get through, except maybe through the Ekimansky Swamp, but that's why it's a swamp, so you can't get through. Who in their right mind would go through a swamp?

At first they thought of fencing off the Cockynork settlement, so they wouldn't come bothering us, but then they thought again and decreed: No, no, we won't give up an inch of our land.

They conferred for a week to decide what tithe to exact from conquered Golubchiks if they entered an armed conflict with a foreign state and won—although they didn't know whether there was another state anywhere. But should the tithe be collected daily, or weekly, or perhaps quarterly?

They canceled leap year for centuries and ages to come, of course.

They issued a special Decree saying that all conjurers, sorcerers, enchanters, magicians, clairvoyants, stargazers, witches, soothsayers, fortune tellers, wicked women, and people who open and close chakras shouldn't even think about engaging in magicianry on a private basis, no, no, not even an eensy weensy bit, heaven forbid. All spellcasters, and especially cloudchasers, will henceforth be considered government workers and should always sleep in their clothes in case they're called out on an emergency.

They worked out a long, formal title for Father-in-law. In official documents he had to be called: Kudeyar-Pasha, General Saniturion and People's Beloved, Life, Health, Strength, Theofrast Bombast, Paracelsus-and-Maria, Sanchez-and-Jimenez, Wolfgang Amadeus Avitsenna Cheops von Guggenheim.

Teterya wanted to be called Petrovich-san, Minister of Transport, Oil, and Refineries. What does that mean? It means that he ordered the guzzelean water to be ladled out in buckets and pails and lugged over to the cellar. You had to admit it was beautiful water, it looked like it was covered with a rainbow. But it was foul-tasting and didn't smell very good. Teterya was Boss of all Transport and Hauling, and of all the Degenerators. Olenka and Fevronia didn't want to be called anything, they only wanted a lot of different outfits, so they could wear a new dress each time there was a public execution, whether it was the wheel or a tongue being cut out, or something else.

It was all so dull.

"... Papa's feelings are hurt, he says you wrinkle you nose at him. Benedikt! Don't wrinkle your nose!"

"Get out of here. I'm reading."

Benedikt waited until every last inch of Olenka had left through the wide doors. She broke his train of thought, the bitch.

"You're wrinkling your nose up at me, I see," said Father-in-law.

"Don't be silly."

"And here we are, friends forever and all time. We swore to it."

"Mmmmmm."

"Where you go, I go. Put that book down!"

"All right, all right, what is it?"

The family was sitting at the table, eating grilled canaries and looking at Benedikt with displeasure, all of them, even Petrovich-san. The children, Bubble and Concordia, crawled under the table, scraping the floor with their claws.

"I've got a mind to reorganize the power structure, my dear boy."

"Be my guest."

"Petrovich and I decided to whip up an internal combustion engine. We've got the guzzelean, I can spark it with my eyes, the rest will take care of itself in the course of things."

"Godspeed. What do I have to do with it?"

"We need a little bit of consolidation," Petrovich-san piped up.

"I don't have any."

"Ay! Help, we need help!"

"I want to remove the Head Stoker," said Father-in-law.

Benedikt thought he'd misheard. He put his finger in the book, and leaned forward.

"Move him where?"

"Where, what do you mean where? Remove him—execute him! Clean out your ears!" Father-in-law sputtered. "You've gone overboard with all that reading, buried yourself in papers, abandoned the government. And you're supposed to be a Deputy! I wish to execute him as a fire hazard. In accordance with the Governmental Decree that took effect ages ago. He's harming the economy: the people have gone to seed, they get their stoves lighted for free, no one's paying the fire tax!"

"Now that we've got gasoline, we cannot tolerate any open flames," confirmed Teterya. "I declare this officially, as Minister of Oil and Refineries. We're an OPEC country now. We have to think about exports, and not all these shenanigans."

"What's more, he's carrying out dangerous excavations and undermining the government. We'll wake up one morning and the country will have collapsed."

"He's erecting columns, interfering with traffic flow—now I'm speaking in my capacity as Minister of Transport."

"The revolution goes on, there's nothing to discuss," said Father-in-law angrily. "Do we need to uphold the purity of the ranks? We do. I'm a medical worker, don't forget. You know what oath we medical workers take? Do no harm. And he's doing harm. Well? So you go on over and see him and tie him up with a rope real quick. Tie him to that column or something, only make sure he's tied tight. I would send my own people, but he'll just huff and puff at them and get away. But he won't huff and puff at you."

"I won't let you execute Nikita Ivanich, what on earth is going on!!!" cried Benedikt. "He's an old friend . . . he made sweet rolls for me, we carved the pushkin together, and . . . he . . . he . . . this . . . and . . . anyway!!!"

He decided not to mention the tail.

"You'll let us, you won't let us—no one's asking your permission!" shouted Father-in-law. "You are the Deputy for Marine and Oceanic Defense, and this is terra firma business. We'll build an engine and drive along the roads! Your job is to bring him in, so he doesn't get away!"

"Up yours!"

"So that's how it is, huh? Cosmopolitan!" shouted Teterya, shoving the table.

"Some cosmetologian you are! You four-legged warty furball!" Benedikt retorted.

"That's how you talk to a Minister?" Father-in-law bent over and tore the book out of Benedikt's hands. He hurled it on the floor and the pages fell apart.

"Jeez! . . . And you, Papa, you just plain stink!"

"Oh, so that's it, is it? Come on, then," Father-in-law jumped across the table in one leap, knocking over the dishes. He grabbed Benedikt by the neck with his strong, cold hands. "Come on, let me hear that again! Say it again—again I say! I'll teach you to—"

And, squinting his eyes, he began to burn Benedikt with a chill, yellow, scratching sort of flame.

"Enough of this outrageous behavior! And in front of the children!" Mother-in-law cried out.

"Control yourself, Papa!"

"What are you? . . . You're just a . . . a . . . a . . . you're the Slynx, that's who you are!!!" cried Benedikt, scaring himself— words just fly out of your mouth and then you can't catch them. He was scared, but he shouted, "Slynx, Slynx!"

"Me? Me?" laughed Father-in-law, suddenly loosening his fingers and letting go. "Nanny nanny foo foo, you got it wrong. You're the one who's the Slynx."

"Me?!?!?"

"Who else? Pushkin? You! You're the one and only . . ." Father-in-law laughed, shook his head, stretched his stiff fingers, and put out the light in his eyes—only reddish glints flickered in the round eyeballs. "Go take a look at yourself in the water . . . in the water . . . hee, hee, hee . . . Yes, the Slynx, that's just who you are . . . No need to be frightened . . . no need . . . We're among friends . . ."

Mother-in-law laughed too, Olenka giggled, and Terenty

Petrovich-san grinned. The children stopped scratching the floor, raised their flat heads, and shrieked.

"Just look at yourself in the water . . ."

He ran out of the room. The family's laughter followed him.

What are they saying! What did they mean! Here's the storehouse, here's a barrel of water. Blocking the light with his hands, he looked into the dark, slimy-smelling water. No, it was all lies. Lies!!! It was hard to see, but you could tell: his head was round, though his hair had thinned; his ears were in place, his beard, nose, eyes. No, I'm a human! A human is what I am! . . . That's right! To hell with you!

He rinsed his face in the barrel: the skin smarted where Father-in-law had burned it with his rays, and it felt rough to the touch, like it was covered with tiny blisters or a rash. He suddenly felt nauseated, as though he'd eaten cheese. He ran to the door and vomited his guts out. Something yellow. Must be the canaries. He'd eaten too many canaries. Ugh, he felt weak.

. . . He should take a walk, no? Get some fresh air. He hadn't walked anywhere in ages. From the city gates. Hiss to the guard. Walk to the hills. To the river. Over the bridge—into the forest, and farther, farther, till he was up to his knees, waist, shoulders in grass, to the place where there are flowers and flies, a hidden glade, and a honey-sweet wind, and the white bird . . . That's right, just wait . . .

He trudged on, shuffling along in his lapty on weakened, sickly feet. He suddenly understood clearly that it was all in vain. There isn't any glade or any bird. The glade was trampled, the tulips torn up, and the Princess Bird, well, she was caught long ago in the snare and ground into meat patties. He ate them himself. He himself slept on pillows of snowy, lacy feathers.

He knew, but he walked on, almost indifferently, like just before death, or just after death—when everything has already happened and you can't fix anything. He plodded past fields planted with bluish turnips, along ravines with their piles of red clay, across canals and pools with worrums. He climbed up the hills with difficulty, slipping on overgrown marshrooms. From the hills you could see far, far away: fields and then more fields, with weeded and unweeded turnips, and new ravines, and dark patches of woods where the blindlie bird hides, and the unbelievably far-off oak groves with their firelings, and then more fields as far as the eye could see. The wind of his homeland blew brisk and warm, grayish clouds turned the heavenly vaults murky, and on the horizon, like a deep blue wall, stood dark clouds ready to sob with summer downpours.

In thickets of brittle August horsetail he found a mirror of dark water, and took another good look at his reflection. He touched his ears. Regular ears. The family's talking nonsense. Nonsense. He patted his cheeks—his palms were covered with pus from the burst blisters. His palms were normal too, rough; across his entire palm and his fingers was a wide callus from the hook. He took off one of his lapty and checked his feet. His feet were just plain feet too: white on top and dark underneath from the dirt, that's what a foot is for. He checked his stomach. Rear end. No tail or . . .

Wait. Just a minute. The tail. There had been a tail. Jeez, there was a tail. But people weren't supposed to have . . . So what did that? . . .

He vomited again, more canaries. No, I'm not the Slynx. No!!!

. . . No, you're the Slynx.

No!

. . . Just think about it . . .

No! I don't want to! That's not the way things happen! I'll go back right now, I'll run home to my bed, to my rumpled warmth, to my beautiful books, to my books where there are roads, steeds, islands, conversations, children with sleds, verandahs of colored glass, beauties with clean hair, birds with pure eyes!

"Ah, Benedikt, why did you eat meat patties made from my white body?"

I didn't mean to, no, no, no, I didn't mean to, they just kept stuffing me, I only wanted spiritual food—they stuffed me full, caught me, confused me, stared at my back! It was all the . . . it never rests . . . It crept up behind me—and its ears were flattened, and it was crying, and it wrinkled up its pale face, and licked my neck with its cold lips, and searched with its claw,

looking to hook the vein. Yes, it's the Slynx! It ruined me, aaa
. . . aaa . . . aaa, ruined me! Maybe I'm only imagining, maybe
I'm really lying in my own izba in a fever, in Mother's izba;
maybe Mother is leaning over me, shaking me by the shoulder:
wake up, wake up, you were screaming in your sleep, Good
Lord, you're all wet, wake up, son!

I only wanted books—nothing more—only books, only
words, it was never anything but words—give them to me, I
don't have any! Look, see, I don't have any! Look, I'm naked,
barefoot, I'm standing before you—nothing in my pants pockets, nothing under my shirt or under my arm! They're not stuck
in my beard! Inside—look—there aren't any inside either—
everything's been turned inside out, there's nothing there! Only
guts! I'm hungry! I'm tormented! . . .

What do you mean there's nothing? Then how can you talk
and cry, what words are you frightened with, which ones do you
call out in your sleep? Don't nighttime cries roam inside you, a
thudding twilight murmur, a fresh morning shriek? There they
are, words—don't you recognize them? They're writhing inside
you, trying to get out! There they are! They're yours! From
wood, stone, roots, growing in strength, a dull mooing and whining in the gut is trying to get out; a piece of tongue curls, the torn
nostrils swell in torment. That's how the bewitched, beaten, and
twisted snuffle with a mangy wail, their boiled white eyes locked
up in closets, their vein torn out, backbone gnawed; that's right,
that's how your pushkin writhed, or mushkin—what is in my
name for you?—pushkin-mushkin, flung upon the hillock like a
shaggy black idol, forever flattened by fences, up to his ears in
dill, the pushkin-stump, legless, six-fingered, biting his tongue,
nose in his chest—and his head can't be raised!—pushkin, tearing off the poisoned shirt, ropes, chains, caftan, noose, that
wooden heaviness: let me out, let me out! What is in my name
for you? Why does the wind spin in the gully? How many roads
must a man walk down? What do you want, old man? Why do
you trouble me? My Lord, what is the matter? Ennui, oh, Nina!
Grab the inks and cry! Open the dungeon wide! I'm here! I'm
innocent! I'm with you! I'm with you!

▪ ▪ ▪

Soaking wet from his head to his soggy shoes, Benedikt banged on the doors of the Red Terem, knowing they wouldn't let him in, that they'd deliberately bolted the doors, that they knew how to get to him. It was pouring, as it does only in August, in a stormy, foamy surge that washed the yards clean of trash, kindling, and peelings. The murky foam swirled with rags and carried them under the gates to the streets and out of the settlement. Way up high Olenka opened a window, screamed a curse, threw out a dozen books — there, go read! — and slammed the shutters. Benedikt rushed to save them, he picked them up and wiped them off — he ought to kill the bitch. But then another window opened and this time Terenty Petrovich, the Minister of Oil and Refineries, tossed out pristine white books with pictures bound with thin, delicate paper over them, the rarest of books . . . Benedikt couldn't grab them all and the treasures splatted into the swirl of rubbish, squelched, and floated off, spinning . . . and then Kudeyar Kudeyarich began to fling other incomparable items to their death from the top floor, one after the other. Benedikt didn't wait for the end, there was no end in sight; the flattened faces of Bubble and Concordia already hung out of the window, the children held packets of journals in their hands; Mother-in-law loomed behind them holding their sashes. He got it. He understood. It's a choice. Come on, now, who would you save from a burning building? He made his choice right away.

V · IZHITSA

THE DILL had been weeded out hither and yon, the square raked clear, the pushkin's pedestal was surrounded with brushwood and rusht, and they'd tucked logs in and around it. Up high, Nikita Ivanich was bound with rope to our be all and end all, back to back. After the downpour the air was clean and it was easy to breathe. That is, it would have been easy if not for the tears.

Benedikt stood in the front of the crowd with his hat off. A breeze played with the remains of his hair and blew the moisture from his eyes. He felt sorry for both of them—Nikita Ivanich and the pushkin. But the old man went and offered himself up voluntarily, so to speak. Almost completely voluntarily. He displayed an understanding of the moment. Of course, Benedikt had explained everything to him straight and clear: You have to. You have to, Nikita Ivanich. Art is in peril, it's perishing all around us. The honor of sacrifice, so to speak, has fallen to you, Nikita Ivanich. You always wanted to preserve all facets of the past? Well then, be a dear and show everyone an example of how it's done.

Of course, no one's forcing you, you know. You don't have to go. But then the decree will be signed and go into effect, because as soon as a decree is signed, there's no way around it. And there'll be a section reserved for art.

It was an unpleasant conversation. Unpleasant. Of course, Nikita Ivanich could go on living his life. How long he had been allotted couldn't be known. But life requires choices. Are you for art or against it, life asks, and that's it. The time has come to answer. That's the way the cookie crumbles.

Having cried his eyes out on the hill amid the horsetail, having talked it through with himself—just like someone else was there, but that was just a regular sort of illusion—Benedikt's spirits rose and his head cleared. Or his reason. He observed everything with much greater calm—and in books they write that's a sign of maturity. He used to want everything himself! Himself! To be higher than the Alexander column! The second man in the government! I sign decrees! Decrees are all fine and well, but somehow, in the shadow of the table, or maybe the bed, Petrovich-san grew unnoticed, that scum, that stinking animal. Before they could turn around he was in charge of everything. How did that happen? Why? Benedikt used to have a close relationship with Papa, that is, Father-in-law. They worked and played together. They swore an oath. Now Petrovich-san had all the keys, all the chits, the guzzelean, and now he had art too. And he gave you that rotten look, and smiled with those shiny yellow teeth, not like other people's; and he's even proud of those teeth and says: "I put the yellow stuff in ages ago, and it's still there."

The bastard pushed him to make a choice. For instance, Nikita Ivanich had agreed to burn on the "Nikita's Gate" pillar, but the family wouldn't hear of it. Let him burn on the pushkin. It was as clear as a bump on a log that this was what you call Terenty Petrovich's doing, or, to put it scientifically, the result of palace intrigues. It was just to make Benedikt do the deciding: if you want to preserve art, then say goodbye to the pushkin. Either or.

But Benedikt's spirits rose and his head cleared, he looked at things with greater calm, so he made this choice immediately too, without looking back: Art was more precious.

But you couldn't exactly control the tears, they flowed by themselves.

Nikita Ivanich stood on the firewood fit to be tied, shouting a tirade and cursing the whole world. Well, he was anxious, you could understand. A lot of people had gathered for the death by execution.

There were some people Benedikt knew, though not many—most were being treated. He could see Lev Lvovich making faces, and Poltorak shoving Golubchiks along with his third leg. Ivan Beefich's friend had brought him on piggyback.

Olenka and Fevronia sat in summer carriages under lace parasols, all fancy and so fat the axles had bowed under them, and the wheels were turning into squares.

Kudeyar Kudeyarich personally placed rusht under the brushwood and straightened the logs. "That's it! Out of propeller range!"

"What do propellers have to do with it?" Nikita Ivanich argued irritably. "You haven't invented the propeller yet, you frigging mutants! Ignorance, self-importance, stagnation!"

"Shut up, Oldener," Father-in-law interrupted. "The General Saniturion himself, Life, Health, Strength, is assisting you with his own personal hands! And he could have stayed at home in the warmth! You should say thank you!"

"Stoker Nikita, don't get uppity, just do your job and burn!" came the weak voice of the aging veteran Jackal Demianich, God knows from where.

"Now listen here, Jackal, if I've told you once, I've told you a hundred times, don't get familiar with me," said Nikita Ivanich, stomping his foot. "And don't give me orders! I'm going on my fourth century now! I'd already had it up to here with your nastiness before the Blast! Be so good as to have a little respect for the individual!"

"What are they scorching him for?" people in the crowd asked.

"He fornicated with a mermaid."

Father-in-law gave a wave of his hand, aimed the rays from his eyes, and gritted his teeth.

"Papa, Papa, careful now, you'll overdo it," Olenka worried.

Kudeyar Kudeyarich crossed his eyes, guided the rays into one point on the rusht, and tensed his neck. A little bit of white, acrid smoke rose, but there were no flames: the rain-soaked logs wouldn't catch.

"Splash a little guzzelean," the crowd muttered, "it needs a little guzzelean."

"Gas-o-line," shouted an angry Nikita Ivanich from above, "how many times do you have to be told, to be taught: GAS-O-line, or, as it is occasionally referred to, petrol, or benzine, that's B-E-N-zine, you blockheads!"

Benedikt, rubbing his eyes with his fist, flinched, like he'd been called by name. "It doesn't matter, Nikita Ivanich . . . What's the difference?"

"Yes, it does! It does matter! Is it really all that difficult to assimilate orthoepy?"

Terenty Petrovich rolled out a little barrel of guzzelean.

"We'll show you . . . Now we'll have a real bang-up fart! Regards from the Sixth Taxi Fleet!"

The crowd pushed forward, shouting, stepping on each other's feet, shoving. Benedikt leaned forward and saw the Minister break off a piece of the swollen lid. He's going to pour the water on the kindling, Benedikt guessed. But why? How could water and fire mix? Benedikt had lived a whole life—and he still didn't understand. And there was something else he didn't understand. There was something important . . .

"Nikita Ivanich!!"—Benedikt leapt up—"I completely forgot! I could have gone and missed it! I've got a head full of holes! Where do I look for that book?"

"What book?"

"That one. Where they tell you everything!"

"Out of propeller range!" Father-in-law cried out again.

"The one you told me about. Where is it hidden? What's the point now? Admit it! Where it says how to live!"

The rainbow water splashed, drenching the brushwood, and running down. The foul smell filled the air. People rushed off in all directions, spreading the guzzelean with their lapty. A crowd of Golubchiks grabbed Benedikt against his will and carried him away from the pushkin into the streets.

"Nikita Ivaaaaanich! Grandfather! Where is the booook! Tell me quiiiiick!"

"Study your letters! The ABCs! I've told you a hundred times! You can't read it without your letters! Farewell! Take ca-a-aaaa-re!"

Turning his head, Benedikt saw Nikita Ivanich inhale deeply and open his mouth; he saw Terenty Petrovich jump back from the pillar, but too late. *Whooooosh!* A rolling ball of fire, like some jeopard tree gone berserk in spring, covered the pushkin, and the crowd, and the carriage with Olenka, and breathed its heat straight in Benedikt's face, spreading out like a red wing, like some bird of vengeance or a harpy, over the amazed, fleeing crowd.

Boom! Baboom! The sound hit his back. Turning as he ran, Benedikt saw the fireball rise up and charge down the streets, exploding extra barrels of guzzelean, swallowing up whole izbas in one gulp, throwing itself like a red yoke from house to house, licking the palings and fences, heading in one direction as though following a thread—right to the Red Terem.

Then he fell in a grassy ditch, covered his face with his cap, and didn't look again.

Toward evening Benedikt lifted the cap off his face and looked around with dull, empty eyes. The plain still smoldered with gray pockets of smoke, but the fire had had its fill and settled down. In some places the charred skeleton of an izba stuck out, in others an entire street was untouched amid grass yellowed and curled by the heat. But there, in the distance, where the red towers had always risen with their carved fripperies and decorative frilleries, nothing could be seen and nothing rose at all.

> My steppe is burned, the grass is felled
> No fire, no star, no road,
> I'm not to blame for kissing,
> Forgive me, my betrothed . . .

What was once the pushkin stood above the yellow, burned field like a black boil. Beriawood is a sturdy wood, we know our carpentry. Benedikt made his way to the poet's remains and looked up at what had been his features, now blistered and blurred by the heat. His sideburns and face had baked into a single blob. On the swell of his elbow lay a pile of white ash with flickering coals, but all six fingers had fallen off.

At the base of the pedestal a scorched corpse was doubled up. Benedikt looked and poked it with his foot—Terenty. Yep, those were his teeth.

It smelled of burning. Life was over. Behind the idol's back someone spat and moved.

"Give me a hand, I'll get down. It's too high for me," croaked Nikita Ivanich.

As black as the pushkin, just the whites of his eyes red from the fumes, hairless and beardless, creaking and still smoking, Nikita Ivanich leaned on Benedikt's numb hand and climbed down from the crumbling, seared braces. He spat out some coals.

"Life is over, Nikita Ivanich," said Benedikt in a voice that was not his own. The words resounded in his head, as though spoken in an empty stone bucket or a well.

"It's over . . . so we'll start another one," the old man grumbled in reply. "You could at least tear me off a piece of your shirt, to cover my privates. Can't you see? I'm naked. What are young people coming to nowadays?"

Lev Lvovich of the Dissidents wandered among the ashes,

clutching his shaggy hair with both hands, looking for something in the grass that was no longer there.

"Lyovushka! Come over here. So, where were we?" asked Nikita Ivanich, wrapping his loins in a piece of Benedikt's vest. "I could use a clothespin. What lazy people . . . Can't even invent clothespins."

"A safety pin!" said Lev Lvovich reproachfully, running over. "I always said: a safety pin! A marvelous, civilized invention."

"There's no civilization, Golubchik. We have to do it ourselves, with our wood one."

"Now that's nationalist claptrap," cried Lev Lvovich. "That stinks of the newspaper *Tomorrow*. Vulgar spiritualism! It's not the first time I've noticed! It stinks!"

"Listen, Lyovushka, knock it off, will you? Let's retreat, let's soar above the sands. Shall we?"

"Let's!"

The Oldeners bent their knees, held hands, and began to rise in the air. They were both laughing—Lev Lvovich shrieked a bit, as though he were afraid to swim in cold water, and Nikita Ivanich laughed in a deep voice: ho-ho-ho. Nikita Ivanich brushed the soot from his feet—foot against foot, quickly—and dropped a little of it on Benedikt's face.

"Hey, what're you up to?" cried Benedikt, rubbing his eye.

"Nothing!" they answered from above.

"Why didn't you burn up?"

"Didn't feel like it! Just didn't feeeeel like it!"

"So you mean you didn't die? Huh? Or did you?"

"Figure it out as best you can!"

O joyless, painless moment!
The spirit rises, beggarly and bright,
A stubborn wind blows hard, and hastens
The cooling ash that follows it in flight.

Moscow, Princeton, Oxford, Tyree, Athens,
Panormo, Fyodor-Kuzmichsk, Moscow
1986–2000

275

POETRY QUOTED IN

The Slynx

Translations by Jamey Gambrell. Most of the poems are untitled.

PAGE

16 *Mountain summits:* Mikhail Lermontov, translation from Goethe

Insomnia. Homer. Taut sails: Osip Mandelstam, "Insomnia"

17 *Spikenard, cinnamon, and aloe:* Alexander Pushkin

O spring without end or borders!: Alexander Blok

25 *Hiccup, Hiccup:* based on Russian folk nonsense rhymes

27 *On the black sky—words are inscribed:* Marina Tsvetaeva

32 *Life, you're but a mouse's scurry:* Alexander Pushkin

33 *The reed pipe sings upon the bridge:* Alexander Blok

In the district where no feet have passed: Boris Pasternak

39 *From the dawn a luxurious cold:* Yakov Polonsky

63 *Winter shows its anger still:* Fyodor Tiutchev

76 *The heart of a beauty!:* Verdi, "La donna è mobile," from *Rigoletto*

86 *Not because she shines so bright:* Innokenty Annensky

87 *The flame's ablaze, it doesn't smoke:* Bulat Okudzhava

I want to be bold, I want to be a scoffer: Konstantin Balmont

88 *No, I do not hold that stormy pleasure dear!:* Alexander Pushkin

You lie in silence, heeding ne'er a sound: Alexander Pushkin

134 *But the hand behind your back is stronger:* Natalya Krandievskaya

189 *O tender specter, happy chance:* Natalya Krandievskaya

190 *O city! O wind! O snowstorms and blizzards!:* Alexander Blok
     But is the world not all alike?: Natalya Krandievskaya
202 *Bright thoughts ascend:* Alexander Blok
206 *From the threshold of the gate:* Bulat Okudzhava
208 *February! Grab the inks and cry!:* Boris Pasternak
216 *Oh, the moment, oh, the bitter fight:* Alexei Khvostenko
223 *Our eyes were glued to the tribune:* anonymous Soviet poem,
     c. 1970s
231 *Steppe and nothing else:* Russian folk song
233 *And where is that clearest of fires:* Bulat Okudzhava
234 *The lamplighter should have lit them, but sleeps:* Bulat
     Okudzhava
241 *Beneath a canopy of fetid thatch:* Natalya Krandievskaya
242 *In the stony cracks between the tiles:* Nikolai Zabolotsky
     Life, you're but a mouse's scurry: Alexander Pushkin
     Neither fire nor darkened huts: Alexander Pushkin
245 *O world, roll up into a single block:* Nikolai Zabolotsky
246 *Joy, thou beauteous godly lightning:* Schiller, from Beethoven's
     Ninth Symphony
254 *The trepidation of life, of all the centuries and races:*
     Maximilian Voloshin
     He who draws the darkest lot of chance: Alexander Blok
     What kind of East do you favor?: Vladimir Solovyov
     Is all quiet among our fair people?: Alexander Blok
255 *Man suits all elements, every season:* Alexander Pushkin
274 *My steppe is burned, the grass is felled:* Alexander Blok
275 *O joyless, painless moment!:* Natalya Krandievskaya

ALSO BY TATYANA TOLSTAYA

Pushkin's Children:
Writings on Russia and Russians

"Tatyana Tolstaya . . . deserves as wide a hearing
as she can get." — David Remnick

Most of the twenty wide-ranging pieces on Russian poli-
tics, culture, and character that comprise this book were
published in the *New York Review of Books* between 1991
and 2000. By way of essay-reviews (from *Classic Russian
Cooking* to Francine du Plessix Gray's *Soviet Women*), in-
formed reportage (from Yeltsin's coup to Putin's personal background), and literary analysis (from Alexander
Pushkin to Solzhenitsyn), Tolstaya conveys her strong
opinions, sense of humor, and deep knowledge of her
country and countrymen. ISBN 0-618-12500-0